# HIS DARK GAME

# HIS DARK GAME

## MARRIAGE GAMES | SEPARATION GAMES

### THE GAMES DUET

## CD REISS

FLIP CITY MEDIA INC.

# HIS DARK GAME

# DEDICATION

*This book is dedicated to my sister and brother authors in the indie publishing world.*
*For your sharing, your kindness, your ethical behavior in a chaotic industry that could be so much more brutal—I have one thing to tell you.*
*Come closer.*
*I'm going to whisper it in your ear.*

**You've created something beautiful.**

# MARRIAGE GAMES

# PART I
# ADAM

# CHAPTER ONE

## PRESENT TENSE

THE MORNING my life changed was no different than any other. I woke. I showered. The tie I chose wasn't much different than the other ties in the drawer, and the suit I put on wasn't much bluer than my other blue suit. It wasn't my favorite or my most hated. It fit the same as every suit I'd had made after I got married. Bigger in the shoulders. Smaller in the waist. Sleeves more generous at the bicep. She liked when I worked out, so I did.

The morning everything changed, I felt the same as I always felt, more or less. I had plenty to do, but not too much. She was probably already in a meeting with our other editorial director. I was heading for a sheer drop into death at a hundred miles an hour while I looked up at the clouds.

The morning my life changed, I started a grocery list for the housekeeper.

The loft was bathed in light, trapezoids of sun cast over the hardwood. Twenty floors beneath me, the capillary of Crosby Street coursed the blood of steel and noise on its way to the artery of Lafayette.

My life changed on a weekday, with the gurgling of the coffeepot behind me, my jacket slung over the barstool, and the milk souring on the counter.

I put it away, because she never did.

I had no sense of impending doom. No gut feeling that that day was different from any other. It's unreasonable to expect I would. In an age of science and reason, why should I sense disaster before it arrived?

Yet I didn't see it coming.

Her handwriting—flowery, curlicued, an expansive rendering of Catholic School standards—was at the bottom of a typewritten note. I poured my coffee, assuming it was a deal memo waiting for my signature to go next to hers.

I was wrong.

It was the first time I was wrong about her intentions, but not the last.

*Dear Adam:*
  *I don't know how to say this.*

# CHAPTER TWO

## PAST PERFECT

First times.

The first time I saw her.

I had the power. I held all the cards. The publishing empire her parents had built was crumbling with the entire industry. They had one willing buyer. Me. She walked into the conference room behind her father, John Barnes, who left his oxygen tank and his ego at the door.

The space folded around her.

The first time I saw her, I had to hold my breath.

The first time she spoke, I exhaled.

"Mr. Steinbeck," she said, taking her place among the lawyers and executives. My name was uttered with more respect than I deserved. She was a child of literature. Saying Steinbeck with respect was a habit.

"No relation," I said. "I've never seen a farm."

"Obviously."

Her hair was straight, brown, to her shoulders, and her eyes were the color of broken safety glass.

We sat. Opened our folders. Numbers got flung around. Her father's breathing became more labored. Emphysema. Three-pack-a-day habit stopped too late. She kept looking at him, getting more and more agitated as the meeting went on.

What would she do for him? If I pretended I didn't see her father's distress, would she jump in to help him? Would she make a hasty decision to get him out of the room?

The first time I tested my future wife, she failed. Or passed, depending on how you look at it.

"What you're offering," I said, "is a forty-nine percent stake in a company that no one else in the business believes will make money over the next five years. You've tapped out your credit, and you want R+D to come in, bail you out, and let you keep the keys to the kingdom."

"No one at R+D knows the publishing business and we have some ideas—"

"No one at this table knows the publishing business. But only one of half this table knows *business*. And you're not sitting on it."

I slid her a folder. It contained McNeill-Barnes's profit projections for the following five years. It was ugly. Even the best-case scenario had them drowning.

"You're past a simple bankruptcy proceeding," I said. "You've already cut too much staff to argue for the jobs you'll save. And as far as the chilling effect on American literature, no one gives a shit."

John Barnes's breath caught and he wheezed. He wasn't looking at the folder; he was looking at me.

"What do you want?" he whispered.

"The whole thing. No less. My buyout number's on the bottom of the page."

The first time I shocked my future wife, she didn't show it. Not much. But her lower lip went slack, and she blinked out of cadence. She closed the folder. "You're after the building."

I leaned back. "It's a nice piece of property." My eyes fell to her breasts. I could detect the entire shape of them from the slight shadow at her collar. I wondered what they tasted like.

"It's a converted SoHo warehouse."

She was about to make a point, but her father wheezed again. She lost her train of thought. I felt sorry for her. She loved him. Her devotion moved me. More than the taste of her tits, I wanted a taste of that devotion.

She tapped her pen and picked up her point. "This building? It's a unicorn for developers. For this number, we could just sell it and keep the company."

"Not with the liens."

The first time I cornered my future wife, I thought I'd won a decisive battle in a war I assumed I understood. Five years later, with the syncopated blast of an ambulance twenty stories below our loft and a typewritten note on the kitchen counter, I realized I'd done neither.

# CHAPTER THREE
## PRESENT TENSE

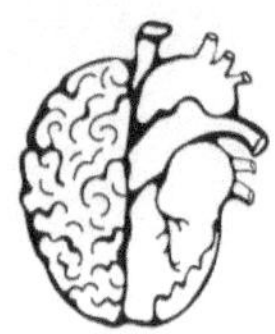



*DEAR ADAM:*
   *I don't know how to say this. But I have to.*
   *I can't be married to you anymore.*

The note was two pages long. I couldn't read it. My coffee chilled in my hand.

Every drop of blood in my body rushed to my face, leaving me with an empty hole in my chest and rigid, white fingers that tingled before going numb.

I crumpled the note until it was a dense, tight sphere of betrayal, and I stuffed it in my pocket. I had to piss. Of all things. I had to walk to the bathroom, open the door, and take out my dick. Do all the things I had to do with this fucking cliff I was driving toward without brakes.

I called her. No answer. Voice mailbox full. Called again. Same. I texted.

*—Where are you?—*

*—We need to talk—*

No reply. I couldn't stare at the phone any longer. She thought she was leaving me, and I still had to piss. I had no time to think, much less manage these absurd bodily functions.

As I stood over the bowl, my thoughts ran out of me, rapping like a playing card in bicycle spokes, downhill faster and faster.

*It's another man.*
*I'll kill him.*
*Check everything.*
*Lock out the banks.*
*Tuesday after the Unicef Gala.*
*Fucked her Tuesday.*
*She came.*
*Did she come?*
*Definitely came.*
*What did I do wrong?*
*It's me.*
*What's his name? I'll kill—*
*Apologize for nothing.*
*Get access to her email.*
*Where is she?*
*Apologize for everything.*
*She didn't mean it.*
*Do something.*
*Do something.*
*Do.*
*Something.*

I slammed the toilet seat down. Fuck pissing. Fuck locking the door. Fuck this fucking walk down the fucking block. It was winter. I cut through the cold like a dull knife. McNeill-Barnes was down the block and I didn't have the bandwidth to be cold. Fuck all the shit I had to do when I should be doing something.

# CHAPTER FOUR

## PAST PERFECT

DIANA. Diana McNeill-Barnes. What would I do to possess her? Would I change my cellular structure? Turn my back on my identity? Walk away from it, never talk about it, burn it so thoroughly into a pile of dust that not telling her wouldn't be a lie?

Would I make a bad business deal for her happiness?

"I'm going to do it," I said.

Charlie and I were at the Loft House—a hip little private club with original art everywhere and a membership waiting list as long as my leg. The top-floor restaurant overlooked the city on four sides. We were on the southern tip, where we could see the point of Manhattan jut into the ocean.

"Break her?"

"I'm going to marry her."

He shook his head, tapping his aboriginal cane. He was a war veteran in his late forties. If you knew history and heard his accent, you might be curious enough to ask him what was the last war Australia fought. He'd tell you "the ones that are bought and paid for," then he'd ask if you wanted to see his war wounds.

Best to decline.

Charlie had been the first to hear about her eleven months before. The first to question my instincts.

"How is it possible she's vanilla?" he'd asked the day after I took her to bed the first time. We were taking a spin around Central Park's six-mile loop, the rattle and tick of our derailleurs punctuating heavy breaths. He was slow because of his leg. "You can't do vanilla. It's not natural."

"What's the big deal?"

"It's like cats and dogs sleeping together. She must be a sub. She might not know it, but she has to be."

"I found her ex-fiancé in some douche Wall Street bar. I got him drunk and asked him a few pointed questions."

"How do you do that?"

"'Oh, hey stranger at the bar…I was just dumped boo hoo were you ever dumped? Oh, really the bitch. My girl wanted yadda yadda in bed etc. etc. did you ever tie her up whatever whatever.' He says, 'She didn't even let me pull her hair when I dogged her.' Done. Confirmed. Took seventy-four minutes."

"All that proves is she's attracted to a closet Dominant, even if the wanker didn't know what he was doing. Did you ask her? Directly? Instead of dancing around the subject?"

"She had a girlfriend in college. Couple of months of light bondage, but she wouldn't let the boyfriend do anything."

He pushed himself off his handlebars to sit straight, arms out. "And you gave up Serena for this?"

This? For Diana. Serena was a child, and our prescribed time had ended already. Once I'd broken her on the last day, I was done with her. Diana was a woman, and she was eternal. I loved her. I'd spent a single night with her and hours over a negotiating table battling her and I loved her.

Between the bike ride in Central Park and sitting with Charlie in the club, drinking whiskey and telling him I was going to marry her, almost a year had passed. Diana was the sky and all the stars in it.

"You're never going to be right with yourself, mate," Charlie said, leaning back into the point of Lower Manhattan.

"That's bullshit we tell ourselves," I said. "It's justification. I don't need justification, and I don't need the lifestyle to have a life."

"Keep paying dues at the Cellar," he said before sipping his drink.

"No need."

"I'll pay them for you. Day will come when you can't deal with power sharing another night."

"I can function just fine."

He smiled. The parentheses around his mouth got darker when he didn't shave for a few days. "Function? My friend, I never questioned your manhood."

"Good idea." I swirled my whiskey around the bottom of my glass. "I could break her, sure."

The thought of it swirled my insides with the drink. It was too good. The idea of her on her knees with her hands behind her back. My balls went into a knot.

I shut out the thought. I loved her. *Wanted* to love her. Needed to love her, and the second she kneeled, she'd be nothing to me.

I put the drink down. "It wouldn't feel right. She's not built for submission."

"You can't just decide to be vanilla the rest of your life. It's not a choice."

"It's all a choice. And I choose her."

He brought his drink to his lips. "She must be quite a piece of ass."

# CHAPTER FIVE

## PRESENT TENSE

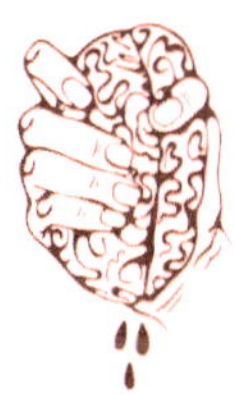

*I can't be married to you anymore. You're a good man. You're good to me and my family. I can never repay you for how you helped us. But I've started to feel obligated, and I think the obligation and gratitude has clouded my judgment.*

We'd started repairing the damage to McNeill-Barnes Publishing by renting out pieces of the building on short leases and putting the staff to work in the smallest amount of space they could manage. Five years later, we'd reclaimed two floors.

I walked through the penthouse with a sucking pain in my gut and a heart wrapped in wire. We'd built this together. Her father had stepped out of the day-to-day and onto the board, while she and I reshaped the business.

"Mr. Steinbeck." Diana's admin, Kayti, ran behind me. A single mom with a nose ring and a sweet smile, she kept my wife organized. "I have a message from—"

"Where is she?"

"Who?" Kayti chased me.

"My wife." I didn't stop walking toward her office. I could see the shadow of a figure between the frosted glass doors and the windows.

"She left a message…"

I opened the door.

"Steinbeck!"

The figure was Zack Abramson, the executive editor. Nonfiction. The stuff that had put us back on the map. He snapped a book closed and put it on the Mission-style coffee table.

Diana liked warm things. Warm colors. Warm lighting. Warm sex.

"She's not coming in," Kayti finished.

Zack was a smug little prick who should have stayed in the acting business. He was sly and untrustworthy. He had a way of looking at people as if he had secret knowledge about them, which he didn't. But he was a formidable editing talent, and despite all that and more, I kind of liked the asshole.

"Did she say why?" I asked Kayti.

"Uh, no but—"

"Shouldn't you know that?" Zack asked, smugly, I might add.

"Marriage doesn't make you psychic." I put my bag on my wife's desk chair because I could.

"That's a really nice suit, Steinbeck."

"What did you want again, Zack?"

"Um, can I finish?" Kayti said.

"No," Zack said.

"Yes," I said at the same time.

Kayti wasn't flustered for long. "Diana said no one knows. Those were her one-two-three words to tell you. No one knows. But she wouldn't say more. So I don't know what that was about. Should I call her and find out?"

"I'll call her," I said. "Thank you, Kayti."

She nodded and left, clicking the doors closed behind her.

"Was there something you wanted?" I asked.

Zack pulled an envelope from his jacket pocket. "I wanted to deliver this personally to one of you. Thank you for the opportunity to work for McNeill-Barnes. Being part of this restructure has been a great learning experience. I'm offering my resignation."

I didn't open it. I'd had one too many good-bye notes that morning. "I'm sorry to see you go, but I won't try to stop you."

"Thanks for that." He slapped my shoulder.

"Any reason? New job? Off to get a real life somewhere?"

"My grandmother back home. In Dayton. She's sick. Dementia."

"And you're taking care of her?" I looked at him from his Tronton boots to his just-slightly-too-long hair. He didn't look like much of a caretaker, but I'd stopped judging people on their looks a long time ago.

"My mother and I."

"Take notes. It'd be a great piece. Actor turned journalist turned editor turned nurse."

He smirked. "I'll bring it here first."

He started out, and I stopped him. "I'm sorry about your grandmother. But your path to the door should not detour to your office. Your laptop stays. Per your contract, you submit all your passwords. Don't make me get legal after you. It's a bore, and you don't want to get served court papers in front of your family."

"Don't worry, my friend. I'm an open book. Give my best to Diana."

Her name cut right through me.

# CHAPTER SIX

## PAST PERFECT

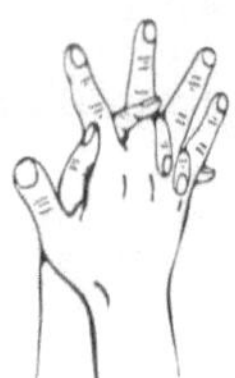

A MAN PUTS on clothes for the place and occasion. A woman dresses
to make a point. When I invited Diana to dinner to discuss the terms of
the deal where I would buy McNeill-Barnes Publishing to sink it or save
it, she dressed to tell me something.

It wasn't just business.

We'd been going back and forth for weeks. She'd fought hard. She
was tenacious and loyal to her parents' vision. It looked as if she'd let the
ship sink before turning it away from the iceberg.

Her dress was New York black, cut to make me wonder about the
shape of her tits yet again. She was too young for her position and her
confidence. At twenty-three, she carried herself as if every one of her
curves fit into the puzzle of the world.

See? Nothing about her was submissive.

"Fifty-one percent of a dying company isn't worth much, Diana."

I wasn't harsh or cutting, just truthful. She deserved the flat truth
without punch-pulling. She'd earned my respect. I wanted to help her
more than buy her company for parts. We were coming to the part of
the negotiation where the deal lived or died. Once I finally said no or she
finally said yes, what then?

"A living company is worth more than a hunk of brick."

"And Cynthia Wilt's entire backlist? And Norton Edge? You can keep it on life support with the IP you own."

She sank a little in both surprise and disappointment. I'd mentioned the company assets numerous times, but never the backlist. I figured she assumed I didn't know the worth of the backlist and was only after physical assets. Now, with her posture deflated, I knew she'd been hoping to use that as a bargaining chip at the last minute. I'd just killed it.

"Let's make a deal," I said.

I'd had a plan back-burnered for days. I hadn't thought about it consciously or run it by any of my team. I'd just let it simmer to see how it cooked down. When she arrived in that black dress, the back burner boiled. Buying the company and kicking her out wasn't an option. I had to see her again. And again. And again.

"Deal? I like that word. It kind of rolls off the tongue." She tipped her wine glass and watched the tears form on the surface. "Let's make one."

"I'll buy fifty-one percent and promise interest-earning cash infusions when necessary. I'll give you five years to get in the black."

She smiled as if this was easily done. She wasn't stupid or naïve, but excited by the idea of a chance, no matter how slim. I didn't know at the time that getting the company in the black was secondary to just keeping it afloat.

"But... " I let it hang to see if her smile disappeared. It didn't. "I'm in the day-to-day operations."

"With fifty-one percent of the vote?" She leaned back, tapping the bottom of her wineglass.

"I'm not shelling out the kind of money you need without oversight."

I didn't admit to myself the real reason the deal included me. I couldn't force myself on her. She wouldn't take what I had to give. She would never crawl to me. Never submit completely. I had enough women who did. I could get Serena back any time. But Diana... Diana was an endless fascination. I just wanted to watch her exist.

She smiled to herself and hid her eyes.

"What?" I asked.

She moved her hand to her mouth and looked at me in a way she hadn't before. "I've had too much wine."

"Two glasses? Come on." I poured her more. "Have another glass and tell me what's on your mind."

"Stop!" She laughed the command.

"You're about to agree to my terms." I put the bottle down. "I think you deserve to get good and drunk."

We clinked. She sipped, put her glass down, drank more, took a deep breath.

"Since we're going to be working together every day, more or less, I want to tell you something that's been bothering me."

"This is going to be great. Please." I moved my bread dish out of the way and leaned forward. "Go on."

She moved her bread dish out of the way and leaned forward. "When you first came to us, I looked you up."

"I'd hope so."

"Marine Park, Brooklyn. Family of electricians. Both parents died in a car accident when you were five. I'm sorry."

"Thank you."

"First in your family to go to college. A real bootstraps story. I couldn't find money anywhere. And here you are." The way she shook her head, like a drill boring into me ever so slowly. She could drill all she wanted.

"Full disclosure—the bootstraps are tainted. My grandparents loaned me money for my first down payment."

"And you're single at thirty-one. Never seen in female company."

"I'm here with you."

"This is business."

"Is it?"

Her finger stroked her pearls, her nail *tick-tick-ticking* against them. The tablecloth shifted when her right knee rocked back and forth. Every woman had a tell for when they wanted to fuck. Diana had ten, and I'd learned all of them.

"You think I'm too old to be single?" I asked.

"No. You're too handsome to be single. Too charming. Too sophisticated."

"Don't stop there. Go for broke."

She smiled, looked into the whirlpool of wine, her cheeks burning with a touch of pink. She bit her upper lip and avoided my gaze.

*She's just looking down. That doesn't make her a sub.*

"I just can't believe you haven't been snapped up."

"You're asking if I'm gay?"

"That would be a horrible injustice for women everywhere."

"I'm nothing if not just. And straight."

"There is a God." She gave me a quick flash of her eyes before she brought the wine to her lips, as if hiding behind it.

"Are you trying to seduce me before the deal is closed, Miss McNeill-Barnes?"

"We just closed it." She put her glass down, tapping the bottom as if she had a cue to hit. "You get to fuck me on my desk every weekday."

She used the word fuck like a piece of dark, bitter chocolate swallowed before it could be savored.

"Just the desk?"

"If that's what you want."

*What you want.*

*She wants to please you.*

*Shut the fuck up.*

I put the top of my foot against her calf and pushed her knees apart. She put her hands flat on the table, opening her mouth in a gasp. She aroused easily. With that, I could take her the good old-fashioned way and like it. It didn't have to be a big deal. It didn't have to be a lifetime of vanilla sex, even though I already wanted that more than anything.

"It's Saturday," I said, running my thumb across her hand and up her arm.

She warmed and bent under me. "Let's pretend it's Monday," she said, eyes at half mast.

"I looked you up too. Immaculate Heart. Volleyball. You've only ever worked at McNeill-Barnes. Met your fiancé while you were failing out of Vassar. Then you dropped him. Why was that?"

"Couldn't bear the thought of fucking him every night."

"Too boring?"

"Too rough. Treated me like a rag doll. But enough about him."

I stroked her arm. I didn't feel any satisfaction or disappointment in being right about how she needed sex. I'd already decided she was perfect. Already knew I'd take whatever she'd consent to give.

"I'll take you home because I've wanted to since I met you. But we're business partners now. This is not me fucking you on the desk every day, no matter how tempting that is. It's this weekend, then it's business. Agreed?"

She rubbed the edge of her wineglass with her ring finger, making a show of thinking. Slipping her hand around the bulb of the glass, she lifted it. "Where do I sign?"

I called for the check.

# CHAPTER SEVEN

## PRESENT TENSE

*I THINK it's clouded my judgment.*

*I'm sorry. I have to interrupt myself. I know the first thing you're going to think.*

*There's no one else.*

*I'm not cheating on you and I never have.*

*This isn't about another man. This is about us. Me. You. Us.*

I'd crumpled the note so tightly the ink had cracked. I couldn't stomach the entire thing in one swoop. She was talking at me. I had no room to disagree or question. I only had room to stop, reread, dissect, panic in the front seat of the Jag, watching the Meatpacking District come alive with restaurant-goers and dog-walkers. Ten at night on Gansevoort was a fucking carnival on cobblestones. What did all these people want?

I called the one man she would tell everything. Her father.

"Lloyd?" I said when I heard the wheezing.

"Adam, how are you?" I knew from his tone that he had no idea. He greeted me like the best son-in-law in the world, as always.

"I'm fine. Have you seen Diana?"

"Not since yesterday. Is everything all right?"

If she didn't tell him, maybe she wasn't serious?

"Yeah. Everything's fine. She's not picking up her texts."

"She's probably at the gym."

"Right. Okay. Thanks."

We hung up.

Did I miss something? A clue? A behavior that should have made me suspicious? Had I been so blind to her misery? I went from angry at her to angry at myself. Then I didn't believe her. This was a cry for help. Then fuck her if this is how she asks me to pay better attention. And did I not pay attention? Did she want more flowers? Why didn't she ask? Why didn't she tell me sooner, before she had to resort to this shitty tactic? When did it start? What did I miss?

I sent my hundredth text.

*—Was it the baby?—*

# CHAPTER EIGHT

## PAST PERFECT

SHE WAS at her father's place again. He lived in a three-bedroom on
Park Avenue in an apartment with maids' quarters. Fifteenth floor,
overlooking the Avenue. He'd struggled to keep the co-op when
McNeill-Barnes nearly went under, but it was where he and his wife had
made their life together, and he insisted on dying where they'd lived.

So romantic.

The doorman greeted me by name. I took the elevator up to fifteen.
The apartment took up the entire floor, so there were two doors in the
hall. One with a welcome mat, thick molding, a table with an ivy plant
next to it, and a little brass mailbox.

The other was just a white door with a rubber mat. Servant's
quarters. I knocked on the plain white door and waited. Rustling.
Voices.

Gilbert answered in his usual suit and tie. "Mr. Steinbeck," he said,
stepping aside. "They're in the kitchen."

The kitchen was through a short landing on the back stairs and
through another door. A shorter walk than the front door. I knew she'd
be there, and she was.

A tea set sat on the kitchen table, and Diana's bare feet were up on
the chair as if she wanted to fold herself into a fetal origami. Her father

sat across from her. He wasn't wearing his mask and tank. His health had bounced back with the business.

"Hey," I said.

Her eyes were swollen and red-rimmed. Still the clearest tempered-glass blue, which made the red stand out and the shine of her cheeks more apparent. She put down her red journal. In it, she asked questions. Just lists of questions.

*Who decided the speed of light?*
*Why can't some people sing?*
*What's in glue?*
*Where do they get the vitamins to make vitamins?*

I was sure it was getting filled with questions about why we'd had to terminate her pregnancy. Some days she read me her questions, but with her curled up in her father's kitchen chair, I didn't ask her to.

She held out her arms for me like a child. Moments like this, I felt the truest bliss of my marriage to her. When I could take care of her, gather her in my arms under her back and knees, and carry her to the couch with her head on my shoulder.

I laid her across me on the couch and held her.

"It's not your fault," I said, taking my handkerchief from my pocket. "It's no one's fault. It happens."

"I hate it," she snuffled. "I hate that it happens."

"I know. I do too."

"I keep wondering what she would have been when she grew up."

"Nothing. It wasn't meant to be."

She spent another few minutes sobbing, and I held her even though my arms ached and I was thirsty. I heard her father behind us as he went to bed, his footfall still slow even though he was feeling better.

"Adam?" she said.

"Yes?"

"Tell me. Honestly. Are you upset?"

"Of course."

"You don't seem upset."

I was unhappy that the baby's spine had grown outside its body. The sonogram had been devastating, and the decision we'd had to make had broken my wife's heart. But it was the right decision for us. We couldn't bring a person into the world to do nothing but experience a few weeks of excruciating pain before dying. Having the baby so we could feel it and touch it would have been selfish.

Once the decision had been made, I wasn't upset about it, because it was right. And because Diana's collapse gave me the opportunity to take care of her. I'd bathed her after the surgery. I'd stroked her hair and fed her. It was as close to dominating her as I would get, and it soothed me. The buzz of anxiety and dissonance that followed me around shut off like a faucet.

"I don't like seeing you like this," I said. "That's the worst for me."

She laid her head back on my chest as if she couldn't look at me. "Will you always take care of me?"

My God. Why didn't she just ask me if I'd allow the sun to rise and set?

"Always," I said. "As long as you let me, I'll take care of you."

# CHAPTER NINE

## PRESENT TENSE

*Part of me wants to just exonerate you, but that's dishonest. You never gave yourself to me. Or maybe you're just not deep. Either way, I can't live with that. I want more. I want to love fully, and there's so much missing. Can't you feel it? I mean, it can't be just me. You're in this marriage too. But then I think you're not and you never were.*

*—Was it the baby?—*

I went on another roll after that, but it was shorter than the others. I only had a half a block to walk to the Cellar.

*—When are you going to talk to me?—*

*—You can't just keep ignoring me—*

Rob saw me before I was even close to the velvet rope. "Holy fucking shit." He held out his meaty hand. He wore a dark suit under a black trench coat that was spotted with new raindrops.

"Didn't you get a real job yet?" I asked.

"And leave this? No way." He undid the rope. "Man, the girls missed you. I did too, gotta say. Everyone's always asking where you went."

"I've been around."

"Are you back now? Back for good?"

"Just seeing some old friends tonight."

I checked my texts in the elevator.

*—When are you going to talk to me?—*

*—You can't just keep ignoring me—*

And a hundred before it that were much the same. Jesus Christ. I sounded psychotic. That wasn't going to work.

*—Diana. If you want to make this about lawyers and money, we can do that. We can do all the things people do when they get acrimonious. But I can't believe you want that. I know because I looked at your email inboxes and outboxes. All your correspondence. No lawyers. You haven't moved any money and you haven't changed any of your passwords. So either you're a very good sneak or you're still the same honest, forthright woman I know. Now is the time to stop playing games. Enough—*

I thought about not hitting Send. I'd just admitted to spending half the afternoon spying on her. I decided that was just tough shit. I'd seen what I needed to see and left her life as it was. She could change her passwords if she didn't like it.

The elevator stopped as I hit Send, and the doors opened when DELIVERED appeared below the message.

That was it. I'd texted everything I was going to text today.

I looked through the elevator doors. Everything in front of me was painted as red as rage.

# CHAPTER TEN

## PAST PERFECT

I LOST my virginity on a park bench at the age of fifteen. Blaire was fourteen and in her last year at St. Mary of the Fields. I was in my first year at Our Lady of Precious Blood High School. We'd been at Fields together, and when I aged out, we felt the brokenhearted sense of urgency common in teens.

I impaled her on that bench. Right under her little plaid skirt and leg warmers, tucked into a corner of the park, just after the sun set. I controlled the motion of her hips. When she moved without my direction, I had a disconcerting feeling I could only describe as not-rightness.

We did it a few more times then broke up. My best friend's mother, Irene, seduced me a few months later, seeing something in me Blaire wasn't qualified to see. Irene had said, "Do what you want to me. We are animals. Treat me like one."

So I did. I never looked back. Not until Diana.

After the dinner where we made our first deal, I took her to my place in Murray Hill. In the back of the cab, she crossed her legs and put on lipstick. Her hands were shaking. Did she know what I was? I'd tracked down her past; had she done the same to me? Had she heard I was a sadist? A Dominant? A punishing fuck?

I hoped she had and still decided to do it.

She snapped her bag closed, and I whispered in her ear, using my Dominant voice, "Open your legs and touch yourself."

She glanced not at me, but the rearview mirror at the center of the windshield.

"The cabbie's right there." She was not amused or coy. She simply didn't want to do what I told her.

I asked myself how badly I wanted her, and I decided badly enough to risk the deal. The risk was greater for her than it was for me.

My condo was on the top floor, with a rooftop garden. I'd bought it to renovate and flip, but the lease on my apartment on Lexington was up and I decided to keep it.

I closed the door and turned on the lights. The place was spotless, but I checked anyway, following her gaze around the windows, the furniture, the curved stairwell to the top floor.

"Very nice," she said.

"Thank you." I only had eyes for her, with her feet perpendicular to one another, legs long below the curve of her hips. "The view's pretty good from here too."

She put her bag on the side table.

*Take your clothes off quietly, get on the coffee table, on your back, and spread your legs so I can see your cunt.*

I bit that back. "Can I get you something?"

"Water, please."

I went to the kitchen and came back with two glasses. Her dress was laid over a chair. She stood in the middle of my living room wrapped in a blanket.

"There aren't any curtains," she said meekly in front of the bare windows.

*Drop the blanket and show New York your body.*

"The bedroom has blinds."

"Is it upstairs?"

*Crawl up the stairs. Second door to the left. Wait for me on the bed with your ass up and spread. I'll be taking that first. You are permitted to prep it with your fingers if you need to. And trust me, you need to.*

I gave her the water. Her hand poked out of the blanket and took it. She drank, clutching the wrap at her chest. She gave the glass back to me, and I put it on the table with my glass. Then quickly, before she could change her mind or I could think better of it, I picked her up, blanket and all, and carried her up the stairs.

She put her hands on my cheeks and put her nose to mine. Her perfume smelled of oranges and orchids. When we got to my bedroom, she wiggled to her feet, still with the blanket around her. I drew the blinds and turned on the bedside lamp.

"Thank you," she said.

When I stood in front of her, she put her chin up and shook the hair out of her face. I took the blanket off, revealing wine-colored lace and a body that made my cock push against my pants. She'd gone all out. Her bra had a little crystal heart between the tits and pushed them up and together. Matching panties shaped like the letter T with an identical crystal heart at the center.

She reached for my jacket to pull it off, and I took her by the wrists.

"Give me a second," I said.

"You don't like it?"

"I want to just look at you for now."

That was true, but I also needed to create a few scenarios before we started. I needed to feel as if whatever simple thing happened, I'd planned and controlled for it.

I undid my tie without taking my eyes off her. Jacket. Shirt. I was working on my belt when she reached for me again, and I reacted by grabbing her wrist again. She stiffened. She wasn't supposed to reach without asking, but then again, she was supposed to do whatever she wanted and I'd reacted too fiercely.

I kissed the inside of her arm, and she relaxed.

"I brought condoms," she said.

*Get on your knees. Take out my cock. Put your hands behind your back and open your mouth so I can fuck your throat. You'll breathe when I want you to say my name.*

"Okay," I said, working my lips to her shoulder, up her neck, her ear, and finally, I kissed her on the mouth for the first time.

She was soft and just yielding enough. I tasted her wine, her water, her ambition, and her loyalty in that kiss.

I was a goner.

# CHAPTER ELEVEN
## PRESENT TENSE

*Whenever I thought of leaving you, I felt two things. I felt relieved. But then I felt worried about McNeill-Barnes, and I couldn't do it. That's not a reason to stay with someone. I know you can understand that. We can figure out the business, but I can't figure out you. I don't feel close to you. When we're in a room together, I'm as lonely as I've ever been.*

I didn't love the club scene, even when I had been a part of it. I didn't like chaos and noise. I understood how much control the free-for-alls took, but I liked intimacy.

The Cellar was a necessary evil though. The club acted as an organization with rules surrounding what would be assault outside its walls.

Every combination on the spectrum was available, depending on which part of the club you were in. Downstairs, in the actual cellar, nothing was off-limits. The sixth floor, where the dominant men and submissive women played, had its share of showmanship and chaos, but it was a more controlled, sedate scene. A bar. A bank of leather couches. A few back rooms.

"Adam?" the bartender said in shock. Norton was an actor and a Dominant. I shook his hand over the bar. "What's happening?"

"Don't get me started."

He put a short glass and napkin on the bar. A young man with grey eyes and conservative haircut sat next to me, talking to an older man I recognized. At the older man's feet curled a woman with a collar. He held her leash taut.

"We missed you." Norton poured me a shot. "How's married life?"

I took the glass. Did I have to answer that? I did, and I had to lie. I didn't want him to know about the note that morning. I still had hope that it was all a big error in judgment, and I only realized it when I couldn't tell the bartender my wife had left me. "Fine."

The room looked over the backside of the district. The windows had been treated so we could see out, but no one could see in. Which was for the best, since a state senator was on her hands and knees, deep in subspace, where dopamine levels were high and pain and pleasure merged. She was in heaven. I envied her Dom. Getting a sub there was the ultimate drug.

"How's the lady?" I asked Norton.

"Naughty." He waggled his brows. He and his wife worked the bar together. She wore his collar and called him Master, scrubbing the floors and wiping the counter when he told her to.

"Where is she?"

"Got a job as a graphic designer. She makes more than I do now."

"Well done." I looked at the couches. Rows and rows of them, with tables. I didn't want to talk about Norton's perfectly kinky marriage where his submissive wife could have it all. It was too close to what I wanted. "Have you seen Charlie?"

"Yeah. He's in aftercare four."

"Thanks."

I took my drink and walked toward the aftercare rooms. On the way, I was greeted with hugs and jovial backslaps. Henry offered me a turn with his sub. I declined.

Aftercare four had a black leather cross on the door with a brass 4 in the center. I knocked gently, expecting he wouldn't answer if it was intense.

"Come in."

I smiled when I heard the accent, and I opened the door.

"Crikey," he said.

A naked woman was draped over his lap, ass bruised and red, slick with soothing cream. Her eyes were closed and a smile stretched across her face.

"I haven't stepped foot in here in years and that's all you have to say?" I closed the door behind me.

"You look like someone wrung you out, mate. Carrie, look who's here."

Carrie opened her eyes, and I recognized her. We'd done a week-long years ago.

She held out her hand. "Sir. Nice to see you again." I took her hand, and we shook as well as she could under the circumstances. She rolled over onto her back. "Do you want a drink, Master?"

"Club soda. And bring Adam a whiskey. Then you need to rest." He dotted the tip of her nose.

Charlie was a Dom like no other. Without the ability to fuck, he had to be more cruel and more tender than any of us.

"What happened?" he asked when Carrie went out.

For the first time since that morning, I wanted to talk about it.

# CHAPTER TWELVE

## PAST PERFECT

THERE CAME a point when the bloody, wrapped up bundles of paper and napkins stopped appearing in the bathroom garbage pail and Diana was walking around the office like a normal person. Once I even saw her laugh through the conference room glass. I watched her talk to Zack as I passed. She was standing, arms crossed, legs apart at the width of her shoulders. Her eyes sparkled as she listened to whatever he was saying, and the sun caught the flyaway hair and bounced off as if flirting with it. Her clothes were more fitted than the sacks she wore after we lost the baby. It was impossible to look away from her.

That was my Diana.

I opened the door. "Are you ready for Easton?"

"Yes!" She gathered a stack of papers.

"Go get 'em, killer," Zack said.

She hopped, literally bouncing out into the hall.

"You seem... what's the word?" I looked up, scratching my head as if second grade vocabulary words had left me.

"Gorgeous?"

We walked down the hall.

"Of course, but also..." I put my hand on the frosted glass door of conference four. "Maybe after the meeting."

I pushed the door open and let her in. We were meeting with an upstate labor relations board over the expansion of a paper mill. Four of them. The mayor of Easton. Two second-rate public relations people. One very litigious and sharp lawyer in a fitted jacket and low heels. The conversation went downhill after the first minute of small talk.

"Our concern," said the balding mayor in the brown suit, "and our bailiwick, if you will, is to render guarantees from you that any new jobs are filled by the residents of Easton."

"We can't give guarantees," I said. "Not for every position you want."

"Why not?" chirped the PR woman with thin lips and straight brown hair. "We have a twelve percent unemployment rate. If we're going to sell the prop to expand the mill, our town needs assurances McNeill-Barnes can deliver jobs and we can deliver tax incentives."

"You can't just come in and build with no benefit to the community," the politician chimed in.

Next to him, a younger woman with a ponytail stared at me as if she wanted to burn holes in me. As I listened to the brown suit talk about his constituency, I dug around for her name.

Becca. Assistant. New hire right out of college.

"Sell them the new income tax base," I said. "Sell them the fact that we're turning an abandoned dump into a functioning structure. We cannot promise all four hundred jobs will go to locals, and the executive positions need to be filled out of Manhattan."

Our plan was to bring in experienced people as temps and train the locals, but we needed that to look like a concession later in the negotiations. We didn't want to tip our hand so far in advance.

"We'll do what we can," Diana said, right on cue. She was the good cop, as always. "We can fill positions from qualified locals first."

"We need it in writing," the lawyer said. "Numbers. As part of the incentive."

"No." I closed my folder.

"Here." Diana handed her a page. "A list of community initiatives. We can build a park and have low cost day-care on site."

She didn't even look at it.

"There's more," Diana said, tapping the page. "Consider it. We have a lot to offer, and so do you."

"We. Have. People." The lawyer poked the paper with every point.

"What you have is an existing structure close to our current site." I sat back and crossed my ankle over my knee. I could do this all day. "What you don't have is talent. We need to hit the ground running. We need people who know the machinery and the software. We need logistics people who know how to transport this particular product. This isn't about putting bodies in chairs. It's about the right people. Believe me. I've done this before."

"You're a corporate raider," Becca sneered. "You don't create jobs. You're like a little boy who buys things just to blow them up."

Becca had obviously gotten caught up in the heat of the discussion. I didn't take her comment seriously, and I was ready to move on when Diana leaned forward as if she wanted to launch herself over the table. I hadn't seen energy pour off her like that since the baby was diagnosed.

"This corporate raider happens to be the best man I've ever had the honor of sharing an office with. He's fair, and he's honest. He looks past the obvious. He finds value where other people see red ink. He's thoughtful and kind, and you need to show him a little respect."

Becca's face went from white to burgundy.

My wife picked up her files and stood. "Anything you need from us is in the folders. I'd like to thank you all for coming. I'm sure we can work something out."

She left. The door clacked behind her.

"Don't worry about it," I said to Becca. "We can reconvene later."

I nodded to everyone, shook a few hands, and went to Diana's office. She was already there, moving things around her desk as if she were a general moving troops over the field. I closed the door.

No word in the English language could describe how happy I was to see my Diana back again.

"You don't have to defend me from petty insults," I said.

"I'm sorry, but fuck them. They—"

I took her face in my hands and kissed her. I hadn't touched her since the baby. Hadn't kissed her anywhere but her cheek. And now with the full scent of her perfume and the feel of her skin, my desire rushed back.

She backed up, panting, lips blush pink. "Jesus, Adam."

I lifted her knee and put it around my waist, pushing my erection against her cunt. She sucked in air and groaned. I knew and loved that groan.

"Shouldn't. Bad professionalism," she said as if she couldn't make a full sentence. I could cure her of that.

"I love it when you're mad." I pushed harder, running the shape of my cock along the line of her cleft.

*Your pleasure is mine. You come when I permit you, and you hold it until I do.*

"I can make you come in seventeen minutes. Open your legs." I'd used my Dominant voice. I hadn't meant to.

"Wait. No."

*The word no does not mean no in a scene. Use your safe word or answer the trigger question incorrectly. Then everything stops.*

"What?" The impatience in my voice must have been thick, because her reaction was sharp.

"I just... I just had this horrible thing happen with my body. I still don't feel whole and I just don't feel... I don't feel intimate, and you have no right to be mad about it."

I let her leg go and took my arms away. "I'm not mad."

"Your voice..."

"I was surprised. That's all. It seemed like you wanted—"

"I'm sorry."

"Don't be sorry."

"I think next week. Let's do next week." She put her hand on my chest, ran her fingers along the edge of my tie and straightened it. "Thank you. I know I'm being difficult."

"You're fine. Now come on. You can be the bad cop."

To her credit, we did have sex the next week. On Wednesday night. She wore garter and lace, came twice, sucked my dick like a champ, and fell asleep in my arms. It was almost like normal for two more years.

# CHAPTER THIRTEEN
## PRESENT TENSE

*I'm miserable. I need to end this before I start to hate you.*

"And you didn't know, mate? Not an inkling? Come on. Nothing happened to make you think she was fucking another bloke?"

Charlie had left his sub to nap, and we'd found a small table by the window. His cane leaned against it. A winter rain had started when I opened my story, and the clubbers and night owls below had found shelter, leaving a cold, empty street below.

"She's not cheating."

"You can't believe that."

"I do."

He looked away, his right foot bouncing. "You know what happened when I got shot, right? With my girl? My sub? I collared her a full year before. Fifteen years we were together, and not once did she care if I fucked her or not. But once I couldn't? Once they shot it off? I couldn't spank her ass red enough. She asked to be shared. Begged. And even then, she was off with four others. *Four.* You cannot trust women when they ask for something. It's never what they want."

"You're dealing with a self-selecting group of women."

"Were you fucking her on a regular?"

"Tuesday. I fucked her Tuesday."

"Did she come?"

"Yes."

"Did you come?"

"What?"

"Not 'did you ejaculate'? Did you *come*? Were you enjoying it? Or were you fucking her missionary while thinking about gagging her with your fist?"

I leaned back in my chair and looked out the window. Manhattan is never truly dark, just shaded differently. What I'd been thinking about on Tuesday night was not what I was doing. Hadn't been for a long time.

Charlie leaned forward and lowered his volume. "Do you think, for once in your life, she might be submissive? And you're not satisfying her? Maybe?"

*No. I love her.*

"You're living in the world of the Cellar like there's nothing outside it."

"All right, look." Charlie put his glass down as if he was just getting serious. "You know I thought this was a mistake, but divorce won't kill you."

"She won't even answer my texts."

"We still have the Montauk place," Charlie continued as if I hadn't spoken. "Take a sub. There are at least a dozen who remember you and a dozen more who heard about you. Take your pick. Do a thirty-day run like you used to."

I let out a quiet laugh. "Shit. The thirty-day runs. They were trouble."

"Just enough time for them to fall madly in love with you, mate."

No. There was no "them." Only one had fallen in love. The last one. Serena. It had ended right before I met Diana, and it hadn't ended well. Serena had been too young, a virgin, and she wanted a perma-Dom. I wasn't interested in loving a sub. The world we inhabited wasn't designed for people to be in love. It was designed for intensity, pain, pleasure, courtesy, and ritual.

"That was never the plan. The plan was to have enough time to get to know how to play them, but not enough time for me to get bored. I was transparent about that."

He shook his head as if there were no words for how fucking thick I was. "The main house is empty. Just do an auction and go out there. It'll be therapeutic."

My phone buzzed on the table, shifting a few inches.

I flipped it.

It was my wife.

# CHAPTER FOURTEEN

## PAST PERFECT

SERENA WAS STUNNING. A long stem rose with the thorns stripped. Pink petals wound tight around a cunt no man had touched, long brown hair ending at the top of her hard nipples. Her hands hung at her sides, and her eyes, which I knew were brown from the dossier, were demurely glued to my shoes.

"Charlie told me why you're here," I said. "But I need to hear it from you, in your own words. What I can do to you, and for you, needs explicit consent."

"I signed the contract, sir. I was pre-law. I understand it."

I dropped the folder on the desk. The back doors were open behind me. I could hear the waves beat the fuck out of the shore. I'd left them open on purpose. In October, the Montauk sky was the flat grey of a tin roof and the ocean wind had the first bite of cold. Goose bumps opened up on the tops of her thighs, but she stayed still, not daring to even shiver. Her discomfort, her stillness as the sheer white shift moved over her, made her submission plain.

"In your own words," I said, stepping toward her. "You went to Charlie. Why?"

"I heard he…" She stopped, drifting off in shame. "I signed it. It's right on the papers."

"You have to say it."

She swallowed. "He trains submissives. That's what I heard. So I went to the Cellar on tryout night to see if I could find him."

"You skipped a step."

I was close enough to smell her shampoo and feel her nerves.

"I want the whole story." I put a finger under her chin and made her look at me. She was about five-ten to my six-one, so her head tilted all the way back. Her tongue flicked over her lower lip. "From the beginning. You don't have to be ashamed here."

The pressure of her chin increased on my finger. She'd relaxed. All she needed was permission to explain how she knew what she was. A first-class masochist. A lovely and educated young woman who liked to be broken with pain.

"I was with my boyfriend, Keith. He went to the boys' school down the road."

"Where was this?"

"Brooklyn. Bay Ridge."

"Go on."

"We were kissing one night in his room. It was a couple of years ago. His parents were out, so he thought he was going to get me in bed. I thought so too. But it wasn't doing it for me. He never did, so I'd never let him touch me. But that time? He put his hands up my skirt, and I figured I'd let him. He put his finger inside me, and I was dry. I was always dry. I thought it was just the way I was. Normal."

"You're safe here," I said, leaning on the desk. I wanted her to feel safe, but not comfortable. There was a difference.

"Keith, well, he didn't think it was normal. He said if I was going to have the sex drive of a child, he'd treat me like a child. He spanked me. Right there in his room while I was looking at his Yankees banners. He called me names. He said I was frigid. He pulled my panties down and kept on spanking me. It was... my pussy..." She tripped on the word but gathered herself quickly. "It felt really good. And I was wet."

"What did he do?"

"I ran out before he could touch me down there again." Pause. "On my pussy."

"Call it a cunt." She looked scandalized. That got my dick hard.

"Pussies are weak. Cunts are powerful. What you have is powerful. Now finish."

"I thought I was crazy or sick. So I looked it up on the internet."

She ended there. The rest was history. She met people who knew people, and she sought out Charlie, who used the word pussy like an invective. He trained her but couldn't fuck her. She was still a virgin. It was my job and my pleasure to relieve her of that. I had thirty days to do it, and I thought I might take twenty-nine just because I could.

"You are crazy and sick, but you don't have to be miserable."

"Yes, sir."

"You have a safe word?"

"Montana."

"Any reason?"

"I hate it there."

"I've never been."

"It's a shithole."

I smiled. I liked a sub with a salty mouth. "When I ask you your age or name, answer honestly if you're all right, and lie if you need me to slow down."

The Dominant asked a simple question when it might be hard for the sub to answer or if it was possible they were too distracted to remember their safe word. It let the sub know the Dom was concerned. It was the equivalent of "hey how are you doing over there?" and the sub had the option of lying or not answering if they weren't doing well. It wasn't as hard a break as the safe word.

"How old are you?" I asked.

"Nineteen."

"Good. That's how it will go. I ask. You answer."

She nodded.

"You have three things you can refuse," I said. "Have you thought about them?"

"Yes, sir." Her fingers flicked at her sides. "Choking."

"No breath play. One."

"I don't like being called a slut or whore or any of that."

Easy. I wasn't much of a name-caller. She was going to be a cakewalk.

"That's two."

"I asked for you," she said. I tilted my head, and she looked up at me before putting her eyes back on the hardwood. "I saw you at Charlie's Black Sword party and I asked for you to be the one."

I remembered her. Sky blue polo. Black pleated miniskirt. Seven-inch heels.

"Nice of him to comply."

"The thirty days..." she said.

"Yes?"

"Is it a hard boundary?"

"You want that to be your third limit? A lack of time limits?"

"I have to go back to school next semester, but..." She swallowed hard. "I don't know what I'm asking."

"The limit protects you, not me."

She licked her lip. The ocean breeze stuck three strands of hair to her lower lip once it was wet, and she didn't move them away. Must have tickled like hell.

"Forget that one. Do another." She balled her hands into fists then laid them flat again. All her emotion was in her hands. "Cross off sharing. Don't share me."

"No sharing. Done." I flipped through the document outlining everyone's boundaries and limits. She'd initialed everything, but I had to check. "You're your mother's primary caretaker?"

"Yeah. She had a stroke in June."

"I'm sorry to hear that."

"Thanks. It's all right. I had to take a semester off until we find a permanent nurse for her. My aunt's around for the month. My brothers and sister are in school. I told them I had a camping trip."

"A month-long camping trip?"

She shrugged. I didn't press her. Logistics were her business.

"You've gone over the rest? My working hours? Your free time? Meals? Everything?"

"Yes."

"And you agree?"

"Yes."

"How do you feel?"

Her right big toe crossed over the next toe, then they all curled. "Really, really excited."

"Good." I tossed the papers on the table behind me. "Me too."

"Thank you." She smiled at the floor. Which was good. She was going to spend a lot of time on it.

"Get on your hands and knees, sweet girl, and crawl upstairs."

# CHAPTER FIFTEEN

## PRESENT TENSE

*I don't know how to say this.*

*I don't love you anymore.*

*It's not there anymore. It's not anything you did or didn't do. I've tried to talk myself out of it. I've tried to rekindle it. But it's not there. I'm dead inside.*

*I'm sorry.*

*~Diana*

Seeing her name on my phone screen, I should have been nervous or tense. The anxiety I felt all day should have twisted tighter, faster, more intensely. I was feeling at home in the Cellar. I could breathe among friends. Her name should have amped me back up to where I'd been that morning.

Instead, I was relieved. Whatever this part of the journey was, it was over. I was going to travel from not knowing into knowing.

"Excuse me," I said to Charlie without showing him the screen. He didn't need to know. "I'm going to check outside."

He leaned forward, looking out the window at the balcony, which was only big enough for a small table with an ashtray and two folding chairs. "It's raining." He crossed his ankle over his knee.

It wasn't just raining. It was cold and pouring fat chunks of icy sludge. But I couldn't talk to Diana in front of anyone. I slid the answer icon over the screen and held my breath as I opened the door to the outside. I was about to hear her voice. It had been years. Hours, even.

"Diana," I said, recalling my goddess name for her. The prayer I said in her honor. "Little huntress."

"Don't."

The first word she said to me after leaving. Don't. There wasn't a submissive on six who would have said that to me.

I sat on the chair. My wool coat protected me from the wet seat but not the slap of the sleet. I moved my back to the wall, into as much shelter as possible.

"Did you read the note?" Her voice was husky and cracked.

"Where are you?"

Silence.

"I won't come. I'll leave you alone. I need to know you're all right."

"I'm fine," she said.

"Where are you?"

"We need to talk."

"I'm not talking about anything until I know you're safe."

"I'm safe."

I didn't answer. I let my silence speak for me. Let the slushy rain splat the balcony rail with tiny wet crowns that rose and disappeared. I tried to listen to her background noise, but it was silent.

She broke first. "I have somewhere to stay."

Loaded. Her statement was loaded.

It was loaded with things she wouldn't say and the things she did. Arranging an apartment in New York wasn't an overnight affair. But she wouldn't say where, or how, or how long she'd planned to move. I knew the market, and it was longer than three days. Which meant she knew she was going to do this, and she still let me fuck her on Tuesday.

"Was that a good-bye fuck the other night?" I stuck the word fuck like a landing so she'd hear it through the phone.

"Don't make this ugly."

"You keep telling me what not to do."

"I'm sorry. I..." She gulped air. "This is so hard."

"I have to tell you something. Is that allowed?"

"Yes."

I bent at the waist until I was jutting forward toward the black bars of the balcony railing. My head was getting rained on and I didn't care. I wasn't relaxed about this. "I don't know what's happening with you. I don't know if this is the baby, or work, or if there's someone else."

"There's no one else."

"But it's gone too far. You let it get too far without talking to me. That's on you. I'm sure I did plenty wrong, but what you've done? You didn't give me a chance. You didn't let me love you the way you wanted to be loved. And make no mistake, Diana, little huntress, I love you. I have loved you from day one. I loved you more each day, and I'm going to keep loving you whether you want me to or not."

"I can't..." She sniffed. "Did you read the note?"

"I read your fucking note."

She was crying. I didn't know what to make of that. It gave me no pleasure, and coming from a man who used to make subs' tears his reason for getting out of bed in the morning, that meant a lot. But I wasn't soothing her. I wasn't going to tell her it was all right. It wasn't all right. It sucked. My socks were getting cold and wet and everything sucked.

A minute ago, I'd been relieved. Before that, I'd been determined, and now everything sucked and I was angry.

I wanted to be one thing for fifteen minutes.

I leaned back into the shelter. I had to piss. That was consistency for you.

"Don't cry," I said. "Please."

She took a deep breath. "I don't love you," she said with determination. "That's the end of it."

"Yeah."

"You don't believe me?"

"Did you tell your father you moved?"

"No."

"There you go. No, I don't believe you."

"I don't want to upset him. He cares about you."

She was baffling. She'd moved to another apartment. She'd left me a two-page note. How long did she expect to keep this a secret from her father? They were close. They talked every day. What was she going to say to him?

"What's your plan, Diana? You couldn't have started this without a plan."

She shot out a nervous laugh. "You know me. I only need half a plan before I start."

That was true. She was a starter. I was a finisher. That was why it was so perfect.

"You'll land on your feet, Adam. You'll find someone else. You're a great guy."

"Shut the fuck up." Maybe it was being at the Cellar. Maybe it was losing control of my life. I used my Dominant voice, the one that wasn't angry but broached no arguments. "Don't talk to me like that. Ever. When you're ninety and I'm a distant memory, don't even think of me with that tone."

And with that, she snapped to attention as if she were sitting right next to me at the Cellar. I didn't know if she gulped down the tears or just stopped on a dime, but business Diana showed up, kicking the door open in her New York black stilettos. She slapped her briefcase on the table and laid it down.

My girl.

"I need to discuss a buyout of McNeill-Barnes," she said with a rigidity that gripped my chest. "In the meantime, you need to excuse yourself from operations. I need full autonomy to run the company."

"No."

"Yes, Adam. This is my family's company. It's mine."

"Still no." I didn't know if I could run the business side by side with her anymore. But I wasn't going to agree to any changes in the fucking rain.

"All outstanding debts to R+D are paid," she said. "We're in the black. It's been five years. I've earned my seat at the table."

"You haven't earned a seat at the head."

"Yes, I have."

I imagined her in the McNeill-Barnes conference room in her power suit and fuck-me-if-you-dare pumps. I knew what her face looked like when she was ripping a printer a new asshole. Business Diana was more manageable than Crying Diana. I could talk to Business Diana. I knew the rules. I hated them, but I knew them, and I had a way to get my disorientation under control.

*Bend over the table. Pick up your skirt. You're getting twenty strokes with my belt. Count them.*

"Go back and read the contract. I'll meet you at the R+D offices at nine to discuss what you missed."

"I might be late. I'm up in Riverside."

Riverside?

The air felt warm on my skin. The sleet was boiling. That was how cold my body became.

I almost said something. Almost asked a question.

But that would alert her that I knew where Zack Abramson lived.

I tapped the red circle to hang up. Her name went grey and I went grey with it, and when it flickered away, the emptiness between us broke into separate universes.

She was beautiful in every way, and I'd been too nice. I'd let her consider leaving me and I hadn't taken a second to wake up to the fact that there would be other men.

Today. Tomorrow. Ten years from now.

Every cell in my body screamed.

I'd been confused and broken. But after the call, I had something I had to do.

# CHAPTER SIXTEEN

## PRESENT TENSE

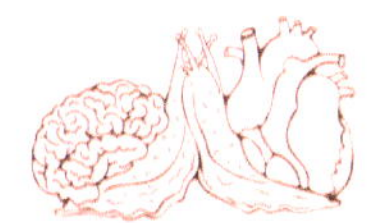

I BARELY PARKED the Jag on Riverside. It landed a foot and a half from the curb, but I didn't have the patience for one more parallel parking maneuver. He could be touching her right now. He could have his fingers in her cunt and his mouth anywhere. And she could be breathing in that way. That sticky-throated way she breathed when she was aroused. As if her throat got wet when her cunt got wet.

He could be on top of her. Pushing his soon-to-be-removed dick inside her.

All that was mine.

Her cunt was mine. Her thick-sexed voice was mine. When she closed her eyes to come. Mine. Her pleasure. I owned it. All of it. For-fucking-ever. Till death, you fucking shit.

"Hey." I smiled at the doorman and lifted a manila envelope. I'd stuffed a galley I'd had lying around the trunk inside it.

"Good evening, sir," he replied. He was a big guy, stretching his shirt at the belly. His long navy tie covered the popping buttons. He sat behind a little podium with closed circuit monitors of the exits and entrances and clipboards with guest signatures.

"Is Zack Abramson in? He's in seven-fourteen."

"I know where he's at. Was at. He left this afternoon."

I hadn't expected that. I'd expected the guard to take it upstairs. Then I'd call Zack and tell him to come downstairs to talk.

"Talking" meant "break his face."

"Can you give this to him tomorrow?" I thought maybe he'd been running errands all day and hadn't gotten back to fuck my wife yet.

"Would if I could. He left town."

"Dayton?"

"I'm not allowed to say. But if you want to leave that here, I'm getting his mail together. Sending next week." He held out his hand.

"I'll send it. Thanks."

I went out to Riverside Drive, crossed the street, and stood behind my car, looking up at the building. The sleet had picked up, going from drops to sheets, but I didn't care. Didn't feel their cold or their cutting friction.

One-two-three-four-five-six-seven.

Seventh floor. Zack had said he had a view over Riverside Drive, so she was in one of those apartments. She wasn't fucking Zack. Not tonight. Maybe never, but definitely not tonight.

I saw her in the second window from the corner, slim and straight. Unmistakable to the man who loved her. She cradled a teacup and looked out at New Jersey through the same veil of sleet I watched her through.

How long was I going to do this? Watch her in the freezing cold? Chase her down? Lie to doormen? Want a woman who'd turned her back on me months ago?

I couldn't shake the jealous rage over any man who touched her. I couldn't let go of the longing or the loss.

But as I got into the car, shivering, I realized there was only one cause for my pain. I didn't have to be a man without anger or jealousy. They were symptoms of another disease. I needed to become a man unburdened by love.

I didn't have a plan yet. I didn't have a beginning, middle, and end. Just a concept without form. I didn't articulate it to myself, but somewhere on the back burners, something started stewing. Something difficult, bold, and utterly callous.

# CHAPTER SEVENTEEN

## PRESENT TENSE

Fɪʀsᴛ ᴛɪᴍᴇs.

The first time I tried to sleep in our bed knowing she didn't love me anymore, I didn't sleep. I barely moved. The noise from Crosby Street rumbled, honked, shouted, clacked, gradually less and less as the moon moved the light from one side of our bedroom to the other. By three in the morning, I could hear the rooftop pigeons across the street coo and flap, rattling their chicken wire coop in the freezing cold.

I stretched across my bed. Was it our bed still? Or was the property transferred when she no longer had a place next to me?

The first time I doubted my decision to marry her, I wasn't sure if I was sleeping or not. How had I missed the manipulation? The calculation? She'd needed me to save her family business. But I was going to save it before she offered herself to me. Way before I asked her to marry me.

It wasn't that.

I owned her. She was mine.

But no.

Vulnerable. Powerless. I couldn't hold what I possessed. The feeling was freefall. The earth coming into sharp focus as I hurtled toward it at the acceleration of gravity.

*I don't need to punish you to paddle you. I don't need an excuse. You're mine, and I can paddle you when I please. Because I feel like it. Now bend over the table, arms out, palms down. Do you need something to bite?*

The first night of the rest of my life, I imagined breaking her. I imagined her crying for mercy. For release. For me. The smell of her skin. The taste of her tears. The color of the parts of her that got my cruelest and kindest attention. How would she beg for my forgiveness? How would I take her then? Gently? Would I bend her body? Her mind?

My fantasies crossed into psychopathic. Anger and dominance had no place together. Revenge and sadism never played in the same scene. The idea was to cause pain, not damage, and rage clouded a Dominant's judgment.

Yet the scenes I imagined with such clarity were familiar. Years before, I'd managed them all with utter control and complete consent.

The first time my wires crossed, I scared myself, and the fear was cathartic.

# CHAPTER EIGHTEEN

## PRESENT TENSE

THE R+D offices were in midtown, in the center of a glass column on the west side. In contrast to the McNeill-Barnes offices, they were sharp and cold, modern and noncommittal. We bought things and either built them back up or stripped them and sold them for parts. I'd started with the Williamsburg, Brooklyn, property my grandparents helped me buy at a fortunate time in the market. I lived in a studio south of Metropolitan and bought another property, then another, leaving little for myself to live on, until the next real estate boom left me with enough to leverage for greater and greater loans.

I made money and explored kink through my twenties. Sometimes I breathed.

The subway wasn't luxurious, but if I wanted to get anywhere at eight in the morning, it was the fastest way to go. No matter how expensive the car, it was still subject to the laws of physics, and the streets were jam-packed with things not even a Jaguar could drive through.

My phone rang in the lobby of my building. Lloyd Barnes. My father in-law. Soon to be known as a guy I wasn't related to by marriage.

"Hey—" I stopped myself before saying *dad*.

"What the hell is going on?" His breath was wheezy. Stress.

"With regard to?"

Lloyd came to me when he wanted it straight. His daughter protected him from anything that might upset him. Even the smallest production glitch was a secret. He only heard about the spina bifida because he called me and I told him without preamble.

"My daughter."

"Is she all right?" I was stalling. I knew what he was calling about.

"She says you're splitting up. What did you do?"

The phone would die in the elevator, so I hung back in a corner of the cold stone-and-glass lobby, away from the push and bustle of people getting to work.

"When I find out, I'll let you know."

"Is she protecting you?"

No. She wasn't protecting me. I had no idea what she was doing except leaving. Maybe it was that simple anyway. Maybe she was just sick of me and wanted to move on.

"She wants out. I have nothing else, Lloyd."

He wheezed. I heard a whoosh and waited as he got his oxygen tubes in his nose.

"I'm not happy," he said.

"Neither am I. But there's nothing I can do about it. Diana wants what she wants, and if she wants to end this marriage, she's going to do it."

"That's her mother, you know. I loved her, but when she wanted something, she wanted it."

"Self-determination's a great quality until it's directed against you."

"You'll stay with us, I hope?"

He meant McNeill-Barnes. Not the family.

"I haven't thought about it."

"Think about it then."

"I will."

I hung up and went to the elevator. What did I want? What was my self-determined desire?

Diana. How was I going to get her back? By her presence or my absence?

R+D ran itself, more or less. My business partner, Eva, took care of much of the day-to-day while we built up McNeill-Barnes. Walking back into the office for the first time since Diana's note felt surreal. I was already a different man; I just didn't know how different.

Eva was a tightly put-together lawyer who had moved into corporate management. She had a short black pixie cut and pant suit. She changed the seven earrings in her left ear to match her suit or her mood. Today she was red.

"Adam," she said, falling into step with me through the reception area.

"Eva."

We went through the swinging doors to the inner offices. We each had a corner, and the other windows were bordered by seven conference rooms.

"Your wife is here with Rhonda Sidewinder. The divorce lawyer."

"They're early."

"What's going on?" She rarely got personal with me, but the concern in her brown eyes was real.

"Everything. Can you grab my contract with McNeill? I'm sure Rhonda has a copy, but I want to glance at it beforehand. And please do it yourself. If you have Brittany pull it, the whole office is going to talk."

She handed me a folder. "I had a feeling you'd need it. Your McNeill-Barnes contract is in there too."

"Great. Thanks."

"They're in conference four." I started to go, but she touched my arm. "Who's representing you?"

"No one yet. Look, this happened yesterday. It was out of nowhere."

"What are you going to do?"

"Fight for her."

I turned away before I had to see the sympathy in her face.

# CHAPTER NINETEEN
## PAST PERFECT

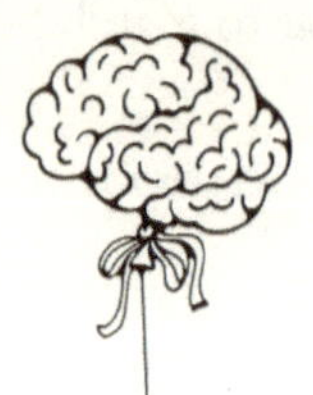

First times.

The first time I saw my wife's face after she left me, she looked different. I thought maybe she'd changed somehow, but I knew I was the one who had changed. Not enough to stop loving her, but enough to see her from far away.

The first time I saw ice in her eyes, I knew it was a thin veneer, put there to make it possible for her to finish the job.

The first time she looked like a stranger to me, I knew it was false. She wasn't a stranger. She was my Diana. My huntress. She was still mine.

And when I looked right at her and she cast her eyes down, I recognized the performance of the gesture as hers. Very much hers. But I'd changed, and I didn't see what I wanted to see. I saw what was always there.

# CHAPTER TWENTY

## PRESENT TENSE

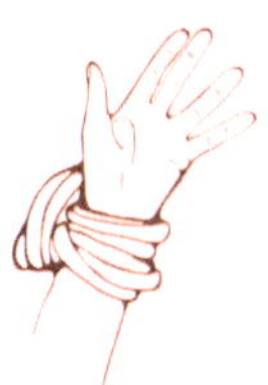

SHE'D TAKEN off her wedding ring. She tried to hide it by folding her right hand over her left, but as the meeting drew on and on, she had to take a drink of water. I caught sight of her left hand before she put it in her lap.

"We understand that the company bylaws fail to provide a clear procedure for valuation of shares in the event of a buyback," Sidewinder said, "but my client would like you to sell her your fifty-one percent of the company at cost."

Diana put the glass down and her right hand joined her left hand in her lap.

"Cost?"

"What you bought them for."

"When the business was underwater and I wanted to break it apart and sell the pieces?" I turned to Diana. "We've been sitting here for an hour for *this*? You want me *out*?"

"My client wishes to appeal to your good will."

"What good will?" I kept my eyes on my wife. "How long did you know?"

Her eyes joined her hands. In her lap. I slapped the table and she jumped.

"How. Long."

"I don't see that it matters," she said.

"Mister Steinbeck, we can reconvene when you've acquired counsel, but this—"

"It matters. I need to know how long I was fucking a stranger."

"—is not acceptable."

"And me?" Diana cried, the fire back in her eyes. "Who was I fucking?"

"Maybe you should make me a list."

"Never, you freak." She leaned forward, left hand flat on the table. "I never. But what were you doing last night?"

The word freak stopped me, and in the pause, Rhonda Sidewinder filled the gap.

"Mr. Steinbeck. I was hoping this could proceed without—"

"What do you mean?" I asked Diana.

"—revealing certain measures we've taken. But last night you were seen walking into a known sex club."

I maintained a steady expression and didn't move. I made sure I breathed. But I felt as though I'd been hit in the gut. I didn't want Diana to know. I didn't want her lawyer to know. I'd kept my past from my wife for as long as I'd known her, and she was finding out how I'd lied to her and myself the entire time.

"How long, Adam?" Diana growled, bottom lip quivering. "How. Long."

"Jesus, Diana, it's almost like you care."

Rhonda Sidewinder was known as a shark who never let an emotional moment get in the way of advocating for her client. "This won't play well in front of a judge. Nor will standing outside and watching her in a window."

"You put someone on me," I said.

"In the interests of—" Rhonda started but Diana interrupted.

"It was Regina's idea, and I'm glad I did it."

"Your *therapist*? She suggested you put a tail on me? Is that ethical?"

"She thought you were cheating." Diana shook her head. "I did it to rule it out, because I thought she was wrong."

"How long have you been going to sex clubs, Mister Steinbeck?" Rhonda asked.

I wasn't answering. Not right away. Diana was upset, and I wanted her to just sit there and feel like I felt for a minute. As if she'd lived a lie for five years. Because fuck her and her ringless finger and her time in Zack's bed. Fuck her detective, her therapist, and her lawyer. Fuck her attempts to kick me out of the business. Fuck her.

I loved her but fuck her. If she'd had the detective on me for long, she would have known I hadn't been to the Cellar since we were married. She had one night's worth of evidence. The night she left me. And it was burning her up from the inside.

Good.

Fuck her.

"As I was saying," Sidewinder continued, "adultery is cause. We intended to make this convivial."

"So you had me followed." I didn't take my eyes off my wife, and hers were glued to me. I didn't know what we were saying to each other. We were just battering rams of hurt and betrayal.

"We can skip the separation and just serve you. But as an article of good faith, we'll go back to irretrievable breakdown status if you agree to sign over the title to the Jaguar."

I turned my attention away from my wife and on to Sidewinder. "What?"

"And the parking spot on Lafayette."

The parking spot in the underground lot was the first thing we had bought together. We laughed about it and fucked in the front seat, in the spot, because it was ours.

"I can't believe this has come down to a car."

"Taxis won't take Daddy's oxygen tanks," Diana said.

"Buy your own car."

"It *is* my car."

I stood. I'd had enough of this bullshit.

# CHAPTER TWENTY-ONE

## PRESENT TENSE

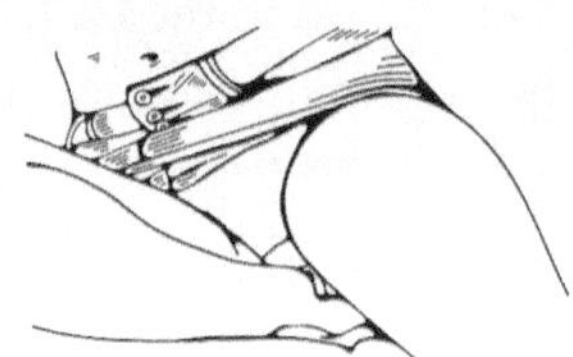



The car, the detective, the terms of the separation, all of those overwhelmed me, but as I walked out of conference four, the only thing on my mind was that Diana knew I was at the Cellar.

Eva saw me in the hall on the way to my office.

"Guess who I just saw in the bathroom," she whispered. "Upset."

"Crusty the Clown."

"What?"

"Random questions get random answers."

"I don't officially advocate you going into a women's restroom."

"You're a piece of work, Eva."

"I know." She walked past me and didn't look back.

Justine, our staff architect, came out of the ladies' room just as I walked down the hall. When she was gone, I went in and locked the door. The clack echoed like a gong.

Diana spun, hands clasping the edge of the counter behind her, the water still flowing. "What are you doing in here?"

"It's my office."

I stepped toward her. She didn't move.

I leaned behind her and shut off the faucet. "Your lawyer isn't interested in anything but her bill. You know that, right?" I snapped paper towels off the roll and handed the piece to her.

"I can't meet you alone." She wiped her fingers. "You're too... I don't know the word. I can't think when you're looking at me. I just—"

"I thought you were fucking Zack Abramson."

Her eyes flashed. Anger or recognition? Couldn't tell anything anymore.

"That's why I went to Riverside Drive," I said. "To kill him if he was."

"From the BDSM club?"

"Directly."

"How could you? You're worried about me with Zack, and you'd just paid some woman to tie you up and spank you or whatever?"

I laughed so loud I thought the whole office would descend on the bathroom to see what the joke was.

"What's so funny?"

"Look, I have nothing against male subs, and the femdom rooms are packed, but—"

"How long have you been into this shit, Adam? From the beginning or after? Is this why you're distracted when we make love? You wish I was something else?"

I stepped back. What she'd said was insulting. She'd missed the entire point and hit the bullseye.

As if sensing the crack in my armor, she went in. "You say you love me. How can you? You had this whole other life and never shared it. What kind of marriage did we have? Tell me, how deep does this go?"

"I'm saying this once to you personally, and once in front of a lawyer if I have to. I shouldn't have to repeat the truth more than that."

I looked her in the eye as she scanned me back and forth, *flick flick flick*. Her eyes couldn't stay still. She could have known me but never loved me, or loved me without ever knowing me.

"I haven't been to the club since before we dated, and you're the only woman I've touched since then. Period."

"You went before? This is a thing for you?"

"Yes."

"Why didn't you tell me?"

*Because I loved you.*

*Because I was afraid you'd like it.*

"Do you want the car?" I asked. "I'll sign it over. One hundred percent."

"What's the catch?"

"You give me five minutes. Right here. Right now."

"I'm not having sex with you."

I smirked. Somewhere in there was an opening. She was interested. Curious what I had in mind. I owned her attention. Her lawyer could have banged down the door and not moved Diana's dial a single notch. "I won't touch you."

She swallowed and tilted her head just a tiny bit. That was the curiosity. "What is this?"

"You'll have to pull your skirt up."

Her brows knotted. "I said I wasn't having sex with you."

"And I said I wasn't touching you. You want to know about me and what that part of me is like? I'm going to show you. It won't hurt. It might even be fun."

She just drilled, pushing her intention forward, trying to see through me.

"Pull your skirt up." I said it without acknowledging the possibility that she'd do anything but what I commanded.

It felt good to use those words and that tone. It felt good when her eyes went to the floor.

"Trust me." I said it so low she was just within range to hear it. "Five minutes. Then we don't have to fight over the car."

I stepped back and set my watch with a beep. It wasn't about the car for her. The Jag was the least of her worries, but it was a tangible justification.

For the downcast eyes. For the way her breathing changed. For what Charlie knew and I suspected but wouldn't acknowledge.

Maybe every bone in her body was vanilla. Maybe.

"Quit any time," I said. "Just say the word."

She laid her hands on her hips.

Curled her fingers.

Gripped fabric.

Pulled up her skirt.

The tops of her thighs came into view then met at the crotch. I was hard already and made no move to hide it. She noticed and stopped moving the skirt.

"Higher," I said as if telling her how to center a picture over the couch. Higher was where it had to be. It wasn't a request.

Up it went. Cotton underwear in a pink so pale they were almost white. Tiny falling raindrops of hair at the edges of the fabric. The surprise of the hair pressed against the base of my balls.

Diana kept herself completely smooth, all the time. It was a priority for her. If she let it grow, that meant one thing. She didn't think anyone was going to see it. Not me, but more tellingly, not Zack or anyone else. Those little hairs were a relief.

"Now what?" she asked.

"How do you feel?"

"Weird, Adam. Really weird."

"Why?"

"Because I'm standing here with my skirt around my waist? Because you told me to? For a car, no less, which is creepy."

She was so honest. I ached for her honesty.

"Not for the car. So you don't have to fight for the car."

"Whatever."

"It's an important distinction. You're not obeying me for an object. You're obeying me so I do something. Take an action or don't."

"You think that's not weird?"

"No, I don't. And we have four minutes." I stepped forward. Part of her discomfort was in the physical distance between us. I'd stepped away so she didn't feel threatened, but my gaze was keeping her from relaxing. I kept my eyes on hers. I could smell her perfume and feel the shortness of her breath. "Are you turned on?"

"Sex isn't going to get me back. I'm sorry—"

"Touch yourself."

I remembered that first night in the cab. She'd seemed so solidly vanilla she wouldn't even play. But alone, in the bathroom, her initial shock and offense lasted only a second before she pressed her lips together and reached down, shoulders angling, hand thrusting as if checking to make sure her cunt was still there.

We have hundreds of bones in our bodies, and sometimes we won't acknowledge the preferences of the ones that scare us.

"Are you wet?"

"A little."

I gripped the edge of the vanity and put my lips near her cheek, millimeters from touching her.

"You don't love me anymore," I whispered. "But I could always make you wet, and you always came for me. Like our Italy vacation. In Florence. Coming back from that club, in the little alley. Against the wall. I ripped through your underwear."

Her breathing got shallow and fast.

"I fucked you in the dark, and when you came, you screamed my name so loud all the lights in the apartments went on."

"That was good." She turned her face toward mine.

When her lips nearly touched me, I pulled away just enough. "I said I wouldn't touch you."

"I changed my mind."

I wasn't fooled. Her arousal was talking. "Are you wet?"

"Yes."

"How wet?"

"Very."

I owned her. She'd do whatever I told her. But I wanted something very simple. I wanted her pleasure. "Take the juice from your cunt and rub it on your clit. Make it wet."

"Adam."

"What?"

"What's come over you?"

"Do it." I felt her arm move against me. "Rub your clit back and forth. Be consistent. One-two-one-two."

When I felt that she had it, I stepped back. She stopped. Her knees were bent slightly and her fingers had taken her cunt from the side of the crotch, not the waistband. She never ceased to surprise me. Her shame was apparent. So was her arousal.

"One-two-one-two, huntress."

"Is this your way of getting back at me?"

"One-two-one-two. Let me see you come. You're so beautiful when you come. You've gone this far."

I didn't think she'd continue with me watching her, but her clit must have been throbbing and hard. Her body must have been able to override her mind, because she moved her finger again, closing her eyes. Her cheeks reddened and her knees bent more deeply.

"In Florence. An hour after we got to the hotel. I came so deep in you that night. I fucked you from behind with your leg up on the dresser. I wanted to thrust my whole body inside you. I loved you that much. And I gave up who I was. Last night, at the club, I remembered what I was. I was a man who was obeyed. I dominated women, and they submitted to me. The result was what you're about to feel. Complete pleasure."

She let out a long, low groan, leaning on the vanity, twisting. I could have fucked her right then. I could have bent her over the counter and pounded her. But that wasn't the point. No. Watching her hand move under her clothes because I commanded it. That was the point.

An *uh* escaped her throat. Years of marriage had taught me that meant she was about to come.

My watch beeped.

"Time's up," I said.

Her eyes went wide. Her hand stopped.

"Thank you," I said. "We're done. I'll send you the title to the car. You might want to pull your skirt down, since I can't lock the door from the outside."

It was hard to walk away from her panting, bent frame without tasting her cunt or even seeing more of her reaction, but I turned the corner, unlocked the door, and left the bathroom.

# CHAPTER TWENTY-TWO
## PRESENT TENSE

IT WASN'T until I got to the corner that I realized I was shaking. Not from the cold, which was significant. Blood had been dumped from my heart and was coloring my entire body hot red. She'd done what I told her. I'd dominated her for five minutes. Owned her. Pleasure and shame, every submissive bone in her body had been mine for that little bit of time.

It all came back in a flood. I was high on dominance. I remembered how it had felt with other women, but it was a hundred times more powerful with her. After such a long time away, the surge of adrenaline and endorphins made me feel like a perfectly tuned instrument.

I stepped onto the street in my flat-bottomed shoes, the melting ice creating new treacheries, and I knew I wouldn't fall.

Walking across, my feet counting one-two-one-two-one with the rhythms of the street, the sounds of the city, the wind on my face, the towering obelisks above, I was threaded into the fabric of the world.

I heard the yellow cab before I saw it. The wheels didn't screech—the street was too coated in melting ice for that. They made a splashing crackle as the hulk of metal barreled toward me out of control, so close. No way to run. No way to jump or dodge.

Yet I was in complete control of myself. I was right in the world. I felt the substance of my existence and the calculations of my thoughts.

I took one step sideways.

The cab missed me by an inch, skidding to a splashy stop.

With that lurching yellow car and the collective exhale of everyone who saw the skid, the door behind me closed. My journey had to go forward, back to who I'd been.

# CHAPTER TWENTY-THREE

## PAST PERFECT

McNeill-Barnes company archives.
Transcript of Lloyd Barnes's retirement speech.
The Claude Hotel Ballroom
June 21st, 2012.
Staff, authors, and their guests in attendance.
Full guest list in appendix.

My wife and I took this company over twenty-five years ago from
another team forged in the bonds of marriage—my wife's parents,
Richard and Bertha McNeill. Dick and Bert were pioneers. Together
they published and nurtured some of the greatest American authors of
the century. True literary giants. And mostly because of Bert's influence,
they published some of the most esteemed female authors of the
generation.

Martha and I tried to maintain that vision, but we had a slow leak in
the business. Technology. Changing tastes. We kept her afloat, working
day and night, but by the time Martha couldn't fight off the second
round of cancer, we were struggling to see a future.

And I can't imagine a future without McNeill-Barnes. The only thing that's kept me alive this past year has been the slow, steady, incremental revival of this company, thanks to my daughter, Diana, and her future husband, Adam Steinbeck.

(raises glass)

(guests cheer)

What a joy to give the day-to-day operations over to my daughter and another husband-and-wife team. It was my dream to pass them a profitable and historically relevant publishing house. I've downgraded that a little.

(cries of denial)

I'm passing them a company rife with potential to create and release important work in this new century. Most importantly, I'm passing it to family. I'll die happy if this company stays alive and in family hands.

You two need to have kids, stat.

(laughter)

# CHAPTER TWENTY-FOUR

## PRESENT TENSE

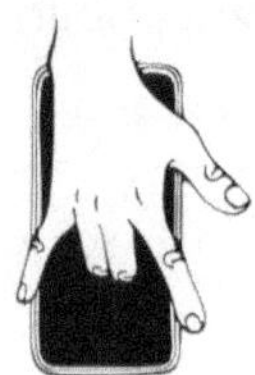

Two days had passed since I dominated Diana in the bathroom at R+D. Since then, she'd worked from home, and I'd jumped between publishing and real estate development.

I carried around five tons of pain where she used to be. But those minutes of submission, as reluctant as they were, they were minutes of heaven I never thought I'd have.

I thought about her constantly.

My wife and I worked because I was a planner and she was the creative mind behind our life together. She had ideas and ran at the starting gun, but midway, she'd get distracted and move on to the next thing.

That worked. Because I liked finishing. She wanted a condo down the street from the McNeill-Barnes building and attacked the purchase single-mindedly. When we talked about reviving the publishing business, she had the idea to diminish the importance of fiction in their catalog and pump new life into long-form journalism based on the questions in her journals. She started both projects. I finished them.

What had there been besides work?

Us, together. In the office, in bed, in the kitchen in the morning, strategizing, coming up with ideas, these were my best memories of Diana.

"Let's sleep in," she'd asked once. Maybe a year into our marriage.

I'd stroked her arm, feeling her eyelashes flutter on my chest. Saturdays were the only day to get anything done, and we had to do it. The financial bloodletting was slowing, but we had to keep pushing.

"We can sleep in tomorrow."

She'd gotten up before I finished the last syllable and she was in the bathroom before I could tell her to stay still a second, another half an hour wasn't going to hurt.

I hadn't gone to her cousin's wedding in Minnesota. She'd only taken two days leave for her aunt's death in New Jersey because we had a pitch meeting in Los Angeles. We'd lost the baby, and beside screwing regularly, we hadn't made any effort to time sex with her cycle.

Every step was another way we failed each other.

I ached. My joints. My head. My heart. I ached with emptiness and helplessness. The pain was physical. I tried to jog it off on the salty streets. Piles of snow built up on the curb, leaving less room for joggers, and I veered right to avoid a stroller. My shoulder brushed against the green subway railing.

Without pausing or missing a beat, I ran down the stairs and got on the Uptown A.

Fucking train. I couldn't tell how fast it was going because it was so goddamn slow. I needed to say what needed saying. We had been too focused on work. That was the problem.

I got off on Riverside Drive and jogged west in the Saturday twilight. I had so many things to say. All obvious. All puzzle pieces clicking into place.

The lights in Zack's apartment were off. I looked at my phone for the time, but I didn't need to. It was dark enough for her to need the lights.

It was almost the end of the month. Did she move out? And to where?

I slid the bar to make a call. She had to answer.

But then I saw a little app that would tell me when a phone was stolen. Was she still on my account?

I sat on a cold bench by the Hudson River and tapped the icon.
In half a second, her phone showed up. Downtown.
At the Cellar.

# CHAPTER TWENTY-FIVE

## PAST PERFECT

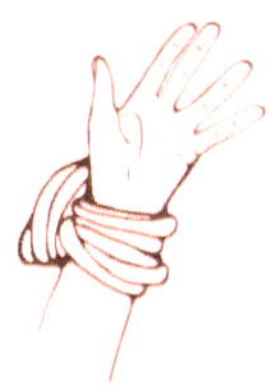

Did you never dominate her? Did she never submit to you, even a little? Take a command? A strong request?

*Open your legs.*

*I didn't shave yesterday.*

*I don't care.*

*Or the day before.*

I open her legs. It's dark. It's late. We haven't had time to breathe all week. We haven't made love in eight days, and the sight of her in the office is driving me insane. Seeing her in the morning as we talk about leasing parts of the SoHo building through the shower doors gives me a boner I never consider relieving because I know the schedule. I know where we have to be and when. But I can smell the delicious tang of her cunt.

I kneel on the bed and open her legs at the knees.

*I'm so tired, honey.*

She is tired. It's not a ploy. I run my hands down her inner thighs, and when my fingers reach her cunt, it's wet. She groans.

I bend her knees up and apart. She is deliciously compliant.

*I can't move. So tired. We have to be up in four hours.*

She can barely make the words.

*Don't move then.*

*Can't.*

*Just let me take you.*

*Okay.*

I fuck her. When she moves, I tell her to stay still. When her eyebrows tense and her mouth opens, I shush her.

*Don't move. Stay absolutely still.*

*Adam. Adam...*

*Shh. Not a word.*

*I love you.*

I can tell she comes when I feel her muscles tense and release. And when I come inside her, I own the world.

# CHAPTER TWENTY-SIX
## PRESENT TENSE

*—Are you at the Cellar?—*

**—What, mate? It's tryout
night. We're at the Loft Club—**

*—Diana's there—*

**—Diana your vanilla wife?—**

*—I'm uptown. I need you to go over
there and make sure she's all right.
I'm coming ASAP—*

**—We're on our way—**

*—Thank you—*

**—You owe us, big time—**

# CHAPTER TWENTY-SEVEN

## PRESENT TENSE

I DIDN'T ASK WHO "US" was. I assumed it was Viktor or another lifer. Another body. Someone who lived by rules and codes. Someone willing to run off to the Cellar on my behalf on tryout night.

I had too much to do in the meantime.

Sweaty gym suits wouldn't get me far in the club, and I was at the northwestern tip of a very crowded island. I wanted to be at the southwestern edge.

*—Diana, what are you doing?—*

I had two hundreds in my wallet and I gave one to the cabbie. "Get me to TriBeCa in five minutes and you get the other hundred."

He took off like a shot.

*—Don't talk to anyone—*

She didn't answer. The signal in the bottom floor—the actual cellar —was notoriously hard core. So was the view. Latex bodysuits and slapping leather. Nipple clamps and tit torture. Scat had a separate room, but some nights you could smell it down there.

That's what I imagined seeing through her eyes. She'd see chaos where I saw control. When I saw it through my eyes, it looked like contented people satisfying their needs. It looked like a place without judgment.

She wouldn't see it that way. She didn't know every stroke was part of negotiation, consent, and contracts. She didn't know there was a board of people who settled disputes with excommunication and fines.

I checked for her phone's location, and no new signal came through. Just the old location.

Tryout nights were tame by normal standards because anyone could show up, but for some in the community, the extra people was the appeal. The increased risk of exposure was a turn-on, and the acts downstairs could get incredibly outrageous just for the sake of it.

She was fine. No one would hurt her or touch her. She was protected by the rules, and she very well might have gone with a friend or two. Maybe she went with a date.

I had to put that out of my mind before I broke something.

The cabbie earned the extra hundred. I promised another hundred if he waited.

I scrubbed down in record time and got into a suit, barely looking at myself in the mirror before grabbing the jacket and running out.

There was a crowd outside the velvet ropes. Rob and Carol were checking people against a list and letting others in just because they looked as though they'd be scared. Fear was great entertainment. They opened the rope for me.

"It's tryout," Rob said.

"I know." I slapped him on the shoulder and walked in.

My phone dinged.

*—I see her—*

*—On six—*

I went to my phone locator. Found her. New signal. Same place. She was out of the dungeon.

I got into the elevator with a woman in latex pants and a collar and her Dom, who wore ripped jeans and a leather jacket. He held her leash loosely, and when the brass doors closed, I saw the three of us in the reflection. Scenes were not permitted in elevators or halls, so we all stood, facing front, on the way to male domination. The Dom to my right quietly yanked the leash, and the sub smiled subtly.

I fixed my tie in the reflection in the brass.

My ring was still on.

I was about to see her, in the club, on the sixth floor.

Relief-plus-elation-plus-dread.

My lungs weren't big enough for the size of the breath I had to take.

The doors slid open to the red hallway.

# CHAPTER TWENTY-EIGHT
## PRESENT TENSE

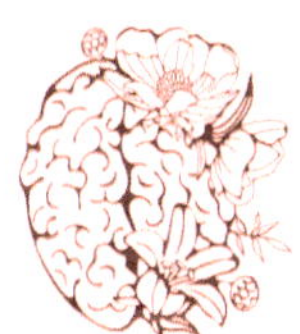

MY SPACE. My room. My world.

Five steps to the door, ten to the bar, and that's how long it took to get my shit together. Diana was under my protection in my domain. Nothing and no one would touch her but me.

I saw Charlie first, and he pointed at the bar. Fucker was just watching.

She sat at the bar between two men. Viktor and Braden. I knew them, and I knew why they were talking to her. She was beautiful and inexperienced. Their intentions were crystal clear to me, and I fought the urge to take their faces off with my bare hands.

I had to hold my breath and mitigate my expectations against the reality.

I expected her to be meek and scared. Kittenish. Overwhelmed. Wide-eyed.

The reality was that she was the woman I'd married. I married a boss. I married a sharp, creative mind. Not that any of those traits kept her from glancing nervously at the nearly naked woman curled at Viktor's feet, but Diana was engaged in a conversation as if everything around her was completely normal.

And she was everything. I couldn't hear her when she spoke, but I knew she sounded clear and confident from the way she made eye contact. Nodded when Viktor answered. Put her drink to her lips.

Her blouse was buttoned all the way, but I could see the heave of her chest, knew the shape of her tits, how to make the nipples hard. The things I could do to her in that club, half a room away.

*Open your cunt. Bend over. Count with me. Beg for my cock.*

I couldn't put them all in order.

She touched her necklace, one of her tells for arousal, but the knowledge that she was wet was pushed away by the wedding ring on her finger. She'd put it back on. Probably to keep men away. That didn't work in the Cellar. If you were there, you were there to play or learn how to play.

*Calmly.* I walked toward her. She saw me a few steps away, and her chin went up a few millimeters. Brazen, like a teenager caught with a cigarette and not putting it out. Viktor, a Dominant who couldn't stand the thought of losing a woman's attention, reached for her face.

I took the last step and grabbed his wrist hard.

Viktor was a Russian oligarch who'd escaped the KGB in a cargo ship, but if he'd touched her, I would have broken that wrist.

"Let go, friend." He elongated friend as if it was a temporary condition.

"She's mine." I let go. "And I don't share this one. Friend."

Viktor picked up his drink. "Shame you feel that way. It's what they need."

He looked down at his sub, who rested her head peacefully on his leg. He stroked her cheek. Her smile widened.

My wife touched her necklace as if frozen. I couldn't gauge her emotions. Mine were muddled as fuck. I didn't want her to be there, but my dick thought it was a terrific idea.

*You don't want her getting any good ideas.*

"Vick!" Charlie's voice cut through the noise.

"You Aussie fuck!" Viktor replied jovially.

Charlie glanced at me and nodded as he shook hands with the man, letting me know he'd saved me and I owed him plenty.

"Diana," I said, "what are you doing?"

She looked at me, lips tight. "I have the right to be here."

"I didn't say you didn't. And you don't have to be defensive. Let's talk about this separate from everything else. Without all the baggage or the divorce. Just talk to me." I put my arm on the bar and motioned for Norton. "What are you drinking?"

"Ginger ale," she said.

"Good choice."

"I felt like I needed my wits about me."

"You do. Do you want to stay or go?"

I wanted her to stay because if she left, I might not see her again. This chance to show her the world I'd left for her wouldn't come again. I didn't know if I wanted to attract her to it or scare her away, but I wanted to know what was possible.

She didn't think about it long, but deep, checking my face, the room, her own breath before answering. "Stay."

I ordered two ginger ales.

She eyeballed Charlie. "Was he at our wedding? The Australian guy with the cane?"

"Yes. And a few other things. Events. Whatnot."

She'd had no idea who he was to me. She'd shaken his hand and made small talk knowing nothing. Of course she looked as if I'd betrayed her.

"You didn't tell me you were coming," I said.

"Neither did you. For five years."

"I stopped when you came along."

"I don't believe you."

"It's true."

"Oh, I believe you didn't set foot in this club. But you were here." She scanned the room, with its ambient music and soft lighting. Men in suits and women doing their bidding. Her gaze landed on Viktor the Russian chatting with Charlie, then moved down to his sub curled at his feet like a contented kitten.

"I knew it was something," she said. "All that time you were phoning it in."

"That's not true—"

"You think I couldn't tell?" She looked right through me, breaking my defenses to bits.

"I love you, Diana." I growled it, taking her arm. "You're not for this. Did you want me to drag you down here? For what? I'd hate myself for ruining you."

"I loved you too. Past. Tense." She yanked her arm away. "And I've been blaming myself for a year now. But it wasn't me. It was *you*."

She snapped her bag off the bar and walked away, twisting on her high heel and speeding off.

Fuck this.

This was my world, and I could do shit here I couldn't do anywhere else.

I took a single step, picked her up, and threw her over my shoulder.

The air went out of her. She beat my back and cried my name as I carried her to the back and around a corner to a bank of doors with leather numbers. One was ajar. I kicked it open with a *slap*. The black room was lit by a single red bulb.

I slammed the door closed with my foot, clicked the *occupied* sign, and dropped her. Her lips were parted and her mouth was twisted into a snarl. She punched my chest so hard the air went out of me. I grabbed her wrists with one hand and pushed her against the wall.

"Don't you fucking touch me!"

I kept my hands where they were and pushed into her.

Her eyelids fluttered. She'd be touching her pearls if her hands were free.

"What did you say?" I whispered. I smelled the arousal on her.

Breathy, without aggression or a struggle to get away, she said, "Don't you fucking touch me."

"You came here to see something? You came here to learn about me? The guy you don't love anymore? Why? What's the fucking difference?"

In the silence that followed, a *thwack* could be heard through the walls. And a long female cry that was a cross between pain and orgasm. And another *thwack*.

"I need to know where I went wrong." Tears glistened on the edges of her red eyes. "And fuck you for lying. You let me think I wasn't good enough."

I let her wrists go and punched the red shade button behind her.

The wall opposite the door opened to a window, and yellow light flooded the room, washing her face in pale yellow. I didn't turn to the window but kept my attention on her as she did.

"You tell me where you went wrong," I said. "Were you not good enough? Or was this just not what I wanted for you?"

I gave her room to face the window. I hadn't known what would be there when I kicked the door in. Could have been any number of kinks, but as it turned out, it was mine.

Diana faced the window. I saw her in the dim reflection, her eyes wide, cheeks slack.

And through it, a sub was bent over a bench, bare feet dirty on the bottoms. Her wrists were tied to a vertical pole on each side of her, and her shoulder blades nearly kissed. Her straight blond hair was tied into a knot out of the way of the tears streaming down her face and dropping onto her parted lips.

Her Dom was in grey slacks, clean shoes, and a crisp white button-front shirt open at the neck and rolled up at the sleeves. I didn't know him, but he was in his late twenties and handled the wooden paddle as if it were an extension of his arm.

She was at an angle to the window so we could see her painfully raw ass and her face. He spoke to her, and she squeaked a response, nodding.

"He's asking her if she's all right, but he's not actually asking. If he said 'how are you,' he'd break the scene. It's a trigger question. He's asking what color the sky is, and if she says 'blue,' it means she's fine."

"Why can't he just ask?"

"He's playing the part of a man who might go to any length to hurt her, and it's her job to trust he won't."

The Dom pressed his sub's lower back down so her ass was high and tight, then he pulled all the way back and paddled her three times, fast on the already wounded skin.

Diana went rigid. I stood behind her.

"Breathe," I said.

She didn't. The sub's face was beet red and wet. He leaned and kissed it, speaking softly. She nodded, and I read her lips. *Please. Yes, please, sir.*

Unexpectedly, and with sadistic relish, the young Dom took one last swipe. The surprise made the sub scream, and I had to reach around and cover Diana's mouth before she did too.

"Hush," I said in her ear.

That perfume. The oranges. Her hair on my cheek. Her mouth on my palm, breaths hard. I put my other arm around her waist and pulled her to me, pushing my hard cock against her.

The Dom touched his sub's raw bottom. She squirmed as he worked his waistband.

"He's going to fuck her now. It's her reward for being a good girl."

I slid my hand down my wife's body, putting my hand between her legs. I'd lost my mind. Everything about this scene was not what I wanted for Diana, but my cock was raging and the heat through her pants was undeniable.

The Dom fucked the sub as the vertical poles shook.

"Every time he enters her, he pushes on her sore ass." I nipped her ear. "I hear it hurts like hell. But look at her. Look at her face. She loves it. She was built for it."

I moved my hand off her mouth and pulled her closer, my hand circling between her legs, mercilessly pushing the shape of my cock against her.

"You want to do that to me?" she asked.

I curved my fingers, getting the tips across her clit, hard and fast. "I love you."

She pushed against my dick, and we moved together. I groaned into the back of her neck, and she spun around, putting her back to the window. Her hair hung in front of her eyes and her shoulders jutted forward.

Behind Diana, the sub came with a cry we heard through the walls and her Dom slapped her ass gently to mix pain with her pleasure. He was good.

Diana put her hands behind her. "Are you this guy? You do what he does?"

"Why are you asking?"

"I want to know what you've been fantasizing about every time we made love."

I didn't want to do this. Every wall I'd built around this life was broken. If I told her what had been in my mind, the very foundation I'd built our sexual relationship on would shatter. "A lot of things."

"Like what?" She stuck her *t* as punctuation. Petulant little girl needed a spanking, and she wasn't taking "nothing" for an answer.

I could salvage this with something mild. Then I could try to get her back under the old rules. Promise the life we had with a little extra. Play the middle.

Or I could draw a line in the sand she'd never cross, effectively pushing her away.

*Play the middle. Play the middle. Play the middle.*

"Like this." I put my hands on the glass and whispered in her ear. "You are on your back. You are tied to the headboard by your elbows and your ankles. Your knees are around your ears, and I see your cunt is already wet. I slap your ass. The backs of your thighs. Sometimes with my hand. Sometimes I use my belt. When your skin is red, I hit harder, until it welts. I put my fingers in your hole, then your ass. You're screaming and squirming as I bring you so close to orgasm, but I don't let you finish. You're begging for an orgasm. Begging for my cock. Then I slap your cunt. Right on it. You scream, but it's not in pain. It feels good. I slap again and again, until your clit is swollen. So when I finally fuck you, my cock gives you pleasure and pain until you can't tell the difference. I own that. I gave you that. Everything you feel is mine and you give it to me. We're connected by your submission."

That wasn't the middle. That was me shredding the foundation of the last five years.

I had an erection that was so sensitive, I was going to explode at the slightest touch. Behind my wife, in the whipping room, the Dom sat on the couch with the sub over his lap as he rubbed lotion on her red bottom.

"You're sick," Diana whispered.

The sub on the other side of the room said something, and she and the Dom laughed together. He kissed her lower back. Her arm flopped over his knee. She looked wiped out and happy. I couldn't give my wife that connection. I loved her.

I pulled back from Diana's ear to look in her face. "I am. And I tried to protect you from that. But you had me followed, then you showed up here. And now that I've told you, your nipples are hard and you're flushed. You're swallowing every half a second."

"So? Just because I'm turned on, you think I'm going to love you again? It takes more than that."

"What will it take?"

"A miracle." She shoved me away. "I felt bad about leaving you. I really thought there was something wrong with me because I couldn't love you. But I don't feel bad anymore. I was in love with someone who didn't even exist."

She swung past me and headed for the door. I put my hand on it. Through the window, the sound of the Dom and sub laughing together. I knew the tension release of a good beating and the hours of laughter that followed. If I ever paddled a woman again, I'd bust my gut laughing. Fuck, I wanted that relief with my wife, but I didn't think I could bear everything leading up to it, or losing her after it.

"What?" Diana asked. More of a demand than a question.

I moved my hand. "Let me walk you out."

"I can find my way."

"Not without being a target for every Dominant on the floor."

"Fine."

She swung the door open. The shades on the window behind us slapped shut, and the hallway light stung my eyes. A few people were exiting rooms, and the hall was moderately crowded. I put my hand on Diana's back and walked her past a security guy who remembered me and out through another wide hallway with a red carpet decorated with white flowers that, if you looked closely, were actually abstractions of bodies twisting around each other in hundreds of sex positions.

That particular hallway was closed to tryouts. I was trying to avoid the bar, but I probably should have walked through it. The hallway was full of people chatting, yanking leashes, draped over each other.

"Adam?" A female voice cut through the conversation, all white noise and ambient music.

"Sir!" The voice came again when I tried to ignore it.

A hand on my shoulder. I turned.

"Serena," I said. I hadn't seen her in five years. She'd been nineteen in the Montauk house. There in the back hall of the Cellar, she was twenty-four.

The bud had blossomed.

She was five-ten with straight brown hair and bangs. Skin like silk. Lips that looked like fresh-risen dough, and a smile sweet and innocent as a child's.

She bowed her head. Bit her bottom lip. This alone told me she was still subbing.

"You can look up," I said.

She wore a collar on her long, slim neck.

"How have you been?" I asked. "Speak freely. As friends."

"Great! I just got back from Paris. I did a shoot with Ingrid Gravenstein for the *Breakout*."

"I have no idea what that is," I said, smiling. It was nice to see her.

"It's a short list of hot designers and their muses," Diana said from behind me.

"Oh, hey. Serena, this is…"

My wife? My future ex? My friend?

"Diana," I said.

The pause was barely discernible, but knowing the woman I loved, she noticed.

Serena bowed her head and bent slightly at the waist.

"Nice to meet you," Diana said.

"I was walking her out," I told Serena.

"Will you come back?"

"Yeah. Give me a minute."

"Thank you."

Still trained like a champ. I nodded and walked Diana to the elevators.

"Well," she said, "who's that?"

"I was with her just before we met."

The elevator doors opened and a crowd piled out. It was getting to be prime time on a tryout night. Worst night to be there.

Diana and I got in with a few other people. She didn't speak to me or look at me. Not even when the doors opened and we flooded into the lobby with the rest. Not at the coat check, except to insist on paying, which I wouldn't allow. Not as we exited into the street.

Only when I started to step into the street to hail a cab did she speak.

"You gave her up to be with me?"

I got back onto the sidewalk. "Yes."

"Do you regret it?"

"Not for a minute."

Her breath made a plume of steam as she exhaled. "Are you going back upstairs?"

"Do you want me to?"

"I have no right to you anymore."

"No. You don't. But..." Fuck it. I was just going to be as honest with her as I was being with myself. "I don't know if I'll go. What just happened with us, just now, it's clouding my judgment. I'm half drunk on it, and I can't tell if that's good or bad. For better or worse, I let you in. I showed you who I am. I'm happy in a way. Really happy. And I'm scared to death."

"You're scared of what?"

"That I pushed you away, and that I brought you closer. Both. Neither. Everything's changed. We aren't us anymore."

"I don't know you," she said. "We were never us."

I put my fingers to the bridge of my nose and pressed the ducts. The cold soothed them. "This was my fault. You leaving. I brought it on myself."

"There's plenty of blame to go around." She sighed another white plume. "I shouldn't have come here just because I was curious. It was completely unnecessary, and it's not going to change anything. We need to just cut the cords and feel hurt over it and move on."

"Let me get you a cab."

"I got it."

She took a step into the street, and a cab pulled up. I opened the back door for her. She slid in and leaned down. She was forlorn in the dark backseat, bag in her lap, nose red from the January cold.

"I'm going to need to come by the condo and get a few things," she said.

"You need to show up at the office," I said. "I won't bite you."

"Not unless you tie me up first." She smirked.

"Ask nicely and I might."

I slapped the door closed before she could joke about asking. A joke like that would get me in the backseat, and she'd either refuse my touch or accept it. Neither option was good.

The cab took off and blended into the river of brake lights.

# CHAPTER TWENTY-NINE

## PAST PERFECT

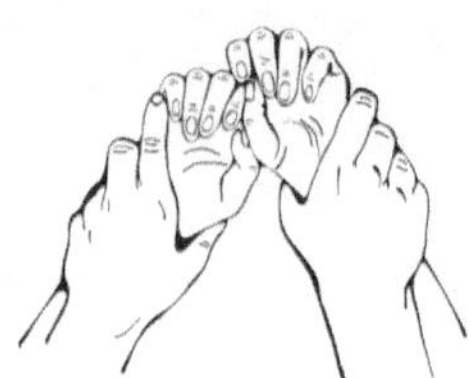

REMEMBER the time it was late? In the office? The time Diana leaned on her desk, crossed her arms, and looked out the window. She watched the last shoppers in the Prada store. She said that if she could change anything about her life—

"I wouldn't change a thing."

That was when we'd gotten Q2 financials back and they were minus .8 YOY, even with the downsize. That was at the bottom. Shit was bleak.

"I'd change these numbers," I said.

She didn't answer for a long time. "I wouldn't."

"Really?"

"We're free." Her form was a silhouette against the lit windows across the narrow street. "We're still privately held. We can do whatever we want. No one would question it, and if they did, fuck them."

I pushed away from my desk and planted myself in front of her. "Tell me, what's on your mind?"

She moved her attention from the checkerboard of light across the street to my face. "Fiction's dead. At least for us it is. We don't have the leverage to break new literary talent, and the genre writers are doing it themselves."

"Right."

"The newspapers can't monetize the internet. They're hemorrhaging. Websites can't pay journalists to research solid, deep pieces."

"All true."

"I think we should kill the literary fiction division. Get out of our contracts."

I crossed my arms. "That feels like suicide."

"No. We circle the wagons around long journalism. Book length. Poach established writers and editors from the newspapers. They'll abandon a sinking ship if we pay them."

"Okay, look, I get it. This shit sells. But stories that work in this genre are unicorns."

Even as I said it, I knew the answer, and the beauty of us was that she knew it too. Her eyes lit up, and together, we laughed.

Her journals with their thousands of questions.

"This is it," I said. "We find the best in the business to answer your questions."

"We put a call out."

"Lists. We list the best ones."

"Long-form answers. Experiential and research-based."

"We throw everything behind it."

We talked over each other for the next ten minutes, an entire plan falling into place.

And that was how we saved her family business.

# CHAPTER THIRTY

## PRESENT TENSE

As Diana's cab disappeared, I thought I'd just go back to our place on Crosby and look at all her things. Maybe digest what the fuck just happened. Take a healthy mental break.

"Hey, mate," Charlie said from behind me. He leaned on his cane. Serena stood a step behind him, averting her eyes to the ground when I looked at her. "We're off to the Loft House. You coming?"

"Sure."

Fuck it. I was pumped full of unanswered questions and undefined emotions. Perfect time to have a couple of drinks.

The Loft House wasn't a sex club, unless you consider money orgasmic, but with an impossibly long waiting list that required recommendations from three members, the sexiness could have sprung from exclusivity.

That night it was sparsely populated, but there was still enough ambient conversation over the experimental classical music to keep our conversation safe. Charlie, Serena, and I were tucked into a corner. Since we were in a vanilla location where I didn't need such a clear head, I moved on to whiskey. Charlie never stopped drinking, and tonight it was rum. Serena drank only water with lemon.

"Who you keeping dry for?" I asked. If she had a new Master, he probably didn't let her drink, or she was only allowed to drink with him.

"I feel better when I have water," she said.

"You look wonderful," I said. "It's great to see you."

I wasn't thinking of her as a potential fuck, but she blushed and looked down, pressing her knees together. She wore a polo shirt, same as always. Sexless and plain. Sometimes she buttoned them all the way.

"She was the most sought-after sub in New York," Charlie said smugly. "Got her pick of the best. And I trained her, thank you very much."

"Never went to law school?" I asked.

"No. I didn't like arguing all the time, and modeling is more fun. More money too."

I knew the truth, and it was sadder. Her mother had died from complications of her stroke. Her father was useless for much besides haranguing her for her failures.

"She socks it away like a squirrel." Charlie was beaming like a proud parent. "Gotta love her."

She smiled. You never forget your first Dominant, they say, and Charlie's praise would always mean something to her. I wondered if I'd made an impression at all.

She excused herself. I must have wondered while watching her walk away, because Charlie cleared his throat as if he had a ream of crumpled paper wads in it.

"The wife," he said. "You back on? You and her?"

"Why?"

"Because I saw her. Same as you. She has potential."

I didn't even want to talk about it. "You said Serena *was* the most blah blah—past tense."

"Why do you care?"

"Making conversation."

"This thing you have?" He put his drink down in pause. "You never loved a submissive."

"I can't."

"Have you tried?"

"Once I break them, it just dies. It's not something I can control. Do you have a point?"

"Serena blames herself. Takes it out on herself."

"It didn't start with her."

"She's been with Stefan going on three years now. That's his collar. The arrangement satisfies her need for punishment and his need to touch everything you've touched."

Stefan was a charming fuck. He was one of the few rich painters in the world. He was educated, talented, and back-breakingly sadistic. Along with Charlie and me, he was one of the three owners of the Montauk house, and he denied hating me.

"Three years isn't spite," I said. "He must care about her."

"I'm sure he does. But they've been having problems."

"Do they both know there are problems?" My voice was laced with bitterness.

"Been tense as the last hour of a cricket match for months."

"And you want me to charm her away?" I asked.

"I like you better than that Scandie."

"I'm married."

"Good thing one of you sees it that way."

"Low blow, Charles. Low blow."

He nodded and waved an apology my way, acknowledging I was right without saying the words. It was enough for me.

"Alayne Kerry was asking about you," he said. "Not a repeat. Take her out to Montauk for a month. The main house is empty. You'll be Master Adam in the first twenty-four hours."

"What's in this for you?"

"Seeing you happy." He leaned back and crossed his legs. "Go. You'll be over your little vanilla wife before the first week. By the end of the month, you won't remember her name until you sign the divorce papers."

Serena came back across the room, head high, legs up to her neck, black polo shirt open to show her fashionable leather collar. I wouldn't try to seduce her away from Stefan. I was soon to be single, and I needed the Cellar. Stealing another Dom's collared sub could get me thrown out.

I was formulating another plan.

# CHAPTER THIRTY-ONE

## PRESENT TENSE

DIANA and I had spent the day at the office acting like adults. We had meetings and made decisions. We didn't talk about anything but work. The activity was a relief, in a way. In another way, I felt as if I were trapped in a bag and thrown in the Hudson.

We were too polite. I'd never felt more awkward in my life.

"I was thinking of coming by tonight to get some things," she said as she slung her bag over her shoulder. The winter sky was charcoal through the window behind her, and the rectangles of yellow light from the building across the street made an orderly grid.

"How long are you living on Riverside?" I moved papers around my desk.

"End of the month."

"Where to then?"

"I don't know. Dad says I can have my old room back."

"Sounds tempting."

"He never took down the One Direction posters."

"You can move back into the loft with me."

She froze with her hand on the doorknob. "I can't. It's too complicated."

"I understand. Come by after eight so I can be gone."

She nodded, rueful. "Thank you."

I had no intention of being gone.

I was back in the condo by seven forty-five. When she came in, she had a suitcase and a duffel. Thank God she was alone. I had a plan if she brought someone, but it wasn't as good.

"Oh, hi," she said when she saw me, keys still dangling from her finger.

"Yeah, hi. I decided to be here."

She dropped the suitcase. It clapped. Hollow. "Why? Did you think I was going to swipe your cufflinks?"

I laughed. "If you want the cufflinks, you can have them."

"I don't want your cufflinks."

"Can we sit? Because I want to talk about what you want."

She tilted her head up, eyes closed in pure annoyance. "I want a divorce. That's all I want."

"No, it isn't. You want that and more. Come on. Sit."

I indicated her own couch, with its cold modern lines and warm colors. I'd kept the light ambient and put a pitcher of water on the coffee table.

"Do I need my lawyer?" she asked.

"I hope not." I sat in a chair and indicated her spot on the couch again.

She kicked her shoes off and sat the way she always did, with her socked feet tucked under her. I remembered the sub in the viewing room, how she went on her toes when her Dom paddled her and how I could see the dirty bottoms of her feet.

I knew where I'd planned to start, but now that she was sitting there, looking at me with eyes the icy color of shattered tempered glass, I couldn't launch into the offer.

"When you got home from the club the other night, what did you do?" I asked.

"I really don't want to talk about the club."

Defenses up already. I was going to have to lower mine to draw her out.

"I need to," I said. "You don't have to do a damn thing for my sake. But I need to."

"Then let's talk about the club. You want to hit my pussy. I don't know what that says about you."

"The fact that I never did says a lot about how I feel about you."

She continued as if she didn't even hear me. "I mean, I know it's not in anger. But it's violence and it's weird. I don't understand how you can want to do that to someone you love."

"I can't do that to someone I love. That's the point."

She wasn't listening, she was looking deep inside herself. "I can't get my head around it."

"I'm concerned you think it's just violence and the sub gets nothing out of it."

"What does she get out of it?" She was leaning forward, drilling again. She wanted all the information. All the words.

I didn't know if it was just Curious Diana or if Aroused Diana was showing up.

"When you got home last night, what did you do?"

"Went to bed."

"Did you sleep?"

"Who could sleep after that? I was all turned around." Her face and posture told a thousand tales.

"You touched yourself."

"Shut up."

"I need to know."

"How is that your business?"

"How is it not?" I asked.

"Did you jerk off?"

"No. I went out."

"Where?"

Shit. I was derailed. How did she do that?

Just by being Diana, that was how she did it.

"I met up with Serena and Charlie, the guy with the cane. From the bar." I sat back, leaning into the new angle the conversation took. "He trained Serena years ago, then sent her to me."

"Right before we met."

"About five weeks before."

"Sent her to you? What does that mean?"

"Did you touch yourself after you got home? Under the sheets? Standing over the toilet? On your hands and knees?"

Long pause. She absently ran her finger along the pressed edge of her cuff. "What if I didn't at all?"

"I'd be shocked."

She spit out a short laugh, looked down. Lordamighty. It's amazing how a man won't see what he doesn't want to see. Was she full-blown submissive? Or did she just have tendencies? How did I not know it?

Charlie's voice answered.

*You knew it, you whacka. You knew it from the beginning.*

"I didn't even get my jacket off." Her eyes were still cast down. "I dropped my keys on the floor and got on my knees. I did it right in the foyer. Then…" She smiled again, looking away as if laughing at herself. "Then I took a shower and made myself come again."

"Just twice?"

When she looked back up, her softness was gone. "What does it mean that he sent her to you? And why did it end? Was it because of me? You told me when we met you weren't with anyone."

"I wasn't with her. Not in the way I meant when I answered. Okay, look, I'll run it down for you." I had to just forget who I was talking to and spit it out. "Charlie trains subs. He finds their limits, tells them what to say and how to act."

"Do they pay him?"

"No, no, there's no money exchanged. It's not that. It's what he loves to do and it's totally with consent. Joyful consent. He's the best, but he can't fuck them. It's a war injury, don't ask. Serena was a virgin. He could teach her to deep throat and take anal using a dildo, but he didn't want to take her virginity with a piece of plastic."

"He's a prince."

"Do you want me to finish?"

"Yes. Sorry."

"She wanted me to take her virginity. So I did. I spent thirty days with her in a house in Montauk I'm part owner of."

"You own a house in Montauk?" she asked.

"Do not even think of suing me for it."

"I won't. Go on."

"Thirty days was the limit, and we agreed ahead of time. We did all the things she was trained to do. She came a lot. I came a lot. On the twenty-eighth day, I took her virginity, and continued to fuck her until she was too sore to walk. On the thirtieth day, it was over and we drove home. The following Monday, I met you in a meeting with McNeill-Barnes regarding a buyout."

I didn't know what she'd think or ask. I knew what I told her had a dozen holes she'd fill with questions, and I knew as painful as it would be, I'd answer them honestly.

"You waited twenty-eight days?" she asked.

"I needed her to be sure. Also, it was torture for her, which we both liked."

"She's beautiful."

"She is. It took a lot of willpower, but it was worth it to see her beg for it."

"Wow."

"Wow?"

"This is... I mean, this is a whole thing. Jesus, I just wanted to get my stuff. I wanted my mom's wedding dress, and I bought underwear last week I never got to wear. And I was going to take the blue stock pot? The Le Creuset one? I had a note all ready in my mind I was going to write on the yellow pad. I was going to offer to get you a new one even though you never cook and now I'm just..." She shot up, standing in her sock feet.

"I'm going to do all that. I'm collecting my things right now. I don't know what your plan is, Adam, but it's not going to work. Getting me all turned on last night and trying to get me jealous today? I get it. But being horny and jealous isn't love. It's being a teenager." She stomped toward the bedroom.

"You're jealous?"

"No! Tie her up and fuck her all night long. I don't even care."

She pivoted on her sock and disappeared around the corner. The bedroom door slammed.

Diana was never jealous. She just wasn't. Not of Eva. Not of the women who flirted with me. She never worried when we were apart. She was incapable of it.

Without rushing, I walked to the kitchen, took the blue Le Creuset stockpot from the cabinet, and went to the bedroom. I opened the door. Her suitcase was spread on the bed and she had a mound of underpants in her hands.

"Adam, can you just leave me alone? You weren't even supposed to be here." She dropped the underpants in her suitcase and opened another drawer.

"I brought you your pot. And you don't even have to write me a note."

She grabbed it without looking at me. "Thank you."

I stood in the doorway, arms crossed, leaning on the jamb. She wasn't particularly graceful when she moved. She stooped and swung, throwing herself into her task as if the only point was to complete it without looking at me.

"How was work for you today?" I asked.

"Fine."

"Really?"

"Yes."

"Do you want to know how it was for me?"

"No." She slapped the suitcase shut. It was so full it bounced open again.

I got out of the doorway and went to the bed. "It was awkward." I closed the case and held it down.

She zipped it shut, poking pieces of fabric into the opening as she went. Still not looking at me.

I continued. "You know we're in for a long fight over the company."

She paused, stuffed in another sliver of cotton, zipped two inches, stopped, zipped... "It's a family business. Why do you even want it?"

"Because I own fifty-one percent of it and put five years of my life into it. And I'm not family. I'm thinking of liquidating. Best for everyone. That building is—"

"I'll buy you out."

"With what? Half a condo and a Jaguar?"

In one motion, she picked up the blue stock pot and threw it at my head. The cover slid off. I ducked before the bottom smashed my head open. It flew past and made a hole in the plaster wall, landing on the floor with a hard clunk.

"You're a motherfucker," she seethed, pointing at me. This wasn't how I'd intended the conversation to go. Not at all. "You have no business fighting over that company. It has my name on it. My father and mother's name. You don't even exist."

"You'd love that. You'd love for me to just disappear. I'm sorry, Diana. It's not my job to make your life easy."

"I know." She yanked the suitcase off the bed and it landed heavily against her calf. "It's your job to withhold for twenty-eight days."

"You *are* jealous."

"Grow up." She started out, right toward me, both hands on the suitcase, using her leg to distribute some of the weight.

I took the handle.

"I have it," she growled.

"Let me help you."

"Get off me." She looked ready to rip out my throat.

"You still have to pack the duffel."

"I just want to go. Can I go, please?"

"Yes. You can go." But I didn't move. I'd just confirmed she wasn't trapped. I put my hand over hers and took most of the weight of the suitcase. "Now let go of the handle."

She dropped it completely and gravity straightened my arm.

"You have the heaviest underwear in the city."

She smiled to herself. "Go to hell."

"I'm sure I will."

She crossed her arms. "You're not moving out of the way."

"I have something to say."

"If you say it, can I go? Not theoretically, but really?"

I switched arms. I wanted my right hand to cup her face from a foot away, to gesture the shape of my words. "You're not the jealous type. I get that. But this needs saying once and once only. For clarity. I don't want Serena. I don't want anyone but you. I've never loved another woman. I know you think I'm a different person than you thought you knew. Maybe you think there's the husband me and the stranger me. But neither guy ever loved her. I love you. Every version of me loves you. Today. Now. Always."

She fell back and sat on the bed, hands dangling between her knees. "I don't know what to say."

"Say you loved me once."

"I did. Adam, I went into this marriage with my whole heart. It's just... what do you want?"

*To not want you.*

"Besides you?"

"Yes. What do you want?" She asked it less defensively, giving me the perfect opportunity to tell her exactly what I'd been thinking.

Nudged to the edge of a tall building with a net I couldn't see past the clouds below, I asked one more time. "What I want? Now? With you on the way out the door?"

"Yes."

"Thirty days," I said, jumping off the side of the tallest building in the city. No turning back now. I leaned into it. "I want thirty days. You and me. Far away. Not a vacation, just thirty days where I show you who I was before I started lying."

The fall was endless. The cloudline below pulled away and closer at the same time, like the horror-movie door at the end of a long hallway.

# CHAPTER THIRTY-TWO

## PRESENT TENSE

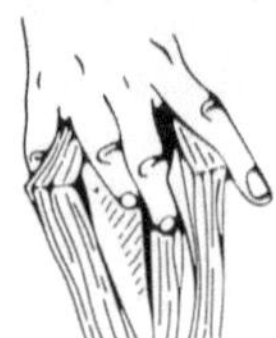

*Where is love?*

In my wife's Unicorn Journals, the query had been embedded deep in questions of how and why. The *where* was most interesting. Nicolla Masta started it as a dissemination on the parts of the body that experienced love. The heart—the historical center, and the genitalia—the evolutionary center.

Zack Abramson killed it. The piece went nowhere. It was DOA. And we weren't sending her all over the world to find where love was. Waste of money and time. It was everywhere and nowhere. We moved on to the underworld lives of garbage men in Naples. Not a bestseller, but not bad.

Of course, I'd been wrong. Love wasn't everywhere and nowhere. It just shifted around. Expanded, contracted, and moved like a nomad.

The morning after my wife refused to go to Montauk, love moved out of our loft, to the offices of McNeill-Barnes. Love was still as awkward as a thirteen-year-old boy with his first public erection. Love didn't fit in the space. Love was uncomfortable. Love wanted out but couldn't find the fucking door.

I could have worked at the R+D office, but I couldn't let her off the hook, and I couldn't make the case for keeping my piece of the company if I stopped showing up.

And I knew she'd say yes to going to Montauk if I played my cards right. It was a question of when.

*When is love?*

Should have attacked that question.

"Do you still need the Montauk place?" Charlie asked at lunch soon after.

"Probably not." I tapped the white tablecloth.

"How's it going with her?"

I shook my head. It was bad. We spoke at work, about work. She'd had divorce papers served and hadn't looked at me for the rest of the day, out of shame and guilt. But she was being strong. I respected that.

I'd gotten myself a lawyer and made it abundantly clear, through him, that I was not going to sign over the company even if she could come up with the value for a buyout. I moved back to my Murray Hill apartment but didn't tell her. Love wasn't in our loft anymore, and its absence made the space seem too big.

"Her father called me. You know what he said? He said, 'Don't give up.' And the more I think about it, it's because he wants me running that business. That whole family runs on that publishing house. Their identity's strung up on it."

"You ever going to let it go?" He speared a piece of meat with his knife and ate off the blade. "Start living? Come by the Cellar for more than a drink?"

When I stopped loving her, I'd let it go.

Or vice versa.

I felt an answer in the intersection of the business and my lies, not in the switch between them, but in the fulcrum where all things pivoted. Our love was there. She loved that publishing house, and I loved her.

# CHAPTER THIRTY-THREE

## PRESENT TENSE

"What's this?"

Diana stood over my desk with a document typed onto my lawyer's letterhead. I glanced at it, then back at the inventory reports.

"A notice."

"You can't do this."

"Yeah, I can."

"We walk out with what we came in with. I came in with this company. We can fight over shares, but it's mine."

I put my pen down and pushed away from the desk. "I came in with a majority interest, which is tantamount to ownership in the great state of New York. See, definitions get muddled. Let's just let the lawyers figure it out." I stood and swung my jacket over my shoulders. "I have a meeting uptown. Do you have the October release meeting under control?"

"Yes."

"Great. Thanks."

I was almost out of the room, hand on the doorknob.

"Adam!"

"What?"

"Why?"

"Because I can."

It wasn't an answer she would understand. Her ambition was always tied to the strings of her heart. She didn't understand the hunger to just *have*.

I did. My attempt to force her into a buyout wasn't about mindless acquisition, but I understood the psychology of it. It had been my mindset until she came along.

"What do you want? Is it money?"

"I told you." I opened the door. "You. Thirty days doing what I tell you."

"That won't change anything."

"Yes, it will. I'll sign it all over to you for nothing. You'll win."

I didn't wait for her to ask for a definition of winning. She wasn't in this to win. She was divorcing me to get out in one piece.

That was my goal too.

Get out in one piece.

# CHAPTER THIRTY-FOUR

## PAST TENSE

"Please."

Serena was the first in her family to go to college. She was synthesized in mediocre education and middle-class values, but she overcame both. When she'd submitted to me, she was released from her responsibility to her education and her family. I was her vacation.

She was intelligent and learned the rules of sophistication quickly. Outside scene, she had a sharp wit that wasn't cruel or cutting. She could choose her future, though in the middle of our stay in the Montauk house, she only had the next hour or so on her mind.

"I have to get back to the city, pet. I'll see you tonight."

She wore only her white gauze gown and her collar. I'd left a polo shirt out for her, but she'd refused it. She was draped over my leg.

"Please." Her brown eyes were as big as saucers, and her light brown lashes curved up at the ends. Her lips parted. When she opened her mouth so I could come in it, I made sure to get some on her bee-stung lower lip.

I didn't love her. I'd never been in love, so I didn't know what it felt like. I didn't feel anything for Serena I didn't feel for any other sub.

But two things were different with Serena.

One, I didn't take her virginity after the first week, or the second.

Two, it became quickly apparent that I'd somehow let her develop feelings for me. She didn't say as much, but I knew women, and I'd inadvertently gotten to her.

"I'll take you when it suits me. Not you." I stroked her cheek.

She turned her head and dragged her lips along my palm. She mouthed *please please please* against my hand. I could see my watch near her lips. We did have time.

"If you ask again," I said, and relief poured over her face before I even finished the sentence, "I'm going to violate you in ways you may not like."

I said it knowing she'd like it. The idea that I could and would do things outside her limits was exciting.

"Please take me."

I sighed as if annoyed and pushed her off me. "Go outside. Get a stick at least a foot long and thinner than your thumb. Crawl back here with it in your teeth. Put it at my feet, then put your head down and your ass up."

She ran out, near naked at the end of September. The front yard was covered in sticks that would do, but if I'd asked her to walk for it, she'd happily die of exposure.

I didn't love her. Couldn't. I'd break her a dozen times before I even took her virginity, and every time I did, I'd feel satisfaction, peace, compassion, and power. But I'd never love her.

I'd never made a choice not to love. I tried, but I felt nothing. I was frustrated with myself, but I was coming to the conclusion that it wasn't the women. It was me.

She came in, closed the door, and got on her knees with the stick in her teeth. She did exactly as she was told and it pleased me. And her.

But I didn't love her. The perfect sub isn't always the perfect match. It was possible no sub was a match.

# CHAPTER THIRTY-FIVE
## PRESENT TENSE

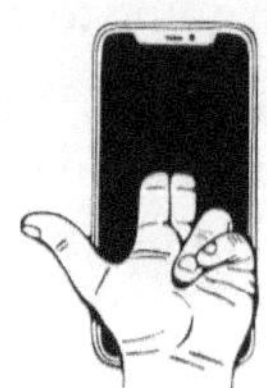

The hardest thing I ever did was stop.

I stopped telling Diana what was on my mind. I stopped trying to get in her way. I stopped chasing her around. Once the lawyer's letter came to her, describing my intention to fight her for the company, I behaved like a calm professional and so did she.

That lasted two whole days. She texted me close to midnight.

**—We need to talk about
this ownership thing—**

A dozen jokes about possession crossed my mind. I tossed them. I couldn't pretend I didn't know what she was talking about.

*—That's fine. My lawyer will relay
the message or we can set up a meeting—*

**—I don't want to talk to lawyers—**

**—I want to talk to YOU—**

I didn't answer. I wanted to talk to her too. I wanted to touch her and whisper to her, but I couldn't.

She found me at the gym the next morning. I was on the treadmill, and she looked as if she'd walked a few thousand miles herself.

I didn't stop the belt. I hit the button to make it faster.

"Are you all right?" I asked, jogging six miles an hour straight into nowhere.

"You're not playing fair."

"How's that?"

"You're being emotionally manipulative and spiteful and it's not okay."

My legs burned, but I didn't stop.

"Did you hear me?" she shouted.

"I heard you."

"You can't demand a price for your shares and offer me less for mine."

She was loud. People were looking. Fuck them.

"Mine are worth more," I said.

"Can you stop that thing?"

"Why?"

She reached onto my panel and hit the emergency stop button. I nearly fell over.

"Because I want to talk," she sniped. "We were talking before, then this started." She waved a piece of paper.

My lowball offer for her shares had been meant to insult her. I'd obviously succeeded.

"It's for the best." I snapped my towel off the machine. "The only thing talking was doing was getting you to feel good about leaving."

"Can you explain this?" She snapped the paper in front of me, jogging to keep up. "How are your shares worth more?"

"They come with me attached. I made that business work."

"*We* made it work."

I put my hand on the door to the locker room. "Is irony completely lost on you?"

She gritted her teeth. Man, she was so mad, she could have peeled the paint off the walls. I went into the locker room and wasn't surprised when she followed.

"We were equals. Which means equal share value."

I slapped open my locker. "I'll lower the price."

"Really?"

I peeled off my shirt. Two guys in towels glanced at the woman in the room, but she was Diana and she didn't care.

"Sure."

"Don't say thirty days."

"Thirty days."

"God damn you."

"A halt to new business development for thirty days while we sort this out." I kicked my shoes off and hooked my thumbs in my waistband. "Access to an operating account. Maintenance of the status quo, current production schedule maintained, and limited power of attorney to a third party."

"We can't even do that."

"Maybe." I stepped out of my sweat pants and stood naked in front of her. "My lawyer says between the common assets and the company assets, it'll take at least two years to litigate, so the thirty days might have to be extended." I wrapped a towel around my waist and grabbed my soap. "I'm a long distance runner."

The showers were down a short hall and through a room of bathroom stalls and urinals. She followed me the entire length.

"Is this spite? This is spite. I know it is."

"Call it what you want."

A guy standing at a urinal saw Diana and turned so she couldn't see him piss. "Hey! She don't belong in here."

"She doesn't." I stopped at the entrance to the showers. "Diana, honey, you should go."

"I'm saying this straight," she growled. "My father isn't going to be around much longer. McNeill-Barnes is a family business. It's *his* family business. If you take it from us, it'll kill him."

"Talk about emotionally manipulative."

"No joke," said the guy at the urinal.

The showers were separate rooms all in a row, marked with green or red flags to indicate whether or not they were occupied. I found a green flag and opened the door.

Diana stopped behind me. "He can't die without this company in his daughter's hands."

"Is that what this is about? Your father?"

"Yes."

"Wrong. This is about business. This is not about family. This is not about your mother's death wish. This is about you and me and business."

I tried to close the door, but she stopped it.

"The thirty days you want? That's business? Because it sounds personal."

"You caught me in a contradiction. Oops, okay? Close the door."

"When did you become such a monster?"

There comes a point when you win, and you can either soothe the loser into thinking there was something in it for them or you can kick them while they're down to make sure they know what just happened.

I pulled my towel off and hung it, exposing my cock again. "Wake up, little huntress. I was the one who kicked out leaseholders on a loophole when your 'family business' needed more room. I was the one who called writers to break contracts. I was the one who did the company dirty work for years. Now you're the dirty work. Deal with it."

I closed the door and turned the lock quickly. I was shaking so hard I could barely work the shower knob. I turned it on high and hot.

She pounded the door once, then nothing.

I couldn't gulp air quickly enough. I let the water scald me, letting the pain on the surface match the pain inside me. I never wanted to hurt her, but I had. I never wanted her to feel small or powerless. I loved her. I loved her with everything I had. I'd done the dirty work to protect her from anger and cruelty, and now I had become the very thing I'd protected her from.

I was well past the point of no return.

# CHAPTER THIRTY-SIX

## PRESENT TENSE

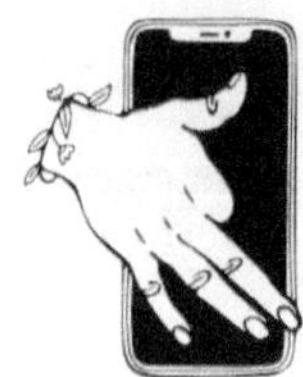

DIANA DIDN'T SHOW up to the office the next day. I checked her phone's location, but she'd shut off the locator service. It didn't matter. The end of the month was approaching.

Do or die.

Sometimes *do* meant wait, and I considered that. But I had a sliver of time between her leaving Riverside Drive and her taking down her One Direction posters.

She'd been right. I was being manipulative. I'd learned how to toy with people as a Dominant, but I used my skills during play and not outside it. I knew better. There was no excuse for me to slap and tickle my wife's emotions, except my hunger to make her feel something. I knew I was wrong, but I did it anyway.

*—The loft—*

**—What about it?—**

*—I moved. You should live in it—*

I slid my phone onto the desk. It was just about dinnertime. I had my coat and scarf on before she answered.

**—Will you be out by
Thursday?—**

*—Already out—*

*—Do you want it? I'll sign
my half over to you—*

Another long pause. I was halfway down the block before my phone buzzed again.
**—For what?—**

I smiled at the screen. She was a learning machine and a worthy adversary. Moments like that, I didn't think about not loving her. I couldn't imagine it.

*—One hour doing what I tell you—*

The phone rang as I got to the front of our building. It was her.
"I'm not a hooker," she said.
"It's a two-million-dollar loft in SoHo. No hooker is that expensive."
"No sex. And don't even try."
"Define sex." I was curious. How did she define it? What exactly were her lines?
"It's not obvious?"
"No."
"We've been married four years."
That was the problem, wasn't it? We'd shared a bed and our bodies for that long and I didn't know what she meant by "no sex."
"I'm not trying to turn you on. I'm trying to talk to you," I said, pacing from the front of the building to the edge of the curb, confusing the hell out of the doorman. "Define what you mean by sex. Is it talking about sex? Describing how much I want you? Is that sex? Is it me

touching you? You touching you? Is it kissing? If I can smell your cunt's arousal, is that sex? If I taste you? Or if I can sense you spreading your legs a little wider under the table? What's that? And if it makes me hard, is that sex? Define it. Draw your lines around it and I won't cross."

A puddle of melted snow had formed at the curb. It reached the height of the sidewalk and no higher. The temperature had fallen with the sun, and the puddle had frozen at the top. I poked it with my foot while I waited for her to answer. My toe made a divot in the crust of ice but didn't break through.

"I don't know," she said.

"Then how am I supposed to know?"

"I feel like if I say no to something, I'm saying yes to everything else. And I just…" She took a deep breath. "I just want to move back into my own place."

I was such an asshole. Constructing ways to eroticize our meeting so I could trade bites of submission for an asset I didn't really want. I was treating her like a whore. She deserved better. She deserved a man who would split everything down the middle and disappear. I wasn't that man. I was much worse. I was a monster. I demanded sacrifice. Recompense. I demanded to be made whole for all the love I'd spent on her. I actually felt compassion for the woman who had shattered my heart.

"Let me define it then," I said.

"Okay."

"I won't touch you unless you ask."

"I won't ask."

"And if I say anything that crosses a line, you can tell me. Just say the word."

"What word? I can't get into spiraling discussions about what's appropriate."

"You pick the word. Make it something that would never come up in conversation."

Her breath changed. I heard a rustle. She was either changing clothes or putting clothes on. Naturally, I got hard.

"I don't know," she said, the phone leaving her ear and coming back. Must be her putting a shirt on.

Or getting one off.

"Just pick a word."

I wondered if she was wearing a bra. Her nipples were thick and hard when she was cold or turned on, and I hadn't given them a good bite in too long. I hadn't thought about them over the phone in months. Years maybe. My sexuality must have been more closeted than I thought. All I could imagine was her naked on the other side of the line.

"Pinochle," she said.

"What?" I'd lost my train of thought.

"If you cross a line, I'll say 'pinochle.'"

"Come over. I'll have dinner ready."

"God, this is so crazy."

"It is," I said before we hung up.

And it was. She'd chosen a safe word.

# CHAPTER THIRTY-SEVEN

## PRESENT TENSE

I ROLLED UP MY SLEEVES, took off my tie, and got to work. I whipped up chicken and a wine sauce with the stuff in the freezer. I wasn't much of a cook, but I managed some green beans and warmed bread. My grandmother had always told me enough butter and salt made stones taste good.

She came in while I was setting my side of the table. Tiny snowflakes stuck to her hair. She'd done nothing to prepare. Her hair was a mess. She wore no makeup. Old jeans. Her favorite button-down shirt. A few bracelets she never took off anyway.

Just the way I liked her. Effortless.

"If I knew what you wanted out of me, this would be easier." She unraveled her scarf. It was blue with embroidered birds.

"I told you already."

"Thirty days for the company and an hour for the condo?"

"Something like that. Look, I'm not going to try to fuck you."

"So what are you going to try to do?" She stuffed the bird scarf in a pocket and pushed her coat buttons through the holes. I got behind her to take it. "Besides be a jerk, which you were totally being at the gym."

"Show you that you might enjoy a month learning about the guy you married. The one I lied about." I hung her coat. "I want to undo all that."

"I'm not going to fall in love with you again."

Would that ever stop hurting?

"I know. But you're curious."

"I am. I read The Book That Shall Not Be Named, of course. And after we were in the Cellar, I did an internet search," she said.

"How was that?"

"Hot sometimes. Scary sometimes."

"You can satisfy your curiosity with me. For an hour."

I pulled out her chair. She didn't go toward it.

I waited.

"I have this choice," she said, looking at the chair. "You have things I want, and you'll give them to me if I do what you want. If I don't, you'll make my life a living hell trying to get those things." She took her eyes off the chair and laid them on me. "When I put it that way, do you understand why it's hard for me to say yes to any of it?"

"I do. But you have more to gain than lose. And I can admit something I couldn't admit before. There's a part of you that might have enjoyed this part of me if I'd been a man and let you in. If I thought for a minute there wasn't a good chance you'd like it, we wouldn't be having this conversation."

"I'm not leaving you over sex."

No, it wouldn't stop hurting. Even when she used different words entirely to say she didn't love me, she still ran me through and twisted the blade. And I realized that it was getting easier for her to say it. She'd become immune to the venom of her detachment, and I kept on asking for the sting.

"The reason you're breaking up this marriage is irrelevant," I lied. "I'm not after 'why,' I'm after 'how.' And the 'how' I'm after is 'not that easily.' You don't have to like it. I don't believe in heaven. I don't believe there's a reward for leaving nicely or being the bigger person. I'm not ready to let you leave with everything. Not easily. Not without payment."

I indicated the seat again, but she didn't sit.

"Would you just sign everything over if you didn't think I was curious?"

The question was one of two things. Either she wanted to gauge whether or not pretending to not enjoy it would make the path easier, or whether or not her curiosity had gotten her and McNeill-Barnes into this situation.

"No. That's not how I do business." I pivoted the conversation back to the matter at hand. "You need to obey me, but I won't ask for anything I don't think you're ready for."

"How do I know you know what I'm ready for?"

"You have to trust me."

She ran her finger over the sharp edge of her front pants pocket. "An hour."

"An hour. And you say pinochle whenever you want."

She nodded. Blinked.

"Is that a yes?" I asked.

Her eyes went to me. Through me. She could hurt me again and again if I let her, because she went a few degrees warmer, seeping tiny droplets of tenderness through the seams in her disdain.

"Yes," she said.

She sat, and I pushed in her chair.

The clock started ticking.

"What did you make?" she asked when I took the cover off the dish.

"Chicken. I think."

"Was it in the container with the blue cover?"

"Yes."

"It's duck." She put her hands on the table. "I need a plate."

She started to get up, but I put my hand on her shoulder and gently pushed her back to sitting. "No, you don't. Just relax."

I sat down and put my napkin in my lap and duck on my plate. I cut it.

"You got an eyeful the other night at the Cellar," I said.

"Yeah."

I speared a piece of meat. "But what you didn't see is what a Dominant really does." I held the fork out to her. She reached for it. "Sit on your hands."

Her hand froze midway. "Literally?"

"When I talk to you like this, you can assume it's literal."

She lowered her hand, shifted her body, and slid her hands under her. I could see her wheels turning. My wife didn't take orders.

"Open your mouth."

She was so scared of herself and me. When she parted her lips, the rest of her face registered nothing but trepidation.

"When you do what I ask you to do, it gratifies me. I have the sense that everything is in its right place. I breathe easier. I think more clearly."

I held out another piece of meat. She opened her mouth.

"Don't open until I tell you."

"Okay. Sorry."

She wasn't supposed to speak, but I couldn't shush her. Too many rules too soon would turn her off. This hour wasn't about my enjoyment. I had to remember that and not get ahead of myself.

"It's all right. Open."

She did, and I fed her.

"Do I have to ask to chew?"

This was why Charlie trained them and I wore them in.

"You're not there yet. You can chew when you like," I said.

"Are you going to eat?"

"I might eat before you, after you, with you."

She took another bite.

"It depends on the guy?" she asked while chewing, and my mood darkened.

Other men. If she discovered she liked this, would she seek it out with other men?

*Shake it off.*

I took a bite of duck. It wasn't half bad. "I'm going to feed you. You're going to eat, and you're going to listen."

She nodded. She was still on her hands. They were going to fall asleep.

"Put your hands on the table."

She did it, palms down. The ring was gone again. I fed her a forkful of vegetables.

"Since we only have an hour and I don't want you to give me

something you're not ready to give, I'm going to tell you what I'm not going to do to you and what I'm not going to ask you to do."

Before she could speak, I fed her a forkful of duck.

"I'm not going to ask you to stand in front of the window and get undressed. Slowly and purposefully, down to the skin. Your nipples would be hard, and your cheeks flushed, but I won't ask you to stand still in front of me, feeling how naked and vulnerable you are while I sit here in my clothes, just staring at how gorgeous you are. I won't ask you to turn around, bend at the waist, and hold your ass and thighs open for me. I'd probably have to tell you to spread your feet apart. This is so I can inspect you. I'd run my fingers over your cunt to make sure you're wet, but I won't tonight. And I won't get my fingers wet so I can slide them in your ass."

She let out a short, hard exhale. I wiped the corners of her mouth with the cloth napkin and tipped the water glass to her lips. She drank.

"The downside is you won't come. Because if you did what I just told you to do, my fingers would graze your clit over and over." I took the glass away. "You can spread your knees if you want."

The tablecloth moved enough to let me know she did.

I stood and got behind her. "I'd tell you to get on your knees and open your mouth. And then, my wife, I'd teach you how to let me fuck your face. Not give me a blow job, but to let me take one from you. With your hands behind your back, you press the back of your tongue down and I fuck your throat. But not tonight. Tonight all I want is your obedience. I want you to let me take care of you the way I'm supposed to."

She was practically panting. I had her.

I took a handful of her hair and pulled her head back hard enough to hurt. Her lips and eyes were open, and I kissed her. I probed her mouth with my tongue, let her groan fill my mouth. She tasted exactly as she always had. Like my wife. My partner. My very heart.

I reached around with my other hand and pulled her shirt open, popping buttons, yanking her bra up over her tits. She let out an *ah* into my mouth, and when I squeezed her nipple harder than I ever had, it turned into a long *aaaahhhh...*

I spoke so close our lips touched. "Define sex."

"Inside me. You inside me."

"I'm not going to fuck you," I said, letting her nipple go and lightly brushing the newly sensitive skin with my fingertips.

"This won't make me love you." The barb came through her teeth.

"I don't want you to love me." I squeezed her other nipple when I lied. I'd never been so cruel to them.

"Oh. God."

"Hush." I broke saying it, because her awakening at this touch was life itself. "Stand up."

I helped her to her feet. Her shirt was askew and her bra squeezed her tits down.

"You all right?"

"Yes." She started to right her shirt, but I held her arms still.

"No. Just like this. Take your pants down halfway to your knees."

She swallowed hard. I'd hit an uncomfortable spot. I could let it go right now. Forget the trade. Tell her I'd give her the condo even if she walked out.

"Go on," I said. "Or say pinochle. Then we can battle it out in court."

I licked one of my thumbs and put the other one in her mouth. She sucked it without being asked. My God. All these years. A long string of a thousand missed opportunities.

"Your nipples are so hard." I ran my wet thumbs over them and pinched. Her eyelids fluttered closed. "I've never seen you like this. You want to finish." It was risky to give up, but I was sure she wanted to come as much as I wanted to make her come. "Trust me with this."

Trust that I'm not holding your financial situation over your head in exchange for sex.

*Hey, we all use what we got.*

"No sex," I said. "My cock won't enter you. You're going to come. After you come, I sign the deed over."

She unbuttoned her fly.

Diana Barnes was meeting me halfway. She was taking everything I'd hid from her and opening herself to it. She pushed her pants down.

I twisted the chair around and sat on it. She couldn't walk well with her pants around her thighs, which was the point, so I guided her to my side. Her expression was open and docile. Waiting to be told what to do next.

"Bend at the waist and relax, darling."

I guided her over my knee, spreading my legs so her head had somewhere to rest. Her bottom was pale and round, soft and ready. I tucked both of her arms at her lower back and ringed the wrists with my fingers so she couldn't move. I slid my other hand along her wet cleft. I put two fingers in her, finding the bundle of nerves inside her wall.

She groaned.

My cock raged against her belly. I wanted to come on her. Mark her back and her pink ass.

I pulled out my fingers, circled her clit, then slapped each ass cheek with a *crack crack*. She squeaked. Groaned. The backs of her thighs went taut.

I put my fingers back in her. She was rigid and tight and—

"Adam!"

Mid-slap when she said my name, my hand landed with a *thwack*.

"Stop!"

I froze.

"Pinochle! Let me go."

I released her wrists. She stood, but her pants restricted her, and when I tried to help her, she pulled away quickly, lost her balance, and fell. She tried to catch herself on a chair, but that only sent it down with her.

Up on the heels of her hands, socked feet, bra half up and off, she was comedic as hell. But I didn't laugh. Sex was funny, and BDSM required an appropriate sense of humor. This, however, was not funny to her. So I swallowed a laugh and scrambled to help her up.

"No!" She pushed me away.

"You can't be surprised at a spanking."

She arched her back and got her pants up. Damn. Fuck, shit, and damn.

"I'm not. But..." Still on the floor, she put her bra back down.

"But?"

Frustration crept into my voice. I'd been snapped backward from the most pleasant free fall. I had to remind myself I was the Dominant here. I was supposed to care for her emotions as well as her body.

She stood and fastened her fly. Her shirt buttons were busted. She crossed the front panels of her shirt across her beautiful body.

I sighed into a deep well of disappointment.

"I'm going." She stepped backward, reaching behind her for her coat. "Don't follow me."

"Diana, I'm sorry."

"Don't be sorry. Just... I'll call you. About this. I'm going to call you about this. Soon."

She threw her coat over her arm and opened the door exactly as much as she needed to get out, then she closed it behind her hard enough to rattle the doorbell. Her blue scarf with the embroidered birds drooped out of the coat pocket and got caught in the door. I walked toward it.

By the time I got there, I heard a click of the key in the lock. I opened the door, bent down for the scarf. Diana stood at the door, waiting. I folded the scarf in two, put it around her neck, and looped it.

"Thank you," she said.

"I like taking care of you."

She walked down the hall without another word.

# CHAPTER THIRTY-EIGHT
## PAST PERFECT

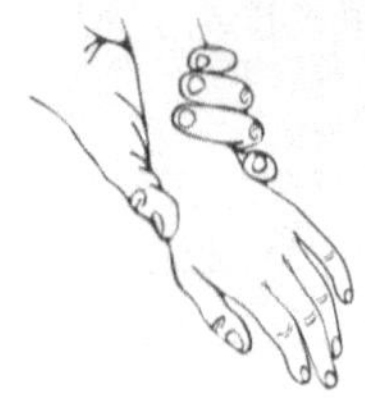

Night.
Crickets.
Her face in darkness.
Pillowcase cool on my cheek.
The blinds clicking in the breeze.
A glint on her eye from the moon.
Our legs twisted together.
*What should we name her?*
*You're not even pregnant yet.*
*But I will be.*
*You're getting ahead of yourself.*
*Lenore.*
*No.*
*It's my grandmother's name.*
*Did your great-grandmother read a lot of Poe?*
*Probably.*
*You want a bunch of ravens circling the building?*
A pinch on my arm.
On top of her.
Her mouth yields in the dark.

The crickets hear her groan.
I suggest a name.
*I like Olive.*
*It's a color.*
*And a boy can be Oliver.*
Kisses wet. Skin sore but ready.
My body trapping hers.
She whispers.
*More please.*

# CHAPTER THIRTY-NINE

## PRESENT TENSE

I PRESSED my ear to the door. The elevator came. I imagined Diana
going down it with her only-slightly-spanked ass and her damaged pride.

That was over. Nice try.

I packed what I could so I could complete my move to Murray Hill.
The rest of my clothes. The toiletries I didn't use every day. Our wedding
album. I flipped through it. We hadn't had a wedding reception. We'd
had a party months after. Fuck that party. Fuck the Lafayette Hotel.
Fuck the first dance and the last. Fuck her mother's white dress. Fuck
the overcooked fish and her cousins from Minnesota who didn't like me.

Fuck all of them. Fuck me. Fuck my stupid decision to try to show
her who I was. Fuck the throb in my balls and her safe word. Fuck my
plan to fall out of love with her. It couldn't work without her. I was just
going to love her forever. She'd always be the woman with her wedding
gown dragging along Fifth Avenue.

I was doomed.

The condo was hers. She'd tried. I'd tried. I failed. I'd sign the deed
over in the morning and be done.

I left the duck and plates for the housekeeper. I started a note about
the change in residents. I wrote down the groceries Diana liked to have,

the way she liked more pillows on the bed, a note to leave the drapes closed and blinds open when she left.

My phone buzzed. I thought it was the west coast printer, but it was Diana.

*—I'm not going to call you—*

*—I can't say it—*

*—Just please swear you
won't show this to anyone.
Even if you marry some
nice submissive girl one day
and want a laugh about
your ex-wife, please don't
show this text—*

*—You don't have to tell me
anything. I get it—*

*—No you don't—*

*—And I'm not getting
remarried—*

*—Yes you are. You deserve
someone who loves you—*

*—Is that what you wanted
to tell me?—*

*—No—*

*—Don't answer until
I say I'm finished—*

—Ok—

*—That's answering—*

*(...)*

*(...)*

The phone rang as I watched the streaming dots indicate she was typing. Her name sprang onto the screen.

"What's going on?" I asked, then I heard street sounds on the other side. "You're not driving, are you?"

"I'm still parked. I just can't type it either. And I can't look at you."

"I decided something," I said, pushing the housekeeper note away. "I'm not sorry. I treated you pretty gently. I checked on you. I'm still your husband—it's not like I'm some stranger. I don't feel a bit of guilt, so if you're about to lay it on, forget it."

"Yeah."

That was all. Then it was street sounds and the car stereo. A podcast. She loved podcasts. Fuck podcasts.

"You can move in tomorrow," I said. "*Nuestra casa* is now *su casa*."

After a deep breath, she said, "Everything about this is bad. You and I are crossing lines. It took a lot of willpower to leave you, and here we are, having sex. Don't correct me. It's sex. And I'm all opened up. I'm allowing things... I run a multimillion dollar company. I brought it back from the brink of a hostile liquidation."

"By marrying the liquidator." That was a lie and this was bullshit. I grabbed my coat and keys and went out.

"Let me finish. I don't need to be spanked like a child. I don't need to take orders from you or anyone. I am your equal. I know all these things are true, and I believed you did too."

She took a long silence. The radio went dead. She must have shut it off. I nodded to the doorman and went into the cold crowded street.

"Can I answer that?"

I had no idea where she was parked, but she wouldn't get a signal from our underground space. There were so few legal spaces I'd probably find her in two minutes. I had the Jaguar's spare key. I clicked the unlock button. The lights would flash when I was in range. She wasn't on the block. I walked east.

"No, you cannot. Because this isn't about you or what you believe or think. I have to put that out of my mind. I had to remind myself that I know all that stuff is true. And so saying that, I have to ask myself what the fuck happened up there. I was all up in my head. I was thinking about how stupid this was and how you're just crazy and I needed to get back and put my stuff in the car and call the west coast printers before they leave for the day." She cleared her throat.

I clicked the car key. No car.

"Then you kissed me. You stupid ass, you always knew how to kiss. And I don't know what happened. I let it all go. I let you own me. No one owns me, Adam. No one."

I rubbed my eyes. For the first time, I thought this was all too complicated. I was dealing with the love of my life leaving me with a note on the counter, but I wasn't. Getting her to submit to me was a distraction from what I should have been doing. Getting the fuck over her.

"I don't know what you want."

"I want my family's company. All the copyrights. All the shares. Complete control. I want you and R+D out without a fight."

"On a strictly business level, that would never be on the table."

"And all debts and loans forgiven. All holdings and assets go back to me. Including the building on Broome."

"You know what you're asking? I put R+D into debt to cover McNeill-Barnes."

"Thirty days. That's the price."

I knew it would be. I knew she'd shoot for the stars. What if I gave it all to her and walked away? It would bankrupt me. I'd survive, but it was bad business. I didn't work that way. I played to win.

If I was going to put the last five years in the negative column and build my holdings back up, I wasn't doing it with a broken heart.

"Thirty days," she repeated, "and then it's over. No sex ever again."

I was about to interject that I'd be happy to never touch her again, but she didn't stop or slow down. The sound of her voice changed. She became more present. More real.

"It's over. No arguing. No more deals. No nickel-and-diming. I'm probably never going to want to see you again."

I spun when I heard her. She was right behind me, coming north on Crosby.

We hung up our phones. The wind bit her cheeks and her breath came in a pouf of steam. Her chin was up a notch and she stood like anything but a submissive.

"This has to be a choice," I said, aware of my contradictions even as I used them to get what I wanted. "I'll give you the contract. It's not legally binding, but it lays out our roles very clearly, and what's expected of you. It's a hard document to read. So buckle in. You can redline three things. They can be broad, but if they're too broad, I'll reject them."

Her eyebrow arched. "We're going to have a contract negotiation over sex?"

"It's not about sex. I might not touch you the entire time. It's about power and trust. These are the rules. No arguing. You come in as a sub. A good Dom respects limits. If you trust me, you'll do exactly what I tell you from day one to day thirty. You'll walk out with every asset we own together and a little more self-awareness than before."

*Because you're submissive, little huntress.*

Behind her, a cab skirted traffic, wheel in the curb, breaking ice and splashing the sidewalk with cold, filthy sludge.

I took her elbow and pulled her out of the way. The flying slush missed her, though I got wet below the knees. Even with all that movement, she and I kept our eyes on each other, testing, asking, feeling for questions we didn't dare ask.

"Send the contract," she said.

"I need you to agree in principle."

"I agree in principle. I'm terrified, but I agree in principle."

"I'll leave it on the kitchen table."

She nodded.

"Let me walk you to the car."

She started walking south. I stayed on her right side so I'd get splashed if another cab attacked. I didn't even think about why I was on that side, it was just what I did. We didn't talk. I remembered wondering how we were going to get a stroller down the street on garbage nights, when even the Michelin two-star restaurant on Crosby put bags of trash on the street for pickup. I'd seen couples wrestle with wheels caught in plastic. Some laughed. Some practically had to dump the kid to get the stroller out. We decided on the little pouches that let the baby rest on her mother's chest. A baby with a spine to hold her up. Not like our baby.

The Jag *blooped* across the cobblestone street.

"Thank you," she said. "For walking me."

I started across the street. "Not done. I'm a finisher. Come on."

She followed, and I opened the driver's side door.

She put her foot on the ledge and stopped before lowering herself in. "I spent the walk asking myself if I trust you."

"Did you answer?"

"I did. I have a lot of mixed feelings about you and about this deal. I think it's weird, but you must need it, and getting out of this marriage without years of litigation is valuable."

"Good."

She got into the car and I closed the door. As I stepped away, she lowered the window.

"I'll make a list of what I expect at the end of the thirty days," she said. "We can make it a rider to your contract."

"A rider to an unenforceable contract isn't enforceable."

"I may not love you, but I trust you."

I got out of the street before I got hit by a car. I was doing it again. Starting over. Reclaiming what I'd been. A pillar of elation built on a foundation of fear. Or the other way around. I couldn't tell them apart anymore because the fear wasn't about something happening, but a fear of who I was.

# CHAPTER FORTY

## PAST TENSE

We—Charlie, Stefan, and I—had decided the main house in Montauk wouldn't have any tools or accouterments on the first floor. We each had a room upstairs we kept the way we wanted and an adjoining room for our subs. Six bedrooms, five baths. Downstairs we had a library, sitting room, an indoor gym, and a room we called the ocean room because it led to the back deck and the short, rocky beach. Kitchen, dining room, office. Everything we needed. Some movable tools in cabinets and hidden hooks, but to the naked eye, the first floor looked as vanilla as anything a real estate broker would show.

We could divide the first floor in a number of configurations by opening or closing pocket doors. In the deep heat of summer, in the years when we all got along, the main house was a hub of kinky parties.

In the off-season, from September to early March, I could work half days in the office and get back to Montauk in under two hours, stay up until two with a sub who begged for a beating, and get to work while she slept it off.

I'd kept that schedule with Serena for two weeks. But on our second Sunday, it changed. We were in the back house, where hooks hung from the ceiling and shackles were bolted to the walls. It was an eight-hundred-square-foot studio space accessed by a stone path behind the main house. The larger room was fit with hooks, crosses, cabinets, whipping benches.

Sometimes I went the entire thirty days without picking up a crop or a lock. Sometimes, if the sub was right and I was on my game, all I needed was time and well-intoned words.

But if I wanted to shackle Serena's wrists to the wall so she was bent over, legs wide, ass up, I had to use the studio.

"She's stunning," Stefan said from behind the one-way mirror.

I was making her wait. She hated waiting, but the anticipation kept her on the knife's edge. "She is."

I picked a soft paddle from the wall. I didn't want to welt her. Then I'd have to wait until she healed to touch her, and taking Serena too far wasn't as much fun as keeping her close to the line. She was too eager to rush over her own boundaries.

"You sharing?" he asked, sitting on a chair facing the mirror/window, legs stretched out and rubbing his chin. He was six-four. Nordic. Dark blue eyes, large nose he played to his advantage, and a bright smile that belied a devilish and unrelenting sadism.

I was glad she didn't want to be shared. I didn't want him to touch her. I didn't have a reason. I just wanted her to myself for thirty days.

"She redlined it."

He waved his hand. He'd come out for a few days to meet an architect about changing the studio into a separate stand-alone with a kitchen so he could live there and paint in the off months. "You have to push the limits, Adam. They're here to be pushed. You can't let them run the show."

"Thanks for the advice." I ended up with a riding crop. A blunt tool compared to my hands, but a little variety was good for everyone.

"She still a popper?"

"As intact as the day she was born." I went for the door.

"You know what I would have done?"

"You?"

"That first day—"

"You would have stripped her in front of a few of your friends, put a dildo on the floor, and made her sit on it so they could all watch her bleed onto it. Then each of them would have fucked her cunt. You'd take her ass that night during aftercare."

He looked back at me with that big Swedish smile. "Something like that."

"That's not how I do it."

"She would have loved it." He turned back to the mirror. "She'd remember it forever. But she wanted you. Two weeks and still a virgin. Too bad."

I pulled a lever on the side of the window, flipping the shades closed. "Jerk off on your own dime."

I shut the door behind me and went around back. Five steps through fallen leaves to the studio door. Five steps in the cold September air. The sound of the ocean behind me, a broken record of rising and falling breaks and whooshes.

Stefan, Charlie, and I had bought this house together, and we used it cooperatively. We joked and got along. Stefan and I had had some differences we worked out. Mostly. He'd found the property and I got roped in, but I didn't trust him.

If he took a sub's virginity the way he described, or enacted any scene in his repertoire for any reason, he talked with the sub first. If he pushed limits outside the sub's comfort zone, he told her he was pushing limits during the scene. He obeyed the rules.

But still, he'd pissed me off.

"Good evening," I said when I walked into the studio.

"Good evening, Master," Serena replied, hair covering her face.

"How are you doing?" I could see the wet sheen between her legs.

"Fine, Master."

"Do you like waiting?"

"No, Master."

"Wrong." I thwacked her with the crop. "You like whatever pleases me."

"Yes, Master."

There was something rote about her answer. Something a little too rehearsed. That wouldn't do. Maybe Stefan was right. Maybe I'd let her have her virginity for too long. I'd let myself become infatuated with her looks and her purity. It wasn't about her anymore; it had become about me. It was never supposed to be about me.

I tossed the crop aside. I didn't want to be Stefan, which in a way, was also about me. I brutalized her that night while I made plans to shock her the following day.

# CHAPTER FORTY-ONE

## PRESENT TENSE

DIANA'S REDLINES came back while I waited for Charlie. He owned a small store that took up half a floor of an old garment factory on 38th Street. It had no name. Just a thick wooden door, a male receptionist, and rooms of every kinky accouterment a deviant could imagine. Every piece was hand chosen. Everything was expensive as fuck. And if you had the money, it was all worth it.

Her redlines came in an email.

1. *You only hit me with your hands.*
2. *I will not crawl or call you sir. I will not be humiliated.*
3. *No gagging with anything. I always need to speak.*

Too broad. A clear case of submissive overreach.

One. It wasn't the sub's place to redline such an enormous number of tools. She could say "no paddling" or even "no wood," but asking me to use only my hands was unacceptable.

Two. Humiliation was too subjective, as well as unpredictable. Sticking my fingers in her mouth was part of the deal, but if she was humiliated by it, that was now on me. Crawling and using respectful names for the Dominant were two totally different things, but they both illustrated the truth of submission. Crossing that much off kept me from achieving the dominance I needed to make this worthwhile.

Three. No gagging was acceptable. But making sure she could always speak? What if my dick was down her throat?

I'd negotiated contracts with her before. This list shouldn't have surprised me. Then I realized what was missing.

Anal. Sharing. Videotaping. Fisting. The dozens of pain-delivery systems that were on the list but I didn't use because they bored me. What about actual sex? I wouldn't have been surprised if she'd crossed that off entirely, but she hadn't.

"Hey, mate." Charlie came into the waiting room with two short glasses of scotch.

He sat on the sage-green brocade chair that matched the couch I was on. A long, low slate-topped table stretched the length of the sofa. The two windowless walls were covered with black-and-white art photos of men and women in the throes of bondage and ecstasy.

He handed me one of the glasses of scotch, and we clicked them together. "What brings you?"

I let the searing heat burn my throat as the scotch went down. "I have nothing at the Montauk house, and I'm taking it until mid Feb. I gave Silver the list."

"Good for you. Main house, right? Stefan's in the studio."

He'd succeeded in converting the small house into his personal painting studio and punishment ward with a kitchen and its own power. I was out of the life and Charlie was fine in the main house, so we allowed it.

"Main house is fine. He alone?"

Charlie laughed to himself and moved to the chair next to me, propping his cane against the arm. "He needs them more than they need him."

"Someone should tell him that."

"What would be the point?"

I took a swig of whiskey. "So it's Serena or another one?"

"I think they're trying to rekindle the old fire."

The Silver Domme came in carrying a wooden box. She balanced perfectly on platform heels in her tight black pants.

"Adam!" she said when she saw me. "I didn't even believe it when I saw your name on the list." She put the box on the table, hugged me, and kissed each cheek. We sat, and Silver put her hands on the box. "I wasn't sure if it was you, but I got your favorite things."

Her smile was lascivious yet not flirtatious. She and I played the same field position. It was a smile of understanding.

Charlie leaned back and sipped his drink. "Mind if I stay for this stroll down memory lane?"

"Stay," I said.

Silver opened the box. "Now, we have another few things I gathered in the back room, but I wanted to bring these out first."

She laid out a birch paddle with three holes in it. A braided brown riding crop. A set of adjustable nipple clamps I couldn't imagine using on Diana, yet—

"The paddle comes narrower, and we have one with no holes and SLUT carved backward—"

"No."

"I remembered." She smiled again, taking out a black stick. "Not your thing. We also have rubber crops. This one's single mold so to prevent breakage, and the handle side also leaves a nice mark."

I leaned forward, tapping my fingertips together as she brought out rattan canes and more paddles in different sizes and colors. I said nothing. Silver was unfazed.

But would Diana be fazed? I had to look at these through her eyes. She'd done internet searches and seen plenty, but if I brought these out to use on her, I was sure she'd be frightened. More than anything, I didn't want to scare her.

"Should I bring out the bindings?" Silver asked.

"Please."

She left the tools on the table and went through the door to the back. I knew how to use everything she'd presented. I knew how to welt skin without opening it. I struck hard, with accuracy, safely. I made them beg for more, because I made sure that the more pain they experienced, the more pleasure it was paired with. In the end, it was about pleasure and freedom. But everything on the table was redlined.

Was I going to accept her line in the sand? Or was I going to rub it out and draw my own?

"Who are you bringing?" Charlie asked. "If I know her, I can pick for you."

"Diana." I said it so softly I barely heard myself.

When Charlie didn't answer, I looked at him. His eyes were slightly wider and his mouth was just open enough for shock.

"Diana," I said with my full throat. "My wife."

"You've got to be fucking with me. The same woman who left you a note on the counter?"

"She's agreed. Saw the contract."

"Wait, wait, wait. *The* contract. The boilerplate? The one with gangbangs and electroshock?"

"Yes."

He fingered his cane, twisting it half clockwise, then counterclockwise, as if he were drilling a hole in the floor. "Do you have any idea what you're doing?"

"I've done it before, Charlie."

"Oh. Done it before, have you? And how did you get her to agree to do this with a husband she wants to divorce?"

I put my glass on the table. "Can we fill that up?"

He looked at me suspiciously. Tapped his phone. A second later, a man swooped my glass away and replaced it with a new drink. Before he'd even closed the door behind him, I downed it and clicked the glass back on the table.

Silver wasn't coming back. Charlie ran the entire operation from that phone. He could have a dozen dancing girls strut in by tapping it.

I picked up the three-holed paddle. The empty circles cut down air resistance so the paddle moved faster, hit harder, pushed the sub's capacity for pain and her ability to submit to the limit. The first time you paddled them, it hurt. If you gave them emotional comfort and a fifteen-minute orgasm, they brought it to you in their teeth the second time and bent willingly for its hard kiss.

I leaned back, feeling its balance in my palm. This tool of domination. Built to help me release the winding knot of a world I couldn't control. Those slices of time in safe spaces where a woman gave herself to me, and I gave myself to her. I missed the emotional connection. It wasn't love. It wasn't ever love, but it was deep and thick, nearly psychic the way a Dom and a sub could click together.

"I own most of her company," I said. "I rescued it. If she wants it back—"

"No," Charlie interrupted. "Absolutely not."

He snapped me away from the memory of that feeling of control. Brought me back to the world where I had to answer to society for my actions.

"*Absolutely not*, what?"

"She's not in a position to consent, mate."

"Believe me, she's capable of reading and understanding a contract."

He put his elbows on his knees, leaning more right than left. I knew it hurt when he bent like that.

"She doesn't know you. You're going to trap her on the tip of Long Island in storm season, with you and a few dozen paddles while you get back in practice? What are you trying to do? Get revenge?"

"It's not revenge."

"You can really hurt her." Charlie stamped his cane. "It's too much. If she's not trained slowly and fully consenting, you can break her mind. Is that what you want?"

"I'm not going to do anything she can't handle."

"Have you ever spent more than a few hours with a sub who wasn't trained and willing?"

"She's willing."

"She. Is. Not. She can't consent cleanly."

"She has the contract."

"You're holding her life's work hostage."

"Hostage? She's holding *me* hostage. She has my guts in her hands. I don't care about the company, I care about her. She's my life, do you understand? Have you ever loved a woman? Have you ever held her at night so tight because you couldn't sleep thinking something might happen to her? Have you ever built a future around a woman? Ever thought of every tomorrow, every year, every decade with her? Dreamed of your old age holding her hand? I can only function with her in my life. I can only breathe if I know she's there. I gave her my fucking soul and she threw it away. Months ago, maybe years ago. She made a decision to throw me away. She's prepared for this divorce, and I'm swinging in the wind. Raw. With nothing. No defenses. Now what am I supposed to do?" I stood and threw my coat over my shoulders. "This is not about money. It's not about some publishing company. Not for me. If I don't do this, I have no chance of recovery. I'm as good as dead."

He didn't stand, but looked up at me from below, still twisting his cane. "No, you're not. Don't do this. You'll get over it. You will."

"Yes, I will. I'll be in Montauk starting Saturday." I went for the door and was almost out before Charlie spoke up.

"You might want to hold off until Serena's gone," Charlie said. "Avoid unnecessary emotional complications."

"I don't have any complications about Serena."

"But Diana might. Seeing your last sub on the property? She's going to be vulnerable as it is."

He was right, but his solution was shit. Everything would change in a week, or days. I had to take Diana now. This moment.

"Thank Silver for me. I'll send a list of what I want delivered."

Before he could answer, I left, striding past the receptionist, into the hall where, thank God, an elevator waited.

What I was doing was wrong. I was treating the love of my life like a device. I was using her against her. I was holding her hostage until she freed my heart.

I knew it. Charlie knew it. Maybe Diana knew it.

The hope that she'd accept my offer and the planning that went into it kept me from breaking down. I feared that breakdown more than I feared a life alone. The inner chaos, the loss of any sense of self outside pain, I wouldn't stand it. I couldn't see through it. Becoming fully saturated in the pain that roiled inside me had to be avoided at all costs. The abyss was too deep. I needed to jump over it.

It was raining ice when I got to the street. I put my back against the building and tapped the cold glass of my phone.

—I accept your redlines—

She came back right away.

149

*—I want one more—*

Of course she did.

*—You only get three—*

*—No scat or whatever
you call it. I don't want
any poop or pee—*

I smiled. God, I loved her. But she was a pain in the ass.

*—Not my thing—*

*—You have no idea
what a relief that is—*

*—Let's meet with Lloyd. We
can put McN-B in his hands
for a month while it's in a
holding pattern. If we have to,
we work mornings from
out there—*

I fell into the comfort of everyday thoughts, everyday talk, business
as usual. To have that again. For it to be a month ago…
It took her too long to answer.

*—Diana?—*

*—We run it as equals.
If we're working you're
not the boss of me—*

What was obvious to me wasn't to her. I didn't know if she'd be able to separate work time from play time, and if I was being honest with myself, I didn't know if I'd be able to either.

*—I wouldn't have it any other way—*

That was the most honest thing I'd ever said to a woman or myself. I wanted her at my side as a partner. That was the abyss I couldn't see past.

I hailed a cab up to R+D before I had to look so far into that vacuum that I fell in.

# CHAPTER FORTY-TWO

## PAST PERFECT

THE REAL ESTATE agent had excused herself so Diana and I could talk.

We stood in the space a few feet from each other. The wood floors shone with new gloss, the white walls reflected the blasting summer sun through the huge windows. Crosby Street passed by, twenty stories below with tires rattling against the cobblestone street. A voice from the sidewalk. Another returning the greeting. An undulating rustle of white noise from blocks away.

"What do you think?" she asked, voice echoing off the emptiness.

"It's pretty big."

"Do you think we can fill it?"

With our stuff. With our life. With our memories. With our children.

"Yes."

She smiled and looked at the high ceiling. "I'm so happy."

"Why's that?" I took her by the waist and pulled her close.

Her eyes were pale and clear in the bright room. Her mouth held all her warmth and expressiveness. She was incapable of lying through it.

"You want the long version or the short version? Pick the long version."

I held her even tighter. "Why go short when long's available?"

"You make me happy," she said. "I can't believe I ever thought I was going to marry anyone else."

"That guy?"

"That guy. He wasn't you, and I must have known it. It was you. Always you. You make me feel loved all the way through. Even the dumb stuff I do. Even when I have a really bad idea, you pay it full attention and you sort through it with me. It's like you know there's a germ of something good there and you want to find it. And can I tell you something else? Sometimes I look at you and I can't believe you picked me. You're so wise. And thoughtful. And handsome. Like, super handsome. I'm sorry but I love you." She closed her eyes again and shouted to the ceiling, "I love you Adam Steinbeck!"

I laughed. She delighted me, filled me, lifted me.

She put her hands on my cheeks and made me look deeply into her eyes. "Promise you'll never leave me."

"I promise. But if you really want me to promise..."

"What?" she asked suspiciously.

"We should probably get married."

Her mouth and eyes went wide.

"Let's!" She said it as if I'd suggested a cruise.

"I have to get a ring."

"Let's do it now!"

"Now?"

"Now! Grab a couple of friends who can witness. Go to city hall. Right now!"

"Wait, wait. Don't you want to do all the things?" I circled my hand in the air as if trying to pull "all the things" out of it. "You know. A bouquet? A party? Walk down an aisle in a white dress?"

"I have my mother's in the closet. I can run home and get it. We can get flowers on the corner. Oh, Adam, let's just do it right now, when it feels so right. Let's not wait for all the stuff. Let's not get distracted by caterers and photographers. I hate seating arrangements. I get stressed out just thinking about it. Let's just get in a cab and go get married."

Her enthusiasm infected me. She was light, life, energy. Everything. What wouldn't I do for her, when she gave me so much?

I would have married her in an instant. So I did.

# CHAPTER FORTY-THREE

## PRESENT TENSE

THE MONTAUK HOUSE had a full-time staff of two that included
Thierry, who drove a long black limousine, and his wife, Willa who took
care of the cleaning and cooking when someone was in the big house.
They lived in a third structure on the east end of the property, took care
of repairs, maintenance, and were unfazed by what they saw.

Thierry pulled the limo up at five o'clock Saturday morning. It was
dark, and the air had the thrum of the day's potential. When he opened
the back door for me, we shook hands and he told me how good it was
to have me back. That was the extent of it. He drove from Murray Hill
to SoHo, to Crosby Street, where Diana and the doorman waited with
—I counted—four suitcases, one trunk, and a toiletry case.

"Take them back up," I told the doorman. I gave him a ten for the
chore.

"Why?" Diana asked as he went into action. "I need—"

"Nothing. You need nothing. I provide you with what you need,
and what I don't provide, you don't need. Think of it as a vacation from
adulthood."

"That's the exact opposite of the way I want to think of it."

I held out my hand. "Regardless. I'll need your phone."

She didn't move. I pointed at her right-hand coat pocket then put my palm up for it.

"What if work calls?" she asked.

"They'll call me, and if it's important, you and I—together—will put the fire out."

She still hesitated.

"Okay, listen," I said. "When you're there, you're mine. Your time, your boredom, your isolation, these are my tools. If you're texting your friends or reading the news, you're not with me. I need you *with me*."

"What if there's work?"

"I brought your laptop from the office."

She took out her phone, weighing its importance in her hand. "This scares me."

"I'm not trying to scare you. But you said you trusted me. If you do, there's no reason to be scared."

She stretched her arm just a little, as if she really wanted to pull it back. I took the phone and put it in my pocket.

"Good." I almost said *good girl* but caught myself. We were still in the world, where that was condescending.

"I want to take my journal."

I thought about it for only a moment. I could cut her off from the world, but I couldn't cut her off from her own thoughts.

"Yes. All right."

"It's in the top bag."

I unzipped it, and the red leather popped through as if it were dying to get out. I handed it to her. She hugged it to her chest.

I held my hand toward the open back door of the car. "Shall we?"

Her hair blew back from her face as she watched her bags being taken back up, and onto her reddened cheeks when she looked at the back of the limo.

"Once I get in there," she said, "everything changes, doesn't it?"

"You wanted change."

"I guess I did."

I left it there, letting her look at the open mouth of the limo, wondering if she'd let herself get swallowed.

She did. My Diana bent her knees and took my hand, letting me help her into the car. I got in after her and let Thierry close the door. The outside world was snuffed out.

The car pushed forward. Diana sat across from me, knees pressed together, hands on them, looking into the space between us. Her wedding ring was where it belonged. I wanted to believe she'd put it on because she kept changing her mind about leaving me, but then I hoped not. If this was over, it was over. I was taking my full thirty days and walking away. I had no intention of looking back.

But that was tomorrow and this was now.

"Diana."

"Yeah?"

"You look beautiful."

"Thank you."

"How do you feel?"

"Scared."

"Thank you for telling me. You should always answer honestly even if you think I won't like it."

Instructing my wife how to speak to me. Was irony or justice being served?

"Do you have any questions?" I asked. I was falling into the natural use of my Dominant voice. I still had to remind myself first, but it took less time to process.

"I can't think right now."

"We'll go very slow."

"Yeah," she croaked.

"Your safe word is 'pinochle?' Is that right?"

"Yes."

"And for the trigger question, I'll ask you your name. You'll say 'Diana.' Your age, your address. If you take too long to answer or say anything but the truth, I'm going to change whatever I'm doing or slow it down."

"I read that in the contract."

She was walking on a wire. Tension surrounded her like a suit of armor. I usually enjoyed a sub's discomfort, but this was something more than that. This was a call for me to help her relax.

"Take your shoes off," I said.

She flashed red for a second, looked away, then slowly shifted her feet until they were out of her pumps. She curled her toes in her black tights as if they embarrassed her. We got on the highway, the seams in the asphalt making a *thup thup* against the tires. No traffic. We'd be there in a few hours, traffic gods willing.

I slapped my knee. "Right foot."

She lifted her foot and I took it by the Achilles, bringing it up to my knee. The sun was rising, washing the black sky blue.

I ran my thumb along the bottom of her foot, the matte nylon of the stockings dry on my skin. Pulling at the toe, I pushed my fingers against the fabric, stretching it into a cone, then I used my left hand to spread the knit apart until it ripped.

She gasped as I shredded her tights up to the knee. She was going to cry. She thought I was going to get very rough before we even got into Long Island.

"Hush," I said, running both thumbs along the bottom of her foot. "This is a foot rub. You have nothing to be concerned about."

She snorted a little laugh that would have gotten another sub welted. But she did it while leaning back and relaxing her shoulders.

"What are you worried most about?" I worked from the tender part of the arch outward with increasing pressure.

She cringed a little when I pressed hard, but she didn't pull away. My wife loved a deep-tissue massage. She went to an old Korean guy with hands the size of dinner plates and forearms as wide as Portuguese loaves.

"Everything," she said.

"Pain?"

"Yes."

"Discomfort."

"Yes."

"Having sex with me again? Which—" I was about to remind her there might not be any sex, but she cut in before I could.

"Not really that. More…" She grimaced then relaxed when I went deep into the ball of her foot. "Ickiness."

"Ickiness?"

"Seeing things I don't want to see. Being something that doesn't feel right." Her face changed as she watched my hand on her foot. "I'm afraid I'll be afraid of you."

I squeezed and pulled each of her toes. This little piggy was mine. This little piggy was also mine. This little piggy got a spanking. This little piggy got the paddle. This little piggy went *yes yes yes* all the way home.

She wasn't afraid of me. Not yet. She might be. If everything worked out, I wouldn't care if she was.

But in the limo to Montauk, I didn't want her to be afraid. I had a box of things in the trunk that had been chosen for their innocuous looks.

I put her foot on the floor and gently lifted the other, putting it on the same knee. I tore open the stockings, and because she wasn't shocked the second time, she wrested her foot through the hole. The foot part came off, and I tossed it aside.

I rubbed that foot the same way, maybe harder. She relaxed.

"The last time I rubbed your feet was in the hospital."

"Yeah." Her voice was no louder than a breath, and her eyes stayed on the hands folded in her lap as if she instinctively knew what to do and just needed to give herself permission to do it.

"Before we lost Olive." I pressed her foot between my palms, curved then squeezed.

"Lenore. And we didn't *lose* her," Diana continued. "We got rid of her."

"She wasn't going to make it. She was going to live a week in extreme pain."

My wife knew this. We'd discussed it. She'd cried for a week then stopped abruptly, as if she'd run out of tears. She focused on getting better as if it was a project she had to complete.

She was terrible at finishing things.

"Taking care of you during that time was one of the most satisfying things I've ever done," I said. "You let me bathe you, advocate for you, tend you. I wasn't happy about losing the baby. But being there for you made me very, very happy."

"I never—" she blurted, then stopped herself, softening her tone. "All that time... I never felt so lonely."

*And there, New York City... there you have it.*

The time I felt closest to her was the time she felt most alone.

I took her foot off my lap. "Did you read the contract carefully? Anything besides the list? I want to make sure you know what's expected of you."

"I did."

"When I walk into a room? What do you do?"

She stuttered. Swallowed. Seemed to shrink inside herself. "Present myself to you?"

"It's not a question."

She nodded slightly. Her hands were folded so tightly the knuckles were white.

"You present me with something to fuck."

"Adam..."

"You don't have to call me sir because you redlined it. But you no longer address me by my name. That's a privilege that's earned. You start from zero. I got into this car after you and you presented me with nothing. You should have been on your knees with your mouth open, at the very least."

Her face was beet red with contained rage. I was going for purple.

"I said I might not fuck you, but that doesn't mean no contact and it doesn't mean you make yourself unavailable. It's not up to you. It's completely up to me." I leaned forward. She looked as if she wanted to become part of the leather seat. "And let me assure you, if I remain unsatisfied in any way, there are going to be years and years of filings before you hold my shares."

"What happened to you?" she whispered.

"Get on your knees."

She didn't move.

I pointed at the floor. "What did you think this was, Diana? Did you think I'd fuck you sweetly once and let it go? Even seeing that contract?"

Her mouth opened but nothing came out.

I reached forward.

Cupped her jaw.

Drew my hand behind her neck.

Up the back of her head.

Made a fistful of hair.

She squeaked.

Her hands gripped my forearms as I pulled her forward.

And down.

Until she was on the floor. She got her knees under her, but I didn't let go, bending her head back so I could see the pores of her cringing face.

"This is what you signed up for. Feel free to change your mind any time."

Her eyes closed. She swallowed so hard I heard it.

"You are my submissive. You will kneel at my feet."

I let her go and sat back.

I thought I was going to have to turn the car around. When she kneeled upright in her ripped stockings, looking at the blurred motion of the trees, I thought she was going to pinochle out. I almost wanted her to.

But she fell forward, put her hands in front of her and her forehead on the carpet. Her ass wasn't up, but she was kneeling, naked toes pointed against the floor mat.

I wasn't going to last the whole month. Submission made her honest, and obviously I wasn't ready for her honesty. Maybe after thirty days I'd be able to hear about how lonely she'd been with me. Maybe I'd grow a thick skin when it came to her, or we'd form an emotional bond I respected and she didn't.

She'd sue me. I'd lose because I'd taken her to a remote house in Montauk to dominate her. The contract and her consent would be inadmissible in court. Everything would go south. My life would be a disaster.

But I'd be over her. I couldn't imagine the day I wouldn't love her, especially not with her submission at my feet. The bare satisfaction of it, the peace, the rightness of my sexual dominance over this woman in a controlled setting was better than any drug.

Worth it. All worth it.

# CHAPTER FORTY-FOUR

## PRESENT TENSE

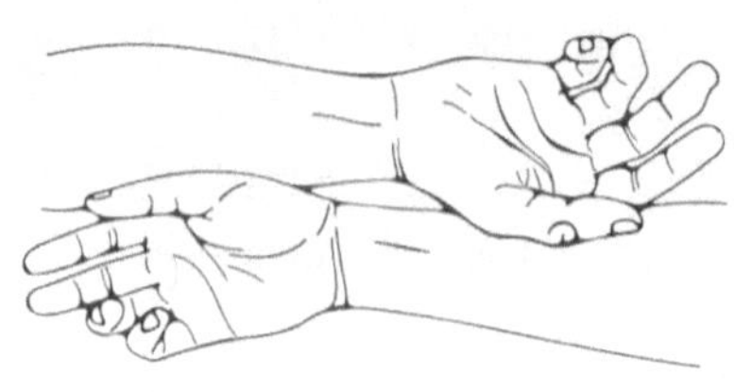

## DAY ONE

AFTER FIFTEEN MINUTES at my feet, she laid her cheek on my shoe. I leaned down and stroked her hair. We were in that position when the car turned onto the private road at the other end of Long Island and stopped at the gate to the house.

Diana looked up.

"You can sit," I said before she could decide to do it herself.

Thierry pressed the number sequence on the keypad while Diana stared at me from the opposite seat. I couldn't tell if she was mad or curious.

"How was that?" I asked.

"I slept a little."

The gates opened and the car pulled forward.

"Were you scared?"

A slight knot at the brow. A tightening of the lips. She didn't know what to make of the change, and I wasn't going to explain it.

"When I looked all this up, I didn't believe you could be that way. When I went to the Cellar, I didn't believe it. Not you. Not my husband."

The car pulled around the circular drive and stopped at the front steps. The two-story house had been built in the late nineteenth century. It had thick wood beams, leaded glass, and porches everywhere.

"And now?"

"I believe it." She put her shoes on her bare feet.

As she spoke, I could see out the window behind her. Two people came from the side of the drive from the studio. I knew who they were.

"You don't have to get out of the car."

Stefan and Serena stopped at the bottom of the front steps. They were both fully dressed in coats and boots. Serena wore a collar attached to a leash.

Stefan yanked the leash, and Serena fell to her knees. Diana turned when the links clicked on the pavement, shock registering on her face when she saw them.

Thierry opened the door. We were blasted with cold. Serena's prone figure on the cold ground. Face hidden. Hair splayed out.

"Thierry can drive you home right now," I said, putting my foot out the door. I thought she was going to stay in the backseat and go back to the city. I could hear the ocean crashing behind the house.

"Adam," Stefan said, holding out his hand.

I got out of the car and shook it. He yanked the chain, and Serena looked up.

I didn't know if seeing Serena's face would inspire Diana to get out of the car, or if seeing that there would be other people around gave her comfort. But slowly, with eyes going from Serena to Stefan to me, she stepped through the car door.

"What do we have here?" Stefan asked.

"This is my wife," I said.

Her stockings were torn and her coat was open.

"Well, well, I assume we redlined sharing?" He said it to her. I didn't want him speaking to her. At all. But his eyes were all over what was mine.

I could hear Thierry behind me, unloading my box of equipment. I wished he'd hurry.

"Mind your own redlines," I said.

"That's a no." One side of his mouth went up at an evil angle. "Us either."

"You're in the studio?" I asked.

"Yes."

"Good. Stay there."

He jerked Serena's leash and made eye contact with my beautiful wife. "Come visit any time."

"Good-bye, Stefan," I said. "And Serena."

A perfect submissive, she glued her eyes to the ground and kept her hands at her sides.

Stefan waved once and turned down the side path, pulling his pet behind him.

"Follow me." I spun and went up the steps. I usually put my hand on Diana's back and let her walk before me, but things had changed. Now it was her job to be at my heels.

Did it make sense that both felt right? That in Montauk, I could let her walk behind me in a subservient position, but in the city, I walked behind her?

It didn't make any sense, and it did.

Once she was inside, I closed the door, shutting out the cold and the wind. Only the sound of the grandfather clock interrupted the silence.

I faced her. She looked all over, taking in everything. The walls of glass, the open rooms, the wood floor, the oversized nature photographs. Willa had left flowers on the hall table.

"We are the only ones in this house except for the following. Thierry and Willa live in the cottage just east." I pointed generally east. "Thierry won't come in without asking, and Willa comes to do some cooking and cleaning. Nothing they see will surprise them, but we are going to work around their times. The studio house on the west is currently occupied by Stefan and Serena, whom you just met. They have no reason to be in the main house unless invited, and the studio is absolutely, positively off-limits to you. Understand?"

"Yes."

I took off her coat, untied her scarf, put it in her pocket, and hung it in the front closet. The stairs to the second floor were by the front foyer, and the office door was on the other side. She faced the back of the house, which overlooked the ocean through high, wood-framed windows. She crossed her arms, looking past the horizon, where her worst fears were.

"Questions?" I asked.

"Will you invite them? Serena and Stefan?"

"Maybe."

"For dinner?"

"For whatever I want." I stood in front of her, blocking the view. "Your room is upstairs. It has a red door and it's connected to mine. Everything you need is there."

"Wait. We're not sleeping in the same bed?"

"No. Not even in the same room. It's your space. There are clothes for you. Unless I have something laid out for you, you can wear what you want. The white nightgown is what you wear to bed unless I say otherwise. You must leave your room for meals and when I need you, but if you're not servicing me, you can go wherever you like except the studio. If you see me, you present yourself."

"Servicing you?"

"We can call it whatever you want."

I used to do this all the time. I'd brought a dozen subs up for thirty-day stretches, and they were typically excited and thrilled. They were usually sucking my cock before I even told them where their room was.

"Can I ask a question?" she asked.

"Yes."

"I didn't redline you sharing me."

"That's not a question. That's a statement."

"I didn't cross it off because I didn't think you'd let anyone else have sex with me."

"How strategic."

"Was I wrong?"

"You might have been wrong."

Her face fell. She'd miscalculated. I didn't want to hurt her, and I certainly didn't want to share her, but she had to accept the rules. She had to do this one hundred percent if it was going to work.

I asked myself if I enjoyed hurting her, and I answered yes and no at the same time. Then I asked myself if I was trying to scare her, and I got the same answer. My responses were tangled up in each other.

"Go to your room and get changed. There's a clock. The alarm is set for five p.m. Be at the base of the stairs before it stops chiming."

She didn't move.

"Yes?" I asked.

No answer. I picked a stack of mail off the side table, sorted through it, and headed out of the room. Still, she didn't move.

"Do you want to go home? I'm not going to ask you constantly. It's up to you. Or I can get frustrated with you and call it off."

She went up the stairs with her head down and her face firm. I watched her ass as she went. She wasn't going to last a week.

And yet, she only seemed scared when I was too brusque.

The more I embraced who I had been—who I was at the core—the more I saw the signs of submission. The downcast eyes, the still hands, the attention to my Dominant voice.

I flipped through the mail and paced the corners and edges of the house like a cat checking his territory. I hadn't been there in years, but I had paid for upkeep with the other two. Not much had changed. It looked like a normal house. The library with its dark woods and stacks of hardcovers. The piano in the corner. The Oriental rug. The hidden hooks in the floor and ceiling. The couch and long table facing the ocean in the open room. The TV room with its rustic furniture. And the kitchen, built for cooks with an island and a six-burner stove with a grill. When we'd had over a hundred people here, it had been really handy, and not just for cooking.

The entire back of the house was skirted by a deck that ended at a rocky beach, thirty feet from the high tide line. I stepped out into the cold and faced the water. I'd had a sub tell me the presence of the ocean and her Dominant in the same place made her feel infinitely small and powerless. She described it as the purest joy. Being under him, infinitesimal in the universe, yet cared for as if she was the most precious being in the world.

Her eyes had fluttered a little when she described the feeling, as if she was re-experiencing the high.

A grunt went up, carried by the wind, made anonymous and sexless in the gusts. It came from the studio. I walked to the other end of the back deck.

The studio building was painted white. The barn doors faced the main house and had windows at the top. On the side, another door and a small porch faced the ocean.

A plane of snow-covered grass tilted between the main house and the studio.

There, thirty feet away in the cold sun, were the residents of the studio. Serena, bare-assed and bent over a huge planter, one naked leg leaning on the edge, one boot on, pants pooled at the ankle. Stefan behind her, thrusting inside her as if he wanted to kill her.

I looked up. A railing above. The narrow balcony to Diana's room was just above me, facing the studio. She stood there, a flat, blurry figure against the darkness of the room behind her.

She was watching from her room. The edge of the porch wasn't in front of her by much, and it was possible she didn't notice me there. I couldn't read her from that angle, but she saw it, and Stefan knew it. She was the reason for the show.

Stefan put his hand on Serena's throat, leveraging himself against it. Pulling her up. Her face went red. I could see it even from far away. She'd redlined choking with me. Had someone pushed that limit? Or was this a first?

I looked up at Diana's window again. She was still there. Stefan's grunts carried over the wind, faster and more intense. When I looked back to Stefan and Serena, his hand was off her throat and her mouth was open wide as if she needed to inhale the atmosphere.

I checked Diana. Still there. Barely a shadow against the window frame. If she saw me, she pretended she didn't.

Serena cried out, barking, "Please!"

Stefan snarled something I couldn't decipher, and Serena's back arched in orgasm. He grabbed her ass with both hands and thrust hard and fast. He went tight, then loose.

When I looked up again, my wife wasn't at the window.

I'd be surprised if she showed up at dinner with anything but a request to go home.

# CHAPTER FORTY-FIVE

## PRESENT TENSE

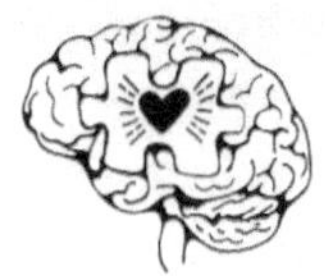

### DAY ONE

THE STUDIO WAS visible from the office room. The sun lit a clear blue sky, warming the air enough to gently melt the last snow on the yard between the main house and the little studio where Stefan and Serena lived. By eleven, strands of dry grass and swatches of dirt came through the white tufts.

I didn't admit to myself that I was watching the studio, even as I looked over my laptop screen whenever there was movement. Diana's room was right above me. I kept it nondescript with white bedding and pale wood furniture. I'd had the door between our rooms left open so she could see my bed, which was higher with posts and beams that could be used for ropes and shackles.

She wouldn't notice the potential of the bedframe as much as she'd notice the blue-and-green quilt, the art on the walls, the Persian carpet. She'd notice how the décor showed our relative places in the relationship. To most subs, the subtle message was a turn-on. To Diana, it would be insulting.

Even the bed sheets made me think I was moving too fast.

I made a hundred plans for her body and mind at dinner, ranging from honest talks to unfulfilling fantasies, then dismissed them all. Having gotten her here, I felt the emptiness of my success. Still so much to do, and I couldn't decide how to do it.

Mostly because I didn't know what I wanted.

I thought I did, but I couldn't commit to it. I still straddled two worlds emotionally. My definitions were contradictory, and the shift had been too sudden. Was I half of a power couple? A Dominant with a submissive wife who didn't love him? Or a single Dominant with insatiable appetites? Neither? Some third, nameless monster?

I could only imagine what it was like for my wife. Except at the end of this, she could go back to being who she was. I couldn't.

At eleven fifteen, one of the barn doors opened. Stefan came out bundled in a wool hat and thick boots. Serena waited in the door, fully dressed in a burnt orange polo and brown pants. A narrow wood crate leaned on her hip. I'd seen Stefan transport his work, and that was a canvas crate. I stood and went around the desk, not even pretending to work anymore.

I watched as he backed a pickup truck up to the door. Got out. Kissed Serena on the cheek when he took the crate. She went into the studio and got another, handing it to him as he came back. He rushed to relieve her of the weight and wagged his finger at her. She didn't get far with the third before he took it.

When he closed the back of the cab, Serena got on her knees, right in the flat, wet snow. She kissed the top of his hand, then the palm. He patted her head and picked her up, led her into the studio, and closed the door.

As he drove away a few minutes later, I couldn't forget that he'd put his hand on her neck until she stopped breathing. That had been a hard limit. Yet the scene I'd witnessed was as warm and normal as any between a Dom and his sub.

I was making a problem where there wasn't one. Serena's lines had moved. Stefan was doing what Stefan did. Serena was a grown-up. She knew how it went. He was giving her what she needed.

Neither Stefan nor Serena needed fixing. If anyone needed fixing, it was Adam Steinbeck, walking across the slope to the little house on the west side of the property with his dress shoes crunching on the old snow and the salt mist freezing in his hair.

The guy with the love of his life biding her time to leave him. The guy who could only get her to spend thirty days with him by holding hostage everything she held dear.

That was who needed fixing.

As true as all that was, I didn't hesitate to knock on the side door. It had been painted since I'd been at the house last. A shiny flat red against the crisp white of the wood siding. A shadow passed over the glass, and Serena opened the door a second later.

"Hi," she said, only opening the door an eighth of the way.

"Hi," I replied. "Sorry to disturb you."

"It's all right."

"You're not supposed to open the door for me or anyone is my guess."

"I didn't know you were going to be here. You and your wife, I mean."

As if Diana and I were on anything more intimate than speaking terms. As if our marriage was more real than a thirty-day stay of execution.

"Are you going to invite me in?"

I was asking for trouble. Her ex-Dom asking to be in the house without talking to her current Dom first? Bad form. We were Dominant and in control. We shared submissives and put our emotions in a locked box. But we had so many ways of stepping on each other's toes. We could release a caged animal with a simple slip, much less an intentional breach of space.

Serena stepped away from the door and opened it wider. She knew what she was doing. It was possible I'd walked across the snow in dress shoes for a good reason.

Before I crossed the threshold, I looked back at the main house, up to the second floor, where Diana had been standing before.

She wasn't there.

# CHAPTER FORTY-SIX

## PAST PERFECT

TWO DAYS after I told Stefan to jerk off on his own dime, he split. Serena hadn't seen him at the house. He had a well-earned reputation and I didn't want her to be nervous. I wanted her to feel as safe as she ever had.

I waited another day. I let her heal, but not completely. I brought a dress back from the city and told her to wear it to dinner. I had flowers brought in. Willa cooked and set the dining room table for two. Everything shone. The tablecloth was stark white and the glasses were nearly invisible.

When she came down, she got on her knees, or she tried to.

"Stand," I said before she fell completely.

I held out my hand. She looked confused, but took it.

"This is your night," I whispered. "It's like your birthday."

"I don't know what you mean, Master."

"Tonight, I'm Adam."

She smiled nervously, looked me in the eye for no more than a flicker before putting her eyes back on the floor. "All right. Adam."

"You look uncomfortable."

"I don't understand. That's all."

"You came to me to lose your virginity, Serena. I'll take it how I see fit."

She nodded slightly. Started to say something. Stopped herself.

"Go on," I said.

"You worry me," she said.

"Why?"

"I don't know what to expect."

A submissive always knows what to expect within certain boundaries. I should have listened to the heart of what she was saying. When I pulled the chair out for her, I was pushing her limits. When I shut off my Dominant voice, I was exploring boundaries. I didn't realize it that night, but I was about to inadvertently stumble on my own redlines.

# CHAPTER FORTY-SEVEN

## PRESENT TENSE

### DAY ONE

PRESENTED with a choice in the moment of its making, I didn't think I was discerning one option from another. When I'd walked Serena up to her apartment in the Lower East Side, kissed her on the cheek, and thanked her, walking out hadn't seemed like a choice. It had seemed like crossing the last *t* and dotting the last *i*. I'd had a project with a start and an end and the end came exactly on schedule.

In the studio five years later, with the space scraped of the vestiges of its past and Serena in her polo shirt, I wondered at the choice. If I'd chosen to stay with her, if I'd given her a chip of my heart, would I have been able to give the entire thing to Diana the following week?

If I'd embraced Serena and given her the time she wanted, how would I have felt about Diana when she walked into the conference room with her father?

I shuddered to think of how easily I could have missed loving Diana. How the richness of my life with her would have been the reality of a parallel existence. One of a million lives not lived. A life created when my mind was blank as the subway rocked in the morning or during the last five tedious minutes on the treadmill. How the fire of my current

existence had been sparked on the kindling of a choice to shut
Serena out.

"I saw you this morning," I said as Serena shut the door behind me.
I didn't elaborate. She knew I didn't mean in the front, by the car.

The studio was painted bright white, from concrete floor to fifteen-
foot ceiling. It was heated to over eighty degrees even though it was the
dead of winter. Absolutely necessary when the occupants could be
exposed and naked at any time.

"Yes. You did." Serena ran her hands along the white counter. The
kitchen was part of the larger room, white and chrome. "Can I get you
something?"

"Water would be great. Thank you."

She got a glass and went to the sink. She was never saucy or
oversexed. She didn't flirt. Ever. Some of us found that very attractive.

Diana flirted. I made the comparison immediately and knew just as
quickly that her clumsiness at it had been the attraction.

I took a few steps into the main room. Stefan's work was neat,
precise, and bold. Tarps were down. Paints covered. The slop sink could
have been used for surgery. I sat on a red chair that looked like a
puncture wound in the white space.

"You'd never know how prolific he was from this studio," I said.

"I think cleanliness is part of the art."

"How many pieces did he take to the city today?"

"Seven. He has a show at Broome." Serena brought me the glass and
stood in front of me.

"Sit," I said.

"I'm sorry. I didn't want to put on a show for you, but I didn't want
to safe out over it."

I tilted my head toward the couch then slid a coaster out of the case
and put my water on the glass table. She sat with her legs pressed
together and her hands folded between her knees.

"I'm fine with it," I said.

"But your wife. Diana."

Serena. Mentioning Diana. Calling her my wife. In the architecture
of my life, there hadn't been a hallway between these women. Now
there was a thoroughfare.

"She's a big girl."

"She was the audience."

The room was so warm my glass already had beads of condensation on it. One at the top inched downward. Stopped in a no-man's-land of clouded frost. Stefan had wanted my wife to see him hammer and choke Serena. Blood rushed to the surface of my skin. The droplet curved a little to the left. Stopped again. I shut down my feelings on the matter.

"I'm not questioning your Dominant. I'm asking you." I looked away from the glass to her big brown doe eyes. "Are you all right?"

"Of course. Why?"

"Unless I'm mistaken, which I'm not, he cut your intake. You have bruises on your neck. Breath play scared you. That was your first redline."

"That was five years ago."

"Our basic fears don't change."

She set her jaw. "My basic fear has always been that no man would ever love me the way I am. We've been together for years, you know. He loves me."

She looked defiant and hard, as if she was challenging me to make the connection between our past and her fears. I wouldn't do it. If I didn't love her, it was because I wasn't meant to. There were no parallel realities. No imaginings created infinite worlds for every possible decision.

She broke our gaze and looked at her knees. I went for my glass. The drop I'd tracked fell another half inch, joined another droplet, and rushed to the bottom of the glass in a line, as it was meant to.

"I'm going to assume it isn't redlined now." I drank, put the glass back on the coaster. "Or I'm going to assume Stefan knows what he's doing."

"I'm glad you approve."

This was code for *I don't care if you approve.* She wasn't much more subtle than that.

"Don't be angry. Or be angry. It's up to you how to feel. Just know, if you ever get in over your head, which you won't, but if you do, you can come to me."

"What about when you get in over your head?"

She wasn't sniping. She wasn't throwing my words back in my face. Her voice was so tinged with regret, it cut right through me.

What I thought I'd hidden had always been exposed.

What I thought I owned had never been mine.

She'd been more perceptive and more in control than I ever gave her credit for.

I swallowed a hundred answers because they all came up my throat in a knot of competing desires. The desire to pretend I didn't know what she was talking about. The desire to confirm what she meant. The desire to tell her I was in as over my head now as I'd been then.

I'd come to the studio to protect Serena, and she'd turned it all around with a few words. The heat had its own weight, and it pressed on me, squeezing my lungs until they couldn't expand. The condensation on my glass was running in vertical lines that looked like a jail cell until two/three/ten drops met and—

A knock at the barn door.

The pressure released as if a valve had opened.

Serena started to get up, but I put my hand on her shoulder and walked across the studio to the big door. The island was dead in the off season, Stefan wouldn't knock, and Diana shouldn't trek across the yard to see Serena. It could have been Willa or Thierry. Or it could have been someone from the other side of the overpass who had noticed Stefan had left his beautiful girlfriend behind.

It had gotten dark in the few minutes I'd been in the studio, so when I opened the door into the bright white room, Diana squinted. She looked genuinely surprised to see me.

So much for her not trekking across the yard.

"Oh. Adam. Hi. I—"

"This building is off-limits."

She blinked in the light. Cold air swept into the studio.

Serena opened the door all the way so she stood in the frame with me. "Come in! It's freezing!"

Serena and Diana in the same room. Not just any room, but the back house of the Montauk property. On any other day, I may have been able to manage the collision of my worlds, but not that day. My sense of control was already chipped away in a situation where I was supposed to have the most control.

"No," I said to Serena, then I brought my attention to Diana, who was shivering. "We're going back."

My wife shot daggers out of her eyes. Who was I to tell her she had to go back?

"Thank you for the water," I said. "Give my best to Stefan."

"Sure." Serena stepped aside as I walked out, stepping into a crevice of ice-cold slush.

My shoes were soaked. I took Diana by the arm, gave Serena a last wave, and led my wife back to the house, along the widening path of yellow light from the open door. When it narrowed and closed with the click of the closed door, Diana pulled away and faced me.

"What was that all—"

"You don't belong over there," I said.

"Why not?"

"Can I ask why you were going there in the first place?"

She crossed her arms. Her breath caught the air in white frost and scattered in the ocean wind.

"Well. You saw." She gestured to the back house, where Stefan had fucked Serena for show. So Diana knew I'd been on the porch below.

"I did."

"I wanted to see if she was all right."

I tried not to smile. She and I had had the same impulse. But hers was born out of ignorance.

"So you know, it's not your place to question what her Dominant does to her."

"Whose place is it?"

It was no one's, really.

"Mine. That's why I was there."

She smiled and looked away, arms still crossed, nearly laughing. Her hair blew back from her face, exposing her high forehead. I didn't think I'd noticed for a long time how high it was, or what a beautiful arch her hairline made.

"What?" I asked.

"I don't understand this world you're in."

"How's that?"

"I didn't know you were there, but when I saw you, I thought you'd gone over there to have sex with her."

"I'm still married to you."

She shrugged. Was she jealous? There was no way of telling. She used to trust that I was faithful, and I'd never betrayed her. With the rules changing, was I about to see a different side of her?

"I figured she'd do things I don't." She let the wind take her hair to the side. "Things you need."

"Come inside," I said. "Willa put dinner out for us, and I'm sure it's getting cold."

I led her back to the house, up the back steps to the dining room. Willa had indeed left dinner out. Two silver circular warming plates crackled, surrounded by a full table setting for two. I took her coat, removed mine, ignored my cold, wet feet. I held her seat out for her. She sat, rubbing her cold hands against her thighs.

Lifting the cover of the first dish, I found tomato soup.

I ladled some into her bowl and stood directly behind her silently for more time than was normal or comfortable.

"Tonight," I said, "we start."

"All right." I heard the tension in her voice crack like an egg.

"Eat your soup."

"Aren't you having any?"

"No. Uncross your legs and spread them when you sit."

Slowly, her body shifted as she uncrossed her legs.

"Your ankles should be outside the width of the chair legs, and your knees should rest on the corners of the seat. The instructions are precise so I know you're listening. Now. Eat."

After a pause, she put her napkin in her lap. She picked up her spoon and ate. I split her hair in the back so I could see her neck, and I ran my finger over the length of it.

"I know what's in your mind," I said. "You want to ask if there's a way you should hold the spoon. Not because you care or want to please me, but because you want to assert my foolishness. My answer to that is, by the end of our time here, you may not submit in your heart, but you'll understand what it means. And you'll understand me."

I let her eat for a second before continuing.

"I know you think it doesn't matter. Maybe it doesn't to you. But it does to me. Maybe you'll understand why you stopped loving me, and maybe I'll accept it."

Her soup was almost finished. Diana ate quickly and efficiently. Always the first one done. It wasn't a competition. She didn't race. She had to begin and finish at the same time. It was how she attacked everything. If she didn't finish before she got bored, she didn't finish.

"What if you don't?" she asked.

"Accept it? I don't see that I have much choice."

She put her spoon down and wiped her mouth. "You might if you slept with that girl."

I yanked her chair out with a loud scrape. "She's not a prostitute." Diana started to look around to me, but I held her face fast in my palms. "I'm not defending her honor. I'm explaining how it works. Stefan owns her. I can't fuck her without his permission, and I won't anyway. I said before and I'll say it until you understand it. I'm married. I love my wife, even if she doesn't love me." I slid my hand down her throat, making her look forward. "Unbutton your shirt."

I felt her swallow hard against my palm before her hand went to her shirt buttons and she worked them open.

"You are not to go over there without me," I said. "Stefan wants to fuck you. One, you're beautiful. Two, you're mine. Three, you're not in our world. He likes innocence. He likes resistance. He likes when people watch him defile something."

I pulled her bra up over her breasts, letting them escape. She gasped.

I let her go and stepped away, still behind her. "You're doing great."

"Thanks, I guess."

"You want to ask me 'now what.'"

"Kind of."

"I'll let you know." I waited, letting her feel her nudity and my presence behind her. I let her imagine what I was going to do. "Look straight ahead."

She stopped watching me to look ahead of her. I knew she could see me from the corner of her eye, but she didn't check me. She wanted to do it right. Maybe this was her way of getting it over with or maybe it turned her on. No way to know just yet.

"Stand up."

She stood, and I stayed behind her. Her hands trembled at her sides.

No way to know if this turned her on, except her posture, her scent, the red flush on the part of her lower back that led to her bottom. She might not understand why she enjoyed this any more than I did, but she did.

"Pull your pants down."

"Adam...?"

"You're using my name."

Long pause. She had no idea of the depths of my patience.

Instead of answering, she unbuttoned. Unzipped. Hooked her thumbs in her waistband and lowered it to her mid-thigh.

"Bend at the waist. Put your elbows on the table."

Her shoulders rose as she took a deep breath, and she bent.

"In my world," I said, "going across the yard to another Dominant's space without permission would get you my belt. It would hurt you, but it would satisfy you. You'd feel right knowing I was in charge. You'd be satisfied knowing I was here to relieve you of responsibility."

I placed my hand on her ass and slowly moved my hand down to her thigh. "Male or female, the more sophisticated and intelligent the submissive is, the more they need to get back to their primal urge to be dominated, and the harder it is to break them."

I moved to her other thigh and up the other side of her ass. "I'm going to spank you six times. Do you understand?"

"Adam..." She caught herself using my name, so I decided not to give her a hard time about it. "Last time. When you spanked me last time?"

"Yes?"

"The second one? I..." Deep breath. "I came."

Of course. The rigidity inside her. The stiffening of her spine. Remembering that night, I should have known she'd had a spontaneous orgasm.

I was glad she couldn't see me, or my face would have given away my elation. I could make her enjoy the month. It wasn't torture for her.

More than simply being aroused, she was actually, really, unequivocally submissive.

It was better than I hoped for.

"Surprise will do that," I said, containing the emotion in my voice. "It's unlikely it'll happen again. But thank you for the warning. Because you're not coming tonight."

I pressed her lower back down so her ass went up. Her hands folded together, still shaking.

"Palms on the table," I said. She laid them flat. "And when you saw me, you didn't present yourself. Two more for that."

I could have invented a hundred more infractions if I thought she could take a raw bottom. I stroked it, running my fingers inside her crack and her folds.

"When did you get wet?" I asked. "When you pulled your shirt up or when I told you to bend over?"

She turned her face down to the table. "When you touched my neck."

I took a handful of her hair and yanked it until she faced forward. She yelped.

I smacked her ass hard, twice, and she yelped again.

"Hush," I said. "Not a sound out of you."

I slid two fingers into her. Soaked. Yanked her hair back again and hit her ass quickly four more times. The skin turned warm.

"How many is that?" I asked.

"Six."

Two more hard swipes on one side. The color. The perfect pink. My cock ached.

Three fingers in her, gathering juice, sliding up to her asshole.

Her cheeks tightened and her anus turned into pure hard muscle.

"No," she said.

"You don't get to say no. You get to safe out."

"Please."

Her voice came from deep in her gut, passing her lips as the size of a wisp and the weight of the world. I stopped moving. I was so still I thought my blood stopped flowing.

*What about when you get in over your head?*

I was running to my limits. I'd forgotten I had them. Again.

I blinked, I exhaled, blood flowed. I put my hands on her hips and kissed her lower back.

*I still fucking love you.*

"Go upstairs," I said. "I'll give you aftercare and tuck you in."

She stood up, looking baffled, hair screwed up, a red mark on her forehead where it had pressed against the table.

*Still. I still love you.*

God help me.

"That's it?" she asked.

"No ball gags and latex body suits tonight, darling."

She pulled up her pants and straightened her clothes with the efficiency of antagonism. She wanted to come, and badly. She opened her mouth as if to speak, shut it, and faced me.

"Go on," I said before she could say whatever it was.

She spun on her heel and paced out of the kitchen. Stopped. "Adam."

"Just go up."

"Are you all right?"

She wasn't supposed to ask me that. I needed to maintain the old rules. I needed those like I needed money in the bank and a house to go home to.

"Why are you asking?"

"You seem different."

"So do you."

She pressed her lips between her teeth and breathed deeply.

I didn't know what I hoped she'd say. But she didn't say anything. Not with words. Slowly, she turned and went upstairs.

I'd hoped she'd say something to release me from the purgatory I'd created for myself. Pinochle. I'll leave. I'll cooperate. I love you.

Standing in the space between the kitchen and the sitting room, watching her legs disappear up the stairs, I knew that of all possible answers, "I love you" was the most desired and the most unlikely.

# CHAPTER FORTY-EIGHT

## PRESENT TENSE

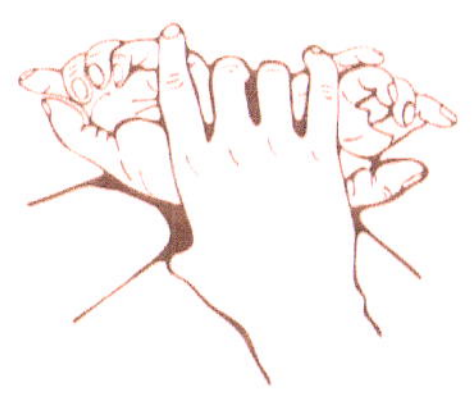

### DAY ONE

I OWED HER AFTERCARE. She didn't really need it. Eight slaps, even if I'd put my back into it, wouldn't require serious coddling. But I had to show her the routine so that when I accelerated the pain, she'd know what was coming.

I stood at the far end of my office, looking out onto the west house. I didn't turn the lights on. The only light in the room came from the moon and the headlights on Stefan's truck as he pulled up the drive.

I was technically giving Diana enough time to get undressed, then I doubled it. I didn't want to go up there and face her. I wanted to watch the empty space between the studio and me.

Stefan got out carrying a package, his slamming door muffled by the wet air. He went inside, hurrying in the cold. The lights in the studio flicked from moody yellow to starkly bright. The windows were set high in the barn doors, so I was spared the visuals.

If I went over there right now, Stefan would ask me to fuck Serena. He'd probably demand it, challenging me to refuse. She'd be a perfect sub for me, quietly taking whatever I dealt. Diana wouldn't care. I'd be one step further away from her, and she'd be a step closer to freedom.

I was a starving man offered a buffet, yet all I wanted were the crumbs my wife offered.

Sensing movement more than hearing it, I turned around. Diana was standing in the doorway. Cast in shadow, I could see the form of her body, with its familiar curves, through the gauzy white fabric of the nightgown I'd left for her.

She was supposed to be upstairs to get aftercare. She was supposed to do one thing I asked without argument. One fucking thing. She owed me nothing and that was what she was giving me.

"What are you doing?" I snapped.

"I was going to tell you I'm fine. Aftercare is optional."

I shook my head and turned back to the window. Worst sub ever.

"Did you love her?" Diana asked.

"No."

"Are you sure?"

Turning away from the window, I tried to read her, but it was dark and I didn't know what I felt besides completely alone. "Why are you asking?"

Arms crossed over her breasts, bare toes pointed, she took two steps into the room. "I think you don't always know what you feel. I think feelings make you uncomfortable."

"I don't need to be analyzed, thank you."

"Why are you looking at her window?"

"Because Stefan just got back."

In the dark, with her body no more than a silhouette shaded in moonlight blue, she shifted her posture, dropping her arms, relaxing her hips. "So?"

"Serena's very clear about what she needs and she knows he pushes limits. No one gets involved with him without knowing that. But she knew I didn't, and five years ago, she asked for me. So this?" I indicated the window and the building beyond. "I just want to watch."

"How long have they been together?"

"Long enough that it's not my business." I laughed to myself. "Long enough that they're bored with each other, from what Charlie says."

*Not as long as me and you, and already they're bored. What does that say about us?*

"You're a good man."

She was lying to soothe me. But I was immune to accusations of virtuousness, especially from a woman I'd taken such pains to lie to.

"Don't mistake me for the man I told you I was."

"I don't understand you. I don't understand all of this. Why you need to dominate women. No, I don't understand that, or why causing pain is even acceptable. But when push comes to shove, Adam, you've always done what was right over what was easy."

"You don't know what you're talking about. Especially when it comes to that girl." I pointed out the window again, and like a magic act, the lights went out, immersing me and Diana in moonlight.

Her silence wasn't space. It wasn't her waiting for me to finish. She wasn't thinking of what to say next. In her silence, she accused me of being a good man, and I wouldn't stand there and listen to that silent accusation without defending myself.

"She was trained by Charlie, and she came to me for thirty days to lose her virginity. She was nineteen. I want you to remember that when I tell you this story."

Silence. Dead winter wind from outside. My eyes adjusted to the low light and I could see the oval of her face and the shape of her breasts through the nightgown. How graphic could I make the truth of what happened? Because that was how she was going to hear it. She needed to be shocked out of the idea that she was leaving a good man with kinky habits.

"Two weeks in," I said, "I decided it was time. I'd fucked everything she had without breaking her virginity. She wanted me to. She begged me to. And I looked at her and thought she was so young. Why did this one thing have to hurt her? Her first time should be sweet. She should know how that feels before she started her life as a submissive. Because once she was fully in our world, there was no going back." I stood behind a wingback chair. "Sit."

Diana sat with her ankles together and her hands in her lap. I sat on the couch across from her. That was, of course, a stall tactic, and once she was still and listening in the way only my Diana could listen, I had to continue.

"I had dinner made. Right there in the dining room, I had candles and music. I got her a dress. She seemed nervous, so I did everything to relax her. Made conversation, all that. I kissed her and carried her upstairs. I was gentle when I touched her. She looked confused. But I figured she'd get it. Well, by the time I got my hand between her legs, she was completely dry. Not aroused at all."

"You're joking."

I smiled. Diana was easy. Always wet. Always ready.

"Nope. So I stopped and asked her what she wanted."

How was I supposed to describe what Serena wanted? Tell it like it was or sugarcoat it? I looked to my wife for the answer, but her expression didn't speak clearly.

"Took two hours, but she finally told me her fantasy. Her dream of her first time. She wanted to fight it. She wanted it to be forced. She wanted to know it was someone she trusted then wanted to forget about that trust. Her fantasy was that it would be a surprise and the more she resisted, the more it would hurt. She wanted the exact opposite of what I planned."

"She wanted to be raped?" Diana's voice was flat, as if she'd made a choice between disgust and emptiness. Or as if she was trying to wipe the shock out of her reaction.

"No," I corrected, "it was consensual. But yes, it would look like rape. Planned but a surprise. Staged but improvised. She needed to act it out in a way that felt safe. Everything but fear. She didn't want to be scared. I know it defies logic—"

"It doesn't."

It was my turn to be surprised. My Diana never ceased to prove she was perfect, and I wanted her more than ever.

*You knew. You always knew there was submission in her.*

Maybe I did. But I never expected her to acknowledge understanding it, even in someone else.

I leaned forward because I couldn't tell the next part in anything more than a whisper.

"On the way west, toward the general store on Breakfront Drive, there's a bridge over the creek. There's a narrow opening in the fence you can squeeze through and go under. It's a shortcut. I told her, if she was walking over to the general, never go that way. Take the long way.

It's dangerous. But after that night when she was dry, I sent her to the store every day with an impossible time limit. If she didn't make it back in time, she was punished. She had to take the shortcut. I watched her. I knew she was safe from everyone but me.

"Twenty-eight days after she came to Montauk, I did it. We had a word I'd use, a dozen safety measures. She was going to fight as hard as she could and I was going to take her. So I did everything we'd talked about. I want you to imagine the most obscene, violent act. Your every fear."

I stopped there, because the act itself couldn't be captured in a few sentences. The dirt. The broken glass. Ripping fabric. Blood. Scratches. Her fist on my face. The sound of my palm on her face as I slapped her, pushed her against the filthy concrete. She was naked, skin marbled with black from being dragged on the ground. She spit at me and I spit back. Called her a whore. Wedged my cock in her tight, virgin hole, head to base in one painful thrust. She cried under me, spit and tears. When she screamed, I stuck my filth-streaked hand in her mouth. Four fingers down, pumping at her, asking if she liked taking it like a slut. Told her how tight she was.

I let go that day. I embraced my violence. Pushed her limits. When she came, I slapped her and her orgasm went on and on.

It took ten minutes to break her, and eleven to break me.

The deal was, I had to leave her there and come around the other side.

I could take care of her after that. I had blankets and broth. I had soothing music and all the words ready. As I crested the rise, I looked back at her lying naked on the concrete. I'd left her there. I was an animal.

I'd wanted to cry, but I couldn't. I wanted to apologize, but there was nothing to be sorry for. She needed me to be strong, and I felt as though I was made of brittle bone.

"I'd been developing feelings for her." Admitting that to Diana was almost as hard as admitting it to myself. "That was why I tried to make her first time gentle. I hadn't realized that until I looked back and knew those feelings were dead. I took care of her as I promised, but I was gone.

She thanked me and told me it was perfect, but I never wanted to see her again."

I sat back because the whispering was done. She already didn't love me with a rabid indifference. Now I had no doubt she hated me with the same vigor.

"That's the man you think is so good," I said, satisfied I'd pushed her away forever.

She shook her head slowly, and all I saw was judgment and disappointment. I was immediately sorry I'd told her about Serena, then glad. I'd pushed her away purposefully. At least I could look at the divorce as something I had a hand in. I wasn't a whimpering victim. No. I was in control of my life again.

Good move, Steinbeck.

"And you met me the following week?" she asked.

"Yes."

She folded her hands together and tapped the thumbs, far away and deeply inside herself. Her eyes narrowed and her mouth tightened as if she was solving a math problem.

Did I just give her ammunition in the divorce?

I hadn't considered that.

Maybe it was time I was punished for the way I'd deflowered Serena anyway.

"Go upstairs," I said calmly. She finally looked at me. "Get in bed. Be at breakfast at seven. You'll get a stroke for every minute you're late or early. And next time I punish you, I won't be as gentle as I was tonight."

She stood and went to the door, brushing her finger on the molding. She stopped before walking across the threshold. She wanted to say something, but I didn't want her to say it. I only wanted to hear that she loved me again, and nothing about the story I'd told earned me love.

"Don't make me say it twice," I said.

She left. I heard her footfall up the creaky stairs. Saw her bedroom light on the last icy vestiges of snow in the yard. It flicked out, and the night was dark again. I waited, feeling the depth of my isolation. Once I thought I'd drown in it, I went to bed.

Having told that story for the first time, I saw myself through Diana's eyes and felt nothing but loathing.

# CHAPTER FORTY-NINE

## PAST TENSE

STEFAN WANTED ANYTHING I HAD. When I got a Mercedes, he got a more expensive one. When Charlie and I started talking about getting a piece of dedicated real estate for "away games," Stefan magically came up with a property he wanted but couldn't afford alone.

We'd met over a sub's body while I was still new in the scene. She was one of his. He never told me her name, so you'd think she didn't mean anything.

Well, I was young and stupid.

I liked making women come. I never felt as dominant as when a woman melted for me. If I could get them off six times in a night, I got them off six times. If I could squeeze in a seventh, I did. To me, the point of pain was pleasure.

The unnamed sub was in the Cellar, past a door separating public fuckery and a private party. I had an invitation. I met Stefan and some of the others, Dom and sub. Half an hour later, the subs were naked, tied, strapped, bent. Stefan's cock was in this particular sub's mouth. She was on her back, her head dropped upside-down, her knees strapped to two poles. She had pearly white lines all over her tits. I'd seen her in the half hour before it began. She'd been excited. She wanted a fantasy fulfilled. A gang bang.

I'd read the rules before I entered the room. There was nothing in there about not making them come.

So I fucked her. I was still figuring out what I liked and didn't. I hadn't gotten bored of the anonymity yet. I hadn't gotten frustrated with how careless it was. I fucked her, and I made her come twice.

The first time, Stefan didn't notice because he was busy with his own sputtering cock. The second time, he looked at me as if I'd taken a dump on his pillow. She was Stefan's. He owned her pleasure. Not me. I was only allowed to degrade her. That was what she'd come there for and that was what Stefan agreed to deliver.

Those rules didn't work for me. I learned that not every peg fit every hole.

So to speak.

Stefan learned... nothing.

"He feels shown up, mate," Charlie said, running his hands over the bare sheetrock in the new toy store. The one I'd visit years later to pick things up for Diana.

"If he wants a pissing contest, we can actually piss."

"There's no need. You both piss in different directions. But from now on, piss away from each other."

He'd taken the metaphor too far, but I got the point. Stay away from Stefan. I tried. I spent the next few years trying and failing. He went where I went, chasing me like a wronged alpha dog, and I just did all the things I needed to without looking back unless he nipped my tail.

# CHAPTER FIFTY

## PRESENT TENSE

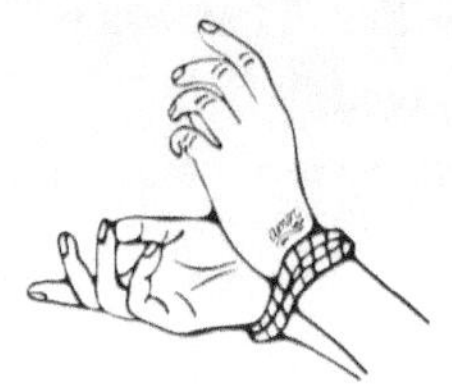

## DAY TWO

I'd gotten up at five thirty and checked on Diana, making sure she was still sleeping. I didn't think I could bear to look at her. I left her a laptop with a note. She had to answer some emails and look at some résumés for Zack's replacement. Not that we could make any offers or execute a contract during the stay, but I knew she'd want to start thinking about it.

I hadn't slept, and I needed fresh air to wake the fuck up. I laced up my sneakers and went for a run.

It was still dark when I jogged the still-icy streets of Montauk. I took a left out the drive and headed toward the general store. Almost exactly a mile. Back and forth three times was a good run. My nose was cold and my hands were frozen into fists. The sky was getting a lighter shade of grey by my second lap and I had exactly nothing on my mind until my wet shoelace untied.

I crouched to knot it. When I looked up, I realized where I was. By the overpass. A steel-grey stream rushed along the tributary. It was colder than the October evening I didn't rape Serena but felt as if I had.

I couldn't take my eyes off the spot, and my happy emptiness was filled with familiar questions.

*What kind of person does that?*

*What kind of person enjoys it?*

I didn't hear the truck slow down behind me.

"Working hard, Steinbeck?" Stefan's voice came from the road. He was leaning out of the driver's side window. "Or are you giving up?"

"You know what my grandfather used to say?" I finished the tie and stood.

"'More please, Mistress?'"

"If you've got nothing nice to say, you probably need to get laid."

He tossed me a water bottle. I caught it. Wondered if he poisoned it. Drank anyway. He got out of the truck.

"You don't like me." He crossed his arms and leaned on the cab. He had on a green doubleknit sweater and mechanic boots that were a dark wet black on the bottom part of the leather.

"What's the difference? I don't have to fuck you."

"We're staying on the same property for a month."

"You stay on your side and I'll stay on mine." I finished the water and tossed the empty back to him.

He caught it and put it in the cab. "Unless you need to ask my sub if she's all right. Then you come over. Make it when I'm not around."

"I'm not apologizing. You're the one putting on shows."

"No apology necessary." He waved as if he wanted me to forget what he'd taken the effort to bring up. "But you care. See? You proved it."

"I care. Fine. I have to finish my run."

"I'm going to the city next week. Few days at most. Feel free to look in on Serena for me."

"I'm sure she'll be fine."

Stefan opened the car door. "She's a good girl, but she needs to know someone's looking after her."

"All right." I was already looking down the road, ready to finish my run.

"If you fuck her—"

My head snapped around to him. "Married. I'm—"

"Whatever. It's permitted. But I own her orgasms. Don't force one."

The discussion was over as far as I was concerned, so I started down the blacktop. He passed me on the way to the general store.

He'd let me fuck his sub but not let her enjoy it. What a shit. I wondered if he was going to instruct Serena to offer herself. As if I'd be tempted. As if presented with an attractive woman, I'd have no choice but to cheat on my wife.

But he was doing nothing wrong. This was the world I was reentering. He was the one following the rules. Constant communication. Openness. Acceptance without judgment. Monogamy optional. I was the one living with abnormal vanilla-with-monogamy-on-top guidelines.

I wanted the old rules back and couldn't have them. I had never been so confused about what I wanted in my life.

I wanted Diana, and I was willing to do anything to have her, but maybe I'd made a mistake. We weren't alone. Serena and Stefan were wild cards, and they were too close. Too sealed inside a way of thinking that I used to share. I couldn't control what they'd do or say. They could poison my wife against me or tempt her with things I didn't want. They could scare her with their very presence.

I saw things through to the end unless the risks outweighed the benefits. In the case of the Montauk experiment, the risks loomed too great to ignore.

I got back to the house at six thirty, seriously contemplating putting Diana in a car and sending her home. Working the divorce out like adults.

Divorce.

I accepted the possibility at the same time as I rejected it. I'd never sit back and work out a divorce like an adult. I knew myself that well. Not while my heart beat for her. Not while she existed in the world.

But maybe there was another plan. If I'd gotten her this far, it was possible I could convince her there was another way to do this. Back home. In New York. Living together again. Falling into old patterns and then...

More of the same.

I got into the shower fully convinced Montauk was right, and equally convinced I'd made a huge blunder.

I made myself scarce the rest of the day, closing the pocket door to the office and staring at my computer screen. I told myself my absence was part of my domination of Diana, but part of me knew better.

I was ashamed of what I'd told her. I didn't want her to look at me.

# CHAPTER FIFTY-ONE

## PAST PERFECT

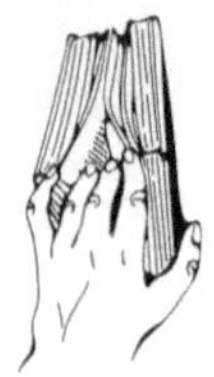

Dinner soured in my stomach. Months to get a reservation at Metropolis for the company's anniversary dinner, and the whole meal had tasted like bark and bile. I threw the keys on the shelf and my bag in the chair.

*Shake it off.*

I'd never felt so distant from my wife. So much like a stranger. The patient had gone code blue. Our marriage stretched out on the gurney with the machine emitting one long beep and a flat green line.

*Had it.*

*I've had it.*

The front door opened before I could even fill a water glass. I thought she'd stay to finish.

"Adam." Diana closed the door. She had a run in her stocking. It accentuated the shape of her calf.

Somewhere in my heart, paddles rubbed together and a shock brought me back to life.

I checked my watch. "Did you pay the bill? I thought you wanted the cobbler."

"Kayti has her card. What happened?"

"I left." I leaned on the counter and drank my water. A nice headache was creeping up on me. I didn't want to fight. She didn't have to know I was upset.

"Because?" She slid her bag onto the counter and sidled up to me, taking my glass and placing it on the counter. The subtle bird pattern on her red satin blouse moved when she did, making the flock look as though it had taken flight.

"I had to manage something for Eva and didn't want to drag it into dinner. Everyone done with their alt-lit dissemination and social critiques?"

*Shut up. Just put a fucking cork in it.*

"The air went out of the balloon when you left."

Her hands under my jacket. Around me. Her lips on the line of my jaw. My bones were china and my muscles were stone. My lungs shrank to the size of fists. My dick was the only part of me aroused. The rest of me battled shame and rage.

With one hand, she slid my belt out of the loop. The other stroked me through my pants. "I thought you came home early to take me to bed."

Sure.

But no. I pushed her hand away.

"Zack didn't follow you out the door?"

She stepped back as if I were made of acid. "What?"

"The way you two look at each other—"

"I cannot even—"

"It makes me sick," I growled. I wanted to push her away. Wanted her to get the fuck out of my sight.

"He doesn't look at me, Adam. This jealousy is bizarre."

"Fuck he doesn't." I turned around and faced the sink. "And you."

"Me what?"

I rinsed the glass.

"Me what?!" She pushed me on the second word.

I put the glass in the rack. "You. That's all."

I pushed myself off the counter and walked to the door, picked up my jacket, my keys, my fucking pride, and closed the door carefully behind me.

I paced the city for hours. When I got back, she was awake in bed, a book in her lap, under the cone of lamplight.

She closed the book. "Are you all right?"

*On your knees. Hands behind your back. Right here.*

"I'm fine. I'm just anxious. I don't—"

*Open your mouth. Push the back of your tongue down so I can fuck your face.*

"—I don't think you want Zack, but he looks at you like you're—"

*You're so beautiful when you're tied down. I can control you with one finger.*

"—a goddess, and it bothers me. Just fucking bothers me. I'm afraid to turn my back on that guy."

"He's not even on my radar." She said it as if I was out of my mind to even think she'd touch him.

I believed her. I always believed her, but I needed a cover story for what was really on my mind.

*Submit to me, and I'll let you come.*

Impossible fantasies. I held them down, tied them up, locked them away, only letting them breathe when I fucked her.

*Submit to me, and you'll be happy.*

I never thought of trotting them out, because then she'd know I was a monster.

*Submit to me, and we will rule the world.*

I'd die not telling her.

# CHAPTER FIFTY-TWO

## PRESENT TENSE

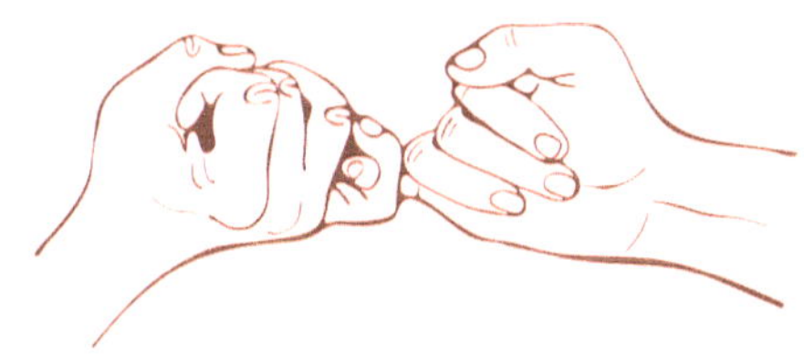

## DAY FOUR

Diana was getting more comfortable, and I was getting further away. After telling her what had happened with Serena, I'd locked myself off. I told her where to put her hands and legs. I gave her easy tasks to execute. I put my fingers in her mouth and corrected her posture. But I didn't have the space in my heart for more intensity. She knew about me. She knew what I'd done. She knew how ashamed I was.

I'd locked myself off before, but this time I knew I was doing it. You might call that progress.

I'd just gotten in the door after my run. Diana was sitting on the steps with her hands folded on her lap. She wore a short black dress that had been in the closet. Everything in the house made her body accessible, and this was no different. She pressed her knees together, but I could see the lace between her legs.

"What are you doing?" I asked.

"Waiting for you. I wanted to talk."

"About?" I leaned on the door and pulled the bow of my wet laces apart.

She watched me, weaving and unweaving her fingers as I worked my laces.

"We haven't gone this long without sex since the first time," she said.

"But who's counting?" I slipped off my right sneaker and worked on the left.

"Do you wanna?" She picked up her skirt, showing me the lace garter she'd put on for my benefit. She'd shaved herself smooth, and she crossed her legs just enough to hide herself.

I dropped my other shoe. "When I want your body, I'll take it."

A flash of rage rippled across her face. She didn't get the game. She didn't intuit the right way to act, and she didn't want to be there.

I was sweaty and loose, faced with an expanse of skin and a cunt hidden between crossed legs. My dick stretched my pants and begged for release.

She started to lower her skirt. I took the hem and I took one of her wrists and lifted it again.

I tapped her toe with mine. "Open your legs."

She did it. A saucy arousal replaced the flash of rage.

"Why do you think I haven't fucked you?"

"What you told me the other night," she said, and my back and arms went rigid. "I think you're worried that I'm—"

"Wrong," I shut her down. I didn't want to hear what she thought I thought she thought.

Ridiculous. She had no fucking idea what I thought. She had no idea what I was worried about, and as a sub, it wasn't her goddamn business. I shouldn't have told her. Part of me had wanted to drive her away by telling her about Serena's first time, but part of me couldn't bear the loss of hope.

"Hands on the bannister," I said. "Bend at the waist. Ass up."

Puzzled, she dropped her skirt.

The bottom step had a winding wood pole at the base that connected to a slightly flourished handrail. When I didn't change my instruction or add to it, she turned slowly and did exactly what I told her. She put her hands on it.

The anger that had started to spin inside me quieted. Not because she did it right. She didn't. She could have been steering a bus. But I was slipping into a place where I was in control.

I put my hands on her waist and pulled her back until her arms were stretched. Kicked her legs open. Pressed her lower back down until her ass was up and the skirt slipped away enough to show me the snaps on the crotch of her underwear.

"So," I said. "You want to fuck?"

"Yes."

"Are you getting yourself off at night?"

"It's not satisfying. Not all the way."

I flipped her skirt over her ass and pulled her damp panties to the side. My God. That cunt. So beautiful. I could smell the bouquet of her sex.

"Show me what you do," I said. When she took too long, I egged her on. "Come on. Let me see."

Her hand left the bannister and crept between her legs. "Can I say something first?"

I went around her until we were face to face. "Yes."

Her eyes were huge and clear. Her lips enunciated each syllable, letting them roll around her mouth as if they were surprisingly delicious. "You are filthy."

She wasn't disgusted. She was turned on. And she didn't take a second to wait for me to react to her comment. Her eyelids fluttered. Her lips parted. Her cheeks flushed. I'd intended to watch her fingers move over her cunt, but her expression was everything. It was complete submission to desire.

I bent to get close to her face.

"Look at me," I whispered. She opened her eyes, grimaced, loosened. "I haven't taken you yet because the next time I do, you're going to submit to me. After that, you're going to compare every man who fucks you to that one time, that first time I owned you. Every guy you bring home for a night. Every man you date. Every one you think might be more than a fling. You're going to compare every fuck to that first time you submitted completely, and every one of them is going to come up short."

Her breath got shallower and her body jerked below the waist. Her fingers gripped the bannister.

"You have to be ready. You have to earn it. I have to be sure I want to give it to you." I took her chin. "Look at me. Eyes open. Good."

A crackling sound came from her throat. I knew her so well. We'd cut our bodies into matching shapes for years. She was going to come. Having her jaw in my hands, I couldn't resist. Not another second. I kissed her while she moaned her orgasm into my mouth. I used my tongue to seek out the taste of her soul. The corners and crevices of her body, the hard and soft, slick and rough, feeling her throat vibrate with the last of her release.

She knew me. She knew the ravaging of Serena ate me from the inside. She knew telling her about it was why I'd shut down, even if I'd told myself another story.

I pulled away a few inches, leaving my spit on her face and my taste on her lips. I had another few weeks with those lips. I could enjoy them as much as I wanted and choose not to worry about our future.

"And yes," I said. "You're right. It was about what I did the last time I was here."

She stood up straight. Her skirt dropped and her right hand was shiny and wet. "Why couldn't you just say that?"

I took her by the right wrist and put her finger to my lips. I sucked it clean, tasting her. She had the same look of awed arousal as she'd had when she told me I was filthy. I dropped her wrist.

"Come to breakfast," I said. "Let's just sit."

I walked across the house to the breakfast table. She padded after me, washed her hands, and sat with me. The hot dishes were already out. Coffee made. Settings laid out. I put eggs and potatoes on her plate.

"Eat," I said.

My wife could pack it away. She'd eat a man out of house and home, but she took a smidgeon of egg and put it on a single sliver of toast.

"That's it?" I asked when she sat.

"Yeah, why?"

Normally, I'd shrug and say, "Nothing," but I wasn't feeling normal. I was feeling like a man who knew a woman better than he had the right to, and I was feeling the need to take care of her. "Because it's breakfast and you're always starving in the morning."

She shrugged and pushed her eggs around.

"That was fun," she said without an ounce of fun in her voice.

"If you're miserable," I said, "just say it."

"I haven't said it."

She had said it. She'd said it in writing and to my face. I'd believed her but hadn't understood it until the breakfast table in Montauk. I hadn't seen the depths of her sadness until that morning, when I told her to finger herself but didn't fuck her.

"You have." I put milk in my coffee to give myself a second to think, but it was too long for her.

"I don't know what to do. I kept hoping these past few months that if I dropped enough hints, you'd catch on and say, 'Yeah, I want out of this marriage,' but you never did. And I thought a clean break would be best. Then this..." She drew her hand over the scene we'd found ourselves in. "I came here because of McNeill-Barnes. I admit it. But a part of me thought if I came, the breakup would be easier for you. I figured, 'How bad could it be?'"

"Has it been bad?"

"No. Not really. I see..." She stopped herself, looked out at the ocean. "I see the appeal. You kissed me back there and..." She put a chunk of eggs in her mouth, eyebrows knotted as if looking for a word. "You haven't kissed me like that in all five years. I mean, ever. And then I think of all the times you seemed so far away. The time we took a vacation in Ojai. We talked about work the whole time, and when we were in bed together, it wasn't... something was off. Were you here? In this house?"

"Yes."

She nodded into her lap. "Were you with someone else? In your mind?"

"Yes."

She blinked. A tear fell. Then another. I hated hurting her, but I couldn't lie. We were past that.

"It couldn't be you," I said. "Do you understand that?"

"I do. I really do. You told me that story, and everything clicked into place. You love me. But why? Because we're a great team and I'm never going to ask you to rape me? I'm safe. You can take that side of yourself and pretend it doesn't exist. Put it where it can't hurt you. But all that time, it's beating down the doors to get out, and it ate at us. It ate us alive. Adam, there is no *us*. There never was an *us*. I loved a man who didn't exist, and you loved me because I wasn't in your world."

She covered her face with her napkin, and I was glad. I didn't want her to read me. This whole project was a mistake. If I hadn't been sure about it before, I was sure now.

But I didn't know how to give up. Even as I told myself I'd had no business bringing her to Montauk, I told myself there must be a way to get her back.

Diana wasn't a blubberer, but she was sobbing quietly into her napkin. I got up and put my hands on her shoulders. She pushed me away.

"Stop it," I said. "We're going through this together."

"No, we're not. I've never lied to you. I loved you honestly."

She wrenched herself out of her chair, standing and running away at the same time. I caught her three steps away and yanked her to me.

"Let go!"

"No. Listen."

"I don't want to listen." Her face and mouth were painted with spit and tears. I'd pushed her, and now I'd gotten exactly what I'd asked for. The truth. "I'm sorry you did that to her, and I'm sorry she liked it. I'm sorry you felt like shit about it. I would have been there for you. If you'd just trusted me, I would have been there for you."

I couldn't bear it. She was right. Every word was right. I'd asked her for trust I'd never given her. Instead of letting her go, I pulled her closer, trapping her in the circle of my arms. I knew it was the last time I would. I knew that once we left the kitchen, we would change.

I was the architect of this marriage and divorce. I was the catalyst. All she'd done was what I'd pushed her to do, then she took the blame for it.

"It's easy to say now you would have been there for me." I squeezed her shoulders.

"I would have."

Monday morning quarterbacking. Pure bullshit, but she believed it, and that was the important part.

"When I'm sleeping next to you, some nights, do you touch yourself?" I asked.

"Yes," she exhaled.

"I know," I said softly into her ear. "I'm not always sleeping. I feel you move the tips of your fingers. I feel you trying to stay still. I feel your muscles tighten."

She swallowed hard.

"I didn't give you what you need. That changes today. I know you throb for it. I know you need it. Let me tell you something, my wife. For the next twenty-six days, I own every single one of your orgasms. If I don't take your pleasure, you don't have any."

She touched my fingers, and I put her hand back in her lap.

"Can I tell you something?" she asked.

"Yes."

"You're really sexy when you're bossy."

"Now you tell me."

Her shoulders hitched with a silent laugh.

"Tonight, we'll reconvene." I kissed the back of her neck, taking in her scent of orchids and oranges.

"I need to go for a walk," she said. "Alone, if you don't mind."

"The general store is open from ten until two. Don't take the shortcut."

She stood. "Tonight then."

"Seven sharp. Winter clothes are in the closet, in the drawers."

She took a step then stopped herself. "Tonight?"

"Yes?"

"I'm looking forward to it."

She skipped away, and I stood in shock.

# CHAPTER FIFTY-THREE

## PRESENT TENSE

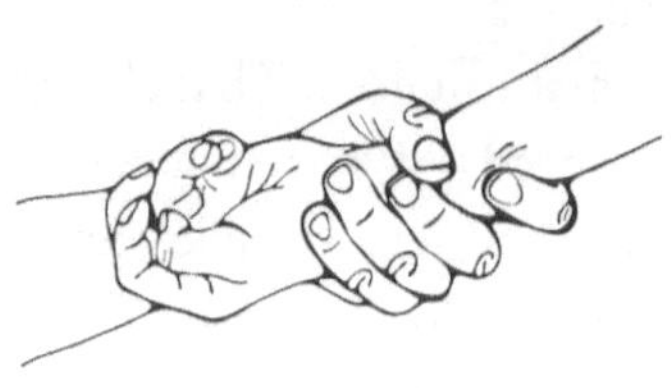

## DAY FOUR

DIANA KNEW how to get to the general store since there were no turns, but I followed her anyway. The town was dead in winter. Year-round residents were known for hunting and drinking. I was a city boy, and I didn't trust the miles and miles of desolation and empty houses.

She trudged along on the side of the two-lane blacktop, head down with a Manhattan tempo. As if she had a meeting to get to or a train to catch. Storm clouds gathered over the horizon, dark grey eating the lighter grey. It would be light and charming. A little snow cover adding to the romance.

She stopped at the underpass, looked at where I'd taken Serena five years before.

What did she think? What was on her mind? Did she really hate me for lying about it, or was the act itself repellent? Maybe both?

She was stepping away from the fence and the icy stream when a truck pulled up. I heard the crackle and roar of it before I saw it. Stefan's truck. I chided myself for thinking he would stop, then I was surprised when he did.

That motherfucker.

He was talking to her.

I couldn't make out what they were saying past the treeline, but she laughed at something he said. Some other shit came out of his mouth and I saw in his rearview mirror that he was smiling. Entertaining her. Charming her.

Oh, fuck this.

Fuck no.

I stomped across the street. As if he could sense my decision, Stefan said good-bye and drove away. I was left exposed in the middle of the road, no truck to block my stalking from Diana's view.

"What are you doing?" she called.

"Following you. It's not safe."

"Then why did you let me go alone?"

"You wanted to. Listen. This is…" I looked down the road. He was a speck in the distance. "Don't talk to him. That's all."

"Why?"

"Because I said so."

She jammed her hands in her pockets, looked toward the general store, then back to the house. Didn't move.

"What?" I asked.

"Either you let me in or you don't. Either you tell me about this other life or you shut me out. You can't have it both ways."

"And if I let you in? Then what? Miraculous healing and a joyful marriage? Is that what you're promising?"

Her breath came out in a long cloud of contradictions. In and out. Desire and repulsion. Thoughts and feelings. Yes and no.

I didn't want the answer. Both would hurt.

No, I don't want our marriage.

Yes, I do want it.

One was a knife, the other was a hope I didn't trust would outlast her curiosity.

"Come on," I said, leaning toward the store. "I have to get gas for the generator. The power always goes out when there's a storm."

"I'm just going to go back, I think."

I let her think she was walking back alone, but I followed to make sure she was all right.

# CHAPTER FIFTY-FOUR

## PRESENT TENSE

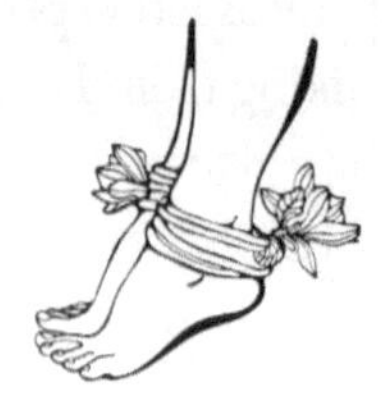

### DAY FOUR

I caught Stefan outside the studio. I had intended to be easygoing but firm with him, and instead I fucking lost my shit. "Stay away from my wife."

"Whoa, there."

"Don't talk to her," I continued. "Don't smile at her. Don't try to do the Scandinavian charm shit."

"I was offering her a ride."

"Stay. Away."

"You forgot. Five years and you forgot that we look out for each other and our subs. We are a village. That's why you go to Serena to check on her and I'm not in your face. I'm grateful. I know you'll make sure she's okay."

Trust this asshole to play the community card and be the bigger man all in a few sentences. I didn't want her near this logic. This was the exact logic that led to sharing subs, to pushing their pain, to situations that could only be rectified with bullshit contracts.

I didn't want this for her. I didn't want it for us.

"It's not going to matter," I said. "I'm sending her home."

"When?"

"Tomorrow."

"I can take her if the truck's ready."

"What's wrong with it?"

"The radiator. That was what I was telling your wife. I'd give her a lift back to the house or as far as the truck would make it. Not far actually, but far enough."

That was why she was laughing. They were joking about the truck. But he was still trying to charm her, and I was still sure he wanted to fuck her.

There was no way she was getting in a car with him all the way to the city. Stefan was good. Very good. The thought of anyone with Diana boiled my blood. The thought of Stefan with her added fear to the rage.

"I'll have Thierry take her tomorrow."

He shrugged. It was a little too fine with him. His smile was shot through with cockiness, as if all my avoidance was useless.

The air was cold and dead calm. The sky was flat cirrus with crystal blue holes. Pre-snow weather. I had to go back to the house and tell Diana she was leaving, and she was going to ask why.

I wasn't going to lie. I was done with lies.

She was in the library with a book, bare feet tucked under her. The diffused light from the window caught on her stray hair.

"Hi," I said when I came in. She faced me. "What are you reading?"

"Steinbeck, of all things."

"Really?" I sat on the arm of the couch next to her.

"I was looking in the stacks, wondering if things would have been different if I'd changed my name. Would it have been harder to leave you? Was I not really committed? And then I came upon this." She held the cover up long enough for me to see *Travels with Charley*.

"'A journey is like marriage,'" I quoted. "'The certain way to be wrong is to think you can control it.'"

"He was married three times." She closed the book.

"That doesn't make him wrong. So." I bent my head forward, putting my hands on my knees. I couldn't face her when I said it. When I looked at her, I wanted her. I needed to be stronger than my desire. Tougher than my love. "You should go home."

"What?" Was she just surprised? Or was there a tinge of disappointment? And was the disappointment over an easy handoff of the company? Or the fact that I was giving up? "Why?"

"I feel better. I feel like we cleared a lot of air between us."

She seemed pensive. I could guess her next questions. Would she still have an easy out for McNeill-Barnes? Was I going to work with her? Did she still get the loft? But none of those questions came.

"Thank you, I..." She caught herself. "When are we going?"

"You. You're going. Thierry will take you tomorrow."

Her head shook slightly as if she was thinking "no" but didn't want to say it. "You're quitting? It hasn't even been a week. And you're staying and I'm going?"

"I need time, Diana."

She crossed her arms and thought for what seemed like a long time.

"Speak," I said.

"I'm leaving tomorrow. Stefan's leaving on Friday. You're staying. And this means you're in the house alone with her?" She jerked her thumb in the general direction of the studio.

"Yes."

"Yeah. No." She stood, clapped her hands as if getting dust off them, snapped up the book, and tapped it on the heel of her hand.

"Yeah, no what?"

"This woman fucked with you so badly you married someone totally wrong for you. She did a number on you. And now? Look, I'm not trying to tell you how you feel, but you're vulnerable. I know what me asking for a divorce has done to you even if you don't show it. You're an open wound. Still handsome as hell, but hurting. You're primed to get involved with her again, and she's going to drag you right back where you were." She slapped the book back into its place. "So no. I'll go back with you when you're ready to go back."

I didn't know what my expression revealed. Shock. Disbelief. Denial. Insult. I didn't try to hide any one reaction because they all came up at the same time with equal measure.

"Wait." I held up my hand. "Are you jealous?"

"No. Of course not."

"You want to stay and make sure I don't sleep with her."

"For your own good."

"For my own good?" I added frustration to the list of emotions. How did I lose control of another conversation?

"I'm not trying to emasculate you," she said without a hint of irony.

Impossible. She was impossible. Was she always such a pain in the ass?

"Thanks for that. You're a fucking gem. I brought you here and you don't fit. You don't want to be here. You have no interest in helping me get my footing, and honestly, I don't blame you. I've never felt as completely fucked in the head about making a deal as I do with this one." I put my hands on the arms of the chair and leaned into her. I needed to take up her entire field of vision. "You know me. I see things through to the bitter end. This is the first thing in my life I've wanted to quit. Can't you respect that?"

"I'm staying."

She was staying to torment me. To expose all my raw nerves. To drag this boneless half-dead shit out into the street.

Well, torment worked both ways.

"Stay. But it's your choice to be in my house. The contract stands. You're my sub. You will kneel when I say kneel and bend when I say bend. Your body is built for me to fuck anywhere I can fit my cock. You have no pleasure I don't allow and it comes with pain. Do you understand?"

I designed the speech to scare her away.

Instead, she swallowed hard and said one word. "Fine."

"See you at seven."

# CHAPTER FIFTY-FIVE

## PAST PERFECT

RESERVATIONS AT METROPOLIS were about as hard to come by as a virgin in a whorehouse, a legal parking spot in midtown, an honest banker—pick your analogy.

Our production director, Georgette, had managed to get us a table for the three-year anniversary of the McNeill-Barnes reboot.

I'd started the evening lighthearted at the round table of eight. Me, Diana, Georgette and her husband, Lloyd, Zack, Kayti. We had a lot to be grateful for. The company wasn't just treading water. It was swimming with the sharks because of what Diana and I had done. She sat across from me in a bright red satin blouse with a subtle bird pattern. When she moved, the birds took flight. I couldn't stop looking at her, seeing how those birds would look with her on her knees.

We were a few bottles of wine into the meal, laughing too loudly and complaining too good-heartedly about the dire fate of publishing. How good books got buried and shit sold like hotcakes to starving men.

"Case in point," Zack said, pouring another glass. "The Books That Shall Not Be Named."

"Glorification of abuse," Georgette slurred.

Zack tried to top up my glass, but I put my hand over it.

"Do you know what my wife would do if I told her to get on her knees and suck my dick?" Georgette's husband—Nick? Ned?—jerked his thumb at his wife.

"Give you five bucks for a hooker?" she asked, and the table went wild with laughter.

I tried to smile.

Kayti held up her hand. "I read them!" Everyone went *ooh* and *aah*. "Hot. They were hot." She fanned herself with her napkin.

"How is getting spanked arousing?" Georgette asked as if she were a reporter on a crime scene.

"Because he's looking at your butt and you know… the other stuff. You're totally vulnerable. It's you and this guy and you can't see him. The tension of it. The anticipation. And the sting is more like… it sensitizes everything. I can *feel* more." She turned red and sat back in her chair. Put her glass near her lips. "Frank and I did a little experimenting."

The discomfort was broken by laughter and chatter about the Books That Shall Not Be Named.

"He was a stalker."

"Creepy."

"Barely consensual."

"But why?" Diana spoke for the first time since the conversation started. "Why read about that? Why invite it into your mind? We've spent a hundred years fighting for equality, and we still get paid less than men. Now we're supposed to let them beat us in the bedroom? How are we supposed to progress when we're saying abuse—literal physical abuse —is a turn-on? Not just acceptable, but desirable?"

Was she asking the table or asking herself?

I didn't know what I expected out of my marriage. I wanted her to bend for me, and I was terrified she might. I wanted to welt her skin and make her scream and beg. I wanted her to want to please me, to give me her body and soul.

If she did let me take all of her, I'd do what I did with every other sub I'd known. I'd throw her away. I loved her too much for that.

But even as I understood that truth, I couldn't let her comment go unanswered.

I leaned toward her with the full force of my intention. I needed her to hear me. Needed her to know that even if I wasn't going to ever tell her why the discussion was personal to me, she was going to know I believed what I said.

"You don't realize this because you're married to me, but most women don't have satisfying sex lives." I must have managed to keep the disappointment out of my face, because most everyone at the table laughed and hooted. "For most women, the fantasy that your husband might actually care about your pleasure is unfortunately just that. A fantasy. So given a novel about a man who loves you, wants you, would give up everything for you... and on top of it pays attention to your needs above his own? I think a little spanking under those circumstances might be a turn-on."

"Now bend over!" Georgette's husband cried, and everyone bellowed except me and Diana.

We were locked over the distance of the table. She had a response. She was waiting until everyone quieted down.

I didn't want to hear it. Couldn't. I didn't know if I'd hate my wife or myself more.

Pretending I had a phone call, I excused myself from the table. I caught a cab and went home.

# CHAPTER FIFTY-SIX

## PRESENT TENSE

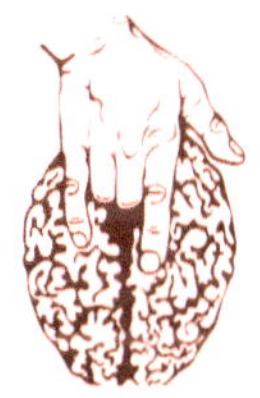

### DAY FOUR

"Hello?"

Her voice came from behind me just after seven o'clock. In the window, I could see the studio lights go on and Diana's reflection from the doorway.

"You're not on your knees," I said without turning around.

"I just wanted to know if I should make us dinner."

I hadn't even eaten lunch, but I didn't answer. I wouldn't until she did what she was supposed to do. The whole scene was getting turned up ten notches. She had to go. She had to beg me to get out of the house.

"Adam?"

"Third time you used my name." I typed complete gibberish into the laptop at a thousand miles a minute. "Now you can take off your clothes and get on your knees. Delay again and you're going to be crying before I even get out of this chair."

Again, she surprised me.

She dropped to her knees without a word, holding up her red journal with a page marked with a ribbon.

I spun in my chair. She hadn't undressed and I should mention that, but I couldn't take my eyes off her bowed head. "You want me to read something in here?"

"Yes."

I took the book and ran my finger along the edges of the pages, opening it. I flipped through dozens of sheets full of questions and landed where the ribbon was marked. There was only one question printed in the center of the page.

*What if I like it?*

I closed the book. Rapped the soft cover over my knuckles. Fast. The same speed as my heart. She was open to this. Not just as a sacrifice or a kindness, but as a path to her own self-discovery.

Some new hormone pumped through my veins. As powerful as adrenaline without the fight or flight. More with the power of "embrace and accept." A tingling desire to run into this particular trouble. Anticipation cling-wrapped tightly and ready to bust.

And still, I wanted her to go. And stay. And go. Make this so hard she'd run like she always did.

I closed the book. "Take off your clothes. Don't do a strip tease. Just get down to your skin."

I sat back down with my back to her and pretended to work. My fingers shook. My heart felt like an alarm going off. I'd filled her closet with things that were easy for me to remove, and lingerie with straps and hooks. She pulled the T-shirt over her head. Slipped out of her bra. Slipped off the skirt.

"Leave the garter," I said with my back to her.

She stopped and stood, straight and nearly naked. I twisted around. Only then did she remember to get on her knees.

Now what?

*Make her want to leave.*

I shut the laptop and got in front of her. "Hands behind your back."

She did it, big broken-glass eyes turned to mine. Lashes black as a lie. Lips round and full with a knife of an opening between top and bottom.

*Run away, huntress.*

I was hard, and my cock was one inch and two layers of fabric from those lips.

She looked up at me and opened her mouth. She was doing what she thought I expected. Wanted. Needed. And she was right. She was giving me the gift of her submission as much as she knew how. Tonight. Now. Maybe this was the last of it. I didn't care.

A shot of gratitude cracked my frustration, disassembling the pieces of it and building a foundation for the authority I needed.

Deliberately, with a purpose to every movement, I unbuckled my belt, undid my pants, and took out my cock. I put it against her bottom lip. Her tongue flicked out, catching the place where the head met the shaft. She reached for it. I grabbed her wrist.

"Open your mouth."

She parted her lips then opened a little more.

I took her jaw roughly, pressing in her cheeks. "What's your name?"

"Diana," she said around my fingers.

I stroked my cock, putting the tip on her lower lip but not entering her. I'd been pent up for days, so it didn't take long for me to shoot my orgasm into her mouth.

Her eyes were shut tight and her nose was wrinkled.

"Swallow."

She shook her head.

"Do it."

She closed her mouth and swallowed. I brushed my thumb on her chin, collecting the last white drop. I put my thumb in her mouth. After a pause, she sucked it clean. Fuck, she was hot. Even in her resistance she was hot. I was about to get hard again.

"Now," I said, buttoning my pants. "Go over to the couch and bend over it from the waist."

She started to speak, but I put my finger over my lips. I didn't want her to say anything. She wouldn't last another day, and I wanted to enjoy every moment before she stormed out.

She stood and went to the end of the couch then bent at the waist.

I kicked her legs open. What a sight. What a beautiful sight. I'd been fucking that cunt for five years and I never appreciated how gorgeous it was.

I took her left hand and put it on her ass. "Open it. Spread out for me so I can see my options."

"Wait—"

"Hush." I took her other hand and put it behind her, using her fingers to spread her ass and thighs apart. Beautiful. Pink and glistening. "I'm going to ask before I check. Are you wet?"

"Yes."

Without prelude, I put two fingers in her.

Yeah. Wet.

"Do you want to come?"

"Yes."

"Yes, what? Is that how you were raised?"

"Yes, please."

I ran my finger along her seam. "When did you get wet? When I came? When you got undressed?"

A third finger disappeared inside her. She groaned and pushed against me.

"When you stood in front of me."

The moment I stood in front of her was the moment I exerted physical dominance. I hadn't expected that answer and I had to hide my surprise by stroking her clit.

I was incapable of loving a submissive. Or was I?

I'd gotten behind her intending to make her come then take her ass for a long, long time. I'd intended to turn her desire to please me against her. I knew if I took that tight, virgin hole, she'd leave. I'd kill all the beauty of her acceptance and turn her against it.

With all four of my fingers pressed on her, she moved her hips with me as I rubbed, then flicked, then rubbed her hard clit until she raised her ass and buried her head in the cushions. I slowed down, extending her orgasm until it drained her.

My fingers were soaked. I could lube her ass with her own juices and fuck it until she begged to go home. My cock was ready.

I put my wet finger against her asshole, pressing just enough. She clamped down.

"Please," she said softly. "I know I didn't cross it off…"

"Hush."

I circled my finger around it. I could do it with only a little pain. Her hurt would be only emotional, and she'd go home.

"What would you do if I insisted?" I asked, gathering more lubrication and drawing it back up.

"I don't know."

One finger. Pressure. Circles. Pressure. Circles. She loosened up.

"Would you leave?"

"Yes," she said as I put more pressure on her ass. "No. Maybe. I…" She didn't finish.

"What?"

"I trust you."

I thought she'd reveal some core dishonesty with herself or me, but she only ever spoke the truth as she saw it, even if one of us was hurt by it. Maybe it was about time one of us was honest.

I pushed inside, sliding against her own juice. One finger, all the way in.

Every woman has a vowel. Diana's was O. The sound came in a long moan, beginning when my finger entered her and continuing until I couldn't go any farther.

My cock throbbed.

"Do you trust me?" I asked, pulling out the finger.

"Yes but—"

Two fingers, all the way in.

She bucked. I took a fistful of her hair and pulled her head back so she could see me.

"If you trust me, there's no but."

"Okay. Yes."

"How does this feel? When you stop worrying about it, how does it feel?"

A smile teased her mouth. "Good, actually."

Diana had arrived. She was still bratty and demanding. She was still barely a novice, but something in her bones had submitted, and the rest of her body liked it. I hadn't expected that, yet I knew it would happen. I held one reality in each hand and balanced the contradiction. Now to balance her and keep her off balance at the same time.

This, I could do. This was my game.

Fuck Stefan, we were staying.

I kissed her lower back and took my fingers out of her. "Let's wash up and eat something, huntress."

We ate dinner, listened to the radio, breathed the same air until bed. I pulled the covers over her and kissed her cheek.

"Stay," she whispered, eyes drifting closed.

"Not tonight. Sleep well. You're going to need it."

I planned the rest of the week in my mind, running through the days and hours.

The only things that could interrupt were work and the pair in the studio. Another week of slight contact. Comfort. Building trust. She said she trusted me, but she didn't even know what that meant.

I had something to do besides feel sorry for myself. Diana's submission was my distraction from Diana's betrayal.

The windows shook with the wind with a *tick tick tick* of driving snow and the sky glowed the flat orange of snowy nights.

I wanted her to go.

I wanted her to stay.

I wanted her on my terms.

I wanted her on any terms.

I wanted to be cured of the disease of love.

I wanted to be cured of want.

PART II

DIANA

# CHAPTER FIFTY-SEVEN

## PRESENT TENSE

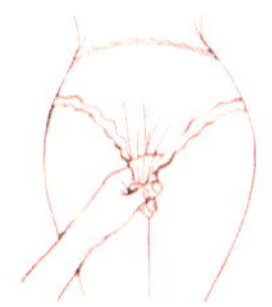

### DAY SEVEN

*How long has it been?*

A week. He hadn't slept next to me. He hadn't put his dick inside me.

*Is that true?*

We hadn't had intercourse, and night seven would be no different.

*What is he trying to prove? That I want him?*

I did and I didn't.

*Am I a monster?*

I asked my journal questions, but they were beside the point. I knew what he was doing. Keeping me off balance. Making me pay attention. Showing me his attention.

Adam was gone, the storm beat the windows, and I could still taste the flat bite of his come on the back of my tongue. He'd just taken my mouth as if he owned it, instructing me how to please him.

Instead of being irritated, I was grateful. If you're going to give a man a blow job, it should please him.

*Doesn't he wonder if I'll use the skill on another man?*

I'd expressed myself in questions since a journaling class in college. It felt less like talking into a void and more demanding the void to fill itself. It also kept me from getting lazy. I may have known the answers, but posing questions meant I never took them for granted.

*What do you want? Do you want him?*

Him, no. Still no. His body? The one he'd barely used to touch me? The one that hadn't fucked me since Manhattan? Only delivered orgasms that were powerful, but somehow left me wanting him more?

Even when we sat together, talking about McNeill-Barnes, I wanted him. Even when we signed payroll checks across the table, the tension in his fingers as he held the pen, the veins in the tops of his hands, the way they moved in and out of me...

*What do you* feel?

I still felt like a monster. I wasn't some careless, unfeeling, heartless bitch, but if you asked me, "Are you a good person?" I'd say I wasn't.

I'd married young because I fell in love young. I married a man with a strong jaw and a heart shaped for me to fit inside. I couldn't resist him, and I admit, in the back of my mind, I thought, "You're young. If you have to bail, you bail and your life won't be over."

So maybe I was a monster.

He just got so far away. I called for him and his body came to me. He showed up physically. But the *him* inside? He was elsewhere.

I shouldn't pretend I understood him, or me, or why I married him besides the fact that I loved him. I loved him so much that when I stopped loving him, it was as if I'd lost an arm or a leg. Not loving him hurt me. I didn't leave to find someone else. I left because he was there, every day, reminding me I'd lost something I cherished. I could deal with the hole in my life if he wasn't there at the edge saying, "Look at this hole, how deep it is, how wide, how empty. Look how our hearts fit into it so well."

I carried guilt and shame. I couldn't even face him because he didn't see the hole. He didn't think it was a hole. He thought it was... I didn't know what he thought it was. He didn't even see it as a hole. He didn't see it at all. He just created it.

I needed out. I only feared the divorce. I was a bad finisher. I was afraid that if he dragged it on, I'd cave and give up anything worth having.

He'd offered the impossible. A cheap ride. An abrupt fall into the heart-shaped hole. I'd heal sooner, start almost immediately the life I didn't know how to imagine and I wouldn't have to risk much more than a month.

I'd have to have sex with him. Probably a lot of sex. I could do that. I wouldn't have married him if I didn't enjoy his body. But I didn't want him to take me to Montauk as a strategy to get me back. I wanted to be clear with him that if he was trying to get me to love him again, he should rescind the offer.

I must have looked like the biggest bitch in town, but I was already hurting him. If I made it worse by being dishonest, I wouldn't be able to live with myself.

*Is that what it means to say, "I care about you, but I don't love you"? Is it another way of saying, "I don't love you, but hurting you makes me feel shitty about myself"?*

*Why do you turn everything back around on yourself?*

My therapist, Regina, always tried to boost me without blaming, but when I told her about the club, she spun it fearlessly.

"Maybe you knew," she'd said with a glint of satisfaction, as if Adam's admissions were her victories. "Maybe you always knew he wasn't what he said he was."

I never told her I'd had an orgasm when he spanked me, or that, at the Cellar, the paddling on the other side of the glass turned me on. I denied it to her. I said it was disgusting. I said, with real conviction, that it undid decades of women's progress and legalized domestic abuse.

Once I decided to join my liar of a husband in a house he'd never told me he owned, I couldn't face her.

I told myself it all happened too fast, but I'd canceled our last appointment before the trip, telling her I was taking a vacation. The fact was, I didn't want to tell her about the offer. I didn't want to tell her I was curious and that I trusted my husband. He'd lied. He'd kept the house and a huge chunk of his past from me. He'd pretended to be a different man than he was, and I couldn't ever forgive him for that. If there had ever been a chance we'd get back together, his lies ruined it.

But I trusted him with my body.

Crazy.

I was crazy.

*You ever going to grow up?*

I put my hand flat on the paper, covering all the questions. I usually asked about the world around me, but the past few month's entries were filled with questions about who I was and what I wanted. I had four pages that asked only one question.

*What do you want?*

The previous night. In the kitchen. On my knees in the middle of the room with nothing but the gauzy nightgown covering my hard nipples. Out the window, the ocean made an eternal meal of the shore.

His feet came toward me. He was fully clothed and I was practically naked. He stood so close I could smell his cologne and the dry cleaner's softener on his suit. His erection stretched his pants. It was right in front of me like a loaded gun.

*Why did it turn me on? Wasn't he just standing still?*

But so close and for so long. The anticipation. The unknown. I stopped writing when I came to the part where he took out his cock. I'd always admired it, but it wasn't just my husband's penis. It was an instrument of domination.

My domination.

My pussy swelled remembering it and I stopped writing, laying my hand on the page like a starfish. He hadn't let me touch him last night. My hands had been behind my back, each hand grabbing an elbow. After telling me how to please him, how to push the back of my tongue down, how to open my mouth and not close my lips around him, how to take it instead of give it, he came down my throat.

*Do you want him to use you? Insult you? Do you want to give up control of what your body's used for?*

When I thought of it that way, that he used my mouth to come in, I was mad. Sure. I was better than that, but my god... I was turned on.

*What do you want?*

# CHAPTER FIFTY-EIGHT

## PAST PERFECT

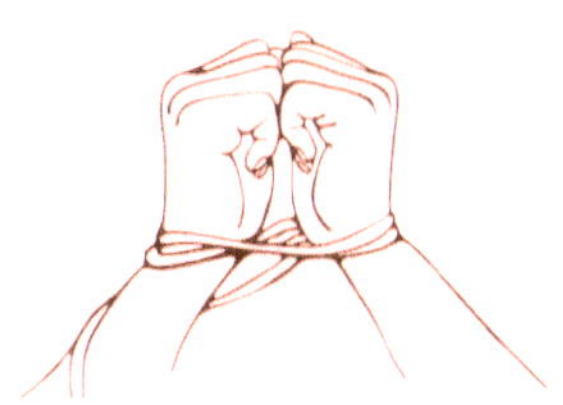

AFTER MY MOTHER DIED, I thought my father would leave their Park Avenue co-op. It was too expensive and too big. Every scrap of wallpaper, every deeply-hidden dust bunny, every swatch of fabric on the upholstery or drapes held a memory of her.

I'd fought with him, cajoled him, shaken my fist at him. He had to move. Start a new life. Instead, he got so depressed I had to leave college and run the business for six months, then forever.

But when Adam and I got rid of our baby because its life was going to consist of a few days of extraordinary pain, I was glad Dad still had the apartment. I needed familiarity. I'd left my first day back at work after two hours, saying I was going home. I didn't clarify where that was.

"What do you want?" Dad asked, turning off the heat on the whistling teapot.

"I want a normal baby. And I want to stop bleeding." I was hunched on a chair, hugging my knees. My tear ducts hurt because they wouldn't stop production for five freaking minutes. They'd been at it all damn day.

"No, I mean what kind of tea do you want?"

"Chamomile."

Dad got a box down from the cabinet. He'd put his oxygen back on when I arrived in tears. I knew I was stressing him out, but I didn't know what to do about it. I needed him.

"Did you call Adam?" he asked, pouring.

"He'll find me."

He would. Eventually. Once he took his head out of the ledgers. After he realized I wasn't at our SoHo place because we'd started talking about the baby on the couch, and sat on the balcony applying for school waiting lists, and named her while listening to the cars out the window. And because I wanted him to come and get me, dammit. I didn't know why and I didn't have to explain it. I needed him to ride in and scoop me up without me giving him instructions on what color the horse should be or how shiny his armor needed to be. He needed to figure it out.

"You should get checked," Dad said when he put my teacup on the table in front of me. "If you have the same thing your mother had."

"I don't. They tested me. Not yet."

He sat and pulled his oxygen tank close to the seat. "Then you can try again."

I nodded into the hot liquid. "I can."

Gilbert, Dad's helper/housekeeper/butler/whatever poked his head in from the back stairway.

"Mister Steinbeck," he said, and opened the door. Dad took his mask off. He hated looking weak in front of my husband.

Adam stood in the frame, looking at me. Disappointment? Pity? I was too blind with sadness to see what was on his mind. But his armor did shine, and his horse was a fine white stallion.

He scooped me up and took me to the couch, placing me on his lap while I cried. He told me it wasn't my fault. It wasn't meant to be. He said a lot of things that didn't mean anything.

The couch faced the window that overlooked Park Avenue. There was nothing out there. Just the building across the street, a polygonal-shaped night sky, a barely visible reflection of us on the couch. But he looked out it. Not at me. He shushed my tears away. And when his hand got tired of cupping my shoulder, he patted it absently, as if comforting a child who had dropped his ice cream.

I stopped crying.
He shushed.
He stared.
He patted my shoulder as if I were a puppy.
And that was the beginning of the end for me.

# CHAPTER FIFTY-NINE

## PRESENT TENSE

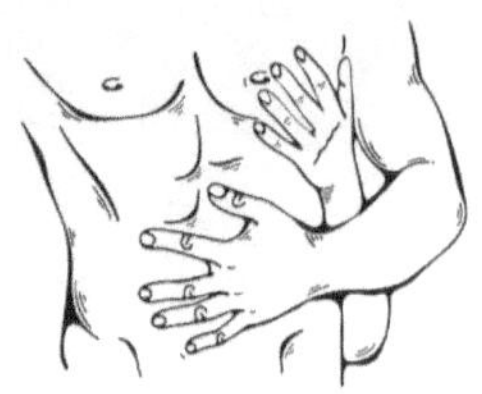

## DAY EIGHT

STEFAN STOOD in front of the stove, where a teapot hissed. Serena sat on the counter in a sage-green polo and a skirt hiked up to her waist. The corners of the tea towel on the counter peeked from under her. Her legs were spread so wide, one rested on the edge of the sink, and the other on the kitchen island with another tea towel under her heel.

She had one hand behind her for balance. The other was between her legs.

I stopped short. I couldn't go in there.

They'd come back the previous night. The motion-sensor light had woken me up briefly.

"I think it's boiling," she said.

"It's not whistling, pet."

She squeaked. I saw the game. She couldn't come until the teapot whistled for no other reason than her Master said so. The scene was disturbing and probably the sexiest thing I'd ever witnessed. I took half a step back. I didn't want to disturb what was happening, but I couldn't walk away. The tension held me. I had to know if she made it. I wanted her to succeed.

"Let me turn it down," Stefan said playfully, turning the knob to lower the heat. He got two cups with excruciatingly slow movements and placed them on the counter.

"Please," she said. "I need to slow down."

"Don't be silly. You can hold it."

"I think the whistle is broken."

He pulled two teabags from a box and swung them into the cups. "It's not broken. Do you want the pekoe or the jasmine?"

"J-J-Ja—"

"Don't you dare come."

His voice was so firm and direct, I probably would have obeyed. The cups ready, he stood in front of her and watched her play with herself.

The teapot whistled.

Serena's head leaned on the cabinet and her ass came off the counter as she opened her mouth and came onto her hand. She didn't cry out or make a sound, but with her mouth open, it looked as though she screamed the sound of a teapot whistling.

When she put herself back on the tea towel, Stefan turned off the burner.

"I knew you could do it," he said, pouring the tea.

She hopped off the counter. "Thank you."

He looked at her with pride and warmth, placing the mugs on a little bamboo tray. "Wash your hands and meet me in the gym."

I stepped into the shadows when he walked out the back door.

"I saw you," Serena said, still rubbing her hands together under the tap. "Diana. It's not a big deal."

Shit. The crust of my shelter cracked and fell away. I was wet from what I'd seen and the object of my arousal could see right through to it.

I stepped into the kitchen. "I was rooting for you."

She shut off the water and dried her hands. "He makes it harder every time. Sometimes I come too soon on purpose."

"Why?"

"He punishes me." She flicked her hair behind her shoulder.

"How?"

She picked up her skirt a few inches. Horizontal welts healed over her soft flesh. She drew a finger over the length of one, then dropped the hem.

The night I came home from the Cellar, I attacked the internet for fifteen minutes before I freaked out and shut the laptop. I'd seen pictures of caning marks, and now, in front of me, was the real thing.

I'd thought a lot of things when I went to the Cellar and when I saw the pictures. My husband was part of that world, so I wanted to understand it. Instead I felt sorrow and anger. When I saw Adam after that, I added betrayal to the list. And with Serena right in front of me, I had to sweep it all away. I couldn't dismiss a living, breathing woman who clearly had her own will in the matter. I was curious.

"You don't get it," she said, half statement, half question.

"No, I don't get it. I wish I did."

She leaned on the counter and put her hands behind her on the edge. Was she getting more comfortable or ready to launch? "What don't you get?"

I didn't get myself. I didn't get why I'd let Adam use my mouth for a sperm receptacle, and I didn't understand why I liked it. "Pain. Punishment. Degradation."

She cocked her head to one side, puckered her bee-stung lips a little, paused as if deep in thought. "My mother wanted me to be a lawyer. She worked so hard. She had three kids and I was the 'smart one.' So I got to go to private school, and she had enough money to send one of us to college. That was me. I got to go. I got my own room so I could study. When I fucked up, she didn't yell at me or punish me. No. She'd say it was all right and she trusted me to fix that B-plus next semester or it wasn't a big deal about that dent in the car. But she'd get all pent up and on edge and she'd yell at one of my brothers for something stupid. I think she was scared of me."

She ran her finger along the edge of the counter, seeming pensive. "And when Mom got sick, it was all on me. I thought I'd break until I found Charlie. Have you met him? He has this old cane he uses?"

"Australian?"

She nodded.

"He came to our wedding."

"He was my first Dom. The first time he told me to bend over his desk and pull my pants down, I was so relieved. I knew I was going to do what he told me, no matter what. No matter how much it hurt. It was like I'd been chained up my whole life and I was free." She looked at me, letting her hand fall from the counter. "Do you get it now?"

She was so vulnerable, I didn't want to cut her down. I wanted to pull her up, but it was hard to pull up someone when you were being dragged down yourself.

"I don't know your parents. I don't even know you. But it sounds like a story you're telling yourself so you have a reason to let men hurt you."

A little smile curled her mouth, and she tried to hide it. "They say masochists and submissives have different brains. Our violence centers are entangled with our pleasure centers. If that's the case, then why deny it? I could be telling myself a story, sure. But if I was wired that way from the beginning, then the story is still true."

Did getting turned on when he spanked me or came on me mean I had a different brain?

"I've been with a few Dominants," Serena said. "Women and men. Your husband can deliver pain better than any of them."

He hadn't delivered pain. A few spankings and a little bondage. But it had been all about me doing what I was told. He'd been all about control the first week, and somehow, I thought that was going to be the last of it. I'd let myself forget the pain part.

"And Stefan?" I asked.

She dropped her voice to a breath. "We've been together a long time."

"Serena." Stefan's voice was taut and deep, making a paragraph-long statement in one word.

She fell to her knees, then her hands, putting her forehead to the tile and her ass up. I backed away.

"It was my fault," I said. "I was keeping her."

"Really," Stefan said with a grin, coming into the room. "I thought she was looking for an excuse to get punished." He put his foot on Serena's upturned ass and gave it a little push. "Is that true, pet?"

"It was my fault," she said to the floor as he rocked her back and forth with his foot.

"Was she entertaining you?" he asked me.

"We were talking. That's all."

"About what?"

His manner was subtly threatening. I didn't like it. The warning was deeply sexual, a promise of something he dared me to enjoy. His ego put me off more than the menace of his manner. It insulted Adam, and I couldn't call him on it because he didn't actually say anything I could pin down.

"She can tell you if she wants," I said with my head held high. "She's a big girl."

"She is. I was about to take her into the gym to reward her, but now I have to punish her."

Did the mention of punishment make Serena feel free from the kitchen floor? Were her chains unbound? The stress released? Had she really wanted to be punished?

"What are you going to do?"

He regarded his sub. "What do you think, pet? What should I do?"

"Whatever pleases you," she said.

"Why does it please you?" I interjected. I wished I hadn't asked, but my curiosity got the best of me.

"The world's a crazy place, Mrs. Steinbeck. Except when she's under me. She makes it sane. Right, pet?"

"Yes, Master."

"Come, then." He stepped back, giving Serena room to turn and crawl toward the door. Stefan bowed to me. "It's been a pleasure. Regards to your husband."

I was left alone in the kitchen, shaking.

That's what you do when you come face-to-face with your fears, and the fears draw you in like a warm cocoon lined with thorns.

# CHAPTER SIXTY

## PRESENT TENSE

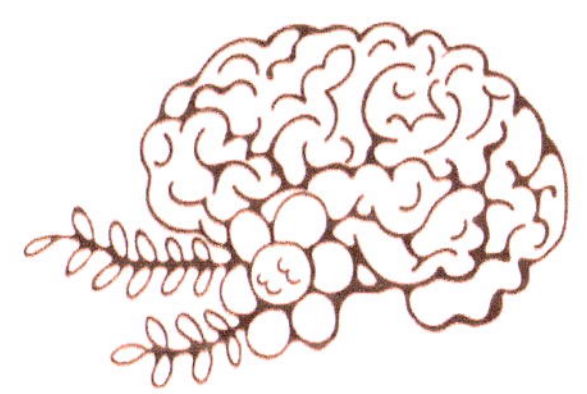

### DAY TEN

*Where is Adam? What will he do today? How much do I love that mouth of his?*

I froze writing the word love.

I never scratched out anything in my journals, but I scored a big, dark i over the o.

The days and nights had passed pleasantly enough. I let him order me around in bed and it was nice. We worked some days the way we always did when we were away. There was very little work to do actually, since we'd put a stay on all new business for thirty days.

*D—*

*The sales staff wants to know why they can't chase new accounts? Lloyd keeps talking about status quo? They're all saying you're getting a divorce and I'm like... no way. Right? That's crazy! Can I have the official word from you guys? They're making me nuts!!!*

. . .

Kayti's email had been sent at two in the morning. She'd be at her desk in an hour, and I needed to answer it. We'd expected this to happen and had prepared a statement. It was a noncommittal stall, but it said enough to hush everyone for a couple of weeks.

Adam was outside, wearing a sweater against the cold, talking to Stefan.

I didn't want to bother him. That was what I told myself. I couldn't bother him with the fact that the prepared statement was two tons of horseshit. No matter how much I was enjoying this month, I couldn't go back to him. Not with the way he was. I couldn't love Manhattan Adam again, and Montauk Adam would be dead in two and a half weeks.

And fuck him for that.

*K—*

*We are getting divorced. It's amicable, but we need to work some things out. Don't panic. Don't tell anyone. Let the rumors be rumors for now. I'll be back in a few weeks.*

Adam and Stefan shook hands and parted.

I hit Send and shut the laptop.

*Why are you hiding it?*

Because telling Kayti we were splitting up wasn't up to me. It was up to *us* and I'd done it anyway.

The front door opened. Boots off.

He appeared in the office doorway with cold-bitten cheeks and ears. "Stefan's going to the city for a week. I'm going to help them load up."

I tried to help load the crates, but the men shooed me away, so Serena and I stood by the barn doors. Hot tea boiled on the stove. Adam had his sweater sleeves pushed up to the elbows so when he lifted his side of the crate, I saw his forearms tense and bulge.

"It's going to get cold in there with these doors open," I said.

Serena stomped snow off the fur of her high-heeled boots. "And the furnace has been acting weird. It's going to take forever to get warm tonight."

"You'll be in the city anyway."

"I'm staying here."

I didn't know what my expression said. Maybe it asked why, or showed a little shock I didn't feel. Maybe no matter what my expression said, her answer would be the same.

"For a whole week?"

"I had a very busy fall. I need the rest. The ocean. Manhattan stresses me. Besides, my Master said Adam would take care of me while he was gone."

Stefan slapped the back of the truck closed.

Maybe my eyes went wider because of gunshot sound and not because my spine turned to ice. Because when she said "take care," she said it with the lush depth of pictures and smells, and her expression— all fluttering eyes and bitten lip—implied more than a pat on the head. His hands on her. His lips. Her eyes looking up at him and his body pressed against hers, naked, loving, rough, and passionate.

*Can't he do what he wants? Didn't you leave him?*

I felt Adam near me more than saw him, because all I could see were Serena's eyes, the sex in them, the anticipated satisfaction. When his earthy scent mixed with her pleasured smile, I panicked.

I met up with Adam as he approached. "Kayti asked if we were getting divorced."

He cocked his head at my timing then nodded. "Did you give her the statement?"

"I told her."

"You told her what?" He raised an eyebrow.

"It's amicable. I told her it was amicable."

His face gave away nothing. Only the length of time it was frozen told me he was hiding his thoughts from me. I decided it wasn't a big deal. It was my news as much as his and if I wanted to tell my assistant, I could tell her.

That didn't wash, even in my own head.

Adam pulled his glove off one finger at a time. I couldn't tell how much of his expression was hurt and how much was anger. "That wasn't what we agreed."

"I know but—"

"Go to the truck. Put your hands on it."

Serena waved Stefan over. Said something in his ear.

"I told her not to tell anyone," I said defensively as the couple stood at the barn doors, watching.

Adam's voice didn't change. "Bend at the waist. Feet apart."

He slipped the glove off and started on the other. I didn't move. When the glove was off, he regarded me fully. Hours and days passed. I made no move to the truck.

"I wonder how many more times you'll betray our agreements." He put the gloves in his pocket. "One, we don't talk about the split until we know who the company is going to. It affects our relationships with vendors and buyers. Two, you do exactly what I tell you for thirty days or I treat you like an adversary."

A lump of culpability grew in my throat. If he wanted to make the divorce ten times more difficult, my impulsivity with Kayti had just made it ten times more possible. I looked like a liar unworthy of trust. I wouldn't be expected to fulfill the terms of any deal.

I glanced at Serena and Stefan, who were still watching.

"Put your hands on the truck. Bend at the waist. Feet apart."

I walked to the truck, heart pounding. Palms sweating even in the cold.

From behind me, he said, "Undo your fly. And don't spread your feet so far I can't pull your jeans down."

He was going to punish me.

He was going to punish me in front of people.

I was turned on and sickened at the same time.

Facing the truck, I wrestled my clothes for my fly. I felt them watching. Heard them step closer. My nipples got hard. My heart felt small and tight, constricting into itself. My breath came in sharp white clouds.

Adam came astride me. I couldn't look at him. My body had gone rigid with fear.

He let out a long breath.
"Go upstairs. Now."
I ran.

# CHAPTER SIXTY-ONE

## PRESENT TENSE

### DAY TEN

I MADE IT UPSTAIRS, buttoning my fly on the way, and couldn't go into my room. I stood in the doorway and couldn't. Just couldn't.

Its plainness offended me. It's not-mineness. Nothing about it reflected me or my personality. It could be anyone's room.

The same could be said of the house. Not mine.

The same of my husband, whoever he was. Not mine. He wasn't even the man I'd married anymore. That guy had slowly faded into memory. I missed him and never wanted to see him again at the same time.

I sat in the hallway with my back against the wall between our two rooms. Adam came up the stairs a few minutes later with two mugs in one hand and a bowl in the other.

He put one of the cups by me and sat across the hall.

"You're an asshole," I said before he'd even settled in.

"Not going to argue."

"Am I in 'trouble' for not going in the room?" I didn't sound as sarcastic as I thought I would. The tea was warm and a deep amber. I sipped it. It was scalding hot and he'd sweetened it the way I liked.

Maybe he wasn't one hundred percent stranger. At least where tea was concerned.

"I said upstairs." He rooted around the bowl and came out with a walnut.

"Nuts? You brought a bowl of nuts?"

"We didn't have lunch, and they were all I could grab. Want one?"

"Sure."

He cracked the walnut between his palms, crushing it just enough to keep its shape while making the nut accessible. The sound reminded me of a time long ago when I was pregnant and he fed me walnut meat out of the shell.

"What happened out there?" I asked.

"I lost my shit."

He tossed me the cracked nut. I picked through it for the meat, leaving the shell pieces in a little pile beside me.

"Why did you stop?"

"Your face. You weren't ready. When I saw that, I knew I'd gone too far. Then I realized the thing I really owe you an apology for." He used a small hand cracker for a hazelnut. "Business is business. I think telling Kayti was incredibly stupid, but it's business. Tanning your ass for it would have been a mixed message."

The last compartment of the nut was trapped behind a sheet of shell. I broke it and picked out the last of the meat. I really was hungry. "Can you break me another?"

He sifted through the bowl and came up with a walnut.

"You think it was stupid?" I asked. "Why?"

"Because first"—he crushed the shell in the heel of his hand, smashing it to dust and shrapnel—"before the divorce is public knowledge, you and Lloyd need to instill confidence that you're not going to go into bankruptcy without me."

The nut couldn't be tossed across the hall. With his palm up so he wouldn't drop it, he shifted to sit next to me. I put my hand out, and he dumped it in.

"It's funny," I said, picking out the good stuff. None of it was caught in the little compartments, so I made quick work of it. He cracked me another, crushing the compartments again. "I thought you were going to say something else."

"I can't imagine."

"I thought you were going to say you wanted to see how this month panned out."

"It's going to pan out." He held out his palm. I picked the nut from it. "You need to get ready to own that company completely again."

The nut stopped in the middle of my throat, and I had to make an extra effort to swallow. I was still confused and a little angry, but when he said he expected to give McNeill-Barnes back, he was saying he expected us to make it thirty days and part cleanly. Exactly what I wanted. Right?

*Your head's all fucked up. You should want to leave him now more than ever.*

When I got that thought out of the way, I was left with satisfaction. Not over getting what I wanted, but that he had faith that I could make it. I craved his approval like never before. So like a child, I asked for it.

"I feel like a failure at this," I said.

"You're not."

I faced him, seeing his profile against the hall window. His jaw moved as he chewed, and the line of his neck rolled when he swallowed.

"I bet Serena would have taken her punishment even if it was business." I hoped the statement would seem like a random musing, but I sounded petty in my own head.

"She would have screwed up the business to get the punishment. What I saw there, outside, was that you were willing to do what I told you no matter what."

"If you hadn't stopped, what would you have done?"

He faced me and took my hand. "You want to know?"

"Yes." The word caught in my throat.

"I would have pulled your pants down, right outside with them watching. I would have made you choose between my hand for twenty, or the belt for ten."

His voice came in three dimensions, putting me back in the scene. The cold. The watching eyes. The tingle of pushing against my own will to do his bidding.

"Your hand. I redlined anything but your hand."

"Twenty takes longer. They'd be watching you longer. Watching me punish you like a child. Seeing your pain and seeing how much you liked it." He brushed his lips on my cheek. "For the length of twenty strokes, they'd see you'd do anything for me. Ten on your ass and ten on the backs of your thighs. Then I'd make you come."

I found myself shifting my hips so my clit rubbed on the inside of my jeans. My fingers pressed against the floor as if I could leverage myself against it.

And still, he kept on. "Hands still on the truck. Ass up in the cold. I'd finger you when I was done. You'd come for me and they'd see who owned you. So. Hands for twenty or belt for ten?"

"Hands. Still hands."

I wanted it, and didn't. The witnesses had turned me on and frightened me at the same time, because I wasn't sure what they'd do. But I could trust Adam. By sending me upstairs, he'd earned more trust than I knew I was capable of.

"Open your fly," he said in that voice. The voice that didn't have room for "maybe she won't."

"What's happening to me?" I asked myself more than him. Neither of us had an answer.

"Pull your pants down to your thighs and get on your hands and knees. I'm going to punish you just because I feel like it."

I unfastened my pants and arched my back to pull them down. Then I rolled to one side to get on my hands and knees on the hallway floor.

He was going to punish me. My whole body begged for his hardest touch.

Behind me, he slid his fingers in my crack, between my folds, putting two fingers inside me. It didn't feel like punishment.

"Were you wet when you came up here?"

"Yes."

With his free hand, he pulled the hood of my clit away, then he stroked the sensitive, nerve-bundled skin with his wet hand. "Do you want to come in this hallway?"

"Yes."

"Don't. Not until I say."

He rolled his finger across my most sensitive parts, slowly gathering pressure and pleasure. I dropped my head, breathing heavily, and when I groaned, he knew I was close and slowed down.

"Can I come?"

"Can you come what?"

"Please. Let me come please."

"No." He took his hand away. "This is your punishment." He slapped my bottom once and stood. "Let's eat something. I'm starved."

I pushed myself off my hands. "You can't leave me like this."

"Yes, I can. Not all punishment is pain. And for telling Kayti, you need to be punished."

He held his hand out to help me up. I took it and got to my feet.

"I don't like this." I pulled up my pants.

"You're not supposed to." He kissed my cheek and went downstairs, whistling.

I shouldn't have told Kayti. It was a monumental blunder, yet he was whistling as if it didn't matter.

As if he knew—no, not just knew. As if he accepted and embraced the fact that he'd no longer be running McNeill-Barnes. As if he'd be signing it over to me when this was done.

*Why aren't you overjoyed?*

# CHAPTER SIXTY-TWO

## PRESENT TENSE

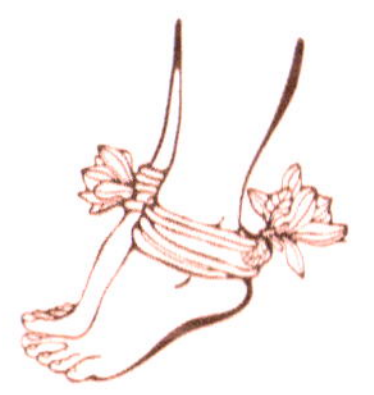

## DAY TEN

He was fully dressed, standing over me at the edge of my nondescript bed, smiling, with an erection stretching his pants. After the walnuts in the hall, lunch in the kitchen, a nap, and a languid dinner, he'd told me to put on a nightgown. I'd spent the past few hours on the couch watching a movie with my head in his lap. It had felt normal, but it wasn't. Whenever I'd tried to close my legs, he opened them as if he was going to let me come, then he didn't. I couldn't have repeated a single thing from the movie. All I could think about was sex.

When the movie was over, he'd told me to go upstairs and get ready for bed, then he watched me brush my teeth and hair. He had me leave the door open a crack when I used the toilet, and made sure he could see me wash my hands. He only left long enough to get a wooden box the size of a stepstool. He placed it under the bedroom window and told me to remove my nightgown. I knew for sure he was going to release the bursting tension between my legs, but I was wrong.

On the bed, with him over me, my nakedness became the whole of my existence. I was aware of every single square inch of skin. His eyes zigzagged over me in swaths, leaving scorched lines behind. My body was crisscrossed with burning lines of his awareness. He set the space between my legs alive. The engorged, unsatisfied throb that begged for release.

For a long time, he didn't say anything. Not with his mouth. He took something from the box under the window, closed it, and turned back to me with black straps dangling from his hands.

I closed my legs.

He opened them gracefully, with a precisely measured pace that was definite, not reactionary, like he was catching an orange rolling off the counter.

Who was this man? This competent, commanding man with no interest in what I wanted or what we'd established as an expected routine. Who was this man, this presence? And what was his agenda?

He sat on the edge of the bed and ran his hand along the inside of my thigh.

I went from solid mass to fluttering energy. "Finish me," I groaned.

"Diana," he said, "you've never finished anything in your life, and for the past five years, I've let you get away with it."

His hand moved to my other thigh without pausing, and I was convinced my pussy's gravitational force could have pulled him in up to the elbow, releasing an orgasm that would snuff out the universe, but he smoothly laid his fingers on my skin and stroked it.

I squeaked. I'd never been so close to the edge of orgasm for so long.

"I can finish. I want to finish." I sounded as if I was begging, because I was.

"We have different definitions of finish, and yours doesn't count. Not in this house."

When he took his hand off me, my body jerked to get closer to it.

"What do you mean I don't count?" I objected. "That's—"

"No talking." He stood and faced me. "Or I *will* gag you."

He knew damn well I'd redlined that. Was it possible the redlining meant the item became optional after a certain point? Was it a test? I read the contract carefully, but did I miss it?

"But—"

I ate my words. His glance at my closed knees quieted me, and I opened them again. Not because I was afraid he'd gag me, but because I didn't want him to want to. I wanted to do it right. To finish this thing his way, no matter how psychotically aroused I was.

"You were going to say something about not counting?" he asked.

I nodded.

"That hurt your feelings. It offended you. Is that right?"

I nodded again.

"This is a game. It's a bedroom game. A Montauk game. We've been business partners for five years. Have I ever made you feel like you don't count?"

My answer was obvious to both of us, but he waited for it, fingering the straps while I stretched naked before him. I didn't feel threatened. If I could dig out a single instance when he didn't treat me like an equal, I was safe to mention it.

"No."

"If the game is too much for you, opt out." He stood over me, exuding a stillness the room revolved around. "But you know I won't push where you won't go. Right?"

I could have said yes. I could have said no. I could have continued the discussion or freaked out or honestly, with the frustration of the orgasm banging at the door, I could have cried and begged. But my voice would be sharp. Even a whisper would have cut through the moment and severed desire from time.

He'd asked what I thought. I wanted the answer to be more than simple, and less than complex, because in throwing it back to me, he made me look at not just what I wanted, but what I needed.

I gave up. But not really. I wasn't throwing in the towel and abdicating. I didn't want to say, "Forget it, I'm out." I wanted to say, "Forget it, I'm in."

So all I did was spread my legs a little wider.

He bent over me, taunting me with the straps in his hand. "You want to come. I understand. You think that's finishing." He gently grasped my right arm. "It's not. Not to me. To me, you're finished when I say. For any reason. And it's going to seem arbitrary. It's not."

He leaned over to get to my left wrist. His body was a hard mass hovering over me, blocking my view of anything else. Like a mothership descending over Manhattan, covering the sky. I let my arms drop and blood flowed back through them, even as it continued to heat my clit.

"P—" The first sound of supplication. The beginning of *Please*. But I didn't finish. I didn't want a useless orgasm. I wanted to do what he wanted, to see where he was going. I trusted him. I trusted whatever he had in mind. It wouldn't be a throwaway climax, but something else entirely.

He centered his face over mine, close enough to kiss. "How old are you?"

He didn't seem to be doing anything rough enough to warrant safe questions, but I answered.

"Twenty-eight."

"Where do you live?"

Where did I live? He'd asked this before, and I still didn't know the answer. "In this bed, in Montauk, in a cottage in snow."

"Do you hate your husband?"

"I never hated him."

"You're about to."

He sat up straight, his eyes between my legs more substantial than warm fingers. He put his hands on either side of my labia, thumbs pressed into the muscle and skin of my ass, fingers in my upper thighs, pressing me open. My legs pivoted outward to the point of discomfort.

Maybe now. Maybe now he'd release me.

Touching me more than he had to, but not where I wanted him, he placed my right arm at my right thigh and snapped one of the straps off his shoulder.

"I'm saving your orgasm for"—he shrugged—"tomorrow, earliest."

"Tomorrow?"

He answered with a stern look and strapped my wrist to my thigh. The nylon weave dug close to my pussy, so close, yet not close enough. He crossed the bed to do my left wrist and thigh.

"I can come both times." I didn't know what I was even asking for. A second ago, I wanted to accept whatever he dished out. That was before "tomorrow, earliest."

"All orgasms aren't created equal." His hands were efficient and businesslike even as my body craved his intimate touch.

He stood. I wiggled, and it came to me what he'd done. Wrists attached to thighs, my legs spread, the storm picking up speed outside the window. I wanted to curse him and please him in one breath.

Adam stood at the foot of the bed, arms crossed, feet slightly apart, his erection outlined in his pants.

"I can't sleep like this," I said. But what I wanted to say, what was flooding my mind, was the sight of his dick and his complete control over it.

He bent at the waist, grabbed my ankles, and pulled me forward until my head rested flat. "Yes, you can sleep. On your back or you can roll over. I'll keep it warm in here in case the blanket falls off. You can sleep knowing you're doing exactly what I'm telling you to do."

"Why would you do this?"

"Because I can."

I'd thought the question would cause reflection, but he relished his answer. That much was obvious.

"I thought this would be different."

Did he smile because he'd surprised me, or because he'd tricked me with my own expectations?

"You're a creative person," he said. "You'll figure out how to get yourself off. After you do, it's your choice to do it or not."

He put his knee on the bed, then his fist pressed the mattress. He thrust forward until his breath cooled the juice on my cunt.

I groaned when his lips found my clit. A quick peck. It was a groan of hope that he'd changed his mind. His eyes made contact with mine as he kissed it again, more slowly, then he kissed where labia and thigh met, near where the strap dug in, checking my reaction.

I thrust my hips into him, but he backed away in reverse. Face, then fist, then knee, until he was standing at the foot of the bed again. With his arms crossed and his erection straight, his attention was riveted on me.

"Can I ask you a question?" I asked.

"Yes."

"You know what I want before I say it. I feel like you're reading my mind."

"I know you. You're my wife."

"Why didn't you know what I wanted before? When I needed you?"

He stiffened, tightened his lips. "Like when?"

"After Lenore."

"You mean Olive?"

"When you came to my father's house and brought me to the couch. You were a million miles away. You were phoning it in."

Did an ounce of his dominion over me leak? Did it fall off him? Any of it? Did I crack his armor?

"I was scared." He stated the fact without losing his dominance. No crack appeared.

"Of what?"

"Of having no control. Of failing. Of you. Everything. And I'd given up the one thing that makes me fearless. I was trying to be what you wanted, but as we now know, I can't be that." He picked up the blanket. "Be good." He threw it over me. "I'm in the next room if you need me. Otherwise, I'll be back in the morning."

He shut off the light and closed the door.

It hadn't occurred to me that he'd be frightened of anything, and if he'd told me that before he told me about taking Serena's virginity, I wouldn't have believed it.

Maybe that was my failure.

# CHAPTER SIXTY-THREE

## PRESENT TENSE

### DAY TEN

THE SNOWFLAKES WERE dry clusters floating down with the speed of
feathers. Some landed gracefully on the windows and dissolved into
tears. I drifted into sleep like one of the clusters on the hot pane,
condensing and warming into a dream where my husband drew a white
feather over my cleft over and over and the white light of my orgasm
flicked on but stayed dim. My wrists were strapped to my thighs even in
the dream, and I strained against them.

I woke to a light from outside.

The motion sensors outside the studio had gone on. There were no
clocks in the bedroom, but I guessed an hour had passed. The torture
between my legs had abated a little, leaving me with only raw potential.
Desire had crouched back into the corner but was ready to spring.

Why would the light go on? A bird? A cat? Too much snow?

Or Serena crossing the yard to fuck my husband?

I trusted him, on the one hand. On the other, the rules of this game
constantly surprised me. I'd thought controlling me for a month meant
he'd constantly fuck me. I'd thought I could just shut down my mind
and heart.

I'd left sharing on the list because he wouldn't share me.

But what if that meant I was sharing him as well?

It shouldn't matter. I'd left him. I'd sent him packing with a note on the counter. I'd assured him repeatedly that I wasn't coming back, ever. That I didn't love or want him.

So I should be fine with her coming over here and letting my husband kiss and touch her and—

A split second passed between the light flashing on and me realizing I wasn't okay with this. No. Not at all.

*Wait. Stop. If you're not okay with it, you have to stay married, and all this trouble will be for nothing.*

Right. I was fine with it. Totally fine. I just wanted to know. Wanted to see if she was coming across the yard. Had to know. My curiosity was a living thing that needed to be fed.

I wiggled out from under the blanket, dropped a foot to the floor, and wrenched myself to standing. It was hard to balance without my arms, and I was bent halfway, graceless, unselfconscious as I put my knee on the bench by the window and looked out.

Serena wasn't coming to fuck my husband. She wasn't even close to the main house.

She was in her own damned doorway, but Adam was standing in front of it, talking to her. He'd gone across the yard. She stepped out of his way, and he went into the studio. She closed the door.

A back-breaking rage filled my heart. A righteous, sour, powerless rage.

I put my forehead to the cold glass. My face twisted, muscles tightened, breath left me. I sobbed.

The motion light went out.

*Didn't you ask for this? Didn't you want to be free of him? Why aren't you happy?*

Not like this. I wanted it to be easier at the same time that I knew the easier it was for me, the harder it was for Adam. As if pain was a zero-sum game. As if there wasn't plenty to go around.

My face was crusted and wet. I couldn't wipe my nose or my cheeks. I yanked at the straps, but they weren't built for me to remove. They were designed to put me under his power.

*While he screws the submissive.*

Fuck him. Fuck Serena. Fuck this whole deal. I wasn't cut out for it. I enjoyed this shit up to a point, but he was crossing a line. All the lines. He was supposed to be in the next room while I was tied up. He said he'd be here, but instead he'd run off to give her what he wouldn't give me.

When I thought of them fucking, my body flooded with petulant and dissatisfied arousal. I couldn't think. Couldn't even be mad because all I wanted was release.

My eyes adjusted to the light, and I scanned the room. The bed's footboard was a low bar across two higher posts. It would do.

I slung my leg over it, nearly falling until I got one knee on the mattress while I leveraged myself against the foot on the floor. I rested my shoulder on the post and lowered my wet pussy against the smooth wood of the footboard.

I sucked air through my teeth. It was good. All good. The friction built tension for a release I had control over. I jerked my hips over the surface of the wood, sliding half an inch one way, then the other, the post biting into my shoulder as I pushed against it.

I fucked the footboard like an animal, back and forth quickly with only one goal.

Finally.

The wood got warmer as the hood over my clit rubbed back and forth, sending blood between my legs, swelling it. My eyes closed and my mouth opened. I rode the bed until my back arched and I came with a long, angry grunt.

Because fuck him for giving her an orgasm and not me. And fuck him for touching her and loving her when he was still married to me. And fuck him for tying my wrists to my thighs and not being where he said he'd be. And mostly, fuck me for leaving him and expecting him not to fuck a beautiful and accessible woman.

Fuck me and my inability to love him.

# CHAPTER SIXTY-FOUR

## PAST PERFECT

My mother said I was the best daughter in the world. I spent my adolescence telling people she made me the man I grew up to be. They laughed and she made her pissed-off face. I joked about it until she was too sick for anger or anything else. She couldn't do much more than breathe in that last month. After three months of shitty prognoses, I was still surprised when the cancer beat her.

I skipped the funeral. I couldn't bear the line of New York's luminaries telling me how *sorry* they were. How they knew how hard she'd fought and what a fine patron of the arts she was. I couldn't bear another story illustrating her wit and intelligence or another friend I barely knew asking me if I needed anything.

I needed my mother back. I was twenty. An adult for all intents and purposes, and a child who needed her mother.

So I went to the Met instead of the funeral. I wanted my mother, so I looked at art. That was where she lived in my heart.

When I was twelve, she'd taken me bra shopping at Bloomingdale's. I was coy and embarrassed, but her businesslike manner and loving touch made the reality of my budding sexuality bearable. With a little brown bag full of A-cups, she took me to a special exhibition at the

Frick. The Fifth Avenue mansion housed great Old Master paintings from a private collection. Mom had been on the board for a while, before every body part that made her female betrayed her.

On Bra Day, the Frick exhibit held Impressionists inspired by Old Masters or somesuch. We made small talk, and she stopped me in front of a particular painting and told me about men. I hadn't been ready to hear it, but I remembered it.

On the day of her funeral, I didn't go to the Frick. I went to the Met to see the same painting. I'd noticed it was on loan from the *Musée de Orsay* that summer, and in some crazy fantasy, I thought Mom would get well enough to see it again with me. She died instead.

The doctors had told me that as soon as I had children, I had to have my uterus, ovaries, and cervix removed. They stopped short of recommending a preventive mastectomy.

*Why is the feminine so volatile? Why don't we get arm cancer? Cancer of the nose? The eyes? Why does femaleness kill so many of us?*

Bra Day.

Funeral Day.

Eight years apart and spun together like loose threads in the sewing box.

On Bra Day, Manet's *Luncheon On the Grass* was probably the first meta-painting I ever saw. Two fully dressed men sit on the grass, picnicking with a naked woman. Behind them, another woman wears a diaphanous white gown. The light and proportions tell the story on an intellectual level. It's a painting about painting, where an artist and a friend step onto the canvas to discuss the image of the naked women bathing.

"What do you think of this?" Mom had asked, flicking her wrist toward the painting. It was one of many, and I didn't know why she was stopping in front of it.

"The lighting is weird," I said, clutching my bag of A-cups.

She raised an eyebrow. "How does it make you feel?"

A naked woman in arm's reach of two clothed men. One of her feet was between the legs of the man in front of her, and she was very close to the man beside her. She looked at the viewer, daring them to take issue. She wasn't uncomfortable, but I was.

"Fine," I said. I was twelve.

"Do you wonder what a naked woman is doing with two men who are dressed? What do you think is the point of that?"

"Manet was just starting to discover photography so—"

"Dominance," she interrupted, turning from me to the painting. She'd had me late in life, and her tightly twisted bun was thirty-percent grey. "It's an expression of man's dominance over women. She's naked to them, and of course in his view, she's fine with it, because it's the proper order to Edouard Manet. The one with the stupid hat? Showing his friend what's between her legs. They'll dominate her, and she'll submit her naked body to both of them."

"Mom..." I tried to shut her up. I was afraid someone would hear her and see the thoughts in my head. The nude leaning back and spreading her legs while the two men stood over her, looking at her body and deciding how to use it.

"Yes?"

"Can you talk more quietly?"

"I'm not saying anything historians haven't. This is how men make women feel."

Like this? Like they have to pee but in a totally different place? I felt swollen and slick, in need of the attention of fully clothed men, and it was terrifying.

I'd been sexually aroused before, especially finding Daddy's porn magazines between the bottom of the bathroom drawer and the casing underneath. The skin and dicks and open mouths. The women in red stilettos and corsets. The stories that taught me the word *cock* and the proper use of the word *cunt*. They were very well-hidden, and I always put them back exactly as they were, until I wondered if he meant for me to find them. I put them back sideways. They disappeared the next day.

"Men," I said to myself on Funeral Day, eight years later.

Manet's painting still aroused me, but it made me angry too. The anger was easier to deal with. It had an object. I couldn't be mad at my mother because she was sick and she died, but I could join her in rage.

"Men will try to dominate you," she'd said on Bra Day. "They think it's their right. Their privilege. They will do everything they can to degrade you. They'll strip you down to body parts if you let them."

I looked at the wood floor of the Met as I remembered the scene at the Frick eight years earlier. I could hear her in my mind as if she was still alive.

"It's not their fault. They're raised that way. You need to find a strong man. Use him to make yourself stronger, and if he loves you, he'll want to be used for your betterment."

"Is that why you married Daddy?"

"Your father is another kettle of fish. I let him use me for his betterment because I love him."

He was my kettle of fish now. I had to be strong for him. I had to take care of him and make sure he had the life my mother would want for him. Everything else was a waste of my strength and my womanhood.

# CHAPTER SIXTY-FIVE

## PRESENT TENSE

### DAY ELEVEN

I SLEPT AT SOME POINT. I'd rolled off the footboard like a clumsy one-night stand, used my feet to get the duvet back over me, and waited for the motion-sensor lights to go back on even as I denied caring.

The sun was reflecting the white of new snow. The brightness was crisp and unforgiving.

"Good morning," Adam said from the door that connected our rooms, fully dressed in slacks and a button-front shirt.

I turned away. I couldn't look at him. Of course he was relaxed.

He pulled the duvet off the floor and threw it on a chair. He opened my legs and inspected me as if checking under the hood. His manner was humiliating and degrading.

*And...?*

Arousing. Oddly. Goddammit.

"Good morning," I said. I didn't want him to know I was mad. I wasn't supposed to care, and I wasn't giving him the power of my jealousy.

He ran his fingers over the sheets, examining the corners at an angle.

I'd admit I was curious about what he was doing, but I was too annoyed to ask.

He crossed to the other side of the bed and stopped at the footboard. Considered the surface with a fingertip. Watching me, he put his thumb in his mouth, releasing it with a pop, and drew his wet thumb over the place I'd ridden.

He put his thumb back in his mouth.

"You still have the sweetest cunt I've ever tasted."

I should have been ashamed of the way he treated me. Of the way he checked on me. Of what I'd allowed him to do to my body. But my shame came from one place only. I'd failed. I'd been weak, and I'd disappointed him. I'd said I'd do what he told me for thirty days. That was the deal and I'd gone into it as payment for a smooth ride out of the marriage. I'd failed to keep my promise. Again.

He sat on the edge of the bed, disappointment pouring off him.

Well, I'd had a reason to get my rocks off.

"What's Serena's taste like?"

He didn't answer right away. He unstrapped my left side. I bent my arm. Stretched. Bent.

"As I recall, her cunt tastes like regular Tuesday cunt."

"Tuesday cunt?"

"Yeah." He got up and went to the other side of the bed. He'd navigated the sides of my bed a dozen times in the past twenty-four hours, and each time, he wound me tighter. "A regular Tuesday cunt. Nothing special. Not funky risky Saturday night cunt." He undid my left side. "Not Sunday godly worship cunt. Tuesday cunt."

Once released, I sat up and rubbed my wrists. "What does mine taste like?"

"A footboard." He stepped back and stretched his arm toward the bathroom. "Get a bath ready. I'll be back in four minutes to clean you up."

He left. He didn't spin off in a huff or back out with a promise of something devilish. He just... left.

The shame of getting caught failing was greater than any other. Not the shame of my nudity, being checked over like livestock, or the humiliation of being turned on by both. Failing was straight shameful.

I turned the bath on as hot as it would go and sat on the little wooden stool, watching the column of water ripple in the center of the steam. I couldn't breathe. I didn't want to cry. I was stronger than that.

But apparently, I wasn't. I didn't know anything anymore. Not about my husband. Not about myself. Nothing.

By the time Adam came back in, the room was in a complete fog and my blubbering had gotten wet and loud. He crouched in front of me, putting his hands on my shaking shoulders.

"Oh, Diana," he said tenderly, pulling me to him.

I couldn't resist. Wanted to but didn't, because I did want to even though I didn't. I held both desires in my mind as he slid along the side of the tub until he was sitting with my naked body stretched across him. I cried harder because I was confused. He confused me. I confused me. My feelings and desires zigzagged all over the place.

I cried and cried. My husband held me, wrapping his arms and legs around me as the bath tap roared and steamed. He didn't say or ask anything, just held me and rocked me.

I let him. I didn't have the strength to explain myself. I let him comfort me. Let him command me. Let him envelop me completely. I cried, but I was dormant inside. My guts had been emptied into him through my tears. When he leaned into the tub to turn off the water, I missed the shelter of his arms but didn't need them anymore.

"I can give myself a bath." I wiped my eyes with the backs of my hands.

"I know." He rolled up his sleeves. "But it's my prerogative."

When his sleeves were rolled up to the elbow, he held out his hand. I took it, letting him help me get in the tub. My skin stung at the waterline as I sank in and stretched out. Adam dunked a washcloth, wrung it, and pressed it to my face.

"Talk about it," he commanded.

He didn't ask me if I wanted to or if I felt all right. He told me what to do, and in that was an odd relief. I didn't have to choose whether or not to be intimate. I didn't have to decide whether or not to burden him or pull back into a shell. He didn't say tell *me*. He took himself out of the equation by commanding me to speak about it, whether it was to him, myself, or the four walls.

"I can't put it in order," I replied.

"Tell it as it comes to you."

I took a deep breath and told it as he ran the washcloth over me. "What you're doing right now? You're washing me like I'm a puppy, or like, your car. You might love those things, but they're objects. Do you see that? How you're just efficient? I don't... I didn't know you were like that. And I'm mad at myself for not seeing it and I'm mad because... I'm mad at myself because it turns me on. All of this shit. I thought I'd just tolerate it, but instead I'm turned on all the time. And last night, I wanted you. I wanted you so bad. I didn't want to hump a piece of wood. I wanted you to fuck me, but you went to fuck Serena. And you had to. You had to fuck her because I left you and why should you give me anything when I took everything from you? I'd fuck her too."

I started to cry again. He worked the insides of my thighs with the washcloth.

"I'm better than this," I said through my tears. "I'm better than a possession. I run a multimillion dollar company with my husband, and I haven't worried about sales or the bottom line for days and days. Who am I now?"

I leaned back and let him scrub my feet.

"You're a submissive." He stated a fact.

"Women aren't naturally submissive."

"Most aren't."

"But I am? Fuck you."

"It's not an insult. It's not a feminist issue. It's a bedroom issue. I've denied this from the minute I met you because I didn't want you to be submissive. Submissives scared me. It was you who opened my eyes to it. Once I did that, I saw you for the first time. You're submissive, and the Dominant in me always knew it." He gently put my foot into the water. "It doesn't have to be shameful, and it doesn't mean we're not getting divorced."

The tap dripped. My skin tingled. His hand brushed the surface of the water, making a rippled *V* behind it.

"It's hard for me to..." I had to stop to clear a lump of gunk from my throat. It threatened to come up in a sob as soon as I spoke. "To be here while you fuck Serena. I'm not saying I blame you. But it's hard."

His expression didn't change. No surprise. No rush to comfort. "Why is it hard?"

"You're my husband." I covered my pussy with my hands. A reflex I didn't understand but was powerless to control.

"And?" He moved my hands away.

"There is no 'and.' There shouldn't have to be."

"Explain it to yourself. Out loud so I can hear it."

I knew what he wanted to hear. The truth. In words. The part of me I shoved aside because it was reactionary and immature.

I couldn't deny him.

"I'm jealous," I whispered.

"Ah." He ran his fingers over the surface of the water again, detouring up my knee, down my leg. "Tell me what makes you think I'm fucking Serena."

"The light went on last night and didn't go back on." I didn't tell him I'd gotten up to see him at the door. I wanted him to deny it. Tell me it was a cat or a bird. Make an excuse.

"I know I told you I'd be in the next room. I'm sorry I left. I did go over there to check on her. The furnace is old. If it breaks in the night and she doesn't feel comfortable coming over here, she could be in trouble."

"You were there for a long time."

The water cooling, he stroked my leg with real affection this time, lost in thought.

"We did talk for a bit. Maybe it was forty-five minutes. She's lonely." He looked at me. "Like you were when you were married to me."

"If you kissed her, would you tell me?"

"No."

"No?" Why did my voice crack? I didn't even love him. I was fighting through the thick dregs of our relationship.

"No. I'd leave you." His hand lay flat inside my thigh and stroked to my center. "I wouldn't touch you again."

But he was touching my legs tenderly, and that was his answer. I'd spent all night telling myself he could fuck her if he wanted, and he was telling me he hadn't.

"It's not fair for me to pull you in two directions," I said.

"It's not fair that Stefan and Serena are here at all. The cold weather isn't fair. Stefan being in the city isn't fair. I can make a longer list if I added everything I've done, but the water's getting cold."

He helped me out of the bath and wrapped me in a thick towel.

"Thank you," I said.

"I still have to punish you for disobeying me."

I looked at the floor, ashamed and annoyed at the same time.

"Talk," he commanded.

"It sounds awful. 'Disobeying' you."

"Did I ever even give you an order before we came here?"

"No."

"Bedroom games. That's all it is. But they're serious, and when played right, everyone wins." He took me by the chin and made me face him. "I haven't felt right in a long time. I need this corner of my world to be under control. You are the one great love of my life, but you don't need this. You might like it, but you don't need it. I do."

I nodded against the pressure of his hand.

"Now, you can safe out, or you can dry off, take care of your business, and be downstairs in your nightgown, where I'll punish you. Got it?"

"Yes."

He dropped his hand and started out. He stopped himself and turned when he was at the door. "You might like it."

"Yes," I repeated. I almost said *sir*, but I bit it back. I'd kept sharing in the contract so I could remove the *sirs* and *Masters*. I wasn't giving it up for a slip of the tongue.

# CHAPTER SIXTY-SIX

## PRESENT TENSE

### DAY ELEVEN

*WHAT IF I pretended it was all right? What if I told myself to go all in?
To not let a hundred years of the feminist fight get in the way? Just forgot
it for the rest of the month? What if I chose to play this part with
everything I had? For fun? Because it wasn't so bad. Because I enjoyed it.
Because I had more to gain than to lose.*

I'd have to choose it very deliberately and consciously. Could I?
*Could I?*

I made a big question mark at the end of the sentence and went
downstairs. A simple breakfast of toast and fruit had been left out with a
handwritten note.

*I'm in the office.*

I ate in front of the wall of windows looking onto the sea. The
backyard and beach were covered in flat white snow. I wanted to go and
wreck it. Write my name in footsteps. My mother and I had built a snow
woman in front of our building once, and the doorman had put a hat
and epaulettes on her until he found out she was a woman. He laughed
and took his hat back as if gender prevented one from opening doors.

265

And there I was, eating toast and wondering if I should get on my knees when I entered the office.

I put the plate in the sink, washed up, and went to the west side of the house. Adam was at the desk. A chair was set up next to it. A robe was draped over the back.

He looked up when I was almost at the door, and he stood, lifting the robe.

"I'm sorry," he said. "We have to break scene. Put this on."

"What does that mean?" He helped me push my arms through the sleeves. I belted the robe.

"It means we have two problems. Which one do you want first? The one we can do something about or the one we can't?"

"The one we can't. This way we can end with something to do."

"Good." He showed me his phone.

*SEVERE STORM WARNING*
*High winds and precipitation.*
*Power and communication outages expected*
*east of Hither Hills State Park.*
*Take precautions.*

"Should we leave? For safety?" I asked when I handed the phone back.

"We should. But Thierry and Willa took the car into Queens yesterday, and if I tell them to come back to get us, all four of us will be stuck."

"Five. Serena's five."

"Five. We've done this before. It'll be fine."

"Okay, what's the other problem?"

"It's a pricing problem on two retailers." He turned the laptop toward me, and I bent to look at it. One of our biggest retailers had discounted a title and the other one had matched it.

"Crap. How much have we lost?"

Adam handed me my phone. "A few thousand. Which one do you want to take?"

"I'll call Lake and you call Shonda."

"Good." He sat down and slid his chair over. I didn't know why until he pushed the laptop halfway over to me. He was making room for me to sit next to him.

"Adam?"

"Yeah?"

What did I want from him? I couldn't get an answer together. He answered me as if reading my mind, his face opening into a knowing smile.

"I'm still punishing... Shonda! Hey, we were just looking at this price and..."

He went on like a normal person. I shook away the submission I'd just accepted and got on the phone. I could accept it again later.

It was half an hour before I realized I'd used his name and he had no problem with it.

# CHAPTER SIXTY-SEVEN

## PAST PERFECT

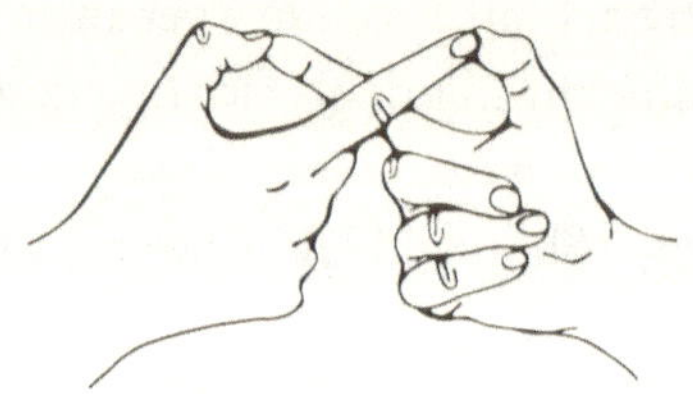

I WAS WEARING my favorite blouse. The one with the flying birds. We'd gotten a table at Metropolis for the company's anniversary dinner, and I wanted to look extra special.

Adam wore a suit, as always: navy blue with a crisp white shirt. Tall and straight, with wide shoulders and a tight waist, he fastened platinum cufflinks shaped like smooth pyramids. He ignored me and spoke to me at the same time. Something about work. Blah blah blah. It was important, but I didn't care. All I saw was his hands, how muscular and wide they were. How each finger was active and articulated when he straightened his cuffs.

As he threaded his belt through the loops, my knees turned to jelly. We'd been together long enough to have bedroom routines, but at least not long enough for them to be tedious.

That day, I wanted something different. I couldn't communicate it, but I felt it in my marrow. I wanted to bend in ways I'd never bent before.

No, I wanted him to bend me. The thought of him pushing me down, moving me, using me turned my insides into a pool of warm liquid.

"Adam." My voice cracked. All I could see were his hands holding the belt.

"Yes?"

I was supposed to tell him what I wanted, but I couldn't. I wanted him to tell me what I wanted then demand it. I wanted to be free of want. Of decisions. I wanted those hands and the beautiful monster that belt locked away.

I still don't know what came over me, but I got on my knees in front of him.

He didn't move. I didn't look at him, because I didn't know what to do. I could have taken his cock out, but that would have broken the spell.

He touched my cheek. I turned toward it, just a little, lips parted, and took his fingers in my mouth.

With an authority that shocked me, he put them down my throat, and I took them. All the way. He shoved them in as if testing how deep he could go. I held back my gag reflex because if he wanted me to take his hand, I would. Just to please him. To prove how much of him I could swallow.

I looked up at him.

He was Adam. Same guy, but different. I didn't have the words to explain it, but I knew he'd heard what I wanted. He took out his fingers, and I breathed.

I wanted him to get his dick out. I wanted him to give it to me. I didn't want to show any aggression.

So I put my hands behind my back. I looked forward, waiting for his hands to come into my vision and undo his pants.

And waited.

"We have to go," he said. "We can pick this up later."

Fear pinched the corners of my heart. I was on my knees in front of him with my eyes cast down and my hands behind my back.

I looked up at him. He was too tall in my vision, rising up in perspective, his crotch huge and his face a tiny dot on the horizon.

I put my hands on my hips. "Fine."

I got up, and we went to dinner, driving to Union Square in silence.

He'd been right. We hadn't had time for a quick blow job. What stuck with me was the pressure on my knees, his fingers owning my mouth, the way my chest jutted forward when I locked my hands behind me. He'd rejected my posture. He didn't want that from me. I was glad we were equals in all things, and when I thought of it, I held his hand as it rested on the gearshift.

When we got to the restaurant, I was cranky. I assumed I was hungry or dehydrated. Even after the first course and a glass of water, I was still sour. I chalked it up to a bad day and didn't connect it to the aborted blow job. That was nothing. That was a tight schedule cutting off a good time and it wasn't new.

I'd bitterly changed my stockings because there were holes in the knees. It bothered me more than I admitted, and the bother had the rank stench of a disappointment you couldn't admit to. So it festered and curdled until I got to dinner, unable to tell myself the truth. I'd wanted to be dominated. I'd wanted to submit and he'd stopped it because, he said, time was tight.

But I knew he was saving me from my worst impulses, and the shame of even having them sealed my lips tight. By the time we got to Metropolis, (early, I'll note) my gratitude and disappointment mixed together to turn my mood muddy and dull.

If the pat on the back on my father's couch was the beginning of the end, that night was the middle of the end.

# CHAPTER SIXTY-EIGHT

## PRESENT TENSE

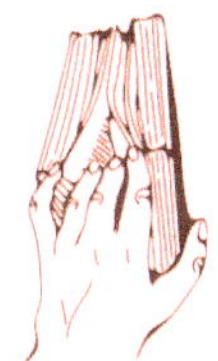

### DAY ELEVEN

THE STOCKINGS WERE black and stretched to mid-thigh. The lace
tops had clear silicone on top that kept them up. After I'd put on a pair
of black stilettos, I looked at myself in the mirror. The stockings made a
border around my triangle, and when I twisted to see my back, my ass
looked rounder and more appealing.

"Turn around," he said from the doorway, catching me admiring
my own body.

He didn't say please or ask. He didn't add an upswing to his voice at
the end to suggest a question. He hadn't even said hello. I turned so he
could see me from behind, then from the side, then front.

I could tell from the way he looked at me, leaning in the bedroom
doorway with his arms crossed, that I was the sexiest thing in his
universe. In five years with him, had he ever looked at me like *that*? He'd
looked at me as if he wanted to eat me alive, looked at me as though he
desired me, but there was an edge to him now, and that edge cut my
own desire, opening it like a wound.

"Last night." He pushed off the doorframe. "You took what was
mine. I trusted you, and you fucked the footboard."

He came in and put his hand under a lampshade, clicking one, two, three times until it was at its dimmest setting. Then he stood behind me. I felt him there, looking, planning. He moved around me, stood in front of me and over me. His silence was predatory. His posture was feral, yet completely in control.

I'd had no idea who I'd married. Had I been stupid and naïve, or shrewd?

"Your breathing's heavy." The back of his hand coursed from my collarbone, over my breast, the hard nipple, to my belly. Inside his manner was the threat of the threat, just enough to bring my awareness to the surface of my skin. "Hands at your side. Legs shoulder width. Don't look at me unless I tell you to. Don't make a move to touch me unless I say."

I dropped my eyes to his shoes. Not being able to look at him meant I couldn't see what he was doing or tell what he was feeling. It was disconcerting, and at the same time, the mystery was sensual. I listened. I felt the air stir. I paid more attention.

"I've been thinking of how to punish you, since I can't use paddles or crops. My hands would get tired giving you all the spanking you deserve."

I tried not to smile. I bit my lips. Pressed them together. Thought about kittens trying to cross Fifth Avenue at noon.

He leaned into me. I resisted the urge to turn around and face him.

"It wouldn't be funny if I really did it the way it was meant to be done." I couldn't swear it because I couldn't see him, but it sounded as if he was smiling too. "Not a stroke count. No. I'd stop when your ass was the right shade of pink and you'd surrendered so fully you stopped begging me to end it."

He grabbed the flesh of my bottom and squeezed. The surprise made me gasp and the flood between my legs came so fast it hurt.

"You want to come so bad, you're going to come. You're going to come until orgasms are agony. You're going to beg for pain."

He stopped. I didn't think he was done, but he cut himself off. I thought to agree. I considered "sign me up," discarded "when do we start?" and opened my mouth to give a simple, "yes," when we were interrupted.

I was working late at the office one night. It must have been eleven o'clock. Adam came in and asked me something. I jolted, surprised to find I'd been sleeping sitting up.

That was how it felt to hear footsteps in the hall. They yanked me from a fugue of sexual promise and churning hormones. I looked over at my husband. His head was turned toward the door, his clenched jaw a fierce line at his throat.

He leapt for the door, blocking it just as Serena showed up wearing a puffer coat, jeans, and boots. She looked at me and I looked back, frozen in place.

It took a second for us to regard each other. Her in boots and a puffer. Me, naked and still, my hands at my sides. When Stefan had pulled her into the driveway on a leash, I'd been disgusted and frightened. She was an animal. A slave. A piece of flesh to be used. And what was I, standing stock-still in the middle of the room in stockings and heels, held still not by ropes or chains, but by a man's will?

An understanding passed between us. She knew why I didn't cover myself in the dim light. She wasn't disgusted with me the way I'd been with her. My shame was my own. In the split second she saw me, I couldn't deny the shame was there and I couldn't blame her for it.

My body broke out into prickly pink heat.

I was ashamed and I was safe at the same time. I felt the shame physically as a weight on my hips. A liquefying warmth. A tightening of my nipples.

"What?" Adam barked, blocking the doorway.

She cast her eyes downward.

*Look at him. You fucking bitch, look at him. Do not submit to him.*

"I'm sorry," she said, hands at her sides. Their position filled me with unreasonable rage. I wasn't the jealous type, especially not over a man I was leaving, but I was boiling over her posture. Even her voice, which wasn't weak or warbly, just submissive, made me want to slap her. "There's cold air coming from the vent."

Adam's shoulders lowered a quarter of an inch. My body reacted by subtly leaning on one hip. I balled my hands into fists.

"Wait downstairs."

She spun and was gone.

Adam took his hands off the doorframe and turned. "It's going to be below zero tonight."

"She needs to fix her own fucking furnace," I said.

He let out a short laugh. "Her mother was the only female plumber in the tri-state area too. You'd think."

"Yeah. You'd think."

He put his hands on my biceps and drew them down, unclenching my fingers to weave his into them. "Give me a minute. It might need to be reset." He circled his arms around me and clasped my hands behind my back, pushing his body against mine.

"The furnace isn't the only thing that's going to need a reset," I groused.

"You're not usually so self-interested."

"I've never gotten this much attention before. It's making me selfish."

My comment was meant to be funny, but it wasn't. I was telling him he hadn't paid enough attention to me when we were married, and though I didn't mean exactly that, and though I would have denied it if he asked, that was the only one way to interpret my comment. I realized the sharpness of the remark as the last syllable came out.

"Lie on the bed," he said before I could rush to apologize. He let go of my hands and stepped back. "I'll be back in a few minutes. If your fingers or the footboard smells like Friday cunt, we're skipping agonizing orgasms and going straight to pain."

As I got my leg up on the bed and he had one foot out the door, I called him back. "Adam?"

He stopped and turned to me.

"What's on Friday?"

"Gratitude."

"What?"

"Thank God it's Friday."

I laughed so hard I didn't hear him leave, but I swore he was laughing too.

# CHAPTER SIXTY-NINE

## PRESENT TENSE

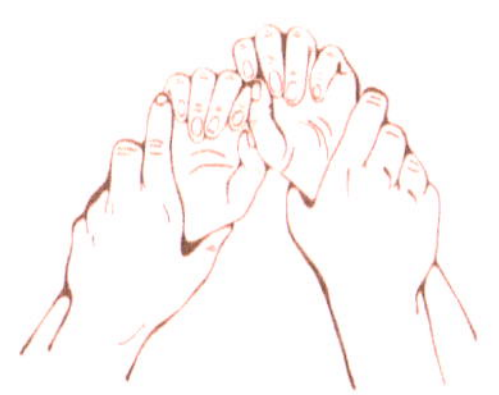

## DAY ELEVEN

Ten minutes had passed since I heard the back door whoosh open and slap shut. Ten agonizing minutes since the front light of the studio had flashed on and nine minutes since it went dark. Six minutes since I'd gotten under the covers. Three minutes since I slipped out of the bed and looked out the window. A minute since I put on pants and a sweater.

Thirty seconds since arriving at the front hall closet. A pocket of cold air surrounded the door, and my nipples tightened when I approached the front window.

I put my fingers on the glass. The sky had turned the orange of low clouds lit from below and the air was heavy with freezing rain and snow.

Wait for him? Do as he commanded? Or satiate the wild, predatory hunger of my curiosity?

The ocean seemed louder than ever, and the breaking waves looked more like toothy jaws ready to eat us alive.

This was more than curiosity. It was bitter cold. Deadly cold. The kind of cold inside the kind of storm that killed children and old people. My husband had been put in charge of a woman who played at incompetence for her own gain, and though I was sure he could handle her, there was nothing wrong with offering him support. I didn't know a damn thing about furnaces, but I could calm Serena down, hand him a wrench, boil water... whatever. Anything but lying in bed doing nothing.

My coat smelled of Manhattan and my scarf poked out of the pocket. It had embroidered hawks on the ends. He'd handed it to me at the door of the loft. I didn't put the coat on right away, just stood there with the lapels in my fists.

I'd given up being his wife, hadn't I? Surrendered my role as partner. Relinquished rights, privileges, and duties. What good would it do to go out there? I'd be taking advantage of my past intimacy with him. Breaking him down and leaving him anyway, and why? Pretending to be his life partner was wrong, unethical, and almost immoral. I was sure it wasn't simple curiosity. I cared deeply. But the curiosity sat in the room with its arms crossed and its foot tapping, saying, "Are you sure it's not about me? *Are you sure?*"

I was fucking sure. I might have given up on loving him, but I'd never promised to stop giving a shit about him.

And I admitted, as I laced up my boots... I wanted my orgasms.

Smirking, I slipped through the dark house and out the side door.

# CHAPTER SEVENTY

## PRESENT TENSE

## DAY ELEVEN

IT WAS COLDER and wetter than I thought possible. Wet snow fell on the ground layer of drier snow and immediately froze to a hard shell. My feet cracked it into ovals as I walked. I hadn't had a hat or gloves on the warm day of the drive from Manhattan, so I wrapped my scarf over my ears and tucked my hands under my arms.

Good thing the little house was just across the yard. Thirty steps at most. I curved my path to match Adam and Serena's steps, putting my feet into the cracked ice of Adam's footprints. The wind burned my exposed skin, and the sleet singed my cheeks.

Snow started filling the footprints. I rushed to step into them, but it was hard to see anything through the storm.

He did right to come back with her. He was a good man.

I got turned around in the wind and wound up on the side of the studio building. The light from the window was diffused by a layer of frost. Was there a door here? I would have sworn there was a side door, but I found no seam and no knob. I rubbed the frost, not feeling the cold glass or anything. Maybe I'd mistaken the warmth of the light for

277

actual warmth. But the heat from inside the house had melted the inside of the frost just enough to let the fractal ice slip down.

Through the window. Quickly. Because I only saw for a moment.

Adam. Pointing firmly and talking.

A painting. Red. In human-not-human shapes.

Serena, hands on a low table. Feet on the floor.

A long cutting board in Adam's hand.

Serena was naked from the waist to the knees.

The cutting board was a paddle.

I wasn't cold, because my anger was so hot.

My feet were no more than weighted blocks, so when I went to lift one to go inside and choke someone, I didn't feel that it wasn't moving. The rest of my body spun around with the intent to move, shifting with inertia and falling on the handrail for the side steps.

The door had been three feet away and I couldn't see it in the snow.

All I had to do was walk up them, but I was falling. The foot that had tripped me—the one that had frozen in place—loosened and I went into free fall, smacking my hatless head on the stone steps.

As my vision erupted into sparks, I had a last question.

*Do you love him?*

# CHAPTER SEVENTY-ONE

## PERFECT

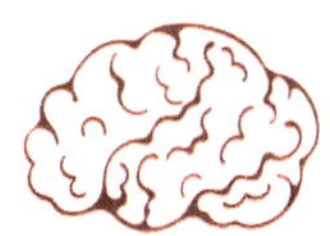

Hold your breath.
You can hear the night birds call.
His face blue in streetlamps.
His feet warming yours.
The breeze clicking the blinds.
A car alarm a million blocks away.
His hand on your cheek.
*What should we name her?*
*You're not even pregnant yet.*
*But I will be.*
*You're getting ahead of yourself.*
*Lenore.*
*No.*
*It's my grandmother's name.*
*Did your great-grandmother read a lot of Poe?*
*Probably.*
*You want a bunch of ravens circling the building?*
You don't care.
You want children before your insides turn into cancer.
He pinches your arm.

You like it.
You like him on top.
Your mouth yields in the dark.
The night birds fall away, and he begins again.
*I like Olive.*
*It's a color.*
*And a boy can be Oliver.*
You'll agree to anything.
He enters you again. You're sore.
You like it.
You whisper.
*More please.*

# CHAPTER SEVENTY-TWO
## PRESENT TENSE

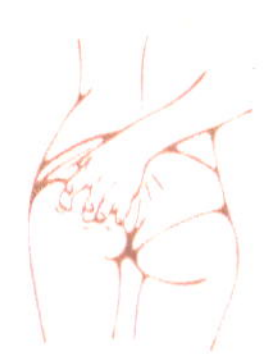

## DAY TWELVE

*When is love? Is love when your heart swells at the sight of him? Is love when you fall asleep on his shoulder? Or when you fold him into sections so you can fit him in your odd-shaped envelope?*

*Did you love him when?*

*Is love when he saved your family's company, or is it when you twisted your bodies into knots in the middle of the night?*

*Did you love him when you told yourself it was time to love him or leave him? When you needed him? When you knew he'd give you children before you had to have your womanhood removed?*

*When he loved you?*

*When it was convenient?*

*Did you only love him when it suited you?*

My head throbbed. I smelled the sheets. Felt damp human warmth all around me. Heard breathing.

Time folded in my unconsciousness.

It didn't fold in half, joining beginning to end in a neat jump. It folded in threes like a letter, past lapping tightly over present, tucking together to fit the shock of my senses.

Her voice.

His.

Warmth.

Blackness.

Nakedness.

Light.

His hard dick against me.

His arms.

Her sobs.

The smell of him slowly finding me, teasing me with half-consciousness. The smell of him in our life together. When I believed I loved him and when I feared I never had.

Folding like a letter left on the counter, signed in a shaking hand one day and kept in a drawer out of cowardice for a week. The edges spread and tucked back ten times until it was finally left for him. The man who smelled like the earth and the grass in it. His arms folded like a letter around me, but without the cowardice or malice of my letter folding.

*My God, what have I done?*

I said it in my sleep, but not out loud. I was only capable of input. The sound of breath and the hiss of the sleet on the windows. The glow of the lamp against my eyelids. The taste of blood in my mouth and the sting of the wound where I'd bitten my tongue.

Spread me like a sheet of paper. Write your life on mine. Fold past and present together like a letter. I am yours.

# CHAPTER SEVENTY-THREE

## PRESENT TENSE

### DAY TWELVE

MY MIND WAS AWAKE, but my body slept heavily on its side. His form against my back was gone, and she whispered so close I could feel the mist of her spit.

"You don't respect me. You think I'm some kind of victim. You look at me with pity. At least you did. When you saw me leashed with Stefan, you had this look on your face. I see it all the time. It's disgust. Like I'm shit on your shoe. Like someone needed to save me but you weren't going to be the one to do it.

"You know I make fifteen thousand dollars a day to walk down a runway, right? I can stuff coke up my nose. I can drink absinthe with princes and kings. But I don't. If I did that stuff, I'd lose myself, and I wouldn't have that *thing* I get from being a slave. Go look at a magazine spread. When you see me, you'll see what I mean. I own that page because I'm owned."

My bottom lip tingled as if she stroked it. I smelled her breath on my face. Her voice was barely audible, but my half-dream wound around it.

"You're afraid. You're afraid I'm taking him away from you, or you're afraid you're the same as me. Or both."

She pulled my lip out and let it go, then she kissed it.

"Lady, you should be fucking shaking in your boots."

Sleep ate her words, digested them, and forgot their specifics, leaving only a vague discomfort behind.

# CHAPTER SEVENTY-FOUR

## PRESENT TENSE

## DAY TWELVE

I WAS GOING to tell him as soon as I got up. Explain everything, probably in one long sentence. As wakefulness came over me, my hands felt warm and dry and the bump on my head felt heavy. I touched where I'd hit it. The throb of it made a rapid smacking sound.

No.

The sound was coming from the next room.

I got up on my hands, shaking off sleep. The storm was fierce. Snow and sleet pelted the rain-rattled windows.

The sheet was warm on either side of me, as if I'd had company. The table night light didn't illuminate much in its dim yellow glow. The lamp shades were square with stained glass squares and rectangles in deep reds and browns. Adam's room.

The rapid-fire smacking, accompanied by squeals and cries, was coming from my room. And a man's voice through the wall. My man.

Fully awake, I sat up straight. My head spun around the hub of the bump on my forehead. The duvet slipped off. I was naked. Adam's bed was higher than mine, with a bench at the end and high posts with bars up near the top. The frame looked innocuous and decorative enough,

285

but there was a track along the vertical posts to adjust the height of the bar.

I wrapped the duvet around me and dragged it behind as I walked toward the adjoining door. The voices got clearer as I got closer.

"Say it," my husband commanded.

"I'm sorry," Serena sobbed right before the smacking sound.

The door to my room was ajar, and though I could only see a slice of what was going on, it was enough of a slice to build a scene.

Serena had her hands on my footboard, bent at the waist with her sock feet apart. Her jacket was hiked to her armpits, exposing the pockets of her designer jeans.

Adam stood over her. "You forgot something."

He hit her ass with the paddle. *Thwack.* Because her jeans were on, it lacked the same snap I'd heard at the Cellar, when the paddle hit the skin.

"Sir." Her tears and groans mixed together. "I'm sorry, sir."

*Thwack.*

"Who else?"

*Thwack.*

"Diana. I'll say I'm sorry to Diana."

*Thwack.*

"I thought you were better than this."

*Thwack. Thwack. Thwack.*

He hit her so hard and so fast I made a noise in my throat, and he turned, paddle in hand, sweat beading on his brow. Our eyes met through the slit of the open door, and when he took it by the edge, I didn't know if he was going to slam it in my face. He was devastating. This was the man he'd been holding back. The man he'd tried not to be all those years for my sake. He was pure power. Pure control. A fucking god.

*Because he's beating a woman?*

I answered my question.

*Because she needs it, and he's a god who delivers it.*

The truth of it went against everything I believed.

I took a step back, because I felt another truth.

I envied her. He was giving her a connection I'd refused. Her basest self was on show for him, begging him to put her right. She trusted him. I thought I trusted him, but not the way she was trusting him. Her vulnerability was raw and painful, and as he beat her bottom, so was his. I wanted that intimacy. I wanted to give him every inch of my skin, but I'd locked myself away.

Standing in the hallway, watching his chest rise and fall in that tight, sweaty T-shirt, I was still wrapped up against him in a thick feather blanket.

I dropped the duvet, letting the white cloud pile at my feet, naked in front of him.

"Stand in the corner and think about what you've done," he said to Serena while looking at me.

I shuffled back to his room.

When I got to the middle of the floor, I spun and faced the doorway. He was already there with his worn T-shirt stretched over his chest and sweatpants that made no secret of his arousal. His erection—the erection I'd lived with as a matter of course for five years—was now a powerful threat of dominance and beautiful pain.

Something in me purred. I had questions, but I could satisfy my curiosity later. He closed the door.

In two steps, he was across the room. He didn't reach for me in tenderness but took a fistful of hair and pulled my head back. He looked at the bump on my forehead.

"It's fine," I said in a breath that begged him to finish what he'd started. "Take me."

He threw me on the bed facedown.

"Show me," he growled.

I reached behind and spread my cheeks apart. He was going to fuck me. Finally. All I wanted was his cock. I felt his fingers in me. Three, pushing in. I shuddered.

"What were you doing looking in the window?" All his vocal control was gone.

"Fuck me."

He pulled my hair again. "I give the orders."

"Yes, sir."

I let go, and he guided himself to my opening.

"You could have died. If I didn't know you. If I didn't know where to look. You could have died."

He didn't wait for an answer before ramming into me all the way. I cried out in pleasure when he pushed against me, stretching me open. I took my hands off my ass and gripped the bedspread, and he redirected them, bending them so they were firmly and uncomfortably upward, pinned behind my back, circling my wrists with two fingers.

Immobilized, secure yet awkwardly positioned, with him using his other hand to yank my head back, I was thoroughly in the moment. I was his. My husband fucked me as he'd never fucked me before. In our relationship and our marriage, he'd never owned me like this. For the first time, I didn't feel loved, I felt possessed. And for the first time, I craved his ownership. He turned me on my back, spread my legs out and up, and entered me again. When I put my arms around him, he pulled them off and pressed my biceps into the bed, thrusting so hard and so deep it hurt. Yet I spread my legs wider to take him to the root.

I cried his name. I thanked him, and when I was so close I thought I'd burst, I grit my teeth and focused on the pain.

"Come," he said through his teeth. "You're so fucking beautiful. Come."

I thanked him again before I stiffened and let the orgasm ripple through my body. Maybe I screamed. Maybe I just opened my mouth. I was sure I was near unconscious all over again.

He let go of my arms and took my legs behind the knees, folding them and exposing me. His cock slid out, and he rubbed the slick length along my seam, where I was swollen and bare. The tide of another orgasm rose. I tried to reach for him, but my arms were behind my knees. He'd twisted me immobile.

"God. God, I'm—"

The sentence got lost in another climax. I strained against him and he held my body still as he ran his shaft along me.

"Stop," I gasped. "Please stop. Hurts. It..."

I came before I finished, surrendering completely to the pain, letting it twist around the pleasure. My screams and my tears echoed both.

Only then did he pull away, and only enough to grab me by the arms and put me on the floor, twisting my loose, pliable body until I was on my knees before him.

I worshipped him. I felt the supplication to a Master in my bones.

This was what it was to submit. To forget. To have my entire world revolve around a single thing. I felt sleepy yet alive. Boneless and ambitious. All the contradictions fused into a simple desire.

Please him.

I put my hands under me, grabbing my ass cheeks and pulling them apart. I bent at the waist, dropping my head between his legs. Without reservation or preference, I lifted my ass to show him his options.

"My fucking God," he said, almost in awe. His T-shirt landed on the floor, and with more authority, he said, "Straighten up. Hands off the floor."

I lurched up. He stood in front of me, cock at eye level. I opened my mouth.

"Take it," he said. "Like I taught you."

I opened my mouth as wide as I could, tongue out, throat open.

"Good girl." He fisted the hair in back of my head with one hand, put his dick at the tip of my tongue with the other.

I only tasted myself for a second. With no slow grind or test thrusts, he shoved it down my throat. I didn't wrap my lips around him. I just kept my mouth open, held back the gags, focused on him and his pleasure.

"Yes," he said. "Keep your mouth open. I'm going to fuck it."

He moved me to his rhythms. My jaw ached and my lungs gulped for air. He pushed my head into him and pulled it away when it suited him. I let him. I became his instrument. We moved together, and his tempo changed to something slower and harder. I knew he was close because I knew him.

He sucked in a breath, pulling out. "I'm going to come down your throat and you're going to swallow it."

I looked up at him and nodded, then he held my head still and fucked my mouth. Five thrusts. I took a gulp of air, and he buried his dick in my face. The base pulsed against my lower lip.

Even as a Dominant, he smiled when he came.

# CHAPTER SEVENTY-FIVE

## PRESENT TENSE

### DAY TWELVE

When I tried to stand, I nearly flopped over. He caught me and pulled me up to the bed, folding himself on top of me. Only in that silence could I hear Serena crying on the other side of the door.

I thought his first words after a monster fuck like that would be poems about love and satisfaction. But her voice reminded me of what had brought us to that moment, and he exhaled in deep resignation of everything that was wrong.

He'd been punishing Serena.

He was mine, and he'd given her something that was mine.

And I let him fuck me.

*Jesus. What's wrong with you?*

I took my arms away from him and let my legs fall away. He must have felt me draw away, because he rolled off me, rubbing his eyes. I felt naked without his body clothing me, but Serena's sobs were a third person in the room.

"What happened?" I asked. "Why were you punishing her?"

"She's topping from the bottom."

"What does that mean?"

"It means I fucked up."

He stood. I twisted to see him. I hadn't seen his naked body in two weeks and I wanted a moment to admire it, but he pulled on his sweatpants.

"Should I be hurt?" I asked.

"Are you?"

"I think so."

Was I? Hurt. Satisfaction. Betrayal. Joy. Warmth. My feelings were a box of puzzle pieces. They were meant to fit together, but it was going to take some work to see the whole picture.

"Are you admitting you care about me?"

"Are you kidding me right now, Adam Steinbeck?"

"Yes. No. Of course not." He took a deep breath and sat on the edge of the bed. "I lost my shit. Serena broke the furnace to get to me. And when I thought about what could have happened to you, I lost control."

"Get to you? Like, how?"

He moved hair from my forehead. "You knocked yourself pretty good. Does it hurt?"

"Only when you touch it." I slapped his hand away. "What does she want from you?"

"Attention. Excitement. Punishment. I think a way out of her relationship with Stefan. It doesn't matter." He paused for a second, and her crying came through the door. "She wants aftercare. She's not getting it."

I'd seen aftercare in the dark room with the window at the Cellar. I remembered the tenderness and intimacy between Dom and sub.

I wasn't the jealous type, but if he gave her aftercare, I would skin them both alive.

Maybe I was the jealous type after all.

"Thirty days," I said. "You're mine for thirty days."

We watched each other for a long time. Everything drifted away. Serena's sounds, the click of sleet on the roof, the rattle of the windows. I didn't shift my gaze from his blue eyes. This submissive shit was so ten-minutes-ago.

"Diana?" he said without shifting away.

"Maybe the contract says you can share me, but I don't share you."

"Do you know you do this thing where you drill into people by just looking at them?"

"And?"

His lips tightened in a smile so slight, I would have missed it if I wasn't watching every change in his face.

"And." He leapt forward and kissed me, surprising me with it even though he was right in front of me. "And I admire the same things about you that I did before you left me." He stood. "Let's take care of business."

He opened the door to my room. Serena was standing in the corner closest to the door, her face streaked with tears.

"Stand here." He pointed at the center of the doorframe.

She stood exactly there. Her legs were closed. She was slouched in a sexless submission.

"What do you have to say?" he asked Serena.

She looked at me through puffy, red, yet strangely satisfied eyes. "I'm sorry."

"Explain what you did."

"I broke the furnace."

"I can make this even less fun, Serena."

She took a deep breath that hitched. "I wanted to come between you and Master Adam."

"I'm not your Master."

"Yes, sir," she said. That bothered me more than Master, because those were my words to him. "My Master is gone and there's no one to punish me. Adam wouldn't do it, so I gave him a reason to."

"If Stefan knew this about you," I said, "why has he been gone so long? He could have come back."

They both looked at me as if they knew something I didn't and they were trying to figure out if I was close to putting together some puzzle. I was outside the circle. I'd always been outside the circle.

I wanted to be inside the circle. I wanted to understand what they understood. I wanted to participate fully in Adam's secret life. I wanted him to be mine inside that life, if that was possible, because we could never go back to who we were.

And I realized that I was inside the circle. I'd claimed a place there.

"Stefan knew," I said. "He knew and he was playing a game with us."

"With me," Adam said, and Serena stood there with her eyes glued to the floor, denying nothing. "Welcome to my world, Diana."

# CHAPTER SEVENTY-SIX
## PAST PERFECT

A LITTLE AD appeared on the side of my screen. A Manet exhibit at the Met. There hadn't been a Manet show at the Met since Mom died. I clicked to see which paintings were included, but found the one I wanted to see was still happily in Paris. Then I went looking for a picture of it. I had to see it.

I let it take up my entire screen. I wanted to crawl into it. Understand it. Live it.

The blanket under her ass. She could probably feel the rocks beneath it digging into her skin. Was it cold enough to make her nipples hard? Her left leg, the way it dropped, the men had to see her pussy.

Were they commenting on how wet she was? Who would take her first? Or would one take her mouth while the other—

"I got your dry cleaning." Kayti came in with a clear plastic trail behind her.

I hurried to shut the browser tab before she saw. "Okay." I cleared my throat and tried to remember what I had been doing before the ad showed up.

"You should wear this one to Metropolis tonight." She flipped the clear plastic up, revealing my red blouse with tonal birds. When I moved, they looked as though they were in flight.

"Good idea," I said, still squirming in my seat from the painting. "Bring your card. We might have to leave early."

# CHAPTER SEVENTY-SEVEN

## PRESENT TENSE

## DAY TWELVE

HE BATHED me for the second time. In five years of marriage, he'd only bathed me when I bled from the D&C. Without the sadness of the lost baby or the tears of the previous bath, his hands were slow and erotic. He touched every inch of slick skin.

"She's been begging me to hurt her every time I go over there. Stefan gave me the green light to fuck her, not paddle her. I've caused a ton of trouble with him. Put your head back."

I faced the ceiling, and he poured water over my head. He was pensive and far away, but different from his distance in Manhattan. He wasn't closed off. He was both vulnerable and commanding in his own thoughts.

"But he wanted you to."

He leaned his forearms on the edge of the tub. His fingertips dripped until he turned his hands over and rubbed his right palm with his left. "He wants to open the door to… things. I want the door closed."

"What things?"

"Things I don't want."

"What? Tell me."

"No!" he barked. He never barked. His voice was most powerful when it was steady and strong.

I drew my knees up like a frightened child and hated myself for it. He was hiding something. A man without secrets didn't have to yell. "You didn't fuck her, did you?"

I hated that I had to ask. Before Montauk, I never would have.

No, not before Montauk. Before I left a note on the counter, I never would have asked such a question. But I'd set him loose.

"Of course not." He put the pitcher aside and sat straight on the stool. "She doesn't want to be fucked as much as she wants to be hurt. You can sit up."

I sat up, and Adam snapped a hand towel off the rack and dried his hands with his elbows resting on his knees.

"You know what this trip has taught me?" He waited for an answer with the front of his shirt bath-wet and the seam between his lips straight and serious.

I wrapped my arms around my bent legs and cupped my hands on my elbows. "I can't imagine it taught you anything you didn't already know."

"I have limits. Hard limits. But I don't know what they are until it's too late. And I just... I'm not ready for this again. The affectation with these people. The overdrawn courtesy. You see what it's covering up?" He flung his arm toward the wall behind him, pointing at an imaginary Serena. "He manipulated her, and she played me. I can't even get on his case for it, because it's so normal. And I should have seen it coming. Should have seen it a mile away and played the game instead of falling into it like a schmuck."

I put my hand on his, letting the water drip onto his pants. "You've been away from it for a long time."

I squeezed his hand. He looked angry and forlorn, holding on to a thousand words until he found the right handful. I slid to the center of the tub, getting up on my knees. I leaned over to him and moved my hands up his arms.

"You're going to be all right," I said with every ounce of conviction I could. "It'll all come back. You're amazing. I mean..." I needed more specific words. Accuracy counted or he'd think I was bullshitting him. "You make me feel safe. I've been walking around in this body my whole life and it's been like dragging around a liability. It's weak, and it wants, and it's built like a magnet for pain. Men look at me on the street... not just me, all of us...women...and it's scary. I'm scared all the time. I didn't know that. I thought it was just how a person felt. Not until you brought me here and I wasn't scared to give my body to you."

"That's you, Diana. You're finding yourself. Don't let the high cloud the reality."

"No." I squeezed his biceps. "I want the high. I want it so badly, and I want the reality."

He shook his head, gave one of my hands a short squeeze, and reached for the towel. "Up."

I stood, and he wrapped the towel around me, tucking one corner tightly under the other until I was snug. I leaned into him and he wrapped his arms around me, resting his chin on my head. I could see a quarter of his expression in the mirror, and even from that oblique angle, his trouble ran deep and turbulent.

# CHAPTER SEVENTY-EIGHT

## PRESENT TENSE

## DAY THIRTEEN

ADAM WASN'T in bed when I woke. The storm had been relentless. Communication held. The power flicked to the generator. Snow drifted to the bottoms of the windows. I felt wrapped in a white cushion of icy batting, protected from the rest of the world. When it stopped, the world went quiet and bright.

By noon, the sun was bright, and a blue plumber's van parked in front of the studio.

Things weren't getting done in New York. Zack's departure had opened up a five-gallon drum of worms, and they were getting out. We couldn't have chosen a worse time to be away from the office.

"Dad's slipping," Adam said, holding his phone to me over breakfast. "He can't keep up."

I read Kayti's email outlining all the line editing, invoicing, and production decisions she still had on her desk. No mention of the divorce. But she wouldn't email Adam about my slip. She'd email me, and I didn't have my email.

"It's a different business than even four years ago," I said. "Do you think they need us to come back?"

"Do you?"

"No. Yes. I don't know. I want to finish. We have two freelancers we can pay rush fees. And I can do the Islands piece myself."

"I can run these invoices. Yeah, you take care of the editing." He nodded to himself, folding his bottom lip in thought. "You should take the office. It's quiet." He turned back to his work and spoke absently, "When the sun is down, you're mine again." I turned to leave, but he grabbed my hand, pulling me down. "And you need to stay away from Serena. You understand why now."

"Yes, sir."

He took me by the back of the neck and kissed me, and though only his lips touched me, he kissed me with his whole body. He hadn't kissed me like that in Manhattan, ever.

# CHAPTER SEVENTY-NINE

## PRESENT TENSE

## DAY THIRTEEN

I TUCKED my laptop under my arm and headed for the office, passing the library. Serena sat in the winged chair there, bare feet tucked under her, flipping through a magazine. I was supposed to stay away from her, but I was so curious I changed direction and went into the library, settling into a thick wooden chair that reminded me I was sore.

"Good morning," I said.

"Hi."

I opened the laptop. A folded piece of paper fluttered out.

"How are you doing?" I asked, opening the note. "After last night?"

*Remember how you got sore. – Adam.*

"Fine. Why?"

I tucked the paper into my pocket, hiding my smile. As if I could forget where the pain came from.

I shrugged. "Just checking. Girl to girl."

She didn't respond right away. Just flipped through her magazine. I started my edit when she spoke up.

"You seemed into it."

"I was."

"I've had a few Masters since him," she said absently, as if mentioning the weather. "But none like Adam. He's got the right balance."

"Of what?"

"Cruelty and compassion." She closed the magazine. "I'm sorry about your head. It was supposed to be more fun."

I closed the laptop halfway. This conversation needed my attention. "It wasn't. We didn't come here to play. Not with you."

"Adam knows how it goes. He knew the minute I asked him to punish me straight out. Which he could have just done."

"I thought Stefan didn't want Adam punishing you."

She shrugged. "Things happen."

Her submission pushed the boundaries of pure aggression. I started to wonder if, five years before, she'd broken Adam on purpose.

"Whatever it is you're playing, I don't want it."

"Why not?" Her dark brown eyes had Venus flytrap lashes that caught my insecurities when they blinked. "You can handle it."

"You're not interested in me. You're interested in Adam. My husband. I'm sorry you couldn't have him, but he loves me."

She hung her head, and while her face was out of my view, I thought she was sad. I was wrong. When she looked up, I saw that she'd been hiding a smile.

The low rumble of an engine cut through the dead silence of the icy world outside. A car door slammed. Voices, muffled through the windows and walls.

Serena stood and pulled down her skirt. "No, he doesn't love you."

"You think you know him so well?"

"He can't love a submissive. Once he breaks them, he doesn't want them. I learned the hard way."

"Serena!" a voice called from across the house. Stefan. "Come!"

Serena's lips went slack and her eyelids fluttered. Just before she spun on her bare heel and ran toward the front door, she let out a gasp that I couldn't deny sounded a little orgasmic.

I needed to see what she did when she saw him, so I got up to follow.

Adam stood in the doorway. I nearly crashed into him.

"Stay in here," he said, pushing me gently back. "Please."

"Why?"

"Just stay and finish editing. I'll come get you."

Without another word, he slid the pocket door closed, shutting me away from the rest of the house.

# CHAPTER EIGHTY

## PRESENT TENSE

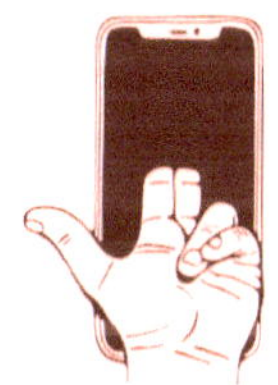

## DAY THIRTEEN

ADAM AND STEFAN stood in the exact center of the yard, in the
middle distance between the houses, as if intuiting the point of no
return to their safe spaces. They talked, but their footprints in the snow
showed their bodies had circled around each other. The plumbers left,
and still they were talking.

I watched from the glass door to the veranda. The same door I'd
stood at when Stefan choked Serena to orgasm.

She'd left the paddle. I didn't realize I was running my hand over it,
feeling its smooth curves, its weight in my hand, the caress of its
warmth.

*What are they talking about?*

I'd waited in the library, behind the closed pocket door, until I
couldn't take it any longer. I slipped into the kitchen and ate something.
The house was empty, or so I thought. Serena was standing in the office,
watching Adam talk to Stefan.

"What are they talking about?" I'd asked.

"Me. Us."

"Who's us?"

"Adam and me."

"There is no Adam and you."

She never answered. I went upstairs. That was when I found the paddle.

I'd watched through a crack in the door as Adam paddled Serena. I was intensely and deeply jealous. He hadn't touched her skin. He gave her no pleasure and took none for himself. Yet the act was intensely sexual. Intimate. The pain. The emotions. His rage. Her shame.

I swallowed, realizing how my hand had drifted over the paddle's surface as if it were a lover. I tapped the edge on the tip of my nose as I remembered the scene, then I pressed it to my lips. Paused.

I kissed it. A blessing. An understanding. Closing my eyes, I accepted the place of that tool in the world.

I put it on the window seat.

The paddle had terrified me and now...

I didn't have a chance to complete the thought. Adam and Stefan headed back to the house. Below me, the door opened, and Serena walked out, hair flowing behind her.

Adam continued into the house. I heard his footfall downstairs. The closet door. The stairs creaking under him.

Outside, Serena reached Stefan. He turned and walked into the studio. She followed. Adam came into my room as the couple disappeared into the side door.

"What's going on?" I asked without turning around.

I felt his breath on the back of my neck.

"Nothing."

I turned. "Nothing? You were talking for two hours."

"Nothing you need to worry about." He reached for the bump on my head.

I slapped his hand away. "I'll decide what I need to worry about. Is he going to punish her?"

Did I sound too eager? Did I sound as if I wanted to be a part of it?

I didn't sound concerned about her, that was for sure. It had taken two weeks for that to change.

Adam folded his lips between his teeth, tilting his head at me, as if considering carefully before he spoke. "You're not part of this world. You never will be. That's by design."

I crossed my arms. The wall between us got thicker and higher, and I didn't know why. I didn't know what had happened in the last two hours to close him off. "Was he mad at you?"

"Of course. But he was more concerned about her."

"Concerned?"

"Why are you challenging me? What's the problem?"

"Me? What's my problem? You and me, we were so close last night, and now you're shut down. You're hiding things. This is the problem, Adam, it was always the problem. You keep things from me."

"No, the problem was you leaving me notes on the kitchen counter."

God, I wanted to punch his face. I walked out. Or I tried to. He grabbed my arm.

"Let me go."

"You want to know what we talked about?"

I jerked my arm away.

"He wanted to punish me through you. Then he wanted to punish her. He wanted to share you to punish me, then paddle you while I watched. Then he wanted you to serve him while Serena watched."

"Serve him?"

"Jesus, you're so curious." He said it as if it were a moral failing.

"You brought me here." I was stiff as a board, a finger pointing up and a jaw set so rigidly I spoke through my teeth. "You held my life over my head. You endangered my family's company. You put me in a car I didn't know you owned and brought me here. All that's bad enough, but I chose to go along because I trust you and I had more to gain than lose. Up until now. As of now, it's all changed. You showed me things I never thought I'd see. You dangled a new way of thinking in front of me, and yeah, I was curious. But now I'm not curious about other people. I'm not curious about your secret life. I'm curious about me. I'm curious about what I'm feeling, and I can look it in the face for the first time. I don't have to be afraid, and I'm so free. I'm so..." I held my hands out to him and tried to grasp the feeling. My face stung with tears, but I held them back. I couldn't let this devolve into crying and comfort. "I didn't know I'd feel like this. I didn't know giving control would make me feel in control. I am fearless, but only because Adam Steinbeck is showing me who I am. Without you, this part of myself that's open now isn't an opportunity. It's an open wound. Every time you shut down, it bleeds. I get small and scared all over again."

I blinked, squeezing out tears. I didn't want to cry, so I grit my teeth together and breathed slowly through my nose. Cleared my throat. Held it together. I needed to finish this conversation. *We* needed to.

As if he understood what I couldn't say, he didn't wipe my cheeks or put his arms around me. He put his hands on his hips and looked down. It wasn't a submissive gesture. He was giving me space to get myself together without his scrutiny.

"You didn't cross off sharing," he said. "You were right when you said I wouldn't share you. But he knows you didn't redline it, so he's trying to hurt me by pressuring me to share. Even if it's not about him touching you, if you even kneel to him from ten feet away, it's sharing." He finally raised his face to me. "He can't force me to, and he can't force you to. But I crossed a line with Serena. I'll get a reputation. It's a small community. But I'm not doing it."

"If it's from ten feet away?"

"No. And the fact that you're even considering it? It's uncomfortable for me."

"I'm just trying to make your life a little easier."

"That's the sub talking, and that makes me uncomfortable too." He took my hand. That little touch cracked me open. I had to hold back another sob.

"Because subs aren't supposed to talk?" I bristled just enough for anger to temper the sobs.

"Because the sub is you."

I had questions about what he'd expected of bringing me to Montauk if not to bring out my inner submissive, but he was missing the point.

"Well," I said, "that was your wife talking."

A door slammed across the yard. Adam and I froze, hearing indistinct voices, the faraway words of a man and the softer cries of a woman.

Adam stood between the window and me. He didn't move.

"Another show?" I asked.

"Probably. But not what you think. Punishing a woman who likes to be punished can get complicated."

I could have shown him I trusted him by showing no interest in what was outside, but my body reacted to the unknown in the way it always did. I stepped toward the window and looked over Adam's shoulder. He moved behind me, and we watched together.

Serena brushed the last of the snow from a picnic chair and spread a blanket over it. Stefan sat down and crossed his legs. She bowed to him and walked to the left side of the yard, where the snow was untouched.

"It's pure devotion," I said. "And she doesn't mean any of it."

"She does."

"She wants you."

"Serving him still satisfies her."

Serena walked into the fresh snow, making grey footprints in the flat white expanse. Adam put his hand on the small of my back. She walked a straight line, then followed it back and jumped to leave a blank space.

"Why is the paddle on the window seat?" he asked in my ear.

"Serena left it."

"Your lip marks are on it."

I looked down at it. In the angle of the winter light, a dull *O* broke the sheen of the wood finish. I could deny they were mine, but what would be the point? The instrument was meant to be used.

He took a deep breath against my neck. I couldn't see him, so I couldn't tell if the sigh was arousal or annoyance.

Serena jumped once, making a single divot, jumped again, and walked a line parallel to the first. She ran back to the start and made a diagonal.

"What you did to Serena last night," I said. "I want you to do that to me."

"Why?"

Serena finished the letter *M* in the snow.

*I'M*

· · ·

I'd been brutally honest when I left him, but I'd been shallow. There was a more brutal, more honest truth to be told.

"I need it." My voice cracked.

Adam took half a step back. When I started to turn to face him, he held me in position, watching Serena in silence.

*I'M SO*

"You need it?" he asked.

"Yes. I can't explain why. Seeing you give that to her... I was jealous, but there was something else. I know you were angry, but I wished I was her. I wanted to be free."

*I'M SOR*

He ran his fingers down my back. "I want to break you right now. I've never wanted anything more in my life. At this point, I don't know whether to take you home and pretend this never happened or take you deeper with me."

"It's too late to pretend it didn't happen."

His hands caressed my ass, running under it and between my legs, getting his finger under my panties.

*I'M SORR*

"This works better if you're turned on already."

My clit was swollen and hungry for him. My eyes closed when he touched it. He was going to give it to me. My fear was the flame under my desire.

"Yes, sir."

He sucked in a breath. "Put your hands on the glass."

I bent at the waist. Adam leaned over me and picked up the paddle, putting it in front of my face.

"Kiss it again."


*I'M SORRY*


I kissed the wood reverently, letting my lips linger on it. The plane that was going to hurt me, dominate me, challenge me to be less and more than I'd ever been.

Adam ran his hand over my ass, up to my lower back, which he pressed down while he tapped my bottom with the paddle.

"Up," he said.

I pushed my ass up for him. The very act of offering him my body for his domination relaxed my muscles and quieted my mind.

How had I ever lived without this?


*I'M SORRY D*


"We go until she finishes your name. Ready?"

I nodded. My body responded with ecstatic vibrations humming with the sound of sexual pleasure.

"Say words."

"Yes, sir."

I heard the whistle in the air before the pain, which was more intense than I dreamed possible. I screamed. Stefan looked up. Serena stopped and met my eyes through the window. Stefan barked at her, and she continued.

Adam hooked his fingers in the waist of my underwear and slid them down, tapping my ankles to let me know I had to step out.

"I don't like screaming, but I understand you might not be able to help it. Open your mouth."

I did. He stuffed my underwear in my mouth.


*I'M SORRY DI*


Stefan was still looking up at us. Serena glanced up when she could take her eyes off her feet. Could she see me? I hoped so. I wanted her to know Adam was claiming me.

"What's your name?" Adam asked, stroking and tapping my ass.

"Eye-ah-uh."

The next stroke hit like a blowtorch, and I screamed into the taste of my cunt, twisting my legs. He pushed me straight, tapped, struck again.


*I'M SORRY DIA*


He rained a series of blows on my bottom and the backs of my thighs, first one side, then the other, then both. Burn on burn. He stopped for a moment to touch me, grabbing raw skin. I groaned from deep in my lungs, and he paddled me again.

Yes, I cried. My face was slick with tears. Tears of relief. I accepted that I needed something in this. Some release that had built up my entire life. A reset button. A reboot. A place where I only had to bend.

I was submissive.


*I'M SORRY DIAN*


. . .

I saw Serena finish the *N* through a fugue. I was floating, and Adam was the rope that held me fast to the earth with his will and his pain.


## *I'M SORRY DIANA*


"What's your name?" His voice cut through the soothing vapor of my surrender, transmitted through the clouds to kiss me with approval.

The high had nothing to do with the pain. The high was pleasing him. The high was from my choice to leave my own will behind, go further, endure more, give more.

I said my name.

My name was a rumble in my throat.

My name was a single, long sound.

My name was the shape of my body leaning on the window.

The light got dimmer as Adam leaned into my face, blocking the window. His hands framed my face.

"You are so deep in subspace," he said as he pulled my panties from my mouth.

I hoped that made him happy, because I wanted him to be happy, and I had no control over the dream state I'd entered.

He picked me up under my arms and knees and carried me to the bed before laying me out on my stomach. I couldn't do more than follow him with my eyes as he got things from the bathroom, arranged my body comfortably, put a blanket over me.

"Was I all right?" I asked, surprised by the huskiness of my voice.

He knelt by the side of the bed to be at my eye level. "Unreal. You're not broken, but I didn't expect you to take so much. Didn't expect subspace."

"Is that good?"

He wiped away tears I didn't know I'd shed. "Just stay still and let me take care of you."

The pain on my bottom was split by a line of cool balm. Adam spread it wherever I burned. Slowly, he worked it in, aggravating the bruises and raising another heat. He pulled my legs apart and massaged the insides of my thighs. I was coming out of subspace and into more familiar territory.

He put his hands on my hips. "Up on your knees."

He helped me move until my ass was up and I was exposed. He spread me apart. I was coming down from the high, and the pain of his touch made me cringe. When he ran his thumb over bruised muscles, I squeaked.

He slapped me lightly. "Shush. Trust me."

Before I could agree, he put his tongue around my opening, circling it. I was on fire, so close that when he sucked on my clit, I burst apart. But he didn't stop. He gave me orgasm after orgasm, until I was awake, aware, and screaming in ultimate pleasure.

I had only had the simplest words.

Good. Yes. Mine. Yes. More.

# CHAPTER EIGHTY-ONE

## PRESENT TENSE

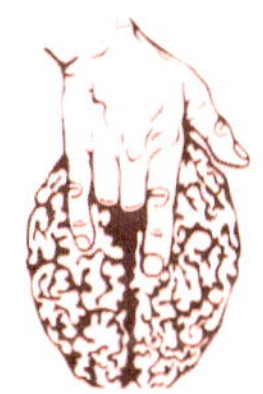

### DAY FOURTEEN

In the hours after he brought me back from subspace, I'd told him about the Manet. I'd never told anyone about it, and when he pulled up the painting on his phone, he said, "Wow. I wonder how many awakenings this thing is responsible for."

He'd fed me dinner in bed, and I fell asleep in his arms. He didn't pat my shoulder or look far away. He was completely, unequivocally present.

I woke at dawn with his hand on my cheek. His lashes flicked and his body rose and fell with his breath. I turned my head and kissed his palm, moving my lips to form words my throat wouldn't agree to make.

*"I love you."*

I loved complying. I loved hushing for him. Pleasing him. Trusting him.

I got out of bed. My body ached, and my ass was black and blue. It hurt to get dressed and walk down the stairs, but in a way, that reminded me of the pleasure of the day before.

The sky was the same deep blue as the ocean, tinged lighter at the horizon. I'd been in the house two weeks and hadn't walked on the beach.

The ocean called me. I felt strong, sure, joyful as I got on my coat and hawk scarf.

*Tell him you love him.*

I was going to tell him, and I was going to stand straight and tall when I did. Then I was going to kneel and he was going to fuck me like he owned me.

It was a plan.

I opened the back door and walked outside, shutting it behind me with a squeak and a slap. The sea was louder than I expected, and the salty wind bit my cheeks. I crossed the wooden deck, its furniture cushioned in smooth snow piles.

Down the wood stairs to the snowy grass, I steeled myself to tell him I loved him. Then we'd go back to Manhattan and...

And what? What if we had the same problems? What if my infatuation with this new Adam was no more than that? An infatuation with excitement and adventure? What if all the same shit reappeared in a week or a year and he was as distant as he ever was? Could I leave him twice? Could I ever screw up the courage again? And how old would I be? How much closer to the day I had to face what my mother had faced?

The backyard grass ended abruptly with a fence. Beyond it, the rocky beach took over. The sea undulated back and forth. The line between wet and dry made a sine wave thirty feet from the fence.

"It's high tide," a voice said in the blustering wind.

I snapped my head in the direction of the sound. Stefan in a pea coat and wooly ribbed cap. His eyes were riveting blue and his hands were in his pockets.

"It doesn't usually get this close. It concerns me."

My decision to go outside the gate was overruled by good sense. "I'm sure you have flood insurance." I put my hands on the top of the gate but didn't open it.

"Of course. But it won't stop the water if the water wants to come. We hold it back and it pushes forward. One for one. *Quid pro quo.*"

He was intimidating even when he smiled. Even when his hands were stuffed in his pockets and he was saying something general and philosophical about the tides.

"I'm sorry about what happened," I blurted. "I can explain."

He shook his head. "Don't. You did nothing wrong. I'm the one who's sorry. I love Serena, but she has a way of creating trouble." He leaned on the fence and looked over the ocean. "Have you seen the rocks on the beach? Schist mostly." He dug into his pocket and pulled out a fistful of small stones. He held them out to me.

I couldn't see the stones well. The sun just peeked over the horizon. It was still not quite daylight, but one stone stood out to me. It looked like a heart. Not a paper heart folded and cut, but a muscle. A living thing.

"This is interesting." I pointed at it, and he rolled it to his fingertips, holding it up. His hands were deft as a magician's.

"Yes," he agreed enthusiastically. "It's quartz. Not special, but this?" He pointed at what looked like a valve in the dark, but it was actually a rough fractal twisting around the smooth shape. "Coral from the Gulf Stream. It can attach to rocks and get carried away to foreign waters."

"It's beautiful."

He handed it to me. "It only lives one summer season up here. Then it dies and leaves this. Take it."

I took it and put it in my pocket.

"I thought he had no business bringing you here," Stefan said.

"And you changed your mind?"

He laughed to himself. "No, actually. But I understand his desperation." He put the rest of the stones in his pocket. "I'm losing Serena." He brushed a line of snow off the top of the gate. "When I leave her alone to respect her space, I lose her. When I pin her down, I feel her leaving me. If I thought a trip to the suburbs for thirty days of vanilla sex would bind her to me, I'd try it."

"Vanilla's a state of mind."

"Touché." He smiled ruefully. "Nothing lasts forever, I guess."

"I'm sorry." I kneaded the rock in my cold fingers. I felt for him in a way I hadn't felt for Adam when I hurt him. I hadn't steeled my heart against Stefan.

"I saw you here and I thought, 'Ah, talk to her. She's in Serena's shoes. She'll tell you what to do.'" He waved off his own stupid ideas. "The desperate strategies of a desperate man."

I put my hand on his shoulder. "It's going to be fine."

"The owner of all your pain and pleasure has arrived," Stefan said, indicating behind me with a jerk of his chin.

Adam was taking big steps across the back deck. He wore a fresh shirt and trousers, but his shoes were untied and he wasn't wearing a jacket.

"I didn't tell you to get out of bed," he said when he was close.

"You never needed to tell me before."

His look crumpled me like a piece of paper with the wrong words on it. The many ways to tell a man to go fuck himself shot up my throat, only to be trapped behind my teeth when I locked my mouth shut.

"I see how much you want to be punished," he said, holding up one finger. He slowly lowered it. "Knees."

Knees? He wanted me to kneel in front of Stefan? Over what? I was touching Stefan's shoulder but there was a fence between us, and more importantly, fuck him.

"Huntress. Do not disobey me."

His tone didn't speak to the Diana who told him to fuck himself. It spoke directly to the part of me that needed his ownership. I couldn't pretend that his voice wasn't a physical force to that need.

I put my knees in the snowy grass.

"So pretty from this angle," Stefan said. The same guy who had just spoken to me in desperation was now the voice of humiliation.

"She is," Adam replied. Then, by a change of tone, he spoke to me. "Crawl back to the house and wait for me in your room. Go."

I'd said I wouldn't crawl for him. I'd stated it explicitly in black and red and white. But I'd also said he couldn't hit me with a paddle and he couldn't gag me. I also said I wouldn't call him sir.

I'd leapt over my own boundaries, and let him leap over the rest.

I put my hands on the cold deck. I had to stop. My heart was beating too hard and my pussy went code red with need. Hands and knees in front of these men, I fell back into where I'd been the day before.

I must have taken too long to think about it. Even as I knew I was going to do exactly what Adam asked, I hesitated.

He unbuckled his belt and yanked it out of the loops in one move. He stood right in front of me, crotch to face, and folded the belt in two. "Open your mouth."

I did, and before the obscenities I had ready came marching out, he put the belt in it.

"Bite."

Stefan laughed derisively, as if he was partnering with Adam in this particular leap over a sub's limits.

My knees were getting cold. I had to decide to obey him or not.

I bit down into the leather of my husband's belt.

"Now. Crawl inside. And keep your ass in the air. I'll see you upstairs." His tone wasn't unkind, but it did reveal an expectation of compliance. He wasn't asking. He was neither impatient nor shrill.

I'd been living with a god all these years and never knew.

He snapped his fingers and I dropped to my hands. "Go."

My body jerked to obey as if his will was a natural force. I moved one hand, then one knee. The shallow layer of ice and snow crunched under me.

My mind fell into a swoon. I was permitted to do this, first by myself, then by Adam. His protection made it possible. I felt them behind me, watching my disgrace as my tongue tasted the leather of the belt. My ass still hurt from the paddle. The thought of the sting of that belt on top of it didn't cause fear, but a hopeful anticipation.

When I got to the door, I had to stand to open it. In the reflection of the glass, I saw Adam standing silently, facing the ocean, in the middle distance between Stefan and me. His back was as strong and solid as a brick wall. I slid the door open and got on my feet.

I took the belt out of my mouth. I probably wasn't supposed to even be standing, much less removing it without permission.

Adam still stood, feet spread apart, hands balled into fists at his side. Stefan hadn't moved either. Only the tide had shifted.

What did he want me to do?

What did he need me to do?

His room faced the back. I ran upstairs. I could be obedient and satiate my curiosity at the same time. But by the time I got to his room and pressed my nose to the back window, they were gone.

# CHAPTER EIGHTY-TWO

## PRESENT TENSE

## DAY FIFTEEN

HE CAME BEHIND ME, swooping into the room with the force of the sun's gravity. He took me by the back of the neck and pushed me down to my knees.

I wouldn't have tolerated that a month ago.

Not the violence or the attitude.

But this was Montauk.

I stayed on my knees, head down, hands on my thighs. He stood over me, snow crusted on his boots and melting sludge onto the hardwood.

"Don't talk to him. Not without me in the room."

Still in my submissive posture, I answered the only way I could. "Are you kidding me?"

"I don't trust him."

"Maybe you should try trusting *me*."

I kept my eyes on my hands. My position contradicted my words, but I had a deep feeling I knew was correct, that Adam would hear me better if we were still in the game.

"I do," he said.

"Really?"

He laid his hands on my shoulders and slid them down my back, hooking his fingers under my arms. He picked me up, and we faced each other. Those lips, those eyes, the stubble on a jaw that defied geometry. I couldn't look at it. I unbuttoned my coat.

"No," he said. "I guess not."

"Now you're talking." I threw my coat on the bed and sat in the upholstered chair. He was making my knees weak. "Stefan and I were just talking. It wasn't anything. He wasn't trying to come between us."

"What were you talking about?"

"Rocks. And Serena. You'd think, with what he does and how he acts, that he doesn't love her. But he does."

Adam sat on the bed. "He does. Of course. What you see is what they need. But that doesn't mean he's not a predator."

"I've handled predators."

"Yeah. Maybe. As the old Diana, you did. But you're changing. I can see it. It's like watching a flower bloom. You're so beautiful when you let go. But you're leaving and you're taking the change with you, and there's not a goddamn thing I can do about it. All I get is the time here. Two more weeks. Then you're on your own, and there are going to be dozens of men like that. Trust me. They're in the fucking woodwork, and when you're single—"

"Wait—"

"—I have to tolerate it, but I can't watch it. Not here."

"—let's—"

Stay together.

Be married.

Start over.

I couldn't choose between them, and the words got caught in my throat.

"I need time," he said, and I cut myself off. "I need to decide if we should finish this."

"Do I get a say?"

He stood. "Technically, yes. But if we go home now because I stopped it, you get everything. Done."

"This stopped being about McNeill-Barnes a week ago."

"It was never about McNeill-Barnes for me."

Right. I knew that. It was about me. Him. It was about our marriage.

"I want to stay," I said.

"I know."

He walked out and closed the door.

# CHAPTER EIGHTY-THREE

## PRESENT TENSE

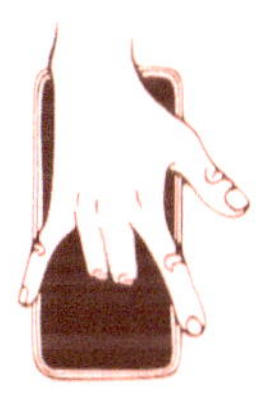

## DAY FIFTEEN

HE'D LEFT me with a feeling of unease. He wasn't telling me everything. I was ready to explode, and he was holding back. When he held back, I held back, and I couldn't do that anymore. He might turn back into Manhattan Adam and a million crappy things could happen, but the idea of signing divorce papers when we got back was absurd.

*What do you want?*

I knew what I wanted. I got dressed, showered, and ran downstairs to tell him.

He'd left me a note on the counter.

*Went into the city to see Charlie. Back by dinner.*

Fine. Actually, this would do nicely. I put bread in the toaster and composed the note in my head.

Stefan came in from the gym. "Hello. How are you?"

"Good. Great, actually."

He leaned on the counter, arms crossed. "I wanted to ask you something about yesterday."

"All right." I hoped he wasn't going to ask me to talk about Adam. I couldn't speak for him. I was about to say something polite in that vein when Stefan's phone rang.

He plucked it out of his pocket and looked at the screen. "My mother. I'll come back later?"

"Knock first."

He took the call and rattled off a good-humored conversation in what must have been a Scandinavian language. He waved and went out the back door, crossing over to the studio.

I rummaged through the drawers in the library until I found a notebook and a pencil. I slid the wingback chair to the dresser, and I began the relationship the way I'd ended it.

*Dear Adam,*

*After everything we've been through, there's no easy way to tell you this. So I'm just going to spit it out.*

*I love you.*

Out the window, the morning sky was a clear glass blue and our way together was in front of us. I rewrote the note a hundred times and finished in the late afternoon, over lunch. He'd gone out to decide whether to stay and finish, but I knew what I wanted and I needed to tell him before he opened his mouth. He needed to know I was committed to staying before he told me his decision.

I left my note on the kitchen counter. Seconds after I turned my back on it, the long black car crunched down the drive.

He was back.

# CHAPTER EIGHTY-FOUR

## PRESENT TENSE

## DAY FIFTEEN

*Dear Adam,*

*After everything we've been through, there's no easy way to tell you this. So I'm just going to spit it out.*

*I love you.*

I ran upstairs when I saw the car. Threw on one of the short nightgowns he liked and went into his room. He'd go to the kitchen to look for me. Get a glass of water. See the note. Come upstairs.

It was going to be great. I didn't have an ounce of remorse for a damn thing. Yes, I'd left him. Yes, it took a lot of balls. Yes, I was going to reverse it, and yes, I felt very good about that.

*Thup.* The car door.

*Scrape.* The bags.

*Click.* The front door.

*Murmur.* Adam and Thierry talking.

*Click.* The front door again.

*Squeak-snap.* The closet door opening and closing.

*Creak.* Footsteps on the stairs.

He didn't go to the kitchen. Wonderful, handsome, caring, dominant man. He came right to me. I got on my knees and elbows, spread my legs, and raised my ass. He was going to have to fuck me without the note. He'd find it after, but I wanted him to find it without warning, the way he'd found the first note. The symmetry made my self-discovery feel complete.

He was in the hall. I could hear him. He opened the door to my room first. Would he come through the hall or the door between our rooms? I adjusted to face the door between the rooms, showing him his options. Serving him.

Those seconds of waiting were the purest satisfaction. Nothing had ever felt so good to me.

He came through the adjoining door. Stopped. I knew from the sound.

My heart was pounding.

I wanted to look at him so I'd know what he thought, how to adjust, how to do everything he needed, the way he needed.

"Perfect," he said.

*Yes!*

He threw his coat on the bed and kneeled behind me. When he stroked my bottom, the bruises ached, and when he ran his fingers along my seam, he touched every ache that had been building since he'd left.

"Everything about this is perfect." He slid his hands up my body and curled his body over mine.

I went flat under the weight of him. "You're staying?"

"If you want."

I fell into the happiness. He'd find the note and know I wanted more than a two-week finish. One bite of joy at a time.

"Thank you," I said. "And thank Charlie."

He spoke softly into my ear. "We have a lot to talk about, but not tonight. You're going to break tonight. You're going to beg me to stop."

"I won't."

He got off me and stood. "Get on the bed. Legs up."

I crawled up the high bed and got on my back, opening my legs for him. The nude woman in the Manet looked right at the viewer and dared them to have a problem with her. She was going to let those two men do whatever they wanted whether anyone approved or not. I was her.

"What's your safe word?" he asked.

"Pinochle."

He took one of my feet and put his lips to the inside of my ankle. Had any kiss ever been so sexy?

"Why?"

"When my mom died, my father and I stayed up late playing pinochle because we couldn't sleep. I felt safe."

He dropped my ankle and pulled down the horizontal bar, sliding it along the track. He rested my feet on it. "You're safe here too."

Adam opened a wooden box, and I heard the clink of metal. He came into my vision with a silver object. It looked like interconnected and fused rings, shined to a flawless polish.

"Give me your hands."

I held up my hands. Adam guided them into the rings, where they crossed together, wrist to wrist, and held them over my head.

He stepped out of my view. I heard him get undressed, buttons, belt buckle, pants sliding down. He took his time, until he stood over me in only his unbuttoned shirt.

"You look terrified," he said. "And aroused."

"Listen to the arousal."

He pulled a long silver chain from the wooden box, slowly so that each little ball in the chain flicked the edge and I could get a long look at the rubber-tipped clamps at the end.

"Charlie convinced me all the shit I was worrying about wasn't worth worrying about."

"Like what?"

"I've never loved a woman I've broken. I can't do it to you. Can't turn you into something you aren't. Something I don't love."

He extended his finger and, with a swift motion, spun the chain, making it helicopter and wrap around, sheathing his finger in ball chain. With the clamps tucked into his palm, he got his shirt off.

"What I feel for you," he said, tossing the shirt away. "It's worth protecting. I hated how I felt when you left, but now I don't want to lose it."

"You won't."

Kneeling between my open legs, he put his hands on my breasts and slid them down, the texture of the chain making a line of sensation on my skin.

"I've never loved a sub. I've never wanted to love a woman who's part of that world. I could never get past the negotiations, the scenes. It felt disposable, and that kept me from loving anyone." He dragged his hands over my thighs and back again, resting them on my tits. "If I can love you, even if you don't love me—"

"But I—"

"Hush. Let me finish. I need to see if it's possible. Only answer yes or no. Will you do this with me?"

"Yes."

"I'm signing everything over even if you say no. Easiest divorce in the world. Will you still stay here? Yes or no?"

"Yes."

He pinched my nipples and pulled. His chained finger hurt my left side in a way that went right to my core. Then he brought his hands down again, and the finger with the chain wrapped around it found my clit.

"Yes," I said as he dragged the tiny silver balls along me, back and forth until he slowly put that finger inside. Every ridge started a new wave of sensation. I pushed against the paired roughness and smoothness, and slowly he pulled out.

"The fantasies I've had these past years," he said, unwrapping the chain. "I couldn't even let myself put you in them." He let the wet chain dangle from his fingertips. There were three clamps. "Destroying you is a dream I was afraid to have."

He took two of the clamps in one hand. Silver. Black rubber tips. About the size of bobby pins. He yanked on my right nipple with the other hand, rough, assured, as if doing a job efficiently.

He clamped it. I must have made a face or something, because when he took the other nipple, holding it out, he said, "It doesn't hurt now.

Just wait," and clamped it. The chain ran down my belly and ended in another clamp.

"Oh," I said. "Oh, no."

"Don't make me gag you."

He bent his head between my thighs and kissed my clit, ending with a suck. It was so good. Adam knew how to work a clit with a flick and a suck. Always. I was nearly lost in it when he pinched the nub and clamped it at the base.

I squeaked and closed my legs.

"Spread those legs. Show me."

I did, and he pressed them back, looking closely at how he'd done. He glanced up at me.

"I'm taking your ass. Not tonight. But before we go back."

He waited for my answer. Or, more accurately, he waited for me to say no. I was so deep in submission I couldn't say no, and still so deeply myself I couldn't say yes either. He smiled as if reading my mind and ran his tongue along the tight skin stretched over my clit. It felt as if he'd licked some deeper pleasure. A pleasure that had always been there, behind layers of skin and membrane.

I groaned deeply.

"You ready, huntress?" He moved the bar back up, letting my feet dangle in midair.

"Yes."

He positioned his cock at my opening and slammed deep into me. Stopped. His eyes closed and he bent his head.

"I'm sorry. I have to say this." He clamped his hand over my mouth and spoke into my ear. "I always knew. I didn't want to admit it, but I always knew this was you. It scared the hell out of me, and I denied it. I needed to love you more than I wanted to dominate you. Don't doubt for a second that I chose to love you."

He took his hand away and jerked his hips. With the hood of my clit peeled back by the clamp, every thrust felt like an explosion, like a kid setting off a mat of firecrackers on July 4th. The popping and cracking went on and on, and when he straightened himself and pulled on the chain that held my nipples and clit, an M80 went off. I strained against the wrist restraints.

"Don't come," he said, thrusting.

"I want to."

"Don't." He pounded me, fisting the chain, letting go, tugging one way and not the other until I thought I'd lose control.

"I need—" The sentence died. I was going to come whether he liked it or not.

"No, you don't."

He pinched one nipple clip then the other, taking them off.

They went on fire in a flush of explosive pain. I thought my breasts were going to burst, but Adam smiled, bit his lower lip, and fucked me harder.

The pain removed the need to come for a minute, but it returned stronger than before, as if the pleasure was too ambitious to let the hurt win. It had to come in a harder, heavier rush.

I barely had a chance to tell him how close I was. He knew. He straightened and pulled my labia open with two fingers.

That pain.

Between my legs.

"No!" I shouted.

"No screaming."

"Please!"

"Breathe through your nose. Look at me when I come inside you."

He took off the clamp. I held my mouth shut like a vise and sucked air in and out of my nose. The blood rushed back, expanding me in fire and pain. I was almost blind as my husband buried his cock in me and came in slower thrusts, groaning deep.

The pain flowed out, leaving a bigger space for the pleasure rushing to take its place.

"Come, Diana. Come."

I stiffened under him, arched, pushing him deeper. I cried and came so hard I didn't feel the cuffs cut into my skin, and it went on so long, I thought I was losing my mind.

~

Hours. He fucked me for hours. He tied me up and took pleasure and pain. He took control. He left me on the edge of orgasm for twenty minutes while he held my head down and put his fingers in my ass. It felt so good I begged him to put his cock in it.

He wouldn't, and I cried because I had no will or want after that.

He'd broken me, and I was so out of myself I didn't realize it until he went downstairs to get water.

He'd broken me and I still loved him.

# CHAPTER EIGHTY-FIVE
## PRESENT TENSE

## DAY FIFTEEN

*Dear Adam,*

*After everything we've been through, there's no easy way to tell you this. So I'm just going to spit it out.*

*I love you.*

*I never thought I'd ever say it again. Believe me, if I thought we had a chance, I wouldn't have written you that other note. But you made the chance. You did it. You showed me the you inside you and the me inside me.*

*My god. We wasted so much time.*

*Let's make it all up. Let's go back home and do this all over again. I'll be everything you need and you'll be everything I didn't know I needed. We'll get the company going again. We'll be partners in the boardroom, and in the bedroom, you'll bring me to my knees whenever you want. You'll be my Master.*

*You win. I lose, but I win. I'm yours again.*

*I love you more than ever,*

*Your Little Huntress.*

• • •

I must have fallen asleep, because it was four in the morning and Adam still wasn't in bed. I was still floppy-limbed, sore, aching, made of dough that had been kneaded but not baked.

Had he found the note?

I didn't know how long he'd been downstairs, but if he went to the kitchen for water, he would have seen it.

What did he think?

Was he writing me a note back?

I got into my nightgown and tiptoed downstairs. He wasn't in the library or the kitchen. I found him in the dark office, framed by a window, facing the darkness between the big house and the studio. He was in pajama pants that hung low on his waist, just below the divots on each side of his lower back. His shoulders were rippled with muscles in tension.

I went in. The floor creaked. He looked around. When I put my hands on his back, he moved away, turning to face me.

"Hey, I was wondering what happened to you," I said. "I left you a note."

He held up his hand. The note was in it, folded into three parts, past over future.

If he'd read it, he didn't look incredibly pleased by what it said. Maybe he didn't believe it, or maybe he'd misunderstood it. Maybe I'd misunderstood. But suddenly I was off balance. I needed him. I was flailing and I didn't even know why. Quicksand or water. Falling fast or drifting slow. Everything in the world had turned upside-down, and I needed him to show me which way our shared gravity pulled.

"Talk to me," I said.

"I know you thought I brought you here to make you love me again."

"I do love you."

He took a breath so deep, his shoulders rose and his chest expanded. "I did something truly evil. I came here with you to break you so I could stop loving you. Then I could cut you loose easily. That's why I waited. I didn't know who I was if I wasn't loving you. I had to let that idea go. Took two weeks."

I didn't get this. He loved me but didn't want to? Was that it? I was confused.

"Did you read the note?"

"Yeah." He tossed it on the desk as if it was a contract with missing redlines. "I did. And it didn't surprise me. I knew it. You loved me, and I loved you."

"Why do you keep using the past tense?"

He flicked my note aside and picked up a piece of paper under it. He wedged it between his index and middle finger and handed it to me. "This was on the counter."

It was a card. I opened it.

*D—*

*We need to talk.*

*—S*

"Okay? So?"

"I decided today that I could do this. You are submissive. You proved that yesterday and I still loved you. I failed to stop loving you, and I hate failing. But I could get something better. You. I could live without lies, and you could be mine. You could make the impossible possible."

"You're freaking me out. What does that have to do with the note?"

"If you'd stop interrupting, you'd know."

I went cold. His tone wasn't dominant with expectation of obedience, but commanding in its disappointment. I'd been on my knees. I'd crawled. I'd offered my body to him as an object to use, but he'd never made me feel worthless.

At home, he couldn't have gotten to me. But in that office in the early morning dark, I was cut open, broken, vulnerable. He'd taken my armor, carefully unlocked it, slipped it off, and hidden it. When he spoke that pointless phrase in that tone of voice, I was in no position to hear it without hurt.

"Go on," I said with no tools to stop the tears from coming.

"This note. I know you're not fucking Stefan. But it presupposes that you're accessible for a chat. That's on him. You didn't do anything wrong. Nothing about it is a big deal, except it told me you've crossed over into the world I left, and then, I just changed." He snapped his fingers. "Like that." He tapped the note on the heel of his hand, pausing to think. "If I wanted you in this world, I would have brought you along. I would have started a little kinky and broken you by our first anniversary. But it's not what I want. Not then, not now."

"You stopped loving me? Over a note?"

"It's not the note. I have love for you, it's not what it was and it never will be again, but what little there is? It's mine, and I'm not giving it up. I'm not going to destroy the only woman I've ever loved. That's why I'm letting you go."

What was my expression? Open-mouthed, head shaking, eyes squinting, brows knotted, I must have been a sight.

"You can't do this," I said.

"I have to."

"You made me love you and now—"

"You never told me you didn't want to split up. I didn't know until it was too late."

"You just... hours... we were doing it for hours. Did you not love me that whole time?"

A tiny crack played across his hard expression. "You were perfect."

"Stop it!" I shouted. "Stop it now. Tell me I'm yours!" I pushed him as hard as I could, but he didn't fall. "You love me! You're mine. Do you understand? You fucking bossy asshole. You prick. You motherfucker, you're mine and you love me!"

He took my face in his hands and leaned down so I could see him clearly. I looked away, but he shifted so the only thing in my vision was him, slowly shaking his head.

"I'm sorry," was all he said.

"Fuck you," I sputtered.

No. We'd entered this room as husband and wife. Dom and sub. Business partners and friends. If we left this room as something else, we'd always be that something else. We'd be ex-things. Ex-partners. Ex-husband and wife. Ex ex ex.

Once we were out of the room, there was no going back.

I took one step closer to him and lowered myself to my knees. I was at war. He hadn't told me to drop, and I did.

"Diana. Don't."

I bent at the waist and pressed my palms and nose to the floor.

"This is what you wanted." I spoke into the floor. "Take me this way."

"Do you think I went to all this trouble to make you kneel? If I needed to get a sub for a month, I would have just gotten one and given you your divorce."

He stepped over me, and I scrambled to get in front of him. I dropped to my knees and put my face and hands to the floor again.

"Last night," I said into the fringed edge of the rug, "what was last night?"

"Get up."

I didn't move.

"It felt like love," I said.

"Diana, you don't have to submit."

"I trusted you. I trusted it was real."

"Get up!"

"Fuck you! Tell me! Was it real?"

He took me by the arms and pulled me up. I was jelly in his arms, but he fought gravity and good sense.

"It was very real, but I realized how toxic it was. To have someone I love in that world. Don't you get it? I'd stop loving you completely."

"You won't," I said. "You love me. I don't know why you're doing this. I don't know what the game is... but you love me."

He let me go, and I stood on wobbly knees.

"Thierry will drive you home tomorrow. I'll fill out the papers. We're done. It's for the best."

"Fuck you," I said. "You love me."

I dropped to my knees again. I was out of breath, heart pounding, tense, and shitty-feeling, inside and out.

He patted my head, leaving me on the floor as he went upstairs.

# CHAPTER EIGHTY-SIX
## PRESENT TENSE

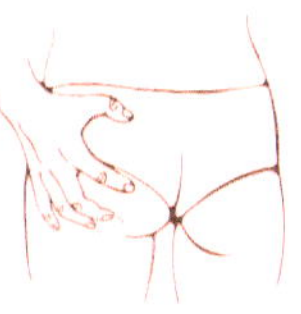

HE'D DISAPPEARED BEHIND A DOOR. Willa had packed for me. Outside my window, Stefan and Serena loaded up his shitty pickup and left.

I got in the back of the limo alone. Thierry didn't ask where we were going.

I was going home.

# CHAPTER EIGHTY-SEVEN

## PRESENT TENSE

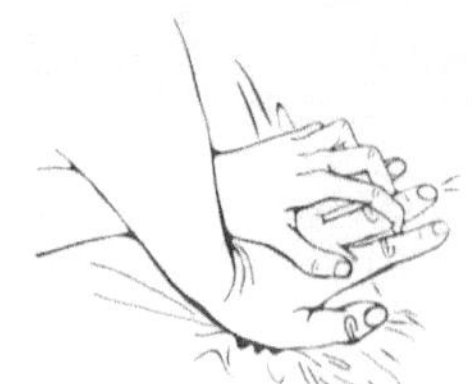

THE DAY my life changed was different than any other. I kneeled and was stepped over. I begged and was refused. I submitted, but no one claimed dominion over me.

The limo was quiet. The tires made no sound over the Southern State. The windows were closed against the wind. My sobs were silent, the way they were before he taught me how to cry.

The day everything changed, I felt different. I had work to do. A life. Bills. A mortgage. But all my routines seemed foreign and futile. Did I ever perform them? Did they ever matter?

The morning my life changed, I sat in the back of a limousine, staring at a small swatch of fabric that lay in the corner like a wound. It took me fifteen minutes to decide to pick it up.

It was a piece of the stocking he'd ripped off me to rub my feet, a million years ago, when he loved me.

I had a sense of impending doom. A gut feeling that I was ruined. I couldn't believe in healing. Not for me. Because I wasn't a victim here. This was my fault.

All of it. I'd been lazy and fearful. I'd left him and told myself I'd been courageous, but I'd been a coward.

And if my pain was my fault, I had to take responsibility for it. I had to fix it. I had to fix myself, of course, but this man I loved needed help too. I scrunched the stocking up in my fist.

*He didn't have a choice.*

*Why?*

*He said to trust him.*

*Why?*

*He told me he's preserving his love.*

*Why why why?*

Something wasn't adding up.

*He can love a submissive. He can and he does.*

I was right with myself for the first time, even in pain, because to submit is to understand your sun and your shadow. To submit is to know your place is not always a *where* but sometimes a *when*. To submit is to accept your power and to embrace that your place is both *now* and *forever*.

To submit is to choose. To hunt. To chase. To decide.

To submit is to dominate.

Adam was mine.

I chose him.

I'd thrown him away, and I could choose him again. I could finish this. I could stand by what I wanted, who I was.

There were two weeks left in our arrangement.

They were mine, and so was he.

# SEPARATION GAMES

# DIANA

# CHAPTER ONE

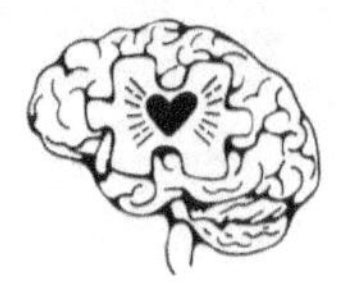

## DAY FIFTEEN

TODAY IS the first day of the rest of my life, and I have no idea how to live it.

Today is the day I make a plan, implement it, and see it through to the end.

Today is the day I prepare to win.

I will take no prisoners but myself. I'll defeat no enemy but my fear.

This is worth it. He is worth it.

Hold your breath.

Hold it for 1,209,600 seconds.

Then.

Breathe.

Because he will be yours.

# CHAPTER TWO

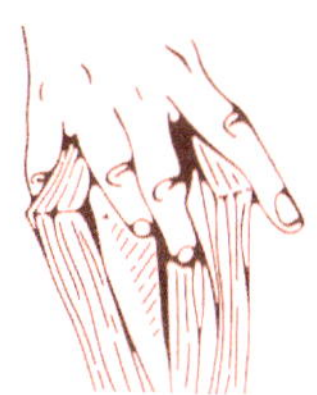

## DAY SEVENTEEN

What can you learn about a man from his office?

I hadn't even had the sense to ask that question when I met Adam, and I should have. His R+D office was stark and clean. It had no history. It gave away nothing. You didn't sense a thing about its owner but the level of his taste.

That was simply the way he ran his business. But standing in his office, with the afternoon sun bending through the glass tabletops, I knew he had run his personal life the same way.

I'd walked past Eva on the way in. She'd warn him I was here. I was ready for that.

The office building across 53$^{rd}$ Street seemed close enough to touch, and the street below seemed far enough away to kill on impact.

My phone said he was a block away. He hadn't shut off the phone tracker after Montauk, and neither had I after he'd found me at the Cellar. Despite everything, we tracked each other. Proof that no matter what the level of our hearts' betrayal, our souls knew where we belonged.

Two days, and I didn't know how I was going to get him back. I'd managed, somehow, to get through the trip home from Montauk. I'd managed to let myself into the loft, walk past my four bags just inside the door, put my keys on the counter. I'd managed to move a chair to the window and sit there looking at the water towers, rooftop gardens, and fire escapes.

Staring was not a plan. It wasn't how a woman in charge ran her life. It wasn't how a person finished a thing. But that was what I had done, and I forgave myself for it. I'd left my husband with a note on the counter. I'd spent months gathering the courage, composing the note, being sure in my head and heart that it was the right thing.

I didn't have months to get him back.

He'd agreed to an easy divorce if I gave him thirty days. Sixteen were gone. It had taken me that long to love him again. The real me loved the real him. It had taken that long for him to fall out of love with me.

Fourteen more days, and I didn't have a plan.

That morning, I'd found stockings and garter in the bottom of my drawer. The bra had a crystal heart between the breasts, and the panties had one to match. I tossed them onto the bed. I shaved myself smooth and put the lingerie on. I stood in front of the mirror and watched myself fall to my knees. I put my ass up, lower back down, forehead to the floor, knees apart. I stayed that way, thinking about nothing but his body until my thighs ached.

Holding that position with that thought cleared my mind enough to do something. Even if it was the wrong thing, it was something.

His phone stopped moving in front of the building. He'd taken a cab.

*Deep breath.*

He had a small table by the couch. The top was made of cracked tempered glass. There used to be a picture of me on that table.

The dot on the map moved again. He'd arrived in the city at the crack of dawn, according to the tracking on his phone. I didn't know what he'd done during the past two days in Montauk. I tried not to think my worst thoughts.

I'd considered positioning myself on my hands and knees when he arrived, sitting with my legs crossed, spread-eagled on the desk, standing like a lady, hiding in the closet. I figured it would come to me when I needed it.

My strategy was set. My tactics were planned. I left room for inspiration in the minutiae.

Even when I knew he was coming down the hall, I hadn't decided.

I heard his voice outside the door. Eva's reply. Business. Did she tell him I was here?

When the door swung open, I was standing by his desk, wringing my hands as if they were made of dough.

He wore a grey suit I hadn't seen before. His shoulders seemed straighter than ever, and his green tie was knotted in perfect symmetry. He looked taller. He walked like royalty. As if he were unstoppable, as if breaking through obstacles was a waste of time. There were no obstacles. Not for him. Not for a Master.

I must have been a madwoman to walk away from him.

He stopped two steps in, seeing me. Eva was right behind him, wearing an emerald-green suit and shoes.

"By the way," she said, winking at me behind his back, "Diana's here."

I dropped my hands to my sides because my heart submitted, and I leaned all my weight onto one hip because my mind was petulant. "Good morning."

He looked me up and down. "Good morning."

"I'll catch you when you're done," Eva said, backing out of the office.

"No," Adam commanded. "Stay. This won't be long."

He came to his desk. Nine steps. Big steps. I didn't move. Eva cocked her head slightly. Our gazes met, and she widened her eyes a little, letting me know she didn't want to run interference.

Adam put his briefcase on the desk and snapped it open. "How was your ride home?"

"Lonely."

"Sorry, I—"

I cut off his meaningless, pat answer. "You should have been there fucking me."

His hands stopped. He tapped his briefcase twice, thinking. His lashes were closed curtains over his emotions.

I continued while I had the upper hand. "Eva being here isn't going to stop me from doing what I came to do."

I put my hands on my jacket buttons, pushing the top one through the hole. He looked up just in time to see that I wasn't wearing anything but a bra under it.

"You kids," Eva said. "This is great fun, but I have a job."

The door whooshed open and clicked shut as she left.

Adam's presence took up my entire world. I leaned on the desk next to him. My skirt rode up enough for the garter to peek out. I wanted him to tell me to do something, anything. Get off the desk. Button your jacket. Walk three steps. Spread your legs. Open your mouth.

"Too bad," I said, hands behind me. My jacket strained against the last button. "I would have done whatever you asked in front of her."

He took a few folders out of his briefcase and slapped them on the desk. "That's the problem, Diana."

"What? That I'll do whatever you want?"

"Yes." He closed the briefcase.

"We have two more weeks. I'm sticking to the agreement."

"The agreement's done. You win." He slid the folders toward me. I didn't even look at them.

"There were only contingencies if I quit. There's no contingency if you quit." I put my hands together behind me and spread my feet. I was uncomfortable as hell, leaning back on the desk with my legs apart.

"You get everything," he said, eyes coursing around the arc of my body. His dick was hard.

"I don't want everything. I want you."

"Diana. I can't... I can't do this."

His body said otherwise. He leaned toward me slightly. His breath had gotten shallow and slow.

"Yes, you can. You can do whatever you want to me. Things you never thought I'd do. You can hurt me. Hurt me so bad, and I'll beg you for more." I throbbed with those words. I wanted to come for him.

He put his hand on my thigh, sliding it inside and upward. I groaned. His touch was magic. I had to hold back from losing my shit right there.

"I didn't want this for you. I didn't want to turn you into this."

"Into what?"

"This." He ran his hand where my panties would be and found nothing but soaking wet pussy. "Look what I've done already. You'd do whatever I asked in front of Eva. In the office. Wearing nothing. I don't want you to be this."

"This what?"

"*This!*" He pinched my clit, and I grunted in surprise and pain. "This," he whispered in my ear while his hard cock pressed on my thigh.

"Your whore?"

He grabbed my hair with his other hand and yanked my head back. No one had ever done that to me, and I loved it. Loved the pain. The domination. The way he growled at me.

"Don't you ever, ever—"

"Your. Whore."

With a sharp breath, he took his hands off me, holding them up as if he had to prove they were empty. "Stand up straight."

He commanded it, so I did it.

"I can't do this." He cut the air with his determination. "Listen to me when I tell you I can spend the next two weeks fucking you blind and beating you raw. At the end of it, I'm walking away and you're going to be worse off. I promise the longer this goes on, the less I'm going to care how much I hurt you. Drop it now, while it's not that bad."

I straightened my skirt. "It's not that bad?"

"Before you get in deeper and there's no way out. Please."

His plea was a command. I'd take a certain kind of order from him. I'd humiliate myself if he asked the right way, but I couldn't stop loving him just because he demanded it.

I buttoned my jacket. He took my pause as agreement.

"You'll see it's better this way," he said, tapping the folders. "I've had my lawyer draft a revised divorce settlement. You should look at it."

"Should I send you back the ashes when I'm done burning it?"

"Diana—"

"Don't Diana me. Don't tell me how I feel. Don't protect me. I didn't ask you to. All I'm asking you to do is finish what you started. Train me. Don't leave me half done."

"I can't."

"Why not?"

"Because if I continue, whatever feelings you have are going to get blown out of all proportion. It's the nature of the game. I'm protecting you."

"From what?"

"From me," he barked.

I tensed from the sudden change in volume.

He pressed his lips into a line and held up his hands as if warding me off. "I don't care if you like it or not, but you'll thank me in the end."

"I'll thank you now." I stood straight and picked up my bag. "I'm going to be in the office. Our office. And you know where I live. You can sign the divorce papers, but I won't file them until our agreement expires."

I turned my back on him and walked to the door. As every step pulled me farther, the tether between us got thin enough to break.

"You can hang onto them then," he said from behind me.

I stopped but faced the door. I couldn't look at him. He pitied me, and it was impossible to truly love what you pitied.

"Take your time," he continued. "You get everything, don't worry about that."

Everything.

Sure. Everything that could be transferred by a piece of paper.

I didn't tell him how woefully inadequate "everything" was, because he wouldn't understand it. I just walked through the door without looking back, down the hall, nodding at Eva in her emerald-green suit and earrings, to the elevator. I kept my chin up, but a cloud of sadness and despair hung over me, ready to descend as soon as I got onto the street.

I pressed the elevator button, and the red light in the center glowed as it was supposed to. It wasn't broken. Press it and the light went on.

Like Adam.

When I'd offered him my body, he lit up like a Christmas tree, exactly as I thought he would. He'd touched me. He'd put his fingers on me. His hands took what his mouth said he didn't want.

Me.

The little red light went out, and the elevator doors rumbled open. They closed with me alone inside, and I went down, giving birth to an idea that was nearly fully formed by the time the doors opened again.

This was doable. I just had to finish what I started.

# CHAPTER THREE

## DAY EIGHTEEN

Dad had put his desk in my office, leaving my space untouched. He hadn't been the more organized of the McNeill-Barnes husband-and-wife team, and obviously that hadn't changed. My inbox was piled high with things that could wait but shouldn't.

We sat on my office couches, and he briefed me from a handwritten notebook on his lap. He wasn't using the oxygen tank, which initially gave me confidence. After a few words, I realized my confidence was his goal.

"Nadine put little Ray over there." Dad pointed at a bright blue blanket with boxes of Legos stacked to the side.

"Why?"

"Just Tuesday and Thursday mornings."

"It's fine. But why?"

"I couldn't just let her call in sick. And he's a good boy."

"Dad. Is. She. All. Right?"

He stopped to take a breath. Talking too much was a strain and I was sorry to make him do it. Not that I could stop him.

"You can write it down if you don't want to talk," I added, but he took a big suck on his oxygen and waved away my concern.

"Gary's making it hard. The divorce. Fighting her on everything. Weaponizing Ray. He hired their sitter in his office two days a week."

"So? What's the problem?"

"He didn't hire her as a sitter. As a marketing intern. So she can't sit for Ray on Nadine's weeks. When she had a hearing scheduled about it, he postponed. So she brings Ray here until she finds someone else."

"Is he all right in the corner? Ray?"

"He just builds with those damn bricks for three hours. It's like a drug. Then her sister comes."

"Okay. Moving on."

"Zack Abramson's back." Dad crossed him off the list of things he had to tell me. "Can't hire him because he left before the freeze. Could use him to move stuff off your desk."

"Agreed. I'll call him."

"And that Kayti girl? She can't keep her mind on a single thing at a time."

"That's her superpower."

He closed his book. Brushed his silver hair into place. Dad hadn't lost his hair as he aged. He was still handsome and well put together, but he'd never shown an interest in a woman after my mother died.

"You're back early," he said. "It wasn't because of the business, I know that. Unless Miss Superpower started with the alarm bells."

"There were no alarms."

"Are you back because the trip failed? Or because it was successful?"

"It's not that simple."

"Are you all right? How is it all with him?"

I closed my notebook. I didn't want to lie to him, but I didn't want to declare the battle won or lost until the war was over. And it was a war. I didn't kid myself about that. I was fighting for the very things I'd thrown away.

"I don't want you asking too many questions because you're not breathing well. So I'm going to just tell you everything I can, all right?"

He nodded and held his hand out as if giving me the floor.

Now I had to figure out what to say and what to leave out. I was his daughter. News that Adam didn't love me anymore, or that he did but just a little, wasn't going to cut it.

"We went. We talked more than we ever have. I learned about him. Things I didn't know. We both changed. There's still stuff that we have to work out. I want to prepare you for the fact that even though I've come around, we might still split up. I love him. I can't tell you how much I do, but it might not matter."

"What can I do to help?"

"Nothing. It's between us. Just... thank you. Thank you for taking care of things around here while we went away."

"You're welcome."

"You can stop coming in if you want."

"Nah. I can come in."

"Dad, I don't want you to tire yourself out. You retired for a reason."

He shrugged, tapped the tabletop with his fingertip, wheezed a little. "Maybe I'll stick around the rest of the week. You need me until you get your feet under you."

Another man protecting me. I was grateful and resentful at the same time.

# CHAPTER FOUR

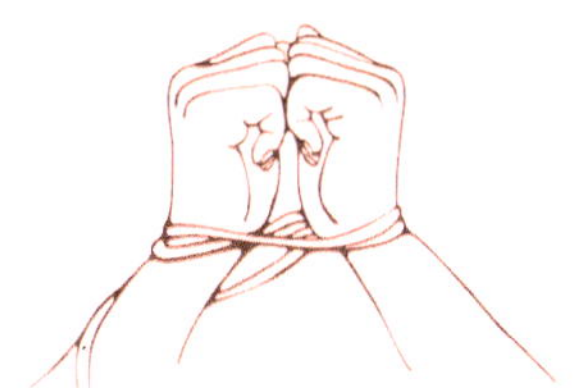

I watched my phone for Adam's movements, obsessing like a tenth grader with a crush on the captain of the football team. I shooed away a constant, humming anxiety that manifested as a twisted stomach. My insides felt like a wet washcloth that had been twisted tight and left in the sun.

He wanted me. His body wanted me and his heart called for me, but his mind had decided to cut me loose. Without him coming to the office, I wasn't sure how to get in front of him so his mind could get out of the way.

Kayti had her bag slung on her shoulder when she poked her head into my office. "Zack's on his way up."

"Leave the door open. Have a good night."

She left me alone. The tracker found his phone in the Meatpacking District.

He was at the Cellar.

My first emotion was anger, then a sense of urgency, then despair, then all the bad things I could think and feel ran together like a ten-car pileup on the FDR. Anger/lust/panic/jealousy/desolation—boom boom boom.

"Hey, there." Zack tipped his head into my office before sliding his whole body in.

I couldn't talk to another human being. All I could do was look at that green dot on a map. I flipped the phone glass-side down.

"Come in."

We gave each other the double-euro kiss. His blond scruff scratched my cheek.

"It's good to see you." It wasn't good or bad, but it was terribly inconvenient, because I wanted to go to the Cellar and curl my body at Adam's feet so no one else could.

Zack and I sat on the couch. He was as handsome and rugged as always, but he looked tired and drawn out, as if he too had been wrung out and left in the sun to dry.

"I'm sorry to hear about your mother," I said.

"It happened so fast. I was there four hours, and boom. It was like she just needed to see me before she died."

"I'm glad you went then."

"Me too. But with the funeral done and my sister in charge of the arrangements, I had to come back. I was going crazy in Dayton. Nice people. Wonderful people, actually. If I could take everybody there and move them to New York, it would be heaven."

I smiled. The fast-paced intensity of the city attracted the most driven people in the world. They weren't always easy to live with. "I can imagine."

I was filling space. I wanted to go to the Cellar or, at the very least, look at my phone again to see if he'd run to some sub's apartment for a fuck.

Zack must have read my mind.

"I heard about you and Adam."

Of course he had. My big blabbing mouth meant I was going to have to say we were getting divorced, or not.

"It's in process."

"Figured as much when you needed to use my apartment but you wouldn't say why."

I'd seen his empty apartment as an opportunity and used it to bulldoze away my fear. I saw it as a sign that I needed to stop delaying the inevitable.

Zack moved on the couch until he faced me completely, draping his hand on the back. "You were miserable. You played the part though." His finger touched my shoulder, stroking it through my blouse. "Played it really well."

I shifted to face him, which showed I was paying attention and got my shoulder away from his finger at the same time. "I wasn't playing. I was trying to hold it together."

"I know. But I could tell. You didn't look at him unless you were talking about work. He had you trapped, didn't he?"

He did, but not enough, obviously. Not enough for me to see why I should be.

Zack's voice was deep and husky with warm admiration. "You were very brave to let him go."

That was the exact story I'd told myself before I left the note. "I was a coward. I told you more about how I felt by asking to move in than I told him."

"He's not the easiest guy in the world to talk to."

Zack made eyes at me. *Eyes* meaning if I wanted to fuck on the couch, I could fuck on the couch. And I did want to fuck on the couch, but I didn't want to fuck him.

I stood and brushed my skirt down. "There's a freeze on new hires, so I can't bring you back. But we're falling behind, and it would be great to have a freelancer we didn't have to train, if you're interested."

He stood in front of me, too close, but the coffee table kept me from stepping back easily. Also, I wasn't going to back away. It wasn't my job to be the only one with an ounce of sense. He should take a hint.

"I'm interested. And when you finally take that ring off, I'm interested in that too."

"I'll make a note."

The loft was a block away from work, but I got in a cab as soon as I knew Zack was gone.

"Gansevoort," I said.

"Got it." And he was off.

I checked the phone. Adam was still there. I had to see him again. The urgency was a physical thing sitting in my gut as if I'd swallowed it whole. I couldn't digest it.

Zack's come-on had pushed me deeper into wanting Adam's touch. The ease with which he'd propositioned me made my position with the man I really wanted feel even more tenuous. Every hour I let pass was an hour closer to the end of our contract.

The cab dropped me on the corner. I walked quickly to the plain building that was the Cellar. A man in a leather jacket stood in front of the black door.

"Hi," I said, trying to act as if I belonged there.

"Hello." His voice was a deep baritone.

"I'd like to go in?"

The door opened behind him, and a couple came out. I recognized Charlie, but not the woman he was with.

"Do you have a member number?" asked the baritone.

Charlie gave me a second look as he led the woman to the curb, then he turned away.

"No, I just—"

"Can't do it."

"A minute. Just a minute."

Was I begging? I didn't want to beg, but I wanted to see my husband. Maybe I'd beg him. Maybe I'd just get on my knees.

"Sorry, ma'am. It's members only tonight."

I turned to Charlie. Did he remember me from our wedding? Did he know where Adam was? Could he get me in? I could beg him too.

But even as I thought he might help, he got in the cab after the woman and closed the door.

"How do you become a member?" I asked the baritone bouncer.

"You need recommendations from three active members," he answered.

"Thank you," I said. "Thank you very much."

I wasn't stalking Adam, but maybe I was. I walked around the corner, wrapping my coat tightly around me. The neighborhood was packed with people going out after work. Laughing, smiling, noses red in the cold, damp night.

Zack thought I was available, and he was a counterpoint to all the women who saw Adam the same way. They'd flock to him. He wouldn't be single another hour. And what was he doing in there? Was he going to leave with someone?

Not on my watch. No way. Whatever he was going to do with whomever he was going to do it with, he was going to have to hide it, because I would stab myself repeatedly with whatever he did. Oh yes, my pain cried out to multiply a hundred times over. If he left that club with someone, I would watch it happen and he would know the level of his betrayal.

I was around the corner when I looked at the phone again. The green dot had moved to the street. I ran, crashing into a lady carrying a little dog, nearly tripping on a garbage pail, navigating patches of ice like a ninja. I ran back around the corner until I could see baritone at the front door and a cab pulling away.

I got my phone out again. It was him.

*Don't text him.*

He was in that cab, and I had no way of knowing if he was alone or with a sub who would do whatever he wanted without the baggage, without the love, without a care in the world.

*Do. Not. Text.*

In the middle of the sidewalk, I watched that cab wait at a light two blocks away, turn north on Tenth Ave., east on 23rd, north on Park Ave., and east again into Murray Hill. Home. He went home alone or otherwise.

—I want to be a member<br>of the Cellar—

I walked south on Hudson, toward home. I had to work off the energy. My body needed something to do besides panic about the fact that he wasn't texting me back.

I stared at my phone. No dots either. He'd gotten the message but wasn't answering.

*Because he's fucking someone else.*

Maybe, maybe not. But why would he go to the Cellar unless it was to find someone to fuck? Maybe he'd gone to talk to Charlie. Maybe he'd just wanted to be among his people. Maybe he'd tried to find someone and failed.

I got all the way home and heard nothing.

He had to be too busy with a sub. A woman with no problem doing what she was told. A woman who could offer her ass without delay. A pure, true, trained submissive who succeeded where I failed.

He couldn't love a sub, but that wouldn't stop him from fucking them.

I took a deep breath when I hit SoHo and emailed Kayti.

*Kayti—*

*First thing in the morning. Pull up the wedding reception invitation list. Not City Hall. The Lafayette Hotel reception. I need phone numbers and addresses.*

He could refuse to touch me, but he couldn't stop me from pursuing my submissive nature. Even after these two weeks were finished and he drifted even further away, I still had a chance to pursue him. Everything about the idea was crazy, but I didn't feel sane.

His text came in just before I went to bed.

**—*You will never be a member***
**of the Cellar—**

It took a ton of effort not to answer his text, because I saw hope inside it. He cared. Even if his dick was wet with another woman, he cared whether or not I was a member.

I didn't sleep well, but that sentiment gave me a couple hours of rest.

# CHAPTER FIVE

*THE JOURNEY of a thousand miles starts with a single step.*

I learned not to expect anything. Or if not that, I learned that what I expected could be wrong, a fantasy, a fear, a bunch of meaningless tropes slapped on a mundane reality.

The old Garment Center red brick building still had brass-fitted mail chutes in the hallways. I stopped by one and pushed the flap. It had been sealed shut. When exactly had the post office stopped using them? Why? And the old glass mail chutes? When had they stopped working?

*You're stalling.*

In the eighties, twenty-three bags of stuck mail had been retrieved from the chute. Years' worth of unpaid bills and business correspondence. Contracts and notices. Thoughts, feelings, typewritten and scrawled. Stamped and stuffed, and in the mass of fluttering business detritus, a woman received a letter from her dead husband. Yet another got a letter her dead husband sent to his girlfriend years before. The emotions were still there on the paper, even if the muscle holding it was long gone.

Was anything stuck in there now? An old love letter, begging for a reconciliation? The declaration of a long-denied love? What was caught in the seams between the floors? In the digital age, messages were lost in the ether. In the analog, a letter could get sealed in a chute forever.

The door at the end of the hallway opened, and a woman in her forties strode out, holding the knob until the door clicked. She didn't look at me as she passed, her heels clopping on the marble, but she'd forced me to look outside my distractions at the brass plate on the door.

*INTERNATIONAL OBJECTS*

I didn't know if a more bland name existed, especially in contrast to what was actually sold there. A wedding invitation had gone there, and I followed the trail by deduction.

The brass knob was warm where the woman had touched it, and I added my own warmth, turning it and entering.

*After the first step, you still have to walk the thousand miles.*

The reception area had been completely bland. Almost insultingly empty. The conference room, however, was completely different. Rich with tapestries and soft cushions, dark woods and a window onto neighboring factory rooftops, it invited the truth.

Which was why Charlie met me in here in his dark denim sports jacket and khaki slacks. I wondered what Adam had meant when he said Charlie had his dick shot off.

"I can't help you," he said, leaning on his cane. Neither of us was sitting.

"Of course you can. You *won't* help me."

"So we agree. It was very nice to see you again. I'll have someone show you out."

Yeah.

Right.

"It means your mind can be changed."

"Ms. McNeill-B—"

"I can convince you."

"I am not going to train you."

"Why not?"

"Are you mad, woman?"

"If you mean angry, no. Not yet. I'm assuming you mean crazy, which yes, I am crazy. Just a little. Adam started to train me and didn't finish. Now I'm supposed to just find my way around? Half done like a runny egg? I don't accept that, and if he's not going to finish, someone has to."

He regarded me for a long time. His eyes were a dark, cloudy grey. They gave away nothing. "He told me you were vanilla. Not a submissive bone in your body."

"He missed a bone, obviously."

"More than that." He held out his hand. "Sit. Please. You're making me tired."

Was he going to sit? Was his order just for me, and why?

"If you can't even take a simple request, Mrs.—"

"Diana." I pulled back a leather chair. It rattled on the casters.

When I sat down, he sat across from me. A little pod of office supplies sat on the end of the table. I folded my hands in front of me and leaned forward. I didn't notice the aggressive posture until I wondered if I should be more submissive. Hands in lap? Eyes down? Knees together or apart?

None of the above. I kept my elbows on the table and my ribs pressed to the edge as if I was going to leap across it. I couldn't second-guess myself all the time, and I thought being myself was safer than trying to be the kind of submissive I wasn't.

"What do you expect to get out of training?" Charlie asked as if he'd asked it a hundred times before.

"Is there a right answer?"

He matched my posture. Hands clasped. Elbows on the table. "There are only wrong answers."

"Wrong answers like 'better sex' or 'a boyfriend'?"

"Those are definitely wrong."

"Why?"

"They're not true, for a start."

"And they're facile and immature."

"Yes. And they can be achieved another way. If you want better sex, find a more compatible partner. If you want a boyfriend, there's always

Tinder. So if you want to do this, you do it because there's no other way to achieve what you're trying to achieve."

"Which is?"

"You tell me. What do you want out of sub training?"

"Adam."

I answered quickly because it was true, and because there was no other way. I was ready to argue my reasons all morning if he'd let me. At the same time, I figured he'd call any answer I gave wrong and dismiss me. Then I'd chase Adam without him or his help. I didn't know how long the chase would last, but I knew it couldn't go on too long before I quit in despair. I was a sprinter, not a long distance runner, so I told myself I had two weeks to do whatever I could.

"I hate to be the one to tell you this." He leaned back. "Fact is, he should be the one telling you and I should kick you out of here right now without another word. But I'm a nice guy."

I pressed my lips together so snarky words wouldn't come out. I practically had to cover my mouth.

"You're wasting your time," he said. "The only woman he ever fell for wasn't a sub."

"That woman was me."

"It was."

"He loves me. I know it. You know it. He's fighting hard to make the biggest mistake of his life, and you're going to let him. How are you going to live with yourself when he's sixty and fucking random submissives he can't love? Do you want that? Or do you not care?"

"This is none of my business, you know." He pushed his chair out and put his hand on his cane. "I'm not getting involved."

I snapped up a pen and pinched a scrap of paper from a pad. "Here's my number if you change your mind."

"I'm not going to call you."

"I'll see you at the club then." I stood.

"You have a membership?" He seemed genuinely concerned.

"No. But I need three members to vouch for me. It can't be that hard."

"Really?" He took his hand off the cane, lacing his hands across his lap. "How easy is it?"

"Tryout night's next week. I can convince someone I'm capable of getting on my knees. There are Doms in the paper looking for—"

"Hold on there, sheila."

"What?"

"You don't know those blokes, and you have no way of checking them. This is a dangerous business."

I shrugged.

"You're going to let some bloke you don't know, never met, no friends in common... let him tie you up? I'm not even talking about fucking. No good Dominant's just going to fuck you without clear consent, but there are bad ones out there. Bad, bad men."

"I can handle it. But thanks."

I couldn't handle it. I was terrified of everything about it. I didn't want to submit to another man, ever. Didn't want to be touched or ordered around by anyone but Adam. Charlie was tolerable because his relationship to my husband meant that no matter what he taught me, he wouldn't touch me.

So I had to go to plan C. I didn't have a plan C, but I was sure I could come up with something. I was halfway through the bland, no-nonsense reception area when Charlie's voice echoed off the walls.

"I can get you someone." He leaned on his cane, a three-legged man against the stark white hall.

"A stranger?" I asked.

"What am I then? I said four words to you at your wedding and you've seen me twice since."

"Adam trusts you, so I do."

He sighed deeply. "I'm going to get no end of trouble for this." He reached into his breast pocket and retrieved a slim card case. "But better this than you running around half-cocked."

With just his thumb, he slid out a card partway, then he held the case out to me. I crossed the distance between us in three steps and grabbed the white triangle, pulling out the rest of the card until the entire rectangle was revealed. On it, just a word in silvery grey.

INSOLENT

I turned it to the back and found a number neatly written in thin black felt tip.

Text: (212) 867-5309

"Give the bloke a fair go."

"You're referring me?"

"You're a brat," he said without insult. "I don't train brats. Don't have the patience anymore."

"Well, thank you. I appreciate the time you took to meet with me."

"Be careful."

"I will," I lied. There was no way to be careful about what I wanted to do. I couldn't do it.

# CHAPTER SIX

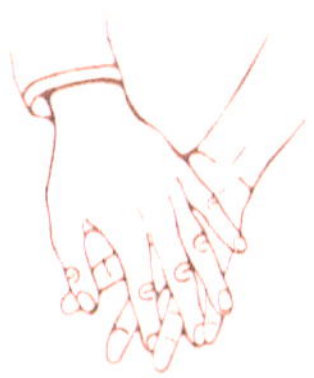

## DAY TWENTY

My father and I had a very open, loving relationship, but he was still my father. He wouldn't want to hear the details of my sexual exploits with Adam any more than I'd want to tell them. Life and relationships were uncomfortable, awkward, and messy in general. Telling your father how it felt to be paddled while people watched from the snowy yard wouldn't bring us closer. It would make him worry.

"I thought the vacation would sort you two out," he said, flipping teabags into white cups. The cups had come from my mother's family, and they were priceless. The whistling teapot was from my dad's father, and it was just old.

"It didn't."

I counted pills and dropped them into his plastic container. *Click click click.* I checked against the calendar and marked off the week I'd allocated.

I kept a log of his meds and prescriptions with refill dates and dosage changes. I was terrible at this sort of thing. I could barely keep a grocery list in one place. But for some reason, I was obsessive about keeping his pills in order.

"And it's him? Not you?"

"I don't know. I mean..." I sighed and snapped the container shut. "I love him, but I think this made him rethink what he needs."

Dad brought our tea to the table. I made an effort to let him do it himself, though I wanted to jump up and take the tray from him.

"He's a good man. He'll make the right decision."

"Maybe." I squeezed my teabag and dropped the dry lump onto the saucer.

"Or." Dad shrugged as if he didn't want to suggest the thing he was thinking and hoped I'd meet him halfway.

"Or?"

"They can take a man's... you know... stuff..." He scratched his head. "Your mother didn't get cancer until later, so maybe it's not worth it."

"Take a man's sperm?"

"Yes. And, you know. Blah blah."

"Artificial insemination?"

"Sure. Yeah. And the other one. In the test tube. You go to a clinic, and they have it frozen. You pick from a catalog. Or... what I'm saying is, I know you were worried."

"I'm still worried." I blew the surface of my tea into crescent-shaped ripples. "Maybe I just don't get to have children."

"You're giving up?" He hacked out two coughs. "Come on."

"It's a race. You lose some races. And if I can't see what I'm racing against? If I have no idea if the cancer is coming tomorrow or never? And what if I make these terms with him? Just a baby, right? He might say yes, but that's letting him off the hook. I want all of him. I'm not splitting the difference. It's all or nothing. I'll give up on this race with Mom's genes, but I won't give up on the dream with Adam."

"This is the man you left." Dad raised an eyebrow, and I detected a little smugness. He'd never wanted me to leave my husband.

"I did it because I wanted time to have a family with someone else. Which was wrongheaded. I'm not making decisions based on how Mom died anymore. If my time's running out and I lose this race, so be it. It's my life to waste, and I'm going to waste it racing with him."

"You seem like you've made up your mind."

I placed my cup in the saucer as if it was the last bingo chip on the winning card. "This is going to the finish line. You mark my words."

He took my hand across the table. His skin was cold and dry. "I'll be here for you. Win or lose."

Dad must have been where I got the strength to stand up to my husband's rejection. His eyes were as sharp and blue as ever, and I could believe in the strong but icy grip of his hand that he'd be there to help me see it through to the end. Adam. A baby. The inevitable fight with renegade cells. He'd taught me how to fight.

"There's always another race," I said.

"I'll be there for those too." He put his cool hand on my cheek and patted it.

He'd never leave me. Never stop. And I'd never stop chasing Adam. Starting tonight.

I threw back my tea in one gulp. "Okay, you're all set." I stacked the containers and picked up my cup and saucer. "I have to go."

"It's nine at night. Where are you going this late? On a weekday?"

"Ready, set, go, Dad." Newly inspired, I put the cup and saucer in the dishwasher. "We don't get to decide when the gun goes off."

"What?"

I kissed his cheek. "See you in the office."

# CHAPTER SEVEN

Monthly tryout night at the Cellar. Anyone could walk in. Last
time, I'd been clothed in anger and disappointment and driven by a
curiosity about what my husband had been seeing when he saw sex.

The second time I went to tryout night, I didn't have that armor or
that drive. I was curious about myself. I was curious about my trajectory.
I wanted to feel what it was like to be single in that world. I wasn't
accepting defeat with Adam, but I was getting a feel for being single and
I didn't want to wait another month to go to the Meatpacking District
to find my place.

This time, I heard every command, smelled the lubricant, tasted sex
in the back of my throat as I got off the elevator onto the sixth floor. I
withheld judgment on everything and everyone. Having been to
Montauk, most of the activity in the room seemed tamer than I
remembered. The clothing was outrageous on some and dowdy on
others. Sitting at the bar, I noticed the ratio of observers to participants
disproportionately favored the observers, who were usually huddled
couples holding their drinks with two hands and sipping through stir
sticks.

I sat with my knees pressed together and my hands resting on them.
I'd worn a blouse and slacks for modesty. As a new submissive without a

Master, I felt vulnerable. Beyond being there, I didn't even know what I wanted out of my trip downtown.

The young Dom I'd seen paddling his sub in the observation room was on the other side of the bar, talking to a man and a woman in black. The young Dom wore a crisp white button-front and grey tie. They could have been talking about real estate.

Our eyes met, and he stopped, tilting his head. I flushed with prickly heat and looked away, hiding behind my ginger ale. I held the glass in two hands, sipping from the rim. Avoiding him. My fingers were cold and wet from condensation, but I didn't let the glass go. His gaze held the promise of dirty feet buckling under the weight of his paddle. The sound of it hitting skin. The knowledge that someone was witnessing my domination and degradation. I wanted all of it, but not with him.

*What do you see?*

At two o'clock, a woman was cuffed to a big X. She was getting her bare ass whipped by two men. At ten o'clock, another woman was sucking off two men, alternating hand and mouth every few seconds. At one and four, collars and leashes, and at every minute in between were observers trying not to stare when staring was the point.

*What are you feeling?*

Lonely. Curious. Aroused in a non-specific-free-floating sort of way.

"What attracts you?"

The voice wasn't in my head, but next to me. Bass-deep and accented in thick Ts and dropped hisses. He'd spoken to me the first time I'd come. Adam had called him Viktor.

I didn't respond right away. All of it attracted me, and none of it.

"I don't bite," he said. "Bark a little, maybe."

I smiled and tilted my glass. The ice had melted into smooth-shaped stones. I glanced at the young Dom. As if he knew I was looking, he turned, and seeing me, he nodded.

"I'm not sure what attracts me," I said, looking squarely at Viktor.

"None of it?"

"None specifically, but in a general way... all of it."

He tipped his drink at the woman on the X. "What do you like? The cuffs or the pain?"

I stayed silent, considering my options.

"This is only curiosity. I'm not in business to give you either. Just to talk."

"I think," I said, watching the woman's behind flush pink, then red. The transformation was gorgeous. Like petals blossoming. "Both together. She needs the cuffs to stay still for the pain. To feel safe."

I shook the ice. My wrung-out lime flopped like a dead fish on top.

"Your drink. You'd like another?"

"Ginger ale."

The bartender was a woman with a long braid that twisted strands of blond, black, and red hair. She wore a corset and platform wedge sneakers. "This asshole bothering you?"

"No. He said he wouldn't bite."

"He barks." She raised a penciled eyebrow.

"I've been warned."

"Ginger ale?" She picked up my glass.

"On me," Viktor said.

"On the house," the bartender parried, filling my glass with fresh ice. "You're Adam's wife?"

"Hey," Viktor said, "put the lid on it."

Some kind of silent message passed between Viktor and the bartender. A conversation the woman with the soda gun won. She slid the glass to me.

"You're being watched," she said. "Protectively. But you're not anonymous here."

"Is this the only club in the city?" I asked, annoyed.

"Ten years ago, three clubs had to merge or the scene would die. Next nearest club is in Newark. Blame gentrification. Call your congressman."

"Could also call your husband," Viktor interjected.

"Someone did that already, I'm sure." The bartender gave me an apologetic face and went to the other side of the bar to help a couple who looked as though they'd taken the train right from their law firm jobs.

"At least you know I'm not trying to pick you up," Viktor said. "And I liked your answer very much."

"So you're watching me?"

"Making sure you don't get into some trouble. We look out for each other and each other's subs."

"I'm not his sub."

"This is between you and him. Ah, and here he is!" Viktor held out his hand and Adam appeared from behind me.

He was wearing a T-shirt and jeans with a coat. He looked as if he'd run the whole way from the gym.

Great.

He and Viktor shook hands. Adam thanked him. I flipped the red stirrer out of my drink and sipped from the rim. I was feeling furious and butch.

"It was nice to talk to you," Viktor said then pointed at Adam. "You take care of this one."

I hid my face behind the glass. My sneer was inappropriate. Viktor meant no harm.

When Viktor was out of earshot, Adam said, "Huntress."

"Fuck off," I said from behind the glass.

He put his hand on the bar and leaned on it, putting his body close to mine. "You know how I feel about you being here?"

"Tell me more about how you *feel*."

The braided bartender smiled when she got to us and folded herself over the bar to kiss him on the cheek.

"The Glenallen," he said. "No ice."

The girl on the big X was taken down. She had a blindfold on, and she was smiling. Her Dom carried her away. I didn't know what to make of it. I hadn't decided how I felt about seeing other people do what I didn't know if I wanted. With Adam, it was all fine. I could figure it out. Without him, I was afraid to experiment, and I was afraid not to.

"I have a right to be here," I said. "I don't need the whole tribe breathing down my neck."

"This isn't you."

"Are you serious? You just spent two weeks showing me that it is. Then you left me hanging."

"I mean it's not you to stalk me."

I almost poured my soda down his pants. "Were you always such a narcissist? I'm here for *me*. I'm trying to figure out who I am, what I like, and what I want."

"You've always known what you wanted. This was never it."

His chest rested against my shoulder, and his breath warmed my ear.

"I want something else. I think. I don't know if I'm submissive or what type and I can't decide from home. If you're going to make me decide without you, I'm going to do what I have to. This place is the first stop for anyone working through this." I faced him nose to nose. "Maybe you're the one who's stalking me."

He put the whiskey to my lips and tipped it. I drank. It made my lips cold and my throat hot.

"Can I show you something?" he asked.

"Isn't that what I've been asking?"

He helped me off the stool and guided me to the back hallway that was for members only, even on tryout nights. The hallway where I'd met Serena. He walked quickly, keeping me on his arm, nodding to a few people but not getting distracted. Leaning on the brass handle, he pushed through a frosted-glass door to a narrower hallway with doors on one side.

He took me down it until he hit an open door. A young man who looked as if he hadn't seen a lick of sun in years furiously tapped a device in the dark room. When he looked up, the light from the device revealed a movie projector.

"Hey," he said. "Looking for something?"

"Number nineteen," Adam said.

"On it." He kicked the door closed.

Adam pulled me to the next door to the left. It opened into a small theater with about two dozen red velvet seats with lights at the bases.

"There was this guy in Marine Park who collected vintage pornography. When he died, one of the clubs uptown took it and preserved it. When all the clubs merged, the reels moved here."

"We're going to watch porn together?"

He guided me down an aisle. "Yes."

"How adventurous of us." I smiled at him, flirting.

He smiled back a little, but was reserved in his enthusiasm. We sat in the center.

"Now I'm sorry I wore pants," I said.

The lights dimmed to black. I took his hand, and he paused before dropping our entwined fingers in his lap.

"I'm trying to illustrate something. I want to talk. So I'm glad you wore pants."

The bullseye countdown appeared. Adam leaned his head back, closed his eyes, and exhaled. They went back to the screen as if all necessary strength had been gathered.

*She's blindfolded, arms tied above her. He's lashing her.*

"These are from the late sixties," he said as the picture flickered. There was no sound. "The stuff here is very real. There's no retouching. It's 16mm, so there's none of the porny quality of video."

*He's wrapping her tits in black tape.*

"I see," I said.

He was right. The frame was raw. The beauty of her submission wasn't on the film. I didn't feel as though I was watching something. I felt as though I was witnessing something.

*He's clamping her nipples until they're elongated meat.*

"This is called tit torture," he said matter-of-factly. "Every step of this was worked out beforehand. You're not seeing the dozen things he's *not* doing." He twisted in his seat to face me. He was backlit, so I couldn't see his expression. "Give me an adjective. What do you think of it?"

"Is this your thing?"

"Answer me first."

I loved him. I wanted him. I'd get on my knees and submit to him.

"It's gruesome."

"It's not my thing." He sat back and faced the screen. The light flickered on his face. "There's so much more though."

*He's putting the business end of a hairbrush in her anus.*

*I've never seen skin that shade of purple.*

*What is she eating?*

In all of them, the submissive may have cried or screamed, but she always came back for more. She kissed the Dominant's hand or looked at him admiringly. Her lips did a dance of gratitude.

*Thank you.*

Ten minutes in, I couldn't hold my questions anymore. "Why are you showing me this? You don't want to wrap me in duct tape."

"Someone might. I want you to know what it looks like first."

"Adam Steinbeck!" I stood and put my fists on my hips. "You fucking shit!"

He crossed his legs, shrugging as if it wasn't his fault. He just worked here. "What?"

"You're trying to scare me."

"I'm trying to inform you."

"To hell with this. I'm going out there right now and getting someone to fuck me with a wooden spoon."

I stomped down the aisle. He grabbed my arm. I spun around to face him. Behind him, a woman was getting choked, and every time she breathed, the ecstasy on her face was unmistakable.

"Let go of me," I growled.

"Look at it. You weren't meant for this."

But he was? But Serena was? Was I too good? Too weak? Too strong?

None of that mattered.

"You love me. Say it, Adam."

"I'm keeping the love I have left."

"Why can't you love a submissive?"

"I don't know."

"You can't love weakness?" I asked.

"I said I don't know."

"You're unworthy of a woman who would kneel for you?"

"What do you want out of me?"

He was hurting me. I jerked my arm away, and he let go.

"I want you to leave me for a reason. A real reason. I left you because I was unhappy. I thought we were incompatible. You're leaving me because you asked me to submit to you and I love it. You're leaving me because you love me a little but not enough. What is all that? It's not a reason."

"I'm protecting you!"

"You're protecting *you*."

No snappy retort. No defense. Behind him, the clips continued.

*She's naked. Blindfolded. Hands tied behind her back and a high collar that forces her chin up. She's stumbling across the room, following his touch.*

"That looks like fun," I said.

When he looked around to see what I was talking about, I slipped away.

"Diana!"

In addition to being easy to keep on, pants were good for running. Which I did at a respectful jog across the hall and into the club. Not too fast. I wanted him to catch me, but I wanted him to chase first.

I ran into Viktor, who kept me from falling on my face. Adam came behind at a slow trot, unfazed. I smoothed my hair and thanked Viktor the Russian for catching me. Adam took my arm without breaking his pace and led me to the elevator.

"I don't want to go," I said.

The doors closed, and we went down. When they opened, Charlie was standing there with his cane.

"Hello, there."

"Hi!" I said, expecting a conversation, but Adam led me out, down a hall and to the street.

He put his finger up to me. "Hear me. I am not training you. Period. And you are not to come back here. Ever. I don't care if it's the only club in the city. It's not open to you."

"You can't expect me to go back to the way I was."

"I loved you the way you were."

"Wake up, Mr. Steinbeck. Your heart's not talking to your head. You still love me."

Like a chariot from heaven, a cab pulled up. I didn't wait for him to deny the truth. I opened the door myself and told the driver to go.

I was in the long game now.

# CHAPTER EIGHT

## DAY TWENTY-ONE

IF I WAS GOING to play a game of cat and mouse with Adam, then I had to make sure I was the only mouse worth chasing. He had to see only me through a field of hundreds of beautiful, submissive women who could satisfy his every need.

When I listed my limitations in my journal, I didn't use the words to become depressed or hurt myself. I didn't fall into despair. I made a calculation that he would have made. Without doing that first, I'd fail. So I didn't get my self-worth wrapped up in the reckonings.

I was inexperienced. Unsure. I carried a ton of baggage with his name on it. He might never trust me again. He might always think I was apt to leave him at any moment. I represented an emotional risk.. On paper, I was the least likely candidate for his affections.

Coming back to me would be crazy. The morning after the tryout at the Cellar, I had a come-to-Jesus moment. I knew him well enough to know he'd told himself leaving me was about protecting me. I was sure he believed that, but I didn't. Without truly understanding what I was saying, I'd told him he was protecting himself. He was legitimately protecting himself from a terrible mistake.

Adam Steinbeck was the jealous type. He still considered me his possession and responsibility, that much was obvious. Best-case scenario, he was telling the truth and wanted to protect me. Worst-case scenario, he wanted me to stay away from the Cellar so he could do/fuck what/whomever he wanted without my eyes on him. Even if that was the case, it proved there a bond between us that hadn't broken yet.

I felt in my bones that the bond would start to fray at the end of the thirty days we'd promised each other. Any legal action would be legitimized. I'd have nothing to hold over him, and we'd split.

Also, I wanted to finish.

Also, he was mine.

Also, every day that passed without me taking action was a day he drifted further away.

I had to take a risk. I had to do something he didn't expect. His reaction would save us or end us. What I was going to do could give him ammunition to justify taking another woman to bed before I could bring him closer to me.

But every day that passed brought us closer to the day he'd find someone else.

Every day, we'd be closer to irreconcilable.

Every day that passed brought us closer to the day he'd stop trying to protect me from someone who could hurt or humiliate me.

My thoughts felt calculating, but my heart was getting closer to panic.

The longer I looked at the card marked INSOLENT as it hung from the refrigerator magnet, the more I knew the panic would get both better and worse if I texted that number.

Success or failure, I had to find out who I was. I still had to understand what my submissiveness meant. How deep it went. How it could complement or destroy my life.

> *—Hello. My name is Diana.*
> *Charlie gave me your number—*

**—Hello Diana. You**
**must be a brat—**

*—Apparently. This makes me<br>hard to train, right?—*

**—"Hard to train" is in the<br>eyes of the trainer—**

He didn't seem very bossy or Dominant. There was nothing sexual about anything he'd said so far. Was I supposed to be attracted to him? I wanted to want him, but it was hard through text and, to be fair, impossible as long as Adam Steinbeck lived and breathed.

*—How's your vision?—*

Maybe making a joke wasn't a good idea. I waited a full minute for a response. Note to self: if the Dom doesn't have a sense of humor or his standard of humor is too high, walk away. I actually got out my journal, started a new page, and wrote that down.

1) Sense of humor
2) Low bar for laughter

Seemed as good a time as any to make a checklist of the perfect Dom.

3) Tall
4) Gentle and hard at the same time
5) Sexy voice
6) Patient with me on the submissive stuff
7) Takes no for an answer
8) Named Adam Steinbeck

Right. Well, I could push hard for the last one, knowing I might not get it. Or I could just pretend that every future man I ever dated could hold a candle to him. The world was going to run out of candles.

My phone rang. I didn't recognize the number, and I would have sent it to voicemail if Insolent's card wasn't right next to it. The numbers matched.

He was calling me. Why?

Should I answer?

Odds his name was Adam? Slim.

Odds he was the man for me? Also slim.

List of what I had to lose? Again. Slim.

I tapped the green button and put the phone to my ear. "Hello?"

"Let's talk."

Not Adam's voice. Bottom line. He wasn't Adam. All I heard was an English accent and the one man he wasn't.

"I can't promise anything."

"It's early for promises. Don't you think?"

"Yes."

Too early, and too late.

# CHAPTER NINE

## DAY TWENTY-TWO

TEN MINUTES on the phone the day before, and I felt as if I'd done most of the talking. I'd been focused on what I didn't want to tell him. Adam's name, for one. My feelings weren't his business, and neither were my intentions. I'd highlighted my inexperience and curiosity. I couldn't tell him what I'd discovered I liked in bed. It felt like cheating on Adam, so I danced around it. He must have seen right through me. Who wouldn't? I was a stumbling idiot.

He said he wanted to go very slow.

God, what was I doing?

This was the stupidest idea ever.

I had to focus. Shed the shame and get the job done. This was my life now.

Facts about Master Insolent

1. English
2. Six-one

3. Fifty-two YO
4. Dark hair/eyes
5. Master's degree—London School of Economics
6. Humor: 6/10
7. Bad humor tolerance: 8/10
8. Dom for 22 years
9. Currently single
10. Goals: break a brat

I didn't want to break. At least, that was my initial reaction. Adam had broken me. He'd shown me my limits of pain, pleasure, and humiliation. He'd dragged me out of myself, folded me into his will, and put me back together.

How could I let someone else do that? I'd lived for years without getting broken. Why did I need it now?

I took the train to Dad's place, rocking with the movement of the subway, submitting to its size and speed. I held a pole in my gloved hand, steadying myself against it, working with the inertia to stay steady.

Could I ever go back to vanilla sex? If Adam got the final word and I was in the cold without him, I would have to decide between being single the rest of my life, leading a vanilla life, or taking on another Master. Could I welcome another man into my bed for a lifetime of nice sex? Good sex even?

No. I couldn't. I'd changed. I was a different woman.

Could I ever let another man beat and humiliate me for pleasure?

No. I couldn't imagine it. There was only Adam.

Staying single forever seemed like the only option. Staying single or getting him back.

And yet...I couldn't make that determination. Not yet.

The train stopped, and I was pushed against the pole. The doors swept open, and a cold blast of air hit me. I stepped onto the platform.

Adam was Adam. I'd worked side-by-side with him for four years. He always got what he wanted. His decisions ended discussions. He decided which result he wanted, made a plan to achieve the result, adapted in process, and won the game every time. If he decided to live without me, I could either accept his decision or stand in the way and get run over. Move with the flow and stay upright, or resist and fall under the train.

I changed my mind with every breath, going from hope to despair and back to hope again. Heart and mind battled, changed allegiances, declared victory, surrendered, and ambushed each other. By the time I got to Dad's apartment, I was exhausted.

# CHAPTER TEN

DAD DEALT THE CARDS, skitting them across the kitchen table.

"You want to bid on a trump, peanut?"

"Just flip it."

He turned the top card. Ten of diamonds.

I fanned my cards, plucked out the tricks, and laid them down, melding a nine of diamonds just to get rid of it.

"Do you want to talk about it?" he asked, laying out his own little fans. He leaned his elbow on his oxygen tank. His mask was looped over the valve by the elastic band.

"No."

"Came back early," he said, sliding a card off the top of the stack.

I could tell from the set of his shoulders that he didn't have another move. I took a card.

"I know." I put the queen of spades next to the king for a meld.

"You don't want to talk about it."

"Not yet."

"What happened?"

"I'm not sure. Can we not talk about it? Pick a card."

He took a card, slid it into his fan, moved stuff around. "Okay. You don't want to talk about it. I understand."

"Thank you."

He threw a royal in diamonds. He was killing me already.

"Then I'm going to bring something else up."

"Good." I took a card from the stack. It was completely useless.

"I want to stay in the office." Dad's card wasn't useless apparently. He laid out a fan of four aces. Damn. "Help out. Learn maybe."

"Learn? Dad, please."

He took a card from the stack and laid it on the table with the rest of his hand. I tossed him my cards to count up with his points. I tapped out my score in three seconds while he separated his counters from his nines.

My phone buzzed. I flipped the glass up while Dad counted.

**—If you're interested in
continuing this conversation,
I'd like to meet—**

It was Insolent. I decided to ignore it. Take an hour or two. Think about it. I didn't have to decide anything right away, right? I didn't have to jump in bed with the guy today, tomorrow, or ever.

Then it dinged again.

**—I have a safe, public place in mind—**

"Hundred forty plus ten for the last trick is a hundred fifty," Dad said.

I put the phone back and noted his score.

"I mean it," he continued. "I feel useful again. Not some old codger puttering around the house. Or dragging my tank to the park to feed the pigeons."

He scooped up the cards for a shuffle. He did seem more lively than usual. His eyes were still red from the constant effort to breathe and he was thinner than I liked, but his voice had real intention and force.

"Do you miss cigarettes?" I asked.

"Every damned day." He shuffled nimbly. "Almost as much as I miss your mother. But they were killing me. Life isn't worth much if you're dead." He dealt the cards, flipping a queen of hearts from the stack. "Hearts trump."

"I remember you smoking in the office."

We shifted our cards around.

"That was before you were born," he said.

"I caught you out on the balcony more than once."

"You were little. Now I can't smoke at all in my own building. It helps actually. You go first."

I had a trick of kings. Laying three down was a guarantee of thirty points, but I didn't put it down. "You still want to smoke? After everything it's done to you?"

"The blood wants what the blood wants."

"Ain't that the truth."

What did my blood want? Did it want Adam, or did it want submission?

To my own detriment, I laid the king of hearts next to the queen of hearts, keeping the other kings close to the vest for later, or never. Or tomorrow.

I picked up my phone while Dad made his moves.

*—That sounds all right—*

Let the queen have her king. The kitchen table could be their tiny kingdom while outside, they broke each other apart.

# CHAPTER ELEVEN

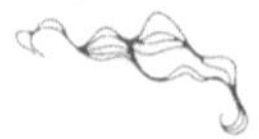

## DAY TWENTY-THREE

In the daytime, as the night, the Cellar wasn't more than a sealed and locked black doorway in the Meatpacking District. I went around to Horatio, as instructed in the latest text, until I hit a brick arch at the entrance to a narrow, clean alley. A brass plate was bolted to the bricks.

## THE GREENS
Members and Guests only

The solid metal gate was open, and I walked past it, heels bucking and slipping on the uneven pavement. The effect of the alley was of something older than me. Older than New York. A place as old as desire.

Insolent knew about Adam. I felt fine manipulating my husband, since it was for his own damn good, but I didn't want to drag someone I didn't know into my personal dramas. Insolent seemed game for the game, but I didn't know how committed he was to winning.

*Be at the Greens at 1:20 p.m.*

*Wear a skirt*
*White underpants. No garter. Nothing fancy*
*Take a cab*
*Do not put a napkin or bag in your lap.*
*Place your phone on the table, glass up.*
*Wear a string of pearls.*
*Sit with your back to the door.*

A heavy metal door stood at the end of the alley. On my right, the red brick of the building, and on my left, windows looked onto a winter garden with patches of snow and twisted brown rosebushes. Since there was no roof, the alley was as icy as February. The bitter air stung my bare legs, and my face and hands were red from the cold.

A handsome man in an open wool coat and a shirt unbuttoned at the collar stepped out of the black door.

"Are you the guest of Master Insolent?" he asked.

*Kick off the heels.*

*Run away run away run away.*

"Yes."

"Come this way."

He led me through the door into a restaurant enclosed in glass. Cool winter sun drenched the white tablecloths, and the low hum of conversation filled the room. It looked almost normal.

The handsome man didn't grab a menu or ask me where I wanted to sit. He took my coat, gave it to someone who whisked it away, and led me to a four-top table in the center of the room. He pulled out a chair for me. I hooked my bag on the back of it and sat.

No water. No menu. Just me in a room full of Cellar members.

I didn't want to be there. Flat out. I didn't want to do what this stranger told me. It wasn't arousing or fun. I wanted Adam. I wanted Adam to tell me to go to some strange glass-encased restaurant that was hidden behind a building. I wanted to know he would be sitting in the seat across from me, not some guy I'd texted. Some guy I'd never seen before.

Was Insolent here? I glanced from face to face. The customers looked like anyone else, with a twist. Business suits. Dresses. Normal voices. A closer look revealed a few collars, a young man with a T-shirt tight enough to reveal nipple clamps. I could tell who was Dominant by their relaxed posture. The submissives had their hands flat on the table, or were sitting on them. Eyes down. A woman in a carefully tailored pants suit patiently fed her tablemate his melon.

A small white plate was placed in front of me. A card stood in the center in an inverted V.

*So it begins.*

My phone buzzed. I could see the preview without touching the glass.

**—*Open the card and read it to yourself—***

As if I needed to be told. Right down to not reading it out loud to a room full of people. Jesus Christ. I was submissive, not stupid.

Annoyance probably wasn't a good way to start. Actually, it was the exact opposite of what I should feel. I was supposed to feel excitement. Trepidation at the very least. This whole experiment was a fail. I was going to leave. This idea sucked.

That being the case, it wouldn't hurt to look at the card. I was curious. I could read it then go.

*Pick up your skirt.*
*Take down your underpants.*
*Remove them.*
*Wrap them around your wrist.*
*Put the crotch out for everyone to see.*

I hadn't been doing this long, but I understood the purpose of the command. I was supposed to get turned on by the exposure. I was supposed to feel a thrill at pleasing him. I was being trained to react like a submissive with a happy master. I was supposed to be aroused.

Right?

Nothing about this was arousing. It was either too soon or I wasn't submissive.

I fished a pen out of my bag and wrote on the back of the card.

*I'm sorry.*
*This isn't working for me.*

I placed it back on the plate the way I'd found it. I was sorry in my heart that this had failed, but I needed Adam to make my submission work.

As if my thoughts attuned me to the tones in the room, I heard his voice. Far away, nearly lost in the ambient noise in the room, his presence tightened my ribs around my lungs. I turned, scanned the room. I had to turn my head almost all the way around to see him with Charlie and Stefan. Their table was against the back wall, and Adam sat in profile, leaning one elbow on the tabletop as he made a point I couldn't hear. The remnants of lunch and coffee were scattered before him, and even at a table with two Dominants, he was the master of the space.

The sight of him opened the floodgates of arousal that another man hadn't been able to tap into. Stefan spoke, and Charlie looked up, making eye contact with me. I froze, wide-eyed, and whipped my head around.

The card sat on the plate.

*What are you going to do?*

I turned around again and shook my head slightly at Charlie. I didn't want Adam to know.

*Yes, you do.*

No, I didn't. But I did. Just not today. Or ever. Or now. What kind of plan was this anyway? I was playing a game I didn't have the intestinal fortitude to win.

Before I turned back to the plate, Adam held up his hand for a waiter, shifting ever so slightly to get his attention. He was going to see me.

Unless I could turn in time.

But he was so beautiful, and the grace of his hand held me.

And as he made the check sign, he saw me.

Shit.

Fight or flight?

His eyes were blue in a world drained of color, and his jaw tightened into angles of fury.

What did he see?

Heels.

Bare legs.

A single card on a plate.

Charlie put his hand on Adam's arm. A calming gesture. It wasn't going to work.

*Fight or flight?*

Stefan followed their attention right to me, and he leaned back in his chair and crossed his arms. I faced forward.

*Fight. It's fight.*

I pushed the plate away. The card tipped and dropped, hiding my writing. I could see the Dom's instructions inside.

<br>

*Pick up your skirt.*
*Take down your underpants.*
*Remove them.*
*Wrap them around your wrist.*
*Put the crotch out for everyone to see.*

<br>

I curled my fingers around the hem of my skirt. Looking straight ahead, I pulled it up.

Adam was watching. I felt it. The arousal I'd been missing flooded me. I was tight as a drum when I lifted my bottom to get at my underpants. I wiggled, sliding them down my thighs.

He barked something, and the volume in the room went down a notch.

Too much. It was too much. I had to look. Charlie clutched Adam's arm tightly. My husband was halfway out of his seat. I couldn't hear what they were saying, but I didn't need to. Like a good sub, I faced forward again.

*Fight, Diana.*

Down my thighs, looser now, past my knees, down my calves, the white cotton underwear dropped, cuffing my ankles together. I reached down, hooked my finger in the fabric, and took my right foot out of its shoe.

"What the hell are you doing?"

His voice. Like a hundred hands on my skin. He'd had the same voice the entire time I knew him, but my reaction to it had changed in Montauk. He could fuck me with that voice.

In the corner of my vision, his hand leaned on the table, fingers flexed against the white cloth, angled in tension. Sky-blue cuff peeking from a navy jacket. Black cufflink with an anchor in silver.

I'd bought him those cufflinks for our first anniversary.

He was my anchor. He was the one who kept me from going adrift.

I'd bought him those fucking cufflinks to express what he meant to me, and he was fucking wearing them to a fucking club and—

*Fight.*

I got my right foot out of my underwear and wedged it back into the shoe. "I'm letting someone else finish what you started."

I took the underpants from my left ankle. I didn't look at him. All my resistance would have drained from me.

"Who?" he growled.

"What's the difference?" I sat up straight with a handful of underwear.

"Huntress." His tone softened enough for my heart to hear him, but not enough for my head to disregard the warning in his voice.

I didn't like it. Not one bit. I made eye contact with him, making sure not to waver. "Don't call me that unless you want to know what I'm hunting."

He didn't break away from my gaze when he snapped up the card and opened it. From below, I could see my note on the back, but he couldn't.

I coiled the underwear around my wrist. The crotch had been bone dry until I heard Adam's voice across the room. I tucked the edges in tight as Adam tossed the card onto the plate.

"Diana?" Charlie's voice came from the side opposite Adam. He yanked out the empty chair next to me and sat in it. "I'm taking you home."

I expected Adam to interject, but he didn't.

"I'm fine," I said steadily, making sure they all understood that I meant it.

Charlie nodded and got up. "You know where to find me."

"I do. Thank you."

Charlie stopped in front of Adam for a beat, just long enough for them to speak without words. He sent a warning to my husband by doing no more than standing there, leaning one side of his body on a cane. Even though the warning was soundless, Adam nodded as if he heard it.

Charlie trudged off. I barely saw him meet Stefan by the exit.

Adam cocked the chair beside me sideways and threw himself into it, crossing his ankle over his knee and leaning one arm on the table. "So."

"Buttons. Sew buttons. You were supposed to be in a meeting. You have to go."

"Why?"

"Someone's coming."

"Yeah. I was curious about that. Those are really nice heels by the way. No stockings. It's thirty-five degrees. The streets are still icy, and here you are. Frostbite and a broken ankle waiting to happen."

"You can't get frostbite at thirty-five degrees."

"What are you hunting, Diana?"

"What?"

"You said you were hunting something. Someone, maybe? Tell me."

*You.*

"Someone to help me finish what you started."

*I'm hunting you.*

He kept his face on mine. He was implacable. Still as deep water.

I continued. "I know that's not what you wanted or intended, but it doesn't matter what you want. You dug up a part of me I need to know. And I'm sorry you have to watch it happen, but this is the only reputable club in the city. So you're going to have to move to the one in Newark or deal with seeing me sometimes."

"I won't sign off on you being a member. As long as there's breath in my body. That's not going to change."

"Your illusion of control is charming."

He attacked, pushing himself forward as if he was capable of biting off my head. "I don't have any illusions. Not since the morning I found a note on the counter. Remember it?"

"I do," I said low in my throat. Probably the least submissive voice on the sound spectrum. "I remember that day. And the weeks after it when you took me away to degrade me so you wouldn't love me anymore. Then you cut me loose just when I knew I loved you. Way to take control, sir."

I said *sir* as if it were the most cutting insult I could muster, and it was. He didn't flinch. Not exactly. His upper lip tightened and his hand stopped fidgeting with the surface of the table. Yeah, I'd gotten to him.

I expected him to answer quickly with some equally cutting tone, but he didn't. He looked at his watch.

"What time is he coming?" he asked, flicking his hand at the empty chair across from me.

"Ten minutes ago."

Adam nodded. "Waiting's a thing. How long you'll stand for it, how still you are, how you react." He laid his palm on my wrist. "How long you'll sit here with your underpants bracelet."

"Fuck you," I whispered.

"Damp," he said, using his thumb to stretch the cotton crotch thin. "When did they get that way?"

"When I heard your voice." I shut down tears. I didn't want his heart to soften. I didn't want pity. I'd been strong for this entire conversation, and I wouldn't ruin it with tears.

"What if I trained you? Just until the end of the contract."

"Too late."

"Why?"

My phone buzzed and lit up.

*—Patient girl. There's*
*a car outside—*

Adam must have seen it. He saw everything. He was an information-seeking missile. But you wouldn't know he'd read it from the way he continued the conversation.

"I know exactly what you need. Let me do it. It's the safest way."

*Yes* would have been the easiest word in the dictionary. He was offering what I wanted. Him.

"I have to go." I picked up my phone and my bag. "And no. You're not safe. Nothing about you is safe."

I walked out with my head high. He was behind me. I felt his presence and heard his footsteps echo mine in the stone alley.

A black limo waited by the curb. A man in a black coat and a felt hat stood by the closed door with his hands folded in front of him. From his posture and manner, it was obvious he wasn't the Dom. He was the driver.

"I'm the only safe one," Adam said from behind me. "And you owe me two weeks."

I spun on him. "You nullified that agreement."

"Kind of. Yes. No. Yes, I did. But you wanted to finish."

I crossed my arms. "What are the terms?"

"The loft is a safe shared space. We play there. You'll have to rethink your redlines. But I'm going to push them hard."

"And sex?"

"No sex."

It wasn't optimum, but I considered it for a second. I could have said maybe, or even yes, but before I could decide one way or the other, he spoke up.

"And no club. I don't want you in the Cellar."

I remembered what he'd said when he found Stefan's note. He didn't want me to be part of that world. The piece of love he held for me would be destroyed by that.

He might believe that nonsense. I didn't.

"Thank you for your kind offer," I said. "But fuck you."

I turned to the limo, and he grabbed my arm.

"Do not get in that car."

"I'm fed up with the mixed messages. Fed. Up."

"Then we can talk about it."

Had he always been this much of an asshole? Even when I left him, I didn't imagine he could be this manipulative and blind to his own motivations. Yet I loved this asshole on the sidewalk more than I loved the nice guy I'd shared a bed with.

"Tomorrow," I said.

"Now. Don't make me tell you again not to get in that car."

"Let go of me." I spoke with such gravity, I felt the words lower in my throat.

He clenched his jaw but let my arm go. "This is a mistake."

His comment wasn't worth an answer. When I stepped toward the car, the driver opened the door, and I got in without looking back. The door shut with finality, and I faced forward. I didn't want to see him. I didn't want to know what he did or if he came to the window to tell me how much of a mistake I was making.

When the driver pulled away, I hit the intercom.

"Hello," I said.

"Hello, ma'am."

"Would you take me home, please? Crosby and Prince?"

"Sure thing."

I shut the intercom and rubbed my eyes. My panties were still around my wrist. I yanked them off and stuffed them in my bag. I couldn't have felt less sexy. I only felt a deep, twisting pain.

# CHAPTER TWELVE

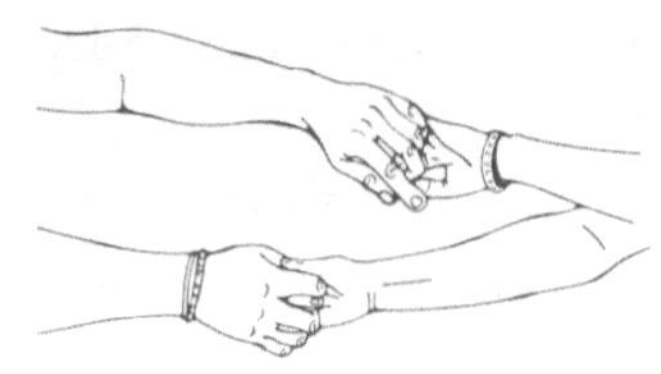

## DAY TWENTY FOUR

I HADN'T LET myself consider what would have happened if I'd done it differently. If I'd sat him down and explained that I was unhappy. If we'd gone to counseling. Opened up communication. Maybe I would have broken through to him.

More likely he would have retreated further, burying his inner Dominant under another few layers of shit, and tried to be the perfect man for me. At least, the man I thought I wanted. No matter how I twisted it in my mind, my only options were this miserable empty bed in a cavernous empty loft with uncertainty in my future and past.

*Stick to the plan.*

I could live like this for another two weeks. That was my cliff. Once I was midair I had to either fly or hit the ground in a mess of blood and bone.

Only his love could stop my trajectory. I was submitting to him in ways he didn't know and I didn't even understand.

Kayti caught me at the receptionist's desk, green eyes wide with the sheer import of what she was about to say. "He's in your office."

"Who?" As if I didn't know. As if I should have been the least surprised.

"Adam," she whispered.

"Thank you," I said. "Hold my calls."

"Should I cancel your ten-thirty?"

It was nine thirty. One hour. "No. I can make that."

The ten-thirty meeting was a perfect excuse to keep my clothes on my body and my knees off the floor.

I strode into my office, letting the door click behind me. Adam stood with his back to the window, hands in his pockets, all dressed up in like a god in a suit.

"What?" I said. "Didn't hear me yesterday?"

"How was it? Your session with what's-his-name?"

"Why?"

"I want to know. I'm your first Dom. It's my job to make sure you're taken care of."

"I don't know if I believe that."

"You don't have to. I see it as my job. That's the end of it."

I crossed my arms and leaned on my desk. I needed more than posture to protect me from him, but my arms and a desk were all I had. "Do you want the gory details?"

He went to the side of the desk chair, two feet closer to me and out of the glare of the morning sun. Close enough for me to see that he hadn't slept. Close enough to smell his cologne and hear the undertone of worry in his voice.

"I want it any way you're willing to tell it," he said.

My throat went dry. He hadn't said anything unexpected or piercing, but I realized my plans were detouring. If we hadn't been honest with each other before the split because of the things we hadn't said, a tidy obfuscation now wouldn't be the right answer.

"I didn't go," I said. "I went home. Not that it's any of your business."

I hadn't realized how tense he was, but his body relaxed noticeably and his smile was one of release.

Which annoyed me. I'd given him what he wanted and he hadn't earned it. Not even a little.

"Get out," I said. "Just go."

"Diana, listen, I—"

"Are you going to tell me you love me?"

"No."

"Then get the fuck out!" I slammed a book on the desk and took inventory of anything on it that I could throw, ready to go full tantrum. "Get—"

Like a wind, he crossed the distance between us. One hand behind my head, the other over my mouth. "Don't yell."

"*—uck oo—*"

"Your safe word is pinochle."

He pushed his body against me, and I was flooded with desire. We were playing now. I hadn't intended it, but we were in the game. I groaned at the thought, discipline flying out the window.

"I was waiting for you to lie about where you went, and you didn't. You told the truth. I'm going to reward you. Do you want that?" His voice was laced with promise.

Yeah. I wanted whatever he had in mind.

I nodded behind his hand. He moved it away.

"How did you know?" I asked.

"What did you think? I was going to let you drive away and not follow you?" In one motion, he pulled my shirt and bra up, exposing my breasts.

"Why? Why did you follow if you don't care? I don't understand what you want."

"I never said I didn't care. Look at you," he said. "So tough. But your breathing is shallow and your nipples are hard."

"You're leading me on," I said. "You know I love you."

"Maybe you don't." He stepped back. "Maybe you think you do. Pull your skirt up."

I was powerless against him. I wanted him. I wanted to obey him. What he was doing was terrible, and I knew it. Yet my body rushed and tingled at his command.

I pulled up my skirt.

"Get on the desk."

When I was sitting on the desk, he grabbed my ankles, pulling them up and out until I fell backward onto my hands. He jerked my knees open so he could see my soaked underwear.

"I realized yesterday that you couldn't go back." He opened my desk drawer and got out a pair of scissors. "There's no more vanilla Diana."

He hooked his finger on the crotch of my panties and snipped them open with the scissors.

"I won't miss her," he said, thrusting two fingers deep inside me before I could feel anything about what he said. "But I'm responsible for who she became. Probably the most desirable submissive in the city." He ran his fingers along my front wall, circling the hard bundle of nerves he always knew where to find. "And the worst trained. Do you want to come?"

"Yes, sir."

"The answer is, 'If it pleases you.'"

"If it pleases you," I gasped.

"It doesn't." He took his fingers out and laid them on my lower lip. "Clean these off." He shoved them in my mouth, and I sucked my taste off them. "I need to teach you what to expect from a Dom and show you how you deserve to be treated." He removed his fingers. "Now what do you say?"

I didn't know the answer. I just looked at him with my tits and wet cunt open for him, wondering how to please this godly creature.

"You say, 'Thank you.'"

"Thank you."

"Good girl. Now." He rummaged around my drawer. "How do you find anything in here?"

He plucked out two silver paper clips and what looked like a credit card but was a membership to some forgotten store.

He pulled a nipple taut and pinned the paper clip to it. "You're going to repeat after me." He clipped the other. The pain spoke directly to my pleasure. "Then you can come."

"This is a reward?" I squeaked.

He slapped me between the legs with the card. I had to bite back a scream. It hurt like the best hurt. Like the ugliest package under the tree that exploded into sparkles and song when opened.

"The reward is, I'm going to train you. Period." He slapped between my legs harder. I clenched my jaw. "This is not negotiable."

"Yes."

"Yes?"

*Slap.*

"Yes, sir."

He tapped my clit with the card just a little. I was on the edge of ecstasy. I didn't care if he loved me. Didn't care if I got hurt. I wanted this drug right now, for as long as I could get it.

"Repeat after me. 'You own me.'"

*Tap. Tap.*

"You own me."

"My body is your toy."

*Slap.*

"My body, oh God. My body is your toy."

"Until the end of our term." He drew the edge of the card over the length of my clit.

"Until... God. Until the end... oh..."

"Diana," he said, his voice deep, rough, yet so sincere I had to look at him. "You're beautiful like this. You're perfect. I want to fuck the breath out of you. I want to hurt you. Mark you. I want you to beg me to stop and love it when I don't." His fingers slid into me again.

"What pleases you." I couldn't do more than squeak.

"Don't come." He reached behind me and swiped things off the desk. "Lie back and hold your legs open."

I leaned back and put my hands behind my knees. He put his slick fingers in my ass, deep.

Looking at my cringing face, he said, "Does it hurt?"

"Yes."

"What do you say?"

"Thank you?"

"That's right." With his other hand, he plucked the paper clips off my nipples and watched me closely.

I knew what was coming, and I knew he had it under control. I trusted him with my body if not my heart. I trusted him with my pain. The stinging came a second later. He bent away from me, digging his fingers in my ass and putting his tongue on my throbbing clit. When he sucked it gently, he put his other hand over my mouth.

Good thing. Because I was lost, and without that hand, my cries as the burning pain turned into a mind-bending orgasm would have brought in the whole office.

"Stop!" I gasped behind his hand.

He heard me. I knew he did, but he ignored me, licking and sucking, stretching my ass, bringing me to orgasm again until I couldn't breathe and my cries dissolved into tears.

I gulped for air when he stopped and removed his fingers. He went into my bathroom. The water ran. I got up on my elbows when he returned with two hot cloth towels.

"I'm fine," I said, but he picked me up and carried me to the couch.

"I know you're fine." He wiped my face, pressing the heat into my tear ducts. "I'm showing you how you should be treated."

He put a towel on my sore nipples. The warmth soothed them. Then he wiped between my legs. I lay back and enjoyed it, closing my eyes against the hard office fluorescents.

"You're going to make it worse," I said. "Even if we don't have sex. Real sex."

"You may hate me when it's done."

"I can love you and hate you at the same time, you know."

A short laugh of recognition escaped him. He must have felt the same when I left him. He might have even felt the same leaning on the couch in my office, shaking his watch down his wrist.

"What time is it?" I asked.

"Ten."

I shot up, bursting out of my post-orgasmic haze like a diver cutting into cold water. "I have to go. *You* have to go." I wiggled out of my shredded underpants and pulled my skirt down. "Shoo."

"Where are you going?"

I pulled my shirt and bra back over my breasts. "Meeting."

His head tilted ever so slightly and his jaw tightened just enough. I had no intention of telling him where I was going or why. I didn't want him to help or hinder the cause.

"I'm going uptown," he said. "We can share a cab."

"No, thanks." I stood. The skirt was long enough to cover the fact that I wasn't wearing underpants. I smoothed it down, and he took my hand.

"You can't go out like that."

"Yes, I can."

"I forbid it."

"Really?"

"Do you want me to train you or not? This…" He waved at me from knees to waist. "This falls under my oversight. You have to put something on under that skirt."

"You shredded my underwear, first of all. So it's your fault. And second, we haven't negotiated the terms of my training." I slung my bag on my shoulder. "This isn't Montauk. I have plenty of options."

He put up his finger and pointed right into me. "You want me to be the one to train you and you know it."

I did know it. I knew it better than he did. But I wasn't going to be a passive recipient of his demands, and I wasn't just going to let him have full control of my future. The next two weeks were going to be his training as well as mine. He just didn't know it yet.

I put my coat over my arm. "Send me the terms."

Before he could answer, I walked out with my head high and tossed my sliced underpants into the office garbage pail.

# CHAPTER THIRTEEN

He didn't follow me out, as far as I could see, though he was probably tracking my phone the same way I'd tracked his. I could remove myself from the list of devices on the account, but that would change the rules.

Once I got into the cab to downtown, I shut off my phone. That should make him fucking crazy. I felt pretty satisfied with myself, then sad we'd come to this impasse. I wasn't sure this was any better than a long, ugly divorce. We were playing a difficult and intense game with unwritten rules. One we could both lose.

I missed Manhattan Adam. The man who loved me beyond all sense. The guy I didn't love but whose company I enjoyed. His good sense, his easy humor, his daily, unintentional beauty gracing the loft and the office. The daily catching up, the quick exchange of advice about important and mundane things. I'd never felt so utterly alone as I did on that cab ride.

Manhattan Adam was my best friend, and I missed him.

The cab dropped me at Metropolis. Stefan sat at a two-seat table by the window, drawing in a black pad. He closed it when he saw me and pulled out my chair like a perfect gentleman. I didn't know if the sadism belied the courtesy or the courtesy cleansed the sadism.

"I ordered for you," he said with his Scandinavian accent. "I hope this is all right?"

"I understand it's standard Dominant behavior." I said it with a smile, so he seemed to take no offense.

"Thank you for meeting me. I wasn't sure you got the note I left."

I'd gotten the note. *We need to talk.* It had tipped Adam into his fear that I was inside a world that had broken him, even as he never admitted to being broken.

"Adam found it."

"Was it a problem? I meant nothing by it."

"Was that the first thing you meant nothing by?"

"Regarding you?" He shrugged. "Could be. I didn't know he was so possessive with you."

"I'm his wife."

*Soon to be ex-wife.*

"All right, Mrs. Steinbeck." He smirked, undaunted, unflappable. "I understand. But I come from a place where we talk about fucking very candidly. Frankly, I would have loved to fuck you. If I had permission, of course. I find you beautiful and interesting." He put his napkin in his lap. "I'm not trying to seduce you."

"You're speaking frankly."

"Exactly." He leaned back to let the waiter put plates in front of us. He'd ordered me a pancetta tartine with goat cheese that looked wonderful.

"And how does Serena feel about you thinking another woman is beautiful and interesting?"

"Usually she would want to know the woman and watch me fuck her." He pulled the toothpick out of his turkey sandwich and laid it on the side of his plate. "It's worked very well for us, this arrangement. You and yours don't have the same. I understand, of course. But it wasn't clear in the beginning."

I focused on my tartine, trying to wrangle crumbs and pancetta that didn't break apart easily. I had so much to learn about Adam's world and my own, where they intersected and what I was comfortable with. I wished he was there to help me with it.

My food went down in a lump. Wishes weren't an alternate reality of a life not lived. They were tricks of the mind, fooling us into believing we had control.

"Is that what you wanted to talk to me about? In the note you left?"

"Yes and no." He sipped his water, considered it, then me. I should have been uncomfortable, but I wasn't. "I wanted to continue our conversation, but Serena and I hit a wall on the way home. Figuratively, of course."

"No seat belts required?"

"My heart needed crash gear."

I let out a short, surprised *huh* that I didn't mean. He raised an eyebrow. No beating around the bush now.

"I thought you didn't have a heart at all," I said.

"Ouch."

"I'm sorry. It doesn't look like love. Not..."

*Not when you do it that way. Not when it's violent and demanding. Not when you're playing with her like she's an object.*

Of course. That was what Adam was reacting to on some level. He should have known better, but the fact was, he didn't. He couldn't separate the violence of his dominance from the love it took to create it.

"Diana?"

"I remember what we were talking about. On the beach. You wanted insight into Serena. She was drifting away the way I drifted away, right? You wanted to ask me things you'd ask her."

"Close enough."

"I'll tell you what I think. But I want you to do something for me." My thoughts were still unformed. I had disconnected words for my feelings.

*Risk.*

*Commit.*

*Me.*

*Separate.*

*Whole.*

"Let's hear it," Stefan said.

"Sponsor me for the club."

"Your Dominant is supposed to ask."

"I know, and he will. Or he might. I don't know. He's not even..."

*mine.* "Whatever. I need three members, and if you help with the application, I'll get a head start."

"What are you playing at, Mrs. Steinbeck?"

I couldn't answer that because I was sure the game didn't have a name. "Serena. Commit to her. Commit to her alone. No sharing. No group... whatever it is. Just her. See if that changes anything."

"It won't."

"How are you so sure?"

"She demands more every time. She is limitless."

He was in awe of her, that much was clear. What had scared Adam away made Stefan worship her. The ability to engage in sex so rough it looked and felt like rape had broken Adam's confidence in his judgment. What she'd asked him to do had driven him to not only marry a vanilla woman, but keep his relationship so kink-free, he could convince himself he was a changed man.

"Have you reached your limit?"

He didn't answer. He just pushed his food around until he gathered a forkful. "I do like you." He put the food in his mouth, chewed, and swallowed. "You are, as they say, a real pistol."

"She wants my husband. She told me as much. I'm invested in keeping you two together."

"The feeling is mutual."

"Sponsor me, and I'll talk to her."

His face betrayed nothing but doubt. His body told another story. He leaned forward, elbows on the table as if getting closer to me gave him hope. "What could you say? She's willful. She won't just take advice from you. Nothing personal, of course."

"No offense taken. And I have no intention of giving her advice."

"She won't respond to threats."

"Stefan. Come on. Threats don't work with anyone. Not even masochists."

He smiled from his perfect white teeth to his sparkling, devilish eyes. "At least not from other masochists."

"Just trust me."

"What's your plan then?"

"Tell her the truth," I said.

"I like this plan."

"Will you sponsor me? Or do you need to see if I'm successful first?"

"I will honor the spirit of the favor. Eat now, would you? Adam will get on my case for not taking good care of you."

We finished lunch while making small talk about Sweden, the endless night, New York snow, and the beauty of Montauk in the winter.

He walked me to a cab. "I want to apologize. For the note. If I'd known he'd act like a child, I wouldn't have left it."

"Don't worry about it. If it wasn't that, it would have been something else."

He kissed my cheek and closed the door. Once the cab got moving, I turned on my phone.

If it hadn't been for the note, would things have been different? Would we have stayed together? He'd come home from the city ready to settle into a life with me. Had that one thing not happened…

No.

I wasn't stupid. If it hadn't been that, it would have been something else. A request to go to the club. A call at an inopportune time. Anything. Adam wasn't ready to love submissive Diana, and he would have found a way to run just as I would have found a way to chase.

The phone connected to cellular. Adam's half-hour-old texts buzzed.

*—Three guidelines. All other
agreements in place, including
end date—*

*—No other Dominants —*

*—You are not to go to the Cellar—*

*—You're at my command
24 hours a day unless
you're working—*

I sent mine without preamble, negotiation, or agreement.

*—No sharing—*

*—I stay in the loft—*

*—Tell me everything. No lying.*
*No leaving stuff out—*

I'd gone from pushing for four redlines to having only two that mattered.

My first was non-negotiable. Whether he thought he loved me or not, letting other people into our relationship wouldn't help my cause. The second was me carving space for myself. And the third was the point of the whole thing. Without it, we had no chance.

*—**Agreed**—*

*—Agreed—*

And thus, he agreed to let me hope that I could fix the mess I'd made.

# CHAPTER FOURTEEN

I **WORKED** the rest of the afternoon and walked home after the sun set. The snow had almost finished melting, and the sound of cars passing and the rumble of the subway underground was cut with water dripping from rooftops and flowing through the street.

I was bone-tired. I could fall asleep to the rippling water or the car alarm. I was going to eat ice cream and watch back-to-back episodes of *Law & Order* until I couldn't keep my eyes open.

I got the mail, took the elevator, walked down the hall until I got to the orange door of our... *my* loft.

A package sat in front of it. Four inches square. Brown paper tucked neatly around the edges. An envelope with the words *Little Huntress* printed on it rested on top.

Taking the box inside, I got my jacket off and barely set it on the hook before I ripped open the envelope. I stood in the foyer in my wet boots with the package tucked under my arm and the envelope on the floor.

*Diana*
*You begin tonight.*
*Do not open this package now. Open it when I tell you.*

. . .

I could hear his bossy voice in my head and fell into a calm, yet excited obedience. That voice was pure pleasure to obey.

*Tonight you will lie down to sleep at nine p.m.*

I glanced at the clock. It was six forty-five. Plenty of time.

*Until then, you will not watch television or look at the computer. No screens. No books. No phone calls. No magazines. You may write in your journal, eat, and take care of the house. I own your boredom.*

*You will take your clothes off as soon as you lock the door. Turn the heat up to eighty-two. Shower. Remain naked for the rest of the night. I own your nudity.*

*Lie down on the floor at the foot of the bed at nine p.m., no sooner or later. You will sleep there. You may lie on the rug or the floor. I own your comfort.*

*Don't touch yourself. I own your pleasure.*

*Don't look in the box. I mean it. I own your curiosity.*

Jesus.

His instructions were hard and cold, yet I tingled for them. Each claim of ownership was sexier than the last. Each demand made me wet to please him.

I flipped the card.

*I intend to come and go as I please, but I don't own the loft. You have control over it. If you need to set a limit, set it now. If I don't hear from you, I'll take it as permission to enter.*

*I'll be in touch.*

*—A*

. . .

Would he enter? And when?

It didn't matter. I was doing this all the way. He could come and go as if he owned my space as well as my boredom, my nudity, my pleasure, and my curiosity.

I stripped down in a state of joy, snapping the curtains closed while fully nude. Let the people in the department store across the street get a good look before I shut them out. My plan was incomplete and my life was a mess, but inside the loft, naked from head to toe, every inch of my skin was alive. My feet felt the woolen texture of the rug and the creaky bounce of the floor. My nipples felt the brush of my arm when I got a plate from the cabinet.

My lips slid against the fork, newly awakened by the fact that they weren't acting out of habit or survival, but for him. Because he'd told me to, and it pleased him.

My shower had a purpose, the towel drying me had a resolve. Each movement was a scene in a larger play that Adam directed. I was complete as long as I was doing what he asked me to do. I was free to feel my own body in space.

The feeling of contentment and peace remained at eight o'clock, but I had an hour to go before sleep and nothing to fill it with.

And the box started to weigh on me.

I shook it, but it made no sound. I peeled the folds back to see how they were fastened. Just tape. Tiny dots of double-stick. I'd never get it back the way it was.

*You could...*

I put the box in the cabinet under the kitchen sink and slapped the door closed.

What was in that damned box?

I took it out of the cabinet. Shook it again.

Was he above leaving me an empty box just to test me? No, he was not, but there was definitely something inside. It had weight.

I put the box to my nose and got a slight whiff of him. A little leather. A bite of something I could never identify. I dropped the box and picked up the note, pressing my nose to it.

Licorice.

That was it.

I went to his bedroom closet. It had been mostly emptied, but once I threw the doors open and stepped in, he surrounded me. Leather and licorice. I opened the drawers, filling every corner of the space with him.

So good. So very good.

I got on my knees and crouched with my cheek to the floor, breathing deeply. I closed my eyes and let him seep inside me.

I loved him. I couldn't speak about the future or the past with him, but in that closet, on my knees, I loved him and it was enough.

The throb between my legs was a growing ache as the minutes passed. I rolled onto my bottom, leaned my hands against the floor, and spread my legs for the empty pole and wire hangers he used to have his clothes on.

How was I supposed to get through the night without touching myself?

I put my head back, surrendering to the mundane difficulties he'd set for me, and spotted something on the top shelf.

Bounding up, I grabbed it.

Packing tape.

I could use that.

The wrapped box sat on the kitchen counter. I picked the edge off the packing tape and carefully unstuck a good section. Sticking it to the top of the box, I spiraled the roll of tape around, letting it scream when I moved it, until the box was a cellophane-wrapped mummy. It would take me so long to get it out that I'd have time to stop myself.

Perfect.

Just to be sure it wasn't staring me in my face, I tossed the entire thing into the freezer.

That was that.

I had thirty minutes.

I checked on the box a few more times. Dusted a few shelves while stark naked. Vacuumed. Brushed my teeth.

By the time I shut off the lights and curled up on the floor at the end of the bed, I was exhausted and completely obsessed with my husband.

I wondered if that had been his plan the entire time, then fell asleep.

# CHAPTER FIFTEEN

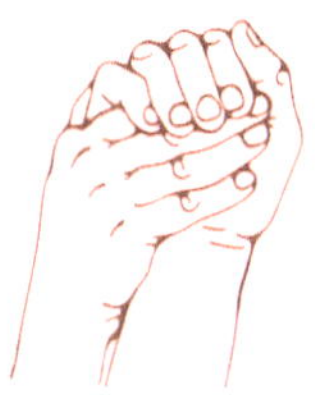

IN THE NIGHT, he came.

In the dark, he whispered.

*You are beautiful.*

*You are perfect.*

*You please me so much.*

He put his lips on my fingers, tasting them, and I sighed out of a dream.

*I'm going to show you how to live.*

*I'm going to make sure you're safe.*

*I'm going to teach you how to be happy.*

He picked me up, put me on the bed, and covered me.

I breathed my gratitude and fell asleep with the shape of his kiss burned into my cheek.

# CHAPTER SIXTEEN

DAY TWENTY-FIVE

WHEN I WOKE UP, the thermostat had been turned down to something less tropical and my robe had been left on the edge of the bed. I put it on. The gunk was still in my eyes when I came into the kitchen. I was alone in the loft, but his smell was everywhere. He'd come to me in the night, said nice things I barely remembered, made sure I hadn't touched myself, and slipped away.

He'd set a robin's-egg-blue box on the counter at an exact right angle to the edge, and the flower on top of it was a surprise. Not a blood-red rose or an exotic lily.

A dandelion.

Where had he found a dandelion in winter?

The square box was still wrapped in packing tape, but it was on a dish that had collected a puddle of condensation from the freezer. A note lay on top.

*Huntress—*

*For the next two weeks, you are to have Kayti send me your work appointments. Outside of those, I own your time.*

*Open the blue box. Wear what's inside all day.*

*Good job wrapping the brown box. It's impenetrable against your curiosity. Carry it with you.*

*I'll summon you later.*

*Be ready.*

*—Adam*

*PS: Do what you want with the dandelion.*

The dandelion was normal in every way. His grandmother, a second-generation Italian, had eaten dandelion salads made with leaves she pulled from the yard, right down to the flowers and the stems with their milky sap. I couldn't see how that connected with me, but the effort involved in finding a dandelion in winter wasn't easily dismissed. He'd left me a puzzle to figure out.

Slowly, because there was no reason to rush the sensual pleasures of a box that particular shade of blue, I undid the white ribbon that held it closed.

I opened it.

Inside was a pearl choker six strands high, held in place with diamond-studded rows. I went to the hall mirror. The robe was high on my neck, so I ripped it off and let it fall so I could put on the choker.

A long chain with a little ruby on the end came from the clasp, and once I had it fastened, I tried to look down at the gem and couldn't. The pearl rows were high, and the bars that held them held up my chin. It didn't *look* uncomfortable. On the contrary, I looked long-necked and proud, even with my hair in a nest of sleep.

He'd said he was going to show me how I should be treated as a submissive.

This wasn't what I'd expected.

I didn't expect to feel so beautiful.

What could I wear with it? Nothing too sexy, but nothing too plain. I couldn't wait to get dressed. I couldn't wait to start the day.

*He's training you to live without him.*

Yes, yes, I said to myself as I wrapped the dandelion in waxed paper and pressed it between the pages of a dictionary, he was doing exactly that. And I was going to train him to love me again.

# CHAPTER SEVENTEEN

I wore a white shirt open two buttons and a grey skirt that ended below the knee. I wore white lace garter and stockings under my clothes. I regretted the high heels. I couldn't comfortably look down as I walked down the street to work, so I had to be slow and careful. I had to feel each step, and with every crack in the pavement, every time I couldn't comfortably look down, every time I felt the weight of the extra box in my bag, every moment I felt a few inches taller, I thought of him.

This was a devil of a way to live.

Serena's agent texted me as I was on the way upstairs. I could see the supermodel on set at eleven o'clock. I had fifteen minutes.

Kayti caught me as soon as I got in.

"Oh my god," she said, putting her hand on her throat. "That's gorgeous."

"Thank you."

"Did he give you that? Or..." She dropped the volume of her voice. "You didn't find someone else already, did—?"

"No. It's from him."

She seemed delighted. "Is the divorce off?"

"No."

"Damn."

I went into my office, narrowly avoided crashing into the couch that had always been there because I couldn't look down, and I put my bag on the desk. "Did you send Adam my schedule?"

Kayti closed the door behind me.

"Add an eleven a.m. with..." Who? I demanded honesty from him but wasn't ready to give it. At least not on the schedule. Not at all. No. I couldn't tell him I was trying to wrangle my way into the club. But I had to. It would be great if I could decide one thing at a time. "Just block out eleven to eleven thirty."

"Okay. So, uh... if the divorce is on...?"

"It's complicated. Is my father in yet?"

"He came in then put a bunch of work in a bag and split. He swore he wasn't sick but..." She finished the sentence with a facial expression that relieved her of saying my father was lying.

I almost said, "Sick? Again?" but stopped myself. My opinion of my father's health was irrelevant, but I could turn this to my advantage. Two birds, one stone.

"I'm going to see him at noon, so just block me out until two. Resend the schedule and tell Adam he owns me after two."

She had no idea how literal I was being.

# CHAPTER EIGHTEEN

Fourteen floors above the street, the roof had been transformed into a garden with a patio and a small greenhouse. The chairs had been pushed to one side so the changing booth could be set up, and the wrought-iron table had been repurposed into a makeup station. A forest of white umbrellas on stands surrounded the scene.

Serena stood on the edge of the roof with her legs spread and her hands on her hips while a photographer with a thick Italian accent ordered her to move a little *zis* way or a little bit *zat*. Huge fans blew her dress between her long legs, and her hair splayed out like a wall of vines.

"Back! Lean back!"

She did, just a little, and collapsed over the edge.

I screamed. Everyone looked at me as if I was a crazy person in a courtroom. The fans slowed and the flashing stopped. A man leaned over the edge of the roof, holding out his hand, and Serena climbed back up with a shoe in one hand.

"*Perfetto*!" shouted the photographer. "*Sirty minote!*"

Another guy in a tight Y-shirt showed up to help Serena back onto solid ground. Once she had both shoes off, she came right to me.

"Aren't you cute?" she said, not unkindly. Her face was caked in makeup. It looked awful and unnecessary.

"I didn't know there was a net."

"I mean with your collar."

Maybe it had been said unkindly. Maybe I was just being naïve and stupid to think she'd have anything nice to say. Good thing the choker kept my head high.

"Is it a bad time?" I asked. "We can do this tomorrow."

"No, no." She waved me toward the changing tent. "I'm going to Tel Aviv for two weeks."

She pushed the flap open for me. Inside, designer clothes twisted on the floor and draped from hangers. Two women, one middle-aged, one in her twenties, discussed a belt. Serena pulled off the white dress and tossed it aside. She wore nothing underneath. Her body was a song to the perfection of the female form.

"Sit if you want." She indicated a white folding chair.

"I'm good."

She threw the dress on it. "Ruby?"

The younger woman looked up. "Yeah?"

"Can I have five minutes?"

They left us alone. Serena didn't reach for a robe or any kind of covering. She just stood fully clothed in no more than her name and her beauty.

"We've been here since five in the morning without a break." She rolled her eyes.

"We never talked," I said. "I never accepted your apology."

"Stefan made me do it."

"Oh, then—"

"It was sincere," she said. "But I wanted to do it in my own way. Stefan turned everything into a game. It was exhausting."

"He said you guys split up."

"Yes." Her hand drifted across the sleeve of a flowing teal jacket. "Enough is enough." She pulled her hand back and crossed her arms. "I've come to see there are better things out there. I've been eating fruit I don't like because I was too afraid to reach for the apple."

She played with a button on the canvas floor, flipping it with her toe. I realized I wasn't the one who should tell her about changing tastes or the limitations of a fruit metaphor when living, breathing, changing people were involved.

"And you found an apple already?" I shouldn't have been surprised. She'd won the genetic lottery. Her world was littered with apples.

"I just had to reach for it." She kicked the button away. "So. How did you like your trip into our world? Short but sweet? You seemed to be enjoying yourself." She smirked. Or I was imagining it. "You left early."

"Yeah. We had to." I had nothing else to say, but I felt like there should be more. My face probably expressed my search for a feasible response.

"You don't need to tell me why. I told you. He can't love a sub. Don't worry. Plenty of them are capable. Or you'll decide to do without love. But you'll be all right." Serena put her hand on my arm and squeezed it. The gesture could only be decoded one way. Sympathy.

I took a deep breath, laying out the plans I'd made in my mind, and threw them all in the trash. "I came to ask you for a favor."

She put her hands on her hips. It was impossible to not look at her body. I found myself casting my eyes down.

"Go ahead."

"I need three people to sponsor me for membership into the Cellar."

"Do you?"

"That's the rule."

"No, I mean, do you really want that?" she asked.

"What do you mean?"

"If he can't love you now, once you're a member and he sees you there? That's not going to fix it."

I knew that as well as she did, and I feared it. If I didn't get him back, my sexual life was going to get very complicated and very messy. But I wasn't going back to vanilla, and I wouldn't let him. Not with me, at least.

And not with her. Never with her.

That was it. My opening.

I thought I'd pitch her Stefan. Tell her how forlorn he was. But no. She didn't want forlorn. She wanted to be beaten under a bridge.

"We may fix it. We may not." I shrugged. "He needs the sweet as much as the kinky. So we'll see."

Her bee-stung lips parted and her perfectly arched eyebrows went up a fraction of an inch. Surprise.

I'd been right. She didn't want him for sweet. Maybe Stefan was too much and she thought Adam was a notch or two more manageable. But Adam said she hadn't gotten aroused for gentle sex. I didn't think my statement would stop her from chasing him, but it would plant a doubt in her mind. That was all I needed.

And I needed to assert myself.

I probably didn't. But I had to.

"When I knocked my head, I was awake. I heard you, and I remember. You're after my husband. Thank you for being honest with me. Now let me be honest with you. You're probably the most beautiful woman I've ever met. You're intelligent, and you don't have any shame. I have no idea why you're so fucking insecure."

I was a good five inches shorter than Serena. I was softer and riddled with aesthetic imperfections, but when our stares locked, it didn't matter. I had the upper hand. Adam was my husband. I knew him. He was mine.

She wouldn't sponsor me. She wouldn't bring me into the world she shared with him. A world that I couldn't access without him. Fine. Let it be then.

Ruby poked her head in. "Can we come back?"

Serena waved them in. "I'm sorry. These ladies need me. We can talk when I get back. I think we can teach each other a lot."

"Yeah," I said. "I think so."

She was set upon by the two stylists, and I backed out of the tent.

She'd said nothing I could pin down. Admitted nothing and threatened nothing.

*Just had to reach for the apple.*

Could something have happened already? Had I lost a battle I'd slept through?

The sun had moved the tiniest bit, but it was enough to send the set into a frenzy of moved scrims and recalibrated light. Men and women in black T-shirts carried reflectors, floods, light meters, shouting numbers and pointing at the sky.

I detoured around them, coming up against the greenhouse. I looked inside as I passed it. Mostly orchids, and a long bed of wheatgrass that was probably sold to a local health food store.

I stopped, because the wheatgrass had taken on a few weeds and, against all odds, they'd flowered.

Dandelions.

# CHAPTER NINETEEN

I was on 57th Street at midday in high heels and a collar. It was cold as hell, and I felt exposed to more than the elements. Exposed by what, I didn't know. By the insecurity I'd accused Serena of.

Dad's texts speared that exposure, getting right in the crack in my armor, puncturing me where I was weak.

*—Guy came with paperwork*
*for Adam. I opened it. Sorry.*
*Probate closed on a property*
*in South Brooklyn—*

*—I'm home the rest of the day.*
*Kayti taught me how to use*
*the internet. Should I have it*
*couriered to him?—*

Fuck this. There was only one reason Dad would go into the office and just turn around and go home. I might be losing my husband to a supermodel. I wasn't losing my company or my father.

"Dad?" I said into the phone.

"Peanut." His breath rattled like an old train.

"I'll give it to him."

"I left it on your desk."

"I was going to come by and tell you this, but I can't. Don't talk. I'm taking care of the company. You can't work anymore."

He coughed, and I cringed at the sound.

"I'm not digging ditches," he said. "I sit on my ass all day and make decisions."

The last vowel came in a wheeze. Shit. The stubborn motherfucker.

"Dad..."

"I stay home when I need to. It's fine. Stop babying me."

"Do you not trust me to run it without Adam? Just say it. Say you think I'm incompetent."

"Peanut, it's a big company in the middle of a lot of change."

"Great. That's just great."

"I'm very proud of you."

I didn't tell him to fuck himself, because he was sick and he was my father. But I was going to. The words were on the back of my teeth and about to break through. So I hung up and waited until the call was cut completely before letting go.

"Go fuck yourself."

Saying it didn't make me feel good. Not even a little. I felt like shit. I stared at the phone, wondering if he'd call back.

He didn't. Good. I wouldn't know what to say to him without fighting. I didn't want to fight with my father.

I caught a cab across town to R+D.

# CHAPTER TWENTY

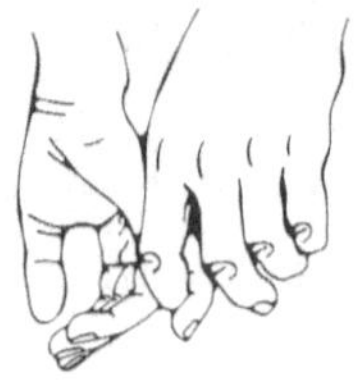

ADAM STEINBECK. My husband. A man I'd shared a bed with for years. A man I would have used fine, fine adjectives to describe a month earlier was now a stranger to me.

If not a stranger, a more evolved form of himself.

Or he was the same, and I had evolved.

Or both/neither/all/nothing.

I'd sat in boardrooms and conferences, obsessed with how I presented myself. Was I strong enough? Confident enough? Was I listening? Talking when it counted? Did I seem bitchy, sharp, entitled?

I should have watched him the way I did from his office. The door was open, and the conference room was across the hall. The blinds were open. He sat at the head of the conference table with four people. Papers everywhere. A whiteboard filled with cryptic lists and notes.

He was everything in his grey suit and red tie. He came from nothing and became everything.

He saw me through the window and the hall as I leaned on his desk. I wasn't being suggestive, but I felt his desire.

The Adam I'd shared a bed with for years was a good man. I would have used fine adjectives to describe him. Trustworthy. Loyal. Steady.

This Adam didn't bring those things to mind. Handsome.

Confident. Powerful. Infusing the spaces he touched with licorice and leather.

I'd come to his office unbidden because my conversation with Serena had scared me. She wanted him, and she'd implied... no... *I'd inferred* too much from my conversation with her and the presence of an impossible dandelion. I wouldn't have bat an eyelash at any of this when I was with the Adam I knew before. But now, I wasn't so sure how much of that guy was left or what this one wanted. How much of his confidence let him cover lies. How much of his power would he abuse?

He got up from the meeting, said a few words, held the door open for his colleagues, and stepped through the hall as if he owned the air.

"Hello," I said when he crossed the threshold.

He didn't answer. He closed the door. Locked it. Dropped his folder on the long table in front of the couch. Closed the blinds to the left, then the right. Only when we were fully alone did he face me.

My heart was going to shatter my ribs, but I stayed still, more or less. Even when his eyes removed my clothes and his body hovered in the space like a predator sizing up its prey, I didn't move.

He rested his gaze on the pearls on my throat. "Diana."

I would have responded if I could breathe. I'd come to challenge him, and I didn't think I'd have the strength to do it.

"Get on your knees."

My knees obeyed, bending, holding my weight, while the space between my legs throbbed. I didn't have a chance to think.

"It's not two thirty." He came close to me. His cock was three inches and a layer of fabric away.

I leaned toward it. "I skipped an appointment."

"Why?"

"I want to talk to you."

He took me by the chin and made me look up at him. "Standard etiquette."

"What?"

"Standard etiquette is I put my cock down your throat then punish you for coming here when you weren't supposed to. I make you wait to talk to me until I'm satisfied you understand your place." He let my face go.

"Understand my place?" Even from my knees, I looked down on him and his attitude.

"Yes." He held out his hand. I took it, and he helped me up. "But you're a whole new way of doing things."

"The old way could get a guy throat-punched."

"Speaking of throats." He touched the pearl choker. "This is beautiful. You look thoroughly possessed."

"I'm thoroughly pissed, actually."

"You may be untrainable, huntress. Sit."

I sat on the couch, and he sat on the matching chair perpendicular to it.

"You were supposed to wait for me to call you," he said.

"I saw Serena today."

"At the shoot?"

I was surprised he didn't give me some open-ended answer like "huh," or "really?" He let me know right off the bat that he knew where Serena was today.

"At the shoot."

"Why?" he asked.

"I had to tell her something, and I wanted to do it in person. And you know what? I got the distinct impression she thinks that when you and I are through here, she's taking over."

"Subs don't take over."

"You know what I mean. And I left thinking she was nuts, but then... I have to ask you something. It's the middle of winter. Where did you find a dandelion?"

"Did you like it?"

"I didn't understand it."

"It was a last-minute inspiration this morning. You're all wound up. It's very sexy." He raised his foot and wedged it between my knees, pushing them open.

"Where did you find the inspiration?"

"Dandelions are the most nourishing weed in the garden. You can practically live on them. If you close your legs, I'll stop explaining."

I opened my legs and crossed my arms. He bent at the waist, put both hands under my knees, and pulled me to the edge of the couch.

"I could have left you a hothouse flower. An orchid or something high maintenance. But think about it. This underappreciated weed grows and grows. You can't kill it. You can try, and it comes back time after time like a big middle finger in the lawn."

"You don't even have a lawn."

He put his hands on my crossed arms and exerted pressure down until I uncrossed them.

"We had one when I was growing up. We ate them with olive oil and salt." He slid off the chair and kneeled in front of me. Pulled my skirt up slowly. "They are delicious." He kissed inside my thigh. "They are tenacious and beautiful, just like you."

He kissed between my legs, pressing his lips to the soaked fabric of my underwear. I gasped and dug my fingers into his scalp.

"Hands under your bottom," he said.

I wedged them under my ass. He pulled my panties to the side and licked the length of my seam.

"I'm not…" I fell into a groan when his tongue flicked me. "A dandelion."

"They come and come and come."

He sucked my clit with a constant pressure, but I wasn't going to give him the pleasure of my pleasure for free.

"Where did you get it?" I squeaked.

"Beg to come."

"Please."

"Beg harder."

He took me with the flat of his tongue then flicked again. I felt every movement, every breath. My body wanted to come, but every fiber of my soul wanted more.

"Please tell me. Just tell me. Please," I said.

"To come, beg to—"

"Tell me, I'm begging you! I forgive you, I promise!"

He worked me like an instrument. I could barely breathe.

"Tell me where you got it. Please."

"I'll tell you. Now come."

His word was good enough. When he laid his mouth on me again, I let loose with an arching back and a scream I had to bite back.

With barely a second to let me come down, he stood and took me by the arm, pulling me to the floor. I was on my knees in front of him before I had a chance to think.

"I own the building the shoot was on. I went this morning to make sure the permits were cleared. The dandelion was in the greenhouse on the roof. You can check the deeds with the city." He tilted my face up to him.

"The owner of the building goes to check the permits? Please. Give me a break."

"She was nervous about the net. She wanted me to look at them. I'm aware that I don't know anything about hanging a net on the side of a building. I know she was manipulating me. But if something happened, I wouldn't be able to live with myself. So I went."

"Did she try to sleep with you?"

"Yes."

"What did she do?" I asked.

"Why are you asking this?"

"I'm curious."

"She got on her knees. I told her to get up. She asked why. I told her I'd had her already. I didn't want a second go round. I was an asshole."

"I don't think it worked."

"That's how it goes with emotional masochists." He stroked my cheek with his thumb. "Open your mouth."

"She thinks when our contract is up, she's going to be yours."

"I said open your mouth." He undid his trousers. "I didn't say talk with it."

His dick was out, and my mouth watered for it.

"Adam, I can't do this if you're making plans for after."

"I'm not making any plans. But Diana, hear me. We can't ever be what we were. I explained this. Do you understand it?"

"If you want my full attention, I need yours."

He took my chin again, pressing his fingers into my cheeks. "You have it. Open your mouth."

I opened, pressing the back of my tongue down for the length and girth of his cock. He thrust into me, taking my throat repeatedly, letting me breathe, then fucking my mouth again.

"Deep breath. I'm coming," he growled.

I took a deep breath and opened up all the way.

He fucked my face, holding me still while he thrust. "Fuck. Coming so hard down your throat. Swallow it." I felt the first spatter on the roof of my mouth, and he slid against it to go deep. "Take it all."

He took his dick out, and I swallowed every last drop.

"There's no one else," he said, running his fingers through my hair as I licked him clean, looking up at his beautiful, satisfied face. "I'm doing this with you. One hundred percent. I'm training you to leave me again."

I took him in my mouth so I wouldn't answer that I was the one who was training him.

# CHAPTER TWENTY-ONE

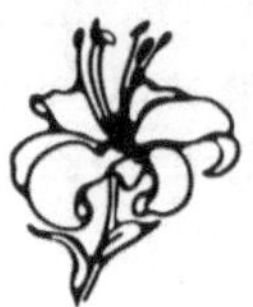

"I PUT something in the mail for you today," Stefan said. Opera came through the phone as I turned the key in my front door.

"Should I be excited?" I swung the door open.

"You're a third of the way to membership in the Cellar."

"Thank you! One down. Two to go." I flicked the lamps on, bathing the loft in warm light. "I spoke to Serena this morning. I don't think I convinced her of much."

"She saw me today. We spoke. That was all I wanted. Thank you."

We hung up without me telling him Adam might have been the reason Serena saw him. There was already too much personal information flowing between the four of us.

As I circumnavigated the loft, I got back to the front door and made sure it was locked.

Two white envelopes had been slipped under the door and pushed forward when it swung open. I opened the one with the McNeill-Barnes logo. Just like Dad said, it was a Withdrawal of Claim and Order blah blah for an address in Brooklyn pursuant to etc etc yada yada.

The other envelope was the size of an invitation. I ripped it open.

The note was in a deeply masculine handwriting, so neat it was nearly generic. The words were underlined in the same felt top pen. I flipped the card, looking for more. Nothing. I put the note on the dining room table and stripped down. Everything came off. Even the pearl choker. I didn't realize I'd been smiling through the whole process until I was putting my underwear in the hamper and caught sight of myself in the mirror.

I would have looked longer, but the lock on the front door clicked. I ran through the big, open space on the balls of my feet and crouched in the threshold between the loft space and the bedrooms, out of the way of the open door.

With my face to the floor and my arms stretched in front of me, I couldn't see. I could only hear his footsteps, the closing door, the lock, his voice.

"I see you were thinking of me."

I didn't want to talk to the floor and I didn't want to move, so I gave him a thumbs-up. He laughed with a tolerance for bad humor I'd never tire of.

The warmth of his hand spread across the middle of my back. "Stand up. I want to look at you."

I stood, keeping my eyes on the floor. He wore his black shoes. The tops were spotted with rain. He picked up my chin and looked at me while he stroked my lower lip with his thumb.

"Did you ever imagine this scene right here?" he asked. "You naked and kneeling when I came in the door?"

"No. Not while we were living together. But since Montauk, it's all I can think about."

He drew the backs of his fingers across my cheek and down my neck. "You took the pearls off."

"Naked is as naked does."

He smiled, brushing his hands across my breasts, tightening the nipples. "Where's the box?"

"In my bag."

He took his hand away and undid his tie. "Do you want to open it?"

"Yes."

"You're not ready." He slid the tie from his collar and came behind me. "Keep carrying it around until I tell you to stop."

He put the tie over my eyes and knotted the back. The world went dark, and I went liquid. Was he going to do the thing I'd seen on the screen? Lead me by his touch?

He put his hands on the sides of my face. I felt his breath and tasted his tongue as he kissed me. Maybe he thought he didn't love me, but his body told me he did. Or maybe together we'd redefined love. Maybe we'd evolved from desire to love to need, because our kiss was nothing if not needy.

He slid his thumb between our lips and put it in my mouth, breaking the lock of the kiss. I sucked his thumb, and he pulled it away. I kept it in my mouth, following into the loft. One step, two, letting him lead me around blindfolded. I trusted him to keep me safe in sightlessness.

The momentum forward stopped and became a right turn, a spin, a disorienting five steps in a direction I couldn't be sure of. Then forward a step. One turn. Two. I was lost, naked, and blind with nothing but his thumb in my mouth to guide me.

I yanked away. "Sorry. Before I forget…"

"Yes?"

"Some legal documents came to the office today. Dad opened them. He was totally snooping."

"Where?"

"Foyer table."

"Don't move."

I didn't. His feet stayed where they were while his hand stroked every inch of my body. I thought he'd forgotten the envelope, but when he'd activated every cell of my skin, making me hot and tingly, he went to the foyer. His heels clicked on the hardwood. Four times. My nervous system sent signals outward, toward his heat as papers crackled, folded, and fell onto the dining room table.

"Lean forward. Hands down. Fingers spread."

Wait. Was I grabbing my ankles? Was I near the windowsills?

As if seeing my hesitation, Adam spoke. "Trust me."

Okay. I was going to trust him. I put my arms out, spread out my fingers, and leaned forward. My hands hit the coffee table, and I laughed to myself. "I thought I was across the room."

He pressed my lower back down, making me raise my ass for the hundredth time. "We're going to really work on your posture. The purpose is to keep you mindful of your body, so... lower back down. Ass up. Legs"—he kicked my feet apart—"at shoulder width. Look straight ahead. It elongates your neck and lets me see your tits."

He pushed me this way and that to get me just right. Every touch was gentle and firm, and when I was perfectly how he wanted me, he cupped my ass and kissed my lower back.

"How is this?" he asked.

"Honestly?"

"Of course."

"Uncomfortable. But if it's what you want, I can remember it."

"You're getting—"

He stopped himself. The table was covered with magazines and mail. I heard a slight ruffle in the space below my chin. I couldn't feel him. He'd made sure at least one part of his body was on mine the whole time, except when he looked at the papers, and without his touch, I felt disoriented and isolated.

"Adam?"

He took the tie off my eyes and held the note in front of them.

*Take your clothes off and think of me.*

"What?" I said. "Was I supposed to do something with it?"

"What is it?" he said as if he were holding all his control behind his teeth.

"A note? Is there another definition?"

"Who wrote it?"

I stood up. Sexy time was done. "You didn't? It was under the door when I came in."

I took it and looked closely, suddenly recognizing the weight and lines of the writing. It was written in very fine felt tip pen, scored with a straight edge. I'd thought it was Adam. Assumed it was, but wishful thinking had shaded my perception. It wasn't my husband's writing at all. I covered my mouth.

Adam thrummed his fingers on the tabletop. I'd done nothing wrong. I didn't owe him an explanation, but he was going to get one.

"Okay. Just stop looking so mad, okay? I thought you left it. That's the first thing. Stop. Stop looking mad."

"I'm not mad."

"You look mad."

"This is not my mad face. This is my 'what the fuck?' face."

"This is my 'calm down' face." I tossed the card on the table and went into the kitchen, where I snapped Insolent's card off the fridge. I put it on the bar that separated the kitchen from the open area.

Adam crossed the room and took it. "Who gave you this?"

"Charlie. Don't be mad. Look! There's the mad face again."

"Is this the guy you were waiting for at the Greens?"

"Yes. I left him a note saying I couldn't go through with it. I presumed he got it."

Adam plucked my phone from the table and dropped it in front of me. "We have a deal. You and I. No one else."

"I'm keeping that deal and you know it."

"Text him and tell him that."

I unlocked my phone, leaning a hip on the counter. "For a guy who doesn't love me, you sure act like you do."

> *—Hi Insolent. Just want to be clear*
> *that this wasn't working for*
> *me and I've moved on—*

"I can't believe you told him where you lived," Adam said as I hit Send.

"He must have gotten it from the driver when I took the car home."

Adam snapped the phone away from me. Looked at my text. "You're too fucking polite."

He tapped the glass. When I realized what he was doing, I came around the counter and reached for the device. He held it away. It dinged with an incoming, and when he looked, I wedged myself in front of him so I could see.

*—My husband is training me.*
*He is my Master. No more notes—*

The new text from Insolent jarred me.

**—*Let me know if it doesn't work out—***

"Charlie sent you this asshole?"

I didn't want him to be angry with Charlie, but it was too late. His own phone was out and he was dialing.

Adam, phone tucked between his shoulder and ear, put his hand on the back of my neck and pulled me into him. I let my naked skin feel the safety of his suit and the firm caress of his hand.

"Charles," Adam said, "who did you send my wife to?"

I couldn't make head or tail of what Charlie was saying.

"You bet it was going to bite you in the ass," Adam said. "Do you know this guy? Is he another war criminal?… Because she told him no thank you and he's leaving notes at the house. Under the door. He knows where she lives, and I don't like his tone."

Adam listened for a long time. I tried to get away so I could put some clothes on, but he wouldn't let me go.

"Yeah," Adam finally said. "Dominic is fine if we can get him."

He said his good-byes and hung up, looking at me with a tenderness I hadn't seen since the day before I left him. It might have been an opening. Was it too small for me to get through? Only one way to find out.

"Why not just tell him it's going to work out?" I asked.

"What do you mean?"

"He said to let him know if it doesn't work out." I slid my phone three inches toward him. "Assure him it's going to work out."

"I'll assure him of more than that. In person. Let's get you dressed."

We went to the bedroom, where Adam opened my top drawer and dug around the back, coming up with a pair of Christmas pajamas.

"Are you serious?" I asked.

"It's cold."

I opened the drawstring pants. I'd gotten them when I was

pregnant, promising to eat a tub of peanut butter cups and get fat as a house. "They have candy canes on them."

He handed me the long-sleeved top. It had a collar with red piping and red buttons down the front.

"I have a perfectly good nightgown."

"You're supposed to do what I tell you."

"Yeah. Stuff that makes sense like 'get on your knees' or 'suck my cock.' This is just weird." I snapped up the nightgown.

"It's too sexy," he said, putting up his hands. "Give me a minute to explain. Just..." He laid his hands on mine, pushing the nightgown out of sight. "Just trust me."

"You can explain, then I'll trust you."

"What's the point of that?"

"Trust me."

He sighed and shook his head a little. "Charlie knows him. Knows where he lives and what he looks like. He and I are going to visit him. Just to make sure he got the message. Which means you're here by yourself. Do you want to be in the house alone?"

"Not really." I was resigned to the scenario before he even finished.

"We're getting someone to watch you. He's going to stay in the living room. Hopefully it'll be Dominic and he'll be here in a minute."

I picked the candy-cane pajamas off the bed, pensively pushing the red buttons through the holes. "I'm sorry. This is my fault."

"No, it's not. You did everything right. You texted. You met him in a public place. You were honest about your intentions, right?"

"Yes."

"And as soon as it wasn't working for you, you let him know."

"I should have texted. A note on the back of the card? So stupid."

"You had every right to assume it would be delivered. And I'm sure it's nothing and I'm overreacting."

"I'm sure."

He kissed my forehead. "Thank you."

"It's too early for bed."

"I was being unreasonable. Wear whatever you want."

"The little elves are so cute."

"They are." He caught my lips in the tenderest of tender kisses.

I could have kissed him like that for another three or four days without interruption or acceleration, but there was a knock on the door.

"Let me get it," he said. "And I meant it. Put on whatever."

I put on the Christmas pajamas because the elves were cute, after all.

# CHAPTER TWENTY-TWO

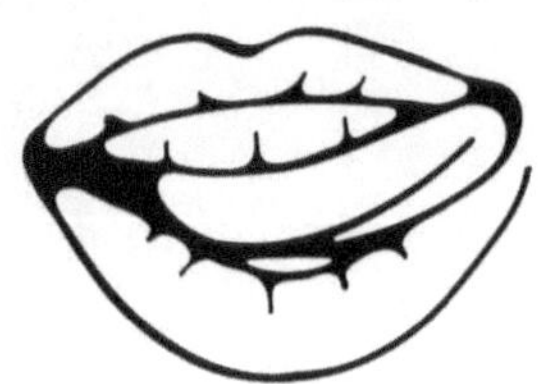

I MET DOMINIC. He was six five, and when I shook his hand, I felt as if I were grabbing a concrete-filled oven mitt. I put on a movie and invited him to watch with me. He declined and went out into the hall. I checked on him a few times. He stood outside the door, listening and waiting. I invited him in, but he said he was fine. He refused food, took water, confirmed he didn't need the bathroom. I watched another movie in my bedroom and fell asleep in the blue light of the TV.

I woke when the light went off. "Adam?"

He sat on my side of the bed and moved my hair off my face. "Go back to sleep."

I pushed myself to a sitting position. I couldn't see the clock. My vision was cloudy with sleep, but my mind was completely awake. "What happened?"

"I can tell you tomorrow."

The light from the moon and the building across the street surrounded his silhouette.

"I can't sleep if you don't tell me."

He turned on the lamp. I squinted and turned away from it, and he put his hand on mine while I adjusted to the light and wakefulness.

He looked fine. Better than fine. Hale and healthy and ready for a day out. I must have been a sight with my crusty eyes, nest of hair, and candy-cane pajamas.

"What time is it?" I asked, rubbing my eyes.

"Two and change."

"What took so long?"

"It wasn't as easy as we hoped."

"Did Dominic stay in the hall the whole time?"

"He's a pro. The best."

I cleared my throat, tilted my head right then left to stretch my neck, then sat up straight. "I'm ready."

He smiled and patted my hands. The gesture wasn't forced or shallow. He wasn't phoning it in. "We went to the last known address. Me and Charlie. Dominant members of the Cellar have to pass a probation period and interview, and Charlie was part of the vetting process. So we figured it was just a misunderstanding."

"Right."

"We got to the place on the Upper East Side. Poor guy, living alone. It smelled like he hadn't left in months."

"Months?"

"Maybe decades. He had Watergate memorabilia all over the house. He had a 'Nixon Now' poster. Framed and everything. He said his mother put it there when Ford took the White House and he hasn't moved it since."

I blinked a couple of times. "Wow."

"We talked. I think you're safe now."

"Thank you."

I was more than safe. If Insolent was actually a smelly, homebound Dominant pretender living in his mother's old apartment, I'd eat my candy cane pajamas. I'd just heard Adam Steinbeck's fantasy of Insolent, and I wasn't about to burst his bubble. I would let him get away with his lie and give him the gift of my unquestioning obeisance.

"What should I do?"

"Go back to sleep." He stood. "Tomorrow, you're moving in with me."

I jumped out of bed. Maybe not that unquestioning. "Wait, wait..."

"I don't like that he knows where you live."

"Murray Hill might as well be the moon. It'll take me an hour to get to work."

"Forty minutes. And it's temporary."

I crossed my arms in my Christmas pajamas with little elves. I didn't know how I expected him to take me seriously in that getup. "How temporary?"

"Until I'm confident he's gone. Or the end of our agreement. Whichever is first."

"So you'll let me move to somewhere on planet Earth after the thirty days?"

His smile was shaped like an orange slice. "Jesus, huntress. It's just the east side."

"Ugh."

"I have two bedrooms. It'll be just like old times. And it'll be easier for me to train you if you're there."

I brushed by him and opened my top drawer. "I'm awake anyway."

My back was to him, so he couldn't see my excited grin. He was making me a part of his life, giving me plenty of opportunities to prove to him that he loved me. On a day-to-day, married people level, we belonged to each other.

My smile turned into a frown.

He was bringing me further into his life and embrace. He was protecting me and treating me as his own. Of course I should be thrilled. That was exactly what I wanted. The more access I had to him, the more likely he'd realize he loved me.

Unless he didn't.

Unless this all backfired completely and training me was the last thing I should let him do. What if I fell more deeply in love? What if this only got harder instead of fixing the rift between us?

"Are you all right?" he asked.

"Sure." I pulled out some more clothes. "I was just thinking about what I have to do at work tomorrow."

I'd lied through my teeth, just like him. We weren't supposed to lie. That had been the problem in the first place. Lies to ourselves and each other had broken us and they had no power to heal.

"You're not going to work tomorrow," he said.

"What?"

"You're staying with me until I know it's safe."

"It's down the block." I thrust out my arm with its fistful of underwear. "Why don't you just stay here?"

"Because this person knows where you live. He doesn't know where I live. Just work from my place tomorrow."

"No. Here's the deal. I stay with you if I go to work. You stay here if you want me to take the day off."

It made no sense. I was basically inconveniencing myself no matter which option he chose. But I couldn't just give up on one of my redlines.

"You're impossible," he said, a stiff second finger pointing at an irritation somewhere in the southern sky. "You're making it very hard to take care of you."

I opened my mouth to say, "I didn't ask you to take care of me," but that was another lie. I wanted him to take care of me. When we were married, and after we got back from Montauk, I wanted nothing more than to feel the weight of his watchfulness.

But that didn't mean I was going to let him eat me alive.

"It's not my job to make it easy for you," I said, dropping my underwear back into the drawer. "The business is about to be mine. If I'm in the city because you sent me home early from Montauk, then I get to prepare the business for the transfer and you just have to deal with that."

He crossed his arms and set his feet a little farther apart. For anyone else, that signified intransigence. For Adam, it meant the negotiations were about to begin.

"The deal was you submit to me. We never negotiated our feelings."

"Sexual submission. That was the deal."

"Place and time were my call."

"The place was Montauk. Wanna go back? Or is it not as much fun without your ex-girlfriend in the house next door?" I slammed the drawer closed. "You knew they were there, didn't you?"

"I did."

"Why did you put me in that situation? On top of everything else, having them there made everything worse."

"Because you agreed to go. They were there and you agreed and I had to choose between taking you to Montauk or not. I decided to take you because I was dying every day. You have no idea how goddamn desperate I was."

If I hadn't had an idea ten minutes before, I did once I heard those last two sentences. His desperation was still there in the soft rattle of his vocal cords and the forward set of his jaw as he tried to hide it.

"I do. I know it. You looked at me and saw someone you loved not loving you back, and all you wanted to do was save yourself. Right?"

He took a long time to answer. I thought I was in for a rant on what I'd done to him versus what he'd done to me. I expected excuses, defenses, and rationalizations.

I got one word, said with a thick undertone of regret.

"Yes."

"I need to make sure my company survives. This is how I'm saving myself." I could have lost him at any minute. My situation with him was that precarious, but winning him wasn't worth losing myself.

"This was supposed to be easy," he said with a smirk.

"It's not. It sucks."

"Right. Yeah. And there's tomorrow." He rubbed his eyes with one hand while the other was still crossed over his chest.

"I have to work."

"The papers your dad opened? It was a Withdrawal of Claim. My uncle Bernard—"

"The hoarder? In Idaho?"

"Yes. He accepted a buyout for the house."

His grandparents' house was a beautiful three-story Cape Cod two blocks from the Belt Parkway. His uncle had wanted the house, but Adam wouldn't sell it so he could "fill it with old newspapers and empty Coke cans." The fight had been bitter and long, but Adam was a tenacious fighter and a patient man. It had obviously paid off.

"I'm going there in the afternoon to see how much of a mess I'm dealing with." He took his hand from his face and flattened it, pointing it toward me. "Come with me. Work in the morning, and come with me after lunch."

Sheepshead Bay was the exact last place I wanted to go, ever. It was far away, residential, isolated, a land of freestanding two-story houses with siding and stoops—and it had nothing to do with me at all.

"Why not just go yourself and let Dominic protect me from evil for a few extra hours?"

His shrug was barely perceptible, and it had the weight of honesty behind it.

"I wouldn't mind having you around." He looked at the floor, put his hands in his pockets, and looked back at me. "It's been empty a long time. I haven't seen it since my grandmother died. I don't..." He stopped himself and shook his head a little as if dismissing a thought.

I believed him, and I felt for him. His grandparents had raised him as their own, educated him, and made him into a man after his parents died. Getting the house meant he had to deal with the place he'd grown up in.

"All right. But I'm sleeping here tonight."

"And Murray Hill tomorrow night."

He'd slipped right back into the negotiation. I couldn't help but admire him sometimes.

"Fine."

"Discussion over," he said, his voice steady and sure, half an octave deeper with an unbreakable rhythm. "You mouthed off." He yanked the end of his belt to undo it, and I was wet in an instant. "Put your elbows on the bed. Feet spread on the floor and your ass up where it belongs. We'll start with your pants on. You're going to count until I tell you to stop."

He snapped the belt free and looped it in one hand. I couldn't stop looking at the way his fingers bent around it. When had he slipped from a human man into the skin of a god? Was it when he rubbed his eyes or when I agreed to his last demand? It seemed fast, but the transition was so smooth, he must have been changing right before my eyes the entire time. My knees were so weak with anticipation that I could barely make it to the foot of the bed, but I did exactly as I was told.

He put his hand on my back, across my ass, between my legs, pressing the fabric against me. He didn't correct my posture, just appreciated it.

"Count with me," he said from behind, and I did.

# CHAPTER TWENTY-THREE

## DAY TWENTY-SIX

THE JAG WAS MINE. I'd earned it in the bathroom at R+D a lifetime ago. I'd touched myself when Adam told me to and stopped when his watch beeped. It was the first time I'd heard his Dominant voice outside a boardroom. It was the first time I'd heard him direct it at me and not at an adversary. It was the first time I'd gotten wet from no more than words.

He'd done what he said he would. Signed the car over to me without another word. Though he could have bought himself another car in a heartbeat, he lived in Manhattan. Cars were unnecessary.

Until you wanted to go to Sheepshead Bay, which was a good hour on the B or Q, four stops from the netherlands of Coney Island. Then you'd want a car, and if you were Adam, you'd drive it even though you gave it to your soon-to-be ex-wife when she played with her clit in front of you.

In the underground garage, I handed him the keys when the valet brought the Jag up from the spot we owned. Adam's coat opened to show his jeans and a cashmere sweater with a button-front shirt underneath. That sweater was winter-sky blue and made the color of his eyes surreal. I could barely look at him as he opened the door for me. I was sure he took that as submissive, but the facts were more mundane and more alarming. The more I looked at him, the more I loved him. I could barely stand it. He'd shaken my body to the core multiple times the night before, then he'd slipped out to the guest bedroom while I slept it off. I woke bereft and irritated that my afternoon had been hijacked.

He snapped the door shut and slid next to me.

"Should I take the Gowanus or the Prospect?" he asked, adjusting the mirrors. He'd picked me up at two o'clock because I needed more time at my desk, and he'd done it without disappointment or complaint.

"I like the Gowanus."

"Always the rebel." He put his arm behind the seat and backed up a little, his body stretching gracefully, his neck elongated as he looked through the back window.

"I like seeing how the neighborhood changed."

He faced front and headed into the daylight. "The warehouses?"

I shrugged. The Gowanus went through a neighborhood of shipyard warehouses that had sat empty for decades as the Port of New York's business dried up. "Except the ones some greedy developer renovated into condos."

"I hear he made a killing."

"You know what I hear?" I said with a hint of gossip in my voice.

Adam took us downtown toward the Battery Tunnel. "What do you hear?"

"I hear his wife can barely sit this morning, he beat her so hard."

"He's a real asshole."

"He's amazing." I regretted it before it was out of my mouth. I shouldn't have been complimenting my husband or getting comfortable with loving him, but I couldn't help myself. Like water flowing downhill, my feelings went in the direction of gravity's pull.

"I hear he's only amazing for the right woman."

I had to stop it there. Fold my hands in my lap. Pretend that didn't mean anything at all. He was just talking, right? Just playing the game. I didn't know how to protect myself from him and win him at the same time.

"Are you ready to get the company back online?" he asked.

"I don't know. It's hard without you, and I haven't been able to hire anyone to replace you with the freeze."

"Yeah. I'm sorry about—"

"No, please."

"Well, I am."

"Fine. Zack is back though," I said. "So we can get the editorial acquisitions up and running quickly."

"He wants to fuck you."

I knew my husband. I knew when he blurted out something he didn't want to by the way he lowered his voice a notch mid-sentence.

"Yeah, well. I'm married at the moment."

We entered the Brooklyn Battery Tunnel with its double line of yellow lights and narrow lanes. There was nothing more to say. I'd added "at the moment" to give him an opening to claim me, but the timing was wrong and he wasn't ready, so we just rode the turns of the tunnel in silence.

The fact that there were other men in the world who were capable of loving me was going to be a sticking point for him. I was poking that flaw as hard as I could, but he knew his weaknesses as well as I did, and he was working on repairing them as hard as I was playing them.

We snapped back into sunlight.

"Let me ask you something," he said. "It's hard to ask. It'll be hard to answer. You don't have to."

"Noted."

"Could you ever go back to regular sex? Not sometimes, but all the time. Just vanilla again?"

He stayed left onto the raised platform of the Gowanus. It was pretty empty in midday, and we went on a good clip toward the outer reaches of the Belt Parkway.

"I don't know. I don't think so. I can't see much outside what's going on with us right now. But we broke something in Montauk. I don't know if I can put it back together."

"What kind of something?"

"Some kind of shell, I guess? I was ashamed. Not like I knew it. I thought I was fine. But I wanted to be hurt and dominated, and I thought if I got all that, I'd hate myself. I thought I'd have to give up who I was. The things that make me, me. I don't know what they are anymore, but I don't feel less like myself. I feel more like myself."

"Do you though?"

"Do I what? Feel like myself?"

"Hate yourself."

I thought about it. Searched for the answer. I'd said I felt like myself, but I didn't tell him whether or not I liked it. I'd thought that was implied. "No, I don't. Not for that."

He drove without comment. We passed the warehouses. Blocks and blocks of big casement windows and stonework.

"Here's yours!" I said, pointing at a slate-grey building with white trim.

"You made me do the white."

We'd been together toward the end of the project, when he was putting on the finishing touches. In the first months of our relationship, he'd brought me there to show off.

"Are you glad?" I asked. "It looks great."

"Yeah. It does."

His grandparents' house was another twenty minutes down the Belt, past the Verrazano Bridge, past Bensonhurst and the train yards at Gravesend, in a nondescript neighborhood built for the working class of the outer boroughs. We turned onto his block as the winter sun got low on the horizon.

The gate across the driveway was locked with a chain. Adam pulled the Jag into a spot across the street and put it in park. He sat there.

Adam's grandmother had died years before we met, and the estate went into probate immediately. The three-story house was unexceptional on the outside. White siding. Screen door. Green trim. A plaster statue of the Virgin Mary inside an arched white cocoon sat in the center of the front yard. He'd paid for the upkeep through his property management company, painting every few years and making sure the patch of lawn in the front didn't get overgrown..

"What are you going to do with it?" I asked.

He shook his head. "No clue."

He got out and came around the front of the car. I waited until he opened my door and helped me out. The street was lined with thick-trunked oaks that would shed hundreds of leaves as big as a man's hand. The curb was crusted with week-old snow and ice Adam insisted on helping me navigate it.

He held my hand as we crossed the street. Ostensibly, the gesture was to keep me from falling. But not really. I knew how to walk on barely icy streets. When he touched me, I knew he needed me. Maybe not in life, but in that moment. He needed me.

He put the code in the front gate, and once we got up the steps, he pulled out a key. "Ready?"

"I've never seen where you grew up."

"It's nothing special." He jiggled the lock, and the door opened with a *creak* and a *whoosh*.

The hall was dark. A stairway led up. A closet on the left and a door to the right. A coat rack had a single fedora with a little feather in the satin band.

"What's that smell?" I asked.

"Sulfur. There's a coal furnace. It stinks up the whole house. My guy came yesterday and started running it. Still works." He took off his coat and helped me with mine. "My grandfather cut the house up into three units. The stairs go to the upstairs unit, which is two bedrooms, and an attic studio. The rent helped them pay for my school."

"Real estate speculator runs in the family."

"Yeah." He hung up my coat and handed me a handkerchief. "It's going to be dusty."

I took it. "Thank you."

He opened the door on the right, and when I went through, I was transported back in time. Not just to Adam's childhood, but to another era. An era of wood paneling and molded pile rugs. An era that was dated even when he was a kid. Pictures of him spanned the hall, broken by a doorway to a room with plastic-covered furniture and a console television. He took my hand again, pulling me so fast I couldn't get a good look at the photos of the handsome boy in the plaid tie with his hands folded in front of him.

Adam went to a larger room with the dining room table. The chairs had mustard velvet cushions covered in more plastic. The fabric matched the drapes.

"They had to really chop this floor up to get it to work," he said, playing tour guide.

He was concealing some anxiety I couldn't pinpoint. I hadn't been around when his grandparents passed. I only knew his grandmother hadn't lasted more than a month without her husband.

"They built this wall and put their bedroom right off the dining room." Adam continued with the tour. "The living room, we passed on the way in. My room used to be the porch." He snapped open the blinds and opened the window.

"Yeah," I said. "Let's get some air in here."

I did the same to the window next to it. I went left and he went right, opening windows and doors. The dust was its own ecosystem, and the sulfur smell had probably gone right through the plastic covers and permeated every porous mass. I opened the windows in the kitchen, and he went around to the porch. We met in the master bedroom with a king-sized bed in front of huge bay windows. The bedspread was silver blue with diamond stitching, and the pillows were stuffed into a hard tube.

"It's like a time capsule," I said.

He snapped his fingers as if remembering. "I had the water turned on."

I followed him into the kitchen, where he stood watching a faucet run pure brown.

"Yuck."

"Toxic," he said. "My grandfather wouldn't switch to copper pipes. He thought lead made you stronger."

"Oh my God. What did your grandmother say?"

"She believed what he told her to believe." He turned away and changed the subject.

He opened the fridge. It stank. A line of brown water came from under it. We looked up. The ceiling was leaking and dripping behind the ancient yellow refrigerator.

We went into action. Adam gripped the appliance by the sides and scooted it one way, then the other to pull it out. I went looking for a pot. Couldn't find one.

"I think something died back here in 1987," Adam said.

I listened as I looked for something to catch the leak.

"Or when Grams died, latest," he said.

Some cabinets were totally empty, and some had odd things in odd places. I opened a cabinet to the left of the sink. On the bottom shelf were wine glasses, above them were dishes, and on the top shelf was a big blue bowl.

Adam continued. "She couldn't do a thing without him. He died, and everything went to shit. This leak could have been here and she wouldn't have gotten it fixed. Not without him."

The blue bowl would do.

"The bills." His voice came from behind the fridge with a particular muffled echo. "The tenants. How she cooked. What she cleaned on what days. I don't know how she made it fifteen minutes without him telling her how to breathe."

I slid a kitchen chair across the linoleum and situated it in front of the counter so I could reach the bowl. I stretched and reached it with both hands as Adam told me more about the dynamics of the people who had raised him.

"I bet she died because he told her to cook him dinner from the grave."

I balanced the ridge of the bowl on the tips of my fingers and lowered myself.

"Stop!"

I froze with my knee on the counter. Adam was half in-half out of the back of the fridge. He held a tea towel in his right hand that was loaded with brown behind-the-refrigerator gunk, and his left was held out to me like a flashing sign at the end of a crosswalk.

"What?" I got my other knee on the counter. "It's for the leak."

I held out the bowl, but he wouldn't take it.

"Not that bowl."

"All right."

He opened the oven. The pots were in there. Obviously.

He took a sauce pot and wedged it behind the fridge to catch the brown drops.

"Adam?"

"This is what I'm talking about. This is exactly what I'm talking about."

"What are you talking about?"

"Just get down. Just…" He held out his hands, one empty, one clutching a gunky tea towel. "Fuck. Where would a normal person put the garbage?"

"Under the sink." I got down so I could reach it, but Adam yanked open another cabinet where an old plastic garbage container was upside down on the shelving paper.

He slapped the tea towel in it. "Nothing ever made sense."

"People get set in their ways." I sat on the counter with my feet on the seat of the chair and put the bowl in my lap.

"You see that bowl?"

He was upset. I didn't know why, but something about that kitchen had set him off.

"This one?"

"We used that every day. And every day she had to have my grandfather get it. Did she ever say, 'Let's put it on a lower shelf instead of the wine glasses? Because, you know, we drink our fucking wine out of fucking jelly glasses?' No. Because he *wanted* it that way and what he wanted he got."

When I was a kid, I used to stand under the light switch and flick it as slowly as I could to see if I could discern the moment the light went from off to on. I never caught the moment. It was too fast. But that moment was happening in the kitchen where Adam grew up.

"And you know why?" he continued, even as the idea solidified in my head. "I figured this out when he died and she didn't know how to do shit. He did that and a billion other things so he'd be indispensable."

"He needed to be needed," I said.

"He didn't want her to function without him."

"He needed to dominate her."

"What?"

"Not sexually. Or maybe. I don't know. But he needed her to submit, and she did."

He cocked his head a little, and I jumped off the counter. I handed him the bowl.

"And when he died," I said, "she had to go too. Right?"

He took the bowl gently, as if he didn't want to break my thought. I didn't let go. "What are you trying to say?"

"You always said she died to make him happy. I never knew what you meant. But now I do." I let the bowl go. "I'm not going to die without you. I'm never going to be so dependent on you or anyone."

"I never said it was like that for subs. You're confused."

He didn't use his Dominant voice to object. He said the words without conviction, as if he wanted me to prove otherwise.

"Intellectually, you know that's the truth. But you can't unsee what you saw with your family. In your heart, Adam? In your heart you can't love a sub because you're afraid they'll forget how to live."

"That makes no sense."

"That doesn't make it false." I put my hands on his arms. I needed to touch him. I needed to feel him connected to me, because I knew I was right. "Your problem isn't that you don't love. Your problem is you love so much it scares you."

He pulled away, and when I went to grasp his hand, he snapped it away. "This is ridiculous."

"What's—?"

"Everything. All of it. Just..." He curled his fingers into fists and closed his eyes. "Just give me a minute."

He left and didn't look back. Through the dining room and down the hall, past his childhood and the plastic-covered furniture in the living room, onto the front porch, where he'd slept as a boy.

# CHAPTER TWENTY-FOUR

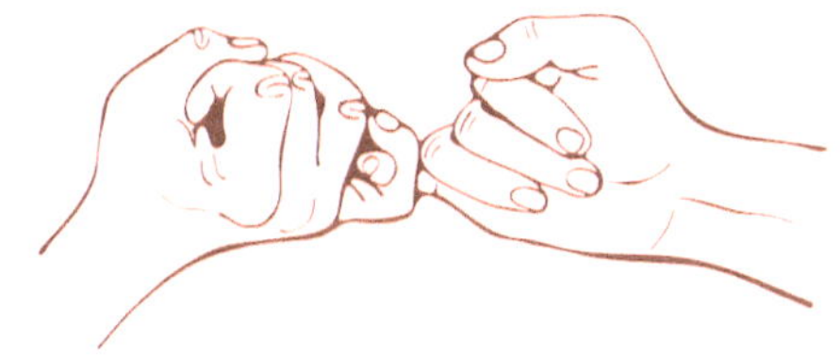

He'd asked to be left alone, so I left him alone. Stranded in an isolated corner of New York in the winter, in a house that hadn't been inhabited in years, with a man who took up more room than space, I didn't know what to do with my body.

Pushed against the wall, the kitchen table had two chairs facing the window. I'd moved the one at the head. A black-and-white TV took up much of the tabletop. Dust coated everything like snow. I opened drawers for no reason. Inexpensive but sturdy silverware and servers, plastic measuring cups worthy of a hipster vintage store. A chrome plate was set into the wall. It had three parallel slits with teeth. I pulled it open to find wax paper, tin foil, and paper towel rolls behind it. I pulled out the paper towels, found some blue liquid in an unmarked atomizer, and squirted the table. The paper towel was black after one swipe. Half a roll later, a third of the table was done, it was getting dark, and I hadn't even gotten to the crevices.

I couldn't clean all this up myself. I didn't have the tools or the time.

Putting down the paper towels and squirt bottle, I followed my husband's path.

Adam was sitting on the bed, leaning on the wall. It was shingled and painted with outdoor paint. When I put my hand on the doorframe, I noticed how thick it was and how it had a big hole for a deadbolt. The light from the wide window was a flat grey that made him an opaque silhouette.

"It's dark in here," I said.

"There's a light switch in the hall."

I leaned out and found it. The switch clacked loudly when I flipped it. An outdoor light by the doorframe went on, bathing the room in yellow. The blue of the crocheted bedspread looked military green, the woods looked like cheap veneer, and the world outside looked dark and unknowable with reflections of us painted on it.

"Yuck," I said.

"Piss was all the rage when I was a kid."

"Has that bedspread been sitting out for five years?"

"Just got it out of the drawer."

I shut off the light, and we sank back into deep blue. The school globe looked rounder, the books and blotter on the desk looked more mysterious, and as Adam faced me, he looked more three-dimensional.

I crawled onto the bed next to him and put my back to the wood siding.

"Definitely got a nice indoor-outdoor thing happening," I said.

"They used to sit on this porch every afternoon. Watch the kids get home from school. Say hi to the neighbors. I remember them being happy on this porch. My grandmother brought Grandpa tea in the winter and iced tea in summer. If you look under the window, you can see the ledge where he rested the glasses. There's still a ring in the paint."

I craned my neck, but though I could recognize that the little shelf in the front of the room used to be the ledge of the porch railing, I didn't see the ring. It was too dark.

"When they took me in, they just closed this thing up and chopped up the house to support me. It was what they did because that was what they did. Not an obligation. Maybe it was cultural. But they had no choice. I was their business. They were close to sixty when they took on a five-year-old orphan. Their entire lives revolved around me, but my grandmother's life revolved around my grandfather. She did a figure-eight around the both of us. When he died, I thought she'd be free. I thought I'd offer to make the porch a porch again. She could sit on it and be happy."

"Why didn't they just take this room out when you moved out?"

"He got set in his ways. They had routines and God forbid one thing was out of place. She was miserable. But when he died, she went right after him. Like she forgot how to live."

The sun had set, and the streetlights came on. I didn't press the point with him. Didn't mention his grandfather's dominance or how it had affected him. A car with a loud stereo drove slowly along the block to the Belt Parkway service road.

"He pissed me off," Adam said. "Sure. But by the end, I was pissed at her too, for letting him destroy her."

"But you loved them."

"Yeah." He rubbed his lower lip. "And she could really cook."

"What was your favorite thing?"

He smiled absently. "You'll make a face."

"Maybe."

"Snails."

I made a face. "Ew."

"She'd make them in this big pot." He flicked his hand to the kitchen, or wherever the pot was, as if he was visualizing it. "But only on my mother's birthday, because she'd loved them. Every year in July. Ten pounds at a time with tomato sauce. We'd pick them out with straight pins, and Grandpa would grouse around the house. Like making something he didn't like was a personal insult and not a way to honor my mother. It was the only thing my grandmother ever put her foot down about. It was for me. Because when I moved out, she stopped doing Mom's birthday because of *him*." He jerked his thumb back at the house as if his bossy grandfather was still there. As if he was physically connected to the stories made in the house.

"Fuck him," I said softly.

"Yeah. Fuck him." He took my hand, putting it in his lap as if it was finally home. "What are we doing?"

"Screwing up."

"Like it's our job."

"If you're going to do something, I say, do it all the way."

He squeezed my hand. I was jarred by the way he looked in the direction of the window, but not through it. He didn't look like the commanding Dominant who had been my partner for the past few weeks. He was as handsome as ever, and graceful and sharp, a leader and a decider, but not the same.

He faced me. "I don't know how to fix this."

The light from the streetlights glinted off one eye. His jaw locked, catching things he'd never say. He looked like a man I knew and abandoned. Manhattan Adam.

"We can't fix it," I said, putting his hand in my lap, watching our clasped hands make a new form. I rubbed the outside of his thumb with mine, feeling its familiar shape, the strength of the knuckle, and the texture of his skin. "We have to build something new. And we can." I looked up from our hands to his face.

Could I make him feel my optimism? Could I take a piece of it onto a fork and lift it to his lips? Would they part? Would he let me lay it on his tongue? Would he chew and swallow, saying "I do. I do believe we can, I do."

He didn't say that. He didn't believe, but his lips needed to touch my belief and his tongue needed to taste my hope.

I didn't know if I kissed him or if he kissed me, but it felt like a first kiss, with full quivering that left me paralyzed by his nearness. The act of two tongues tasting each other was so intimate between strangers, so taken for granted over time, and so rarely was the wonder of it felt through to the bone.

He was licorice. Fennel and leather. And he moved like cool water, reacting to my movements, countering with his hands and his mouth, wrapping me with his attention. The kiss was the sway of sex, the smell of it, the carnal desire without the promise of anything but another dance.

He pulled me on top of him, my knees on either side of his hips as he pushed them into me. My body reacted as if the shape of his cock was new.

I was blind. The world was pitch black.

But him. In a tunnel of light.

We pushed against each other. Our clothes got moved aside,

unbuttoned where necessary and no more. We released our bodies from bondage and joined them. Right in the walled-in front porch built just for him, we made together what couldn't be made separately.

If only for that moment, in that bed, in that dusty old house. We built something as permanent as the night breeze. Something that would go away too soon but would return like the seasons.

I forgot the latent desires and sexual exploration for a minute to look into my husband's eyes and see all his anxiety, his growth, and his intentions. I saw everything he didn't want anyone to see.

He loved me. He was terrified, but he loved me.

I closed my eyes. Felt the strength of his hands as they caressed me. Listened to his tender whispers. His movements under me were as familiar as the sound of my own voice.

Manhattan Adam was still there, and he loved me.

I wanted to cry but couldn't. I was flayed, spread out, raw red, and bleeding. Reality was a serrated knife separating muscle from bone, sinew from skin. It cut away the truth of me from the truth of him.

We were on perpendicular paths. We were crossing at a ninety-degree angle, and soon we'd be traveling on different axes.

Manhattan Adam loved me, and I still didn't love him.

# CHAPTER TWENTY-FIVE

IN MY TEENS, I was infatuated with drawing. The idea of being an artist appealed to me, and since I was forgetful and flighty, I figured I must be the creative type. Music was a lot of work and required a lot of attention. So at fifteen, I signed up for a class at the East End Artist's Studio.

I sat around a platform with twenty other teens. The teacher's name was Len Bellinger. He sat on a stool in the center of the platform. He was big and bellicose with a pencil moustache and combed-back black hair. He held up a soup can and spoke in a European accent I couldn't pin down to any single region.

"What shape is this?" he asked.

"A cylinder!" we chanted.

"Correct. In the third dimension, this is a cylinder. But drawing is in two dimensions. So!" He slapped the can right side up on the stool. "What shape?"

"Rectangle," some of us said, unsure.

"Yes. Now. If I do this… what is the shape?" He held the end up to Hanlon Speck, a foot from his face.

"A circle?" he said.

"Yes!" Len replied. He put the can in front of each of us, and each of us dutifully said it was a circle.

"So!" He placed the can back on the stool. "To draw, you need to live in the second and third dimension. You need to see the circle and the rectangle. You need to know they both exist even if you don't see them." He bent his elbow and made a fist as if catching a fly midair. "You must hold opposite things in your mind at the same time, and you must *believe them both*."

# CHAPTER TWENTY-SIX

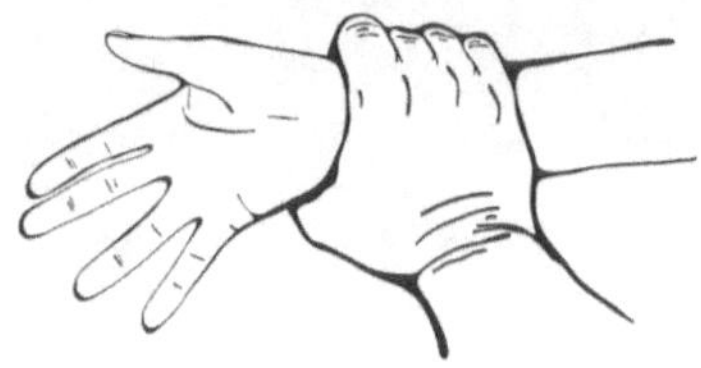

HE PULLED onto the Gowanus and home to Manhattan. Traffic was light, and I was confused about my intentions and my feelings. I felt as if he was going too fast, and I didn't know what I wanted out of him or the next four days. I didn't know if he was going back to being a man who could train me, or if his needle had found the groove of his old self. I held onto the edge of my seat.

He rubbed his bottom lip as he drove. Had he done that in Montauk? Even one time? I couldn't remember. My eyes had been on the floor half the time, and the other half was spent getting my bearings around a stranger.

"You're looking at me," he said with a smirk. Not the devilish smirk that betrayed plans for my body. Just a plain smirk on a devilishly handsome man.

I turned to my window. He was in the reflection. A half mask of blue dashboard lights.

"Sorry," I said, apologizing for nothing.

I'd never finished the drawing class. Never learned to hold two ideas in my head at the same time. Not about soup cans and not about men.

"What happened back there, Adam?"

"Back where?"

How deep was I going to go? Was I really going to shred this thing?
Yeah.

I was.

"What happened? In your old room?"

He looked away from the road for a second, taking my temperature. "We fucked. Why?"

"It was the old way."

"Diana." His voice went deep and slow, but it wasn't the voice that made me feel safe. "Did you think regular sex was against the rules?"

"I want to talk about it."

"Okay."

Wrong answer. Wrong answer a million times. He was just rolling over. He was supposed to tell me that he'd fuck me how he wanted, when he wanted.

Even as my anxiety grew from a pinprick to a full chest pain, I knew I was being unreasonable. I was expecting him to read my mind, and I wasn't respecting his need for five minutes off from bossing me around.

"You're supposed to be training me. Twenty-four seven. That's what you said."

He exited the parkway, eyes drifting past me as he looked behind him for traffic. We were right by the grey building with the white trim. The one he'd bought whole and sold in pieces.

"Did you not want to have sex?"

"No, I mean, y—"

"Did I rape you?"

"No!"

"What's the problem exactly?"

"It's..."

"You think it has to be a power exchange every time?"

"No. I... no, not that."

He pulled up to a metal gate and pushed a code into a panel. "What is it then?" The gate rolled open.

I felt silly. I had nothing concrete to say. I had feelings and intuitions and assumptions. What was I supposed to say? *It felt like you loved me, but you also seemed like the guy I wanted to divorce, so which are you? Because I need to know if I love you or not?*

"Where are we going?" I asked.

"Is that literal or rhetorical?"

It was as if he'd read my mind.

"Both."

He drove into the tiny alley behind the converted warehouse. It had a few reserved parking spaces that surely cost a fortune to rent. The loading bay had been converted into an outdoor eating area with strung lights and big doors leading inside. He parked in front of three garage doors.

"Literally," he said, "here." He put the car into park and looked at me.

I swallowed hard as if that gave a woman strength against a man who loved her.

"Rhetorically? Fucked if I know."

He got out before I could respond, came around the front as always, and helped me out of the passenger side. He didn't make eye contact, but walked to the garage door.

"Adam!"

"What?" he asked over his shoulder, not looking back around.

This was the man with half his attention on me. This was the man who patted my shoulder when I was in pain. The one who made love to me like a nice guy.

I leaned on the garage door so I could see his face as he put in another code. I was in his sight, but he didn't look at me. He was all avoidance and internal energy. Locked away like the crown fucking jewels. Had it been being in his old house? Had it been the memories of his grandparents? The vanilla fuck? Had his love for me turned him back inward?

"Step back please," he said as if speaking to an employee.

I got off the door, and he yanked it up. I was assaulted with the smell of old grease and liquid chemicals. Adam flicked on a light. The garage had room for one car, and it looked to be under a tarp. He walked around it, unsticking Velcro tabs, then he whipped the tarp away.

"Wow," I said.

"That's exactly the word," he replied, rolling up the cover.

"What year?"

"'67. V8. 450."

The Mustang's paint was perfectly red. Not too blue. Not too yellow. The interior was clean white leather and exposed by the convertible top, which had been removed entirely. It had been placed on a ledge by the four wheels, which hung on the wall.

"I took it when the garage started leaking and put it up on blocks. Uncle Bernard never knew. But hell if I was giving up this car." He ran his knuckle along the side. "I figured since you had the Jag, I might as well use this one."

"That's a good idea."

It was a great idea if we were divorced. If we were together, it was stupid to have two cars in the city. We had the money to keep two cars, but we didn't drive enough to make putting the wheels back on the Mustang sensible. And what was the point of having a car like that if you didn't take it out?

Or the point of having a husband who only loved you when you didn't love him?

If this man standing in the flood of yellow light was Adam, we were getting divorced because I didn't love him even though he loved me. I could love the man in Montauk, but this one? No.

I wanted to love him more than I wanted to be loved.

I felt empty without that love. Crippled. A speed machine drained of gas and up on blocks for the preservation of its uselessness.

"I can't…" I stopped myself. I had an end to the sentence, but not the one after it.

"Can't what?"

*Deal.*

*Decide.*

*Understand you.*

*Leave you.*

*Be with you.*

I couldn't fight to be loved and be true to myself. But I could fight to love.

I dropped my bag and took off my coat, which I threw on the hood of the car. The cold air bit my skin and my nipples tightened.

He didn't say anything. He didn't make a move toward or away from me.

I dropped to my knees, keeping my eyes on the concrete floor and my hands to the side. I heard his soles against the floor's grit, and his shoes came into my vision.

Bending at the waist, I put my hands flat on the floor and my forehead between them. My hair spilled around his shoes. My heart thrummed. I stayed still, even as I panicked. On my knees, unable to see him, I wasn't protected. I was vulnerable to emotional hurt. But I didn't know how else to say what needed saying. That I needed him to be Montauk Adam. I needed his control and his dominance. I needed to love him.

"What are you doing?" he asked.

"Whatever you want." My breath hit the floor, and dust blew back up against my chin.

He moved. Grit scraped. He walked far. Then near. To my left. To the other side of the car.

"What if I want you to get up?" he asked from far away.

"I'll get up if it pleases you."

"What if I don't know what pleases me?"

I had a moment of confusion, then I remembered my husband of five years. The man who was afraid to do what he liked to do because he didn't want to lose me. What had he done when he was fearless? When losing me was a foregone conclusion?

I brought my hands around, and with my forehead still on the floor, I unbuttoned my pants and pulled them down, exposing my ass. The shame of it was overwhelming. To talk to my husband by showing him the ways he could fuck me was a deep humiliation, and the only option I had.

The garage door was wide open, and I could hear the *hoosh hoosh* of the expressway. He came around behind me. If he told me to pull up my pants and get in the Jag, I was going to cry, because if I couldn't reach him with this, we were finished.

Doubling down, I put my hands on my cheeks and spread them apart.

He moved. I felt it but couldn't see him. He did it slowly. He knew I was in a dark tunnel. I knew why. To keep me unsure of my own choreography. The garage door rattled down, cutting off the coldest of the wind and revealing the rumbling white noise of a heater.

Forever. That was how long he let me kneel like that. Until I was hyperaware of every sound from the apartments above. The sting of the floor on my knees. The cold air on my sensitive parts. The sound of his breath, revealing his position next to me, on one knee.

"Are you wet?" he asked.

I was so relieved I almost wept. "Yes."

"Yes?"

"Yes, sir."

"I know you're wet. I was checking to see if you still had the ability to answer questions. I asked you something you didn't answer."

"I'm sorry." My breath hitched. I was going to cry. "Sir. I'm sorry, sir."

"Do you want to answer?"

"I forgot the question."

"You said, 'I can't,' and when I asked you to complete the sentence, you didn't. So why don't you tell me what you can't do?"

"I don't remember."

"What do you want, Diana? In the next four days, what do you want?"

I swallowed a lump of cry gunk and sniffed hard. What did I want? I wanted to love him and I wanted him to love me. I wanted the impossible.

"Everything," I sobbed.

"I can give you everything. But not all at the same time."

I nodded by pressing my head to the floor harder. He stood up and slapped his hands clean. I swallowed the rest of my tears. I couldn't break down. Not now.

"Get up on the hood."

Was he back? Was he the man I loved? When I stood and saw the way he took up more space than a normal man and how his posture was perfect and confident, I knew I had him back. He regarded me with curiosity and care, but not love. I was relieved and I despaired at the same time.

I took two unsure steps back with my pants half down, then I got up onto the cold metal of the car.

"Legs out," he said, standing in front of me. When I straightened them he got his hands under the heel of my boot and pulled it off. "Just because I fucked you like a husband this afternoon doesn't mean you're in charge." I was left with a sock half off, and he left it there to pull on the other boot. "You don't kneel to force the issue. I see right through that." The other boot slipped off, the sock with it.

"You were sad and unhappy," I said.

"What makes you think that?" He took my pants by the cuffs and pulled, whipping them off. His erection pushed against the front of his pants.

"You looked... I can't explain it."

He took my underpants down and put them and my jeans over the car door. "Spread your legs."

I did.

"Wider."

I tried.

He grabbed my ankles and pushed them up and out. I fell back onto my elbows, unbalanced on the uneven car hood. One foot leaned on the car antenna.

"You look wet." He put his fingers on the base of the antenna and twisted. "Tell me how I looked."

"Like you were hiding something."

"I'm not hiding anything."

"Not a secret. Not a thing, exactly."

The antenna came out, and my foot fell outward. I thought he was getting it out of my way, but when he swiped the air with it and it hissed through space, I knew different.

"I know you think you successfully psychoanalyzed me back there." He whipped the antenna through the air again, landing it inside my thigh.

The pain was searing. I yelled and closed my legs.

He jerked them open and leaned into my face. "It's not that simple."

What was he trying to defend, when I hadn't accused him?

"Yes. It. Is."

"It doesn't change anything." He spoke through his teeth, as if opening his mouth all the way would let out something he wanted to keep inside. The truth. The fact that maybe something could change.

"Not today."

"What did I look like?"

He really wanted to hear it. Well, I wasn't ready to tell him. I put my head back, exposing my neck, and spread my legs. I felt him stand straight, but all I could see were the yellow lights and the spider webs on the ceiling.

"You want me to break you?" he asked.

"I want to please you. I want you to use me."

I heard the whipping sound before the pain buckled me. Involuntarily, I closed my legs and rolled. He pushed me back and open, whipping from knee to center as if moving the sensation to the core of my desire. It felt good to hurt. So good to focus away from myself and into the immediate moment. I was untouched by worry, and my only desire was for relief from the pressure of my arousal.

He stopped and threw the antenna into the front seat.

"You're the one who's hiding something." He laid his hand inside my thigh and squeezed the raw flesh. I sucked in a breath. "What is it?"

"Yes."

His hand moved, hurting with a promise of pleasure that had to overcome such pain. He opened his pants. Cock out. Fingers inside me. Had I ever been so wet?

"You like it when I hurt you." He tapped my clit with the pad of his finger, and I arched and twisted.

"Yes."

Pulling me forward, he put his dick in me. My mouth opened to scream in gratification, but nothing came out. He gave me two thrusts. I thought I was going to burst between the pressure of the pain and the nearing orgasm that complemented it.

"Are you going to come?" he asked from deep in his throat.

I nodded, unable to form words.

He pulled out and rested his head on my clit. "You don't run this show, Diana. I top. You bottom. Got it?"

"Yes," I squeaked. "I'm sorry. I wanted to talk and I didn't know how else to get to you."

I wasn't sorry. I would have done it again exactly the same way. Either he intuited my insincerity, or he wanted to punish me. Maybe he had some other motivation. My brain was too soaked in sex to discern why he pulled his body away.

"Don't stop!" I gasped. "Please."

He wasn't going to. I could see the satisfaction of control in his face. He almost looked peaceful and content. Gratified with his denial.

I turned to one side so I could get off the car, but he pushed me back down and leaned over me until his face was an inch from mine.

"You want to fuck?"

"Yes."

He flicked my clit with the head of his dick and buried himself inside me, pushing so deep it hurt, then deeper, until his root pressed against every fold and knot.

"I looked like what?" He pulled his full length out and thrust in again.

"God, it hurts. Yes." I clawed at his shirt.

He wrangled my wrists together, crossing them and pressing them against my chest. "What did I look like?"

"Like you loved me."

He slammed me, and it was so good, so painful paired with such a rush of shuddering pleasure that words broke down into syllables, then individual sounds.

"When?"

I had to organize the sounds. Had to do what he told me. "Porch." I spit it out.

Holding me down, he took my body on the hood of the car. He took my will, timing his movements perfectly, as if he knew what I needed and how to deliver it.

"Do I look like I love you now?" he said through his teeth.

I could barely see through my own pleasure or speak through the pain. He'd never driven so deep it hurt. Never ripped through me like this.

"Answer," he demanded.

"I'm. Come. Going—"

"Do not come. Answer. Do I look like I love you now?"

"No." I thought it would come out in a shout, but it was a whisper.

"Good girl. Come for me. Say my fucking name."

His name boiled in my core and flowed past my lips. Pleasure exploded, overtaking the pain, mating them into a blinding whirlpool of soul-shaking ecstasy.

He put his free hand on my face, pushing me down with his weight on my wrists, sternum, head, possessing my body completely, holding me still so he could use me.

With a jerk, he came inside me. Framed by his fingers, his surrender was visible in his hooded eyes and slack lip. His dominance was in his clenched jaw and the ropes of strain in his neck. He was both in that moment of ultimate vulnerability.

He chanted my name as if it were law, then fell on me, his chest rising and falling with mine.

In one second, he'd shift his weight.

In three seconds, he'd get up.

In ten seconds, he'd look me in the face.

In thirteen seconds, he'd speak.

In fifteen seconds, I'd realize he didn't love me.

"Get off me."

He propped himself up on his hands so he could see me. I was right. He was Dominant Adam, with nothing but confusion in his heart.

He stood back and got his dick in his pants. I snapped my underwear off the convertible door. He grabbed it.

"I have it." He held out my underwear so I could get my feet in the holes.

I pulled the sock off and put my feet in, then I jumped off the car to get them up my thighs.

"No. You don't." I snapped my jeans away from him. "All the tender shit is lies. You shred me then take care of me like it was an act of love. But it's not. Not for you. You're just playing a part."

I hopped into my jeans. He stood back with his arms folded as if he was passing judgment on my delivery.

"When I'm gentle, it's a lie? Is that why you can't stand it?"

"The problem is this. When you dominate me, I'm in love. But when I submit, your love dies." I got my jeans around my waist and buttoned them as if I were trying to fling the sides together. I missed and slowed down to fasten them correctly. "We are the two most incompatible people who ever lived." I bent down and got my other ball of a sock and poked the toe through the ankle. "Do you agree or not?"

I snapped the sock, trying to uncurl it. It wouldn't go. I did it again, getting frustrated. Adam took the sock.

"You have a lot to answer for," I said. "With everything. Lying the whole marriage and taking me to Montauk to get over me."

"I didn't think you'd love me."

"I know. I believe you."

"This is not what I wanted." He held out my untangled sock. "It's an unmanageable clusterfuck."

"Epic." I snapped the sock away. "And I wanted that old Adam back so he'd love me, but I just…" I shook my head and studied the stitches in my stupid sock. "I'd only hurt him again. I can't do it all again. It's too much."

He put his hands on my shoulders. I didn't look up. If I looked at him, I would love him or not depending on who I saw.

"Do you think I can't love someone who loves me?" I asked.

"Huntress."

"I mean it. Because if that's the case, I am royally fucked."

"And I am too."

A teardrop fell on my sock. I wiped my eye with my wrist and sniffled loudly. He put his hand on my jaw and made me look at him. He didn't look dominant and assured, but he didn't look locked up like Manhattan Adam either.

"I need you," he said. "I don't know how to love you, but I don't know how to live without you either. For now, can we just need each other?"

"I don't want to get stuck. I don't want to wake up in a year in this weird in-between place. We need to finish this the way we planned, when we planned. It's not going to be easy, but it's the only way."

I wanted him to fight for me, but he wasn't going to. A sinkhole of despair opened up inside me.

*Don't say it.*

"You're as trained as I can get you in the time we had."

*You're saying it.*

"If I ever love a sub, it's going to be you." He stepped close to me and put his fingertips on my collarbone, brushing my skin with a light, preoccupied touch. "Today I felt close to you. Very close. And at the same time, I can't. I've tried. Every time you submit to me, it's like I'm waking up from a dream and the reality is that I'm fucked up."

He hurt me. Every word opened me to hopelessness. But my overriding emotion wasn't self-interest. It was compassion. He was truly pained and utterly confused. He couldn't explain it to himself any more than he could explain it to me.

I felt sorry for him.

I also felt a responsibility to him.

And though he could hurt me worse than any other human being could, I decided to put my own pain away for a minute. I'd feel it later. I'd feel his lack of love like a punch to the chest. Later.

I pounded my feet into my boots. Later.

I'd left him once. I knew what it took to admit the bond was gone. To say it out loud. To be responsible for the vacuum where love used to be. Even if he left me on day thirty-one, his suffering was greater than mine.

I reached down for the garage door handle and yanked it up. It rattled, and the whoosh and white noise of the expressway filled the room.

"We should stop," I said. "We're just making it worse."

I didn't want to see his reaction. If he agreed, I'd choke on my loss. I couldn't bear it, so I walked out to the Jag without looking back.

He got in front of me, wedging himself between the car and me, holding my elbows with an unexpected intensity. "Give me a chance. Give me the days we have."

I held two things in my mind. He was making me crazy. He was confusing me. He was yanking me toward him and pushing me away at the same time. I was angry, frustrated, vulnerable, defensive, and broken.

And I saw this for what it was. The obfuscation before clarity. Everything had to come out of the closet before it was rearranged. This was the mess where every emotion was strewn on the carpet, waiting to be put back in an orderly fashion. Through all my confusion, I made the calculation that this was a necessary stage.

Fear was hitched on the back of that calm assessment, because the emotional certainty that was to come might include love and it might not.

"What are you fighting for?" I asked, pushing him toward the lucidity I feared.

"Us. Me. I don't know."

"You just said—"

"I know what I just said. Then you walked away and I thought it might be the last time you left, and I made up this thing in my head that if you got to the car before I caught you...I got scared."

He didn't recognize his own scramble of emotions, and I didn't recognize the woman who made the calm assessment that this was part of his journey either toward me or away from me. But though she coexisted with a hysterical panic, she was in charge.

"What were you afraid of?" I asked.

"That I'd never see you again."

"That's not love?"

"I don't know what it is." He drew his hands down my arms pensively. "Maybe it's just the opposite of indifference."

Can a body survive on scraps?

Can a woman pick the meat off dry bones and live?

How long would we do this to each other?

"Four more days," I said.

Love or bust in four days.

# CHAPTER TWENTY-SEVEN

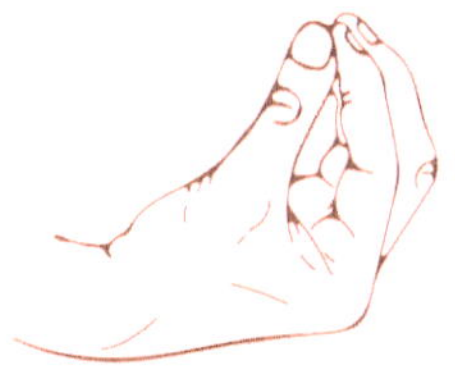

DAY TWENTY-SEVEN

I got to work at ten.

The night before, Adam had helped me pack things, take perishable food out of the fridge, and lock up. We took a cab to Murray Hill, where I reacquainted myself with the apartment he'd had when we met.

Three bedrooms with casement windows and a four-foot-wide wraparound veranda that wasn't good for much more than standing. He'd done it to flip then kept it, so the fixtures and finishes were flashier than what we'd chosen for the loft.

After he fucked me on the rug, leaving me more sore than I'd ever been, I went to the room closest to his, just like in Montauk. Alone. I tried to cry. I tried to feel the pit of my grieving and sadness, down where it was the thickest black. I'd tried to dig it out, but I couldn't find where it ended, and I'd fallen asleep before touching bottom.

"Dad," I said when I walked into my office. "How are you doing?"

"Fine," he wheezed, hunting and pecking at his email.

"I moved temporarily, just so you know. It's temporary, so—"

"Where?" He barely looked away from his screen.

"Murray Hill."

He peered at me over his glasses. If I'd hoped he had forgotten where Adam lived when I was single, it was dashed with that look.

"Temporary," I restated.

"Why?"

*Because a Dominant I contacted to train me as a submissive makes my Dominant husband nervous for my safety.*

"There have been security problems at the loft." I put my bag on my desk and unraveled my scarf. "We're just being safe."

He turned back to the screen. Hunted. Pecked. Two pointer fingers tapped keys like a sparrow seeking seed in the grass. "That's pretty far east. You going to make it on time for the thing at the Intercontinental?"

*The thing the thing the thing...* ooh. The thing. The Literacy Project event. McNeill-Barnes donated big. Mom used to be the development chair. Mom and Dad had gone to the black tie gala at the end of the campaign for years, then Dad took me until Adam came along. Then he and I went. It was a family tradition.

"Can you come with me?" I asked.

"Yeah. Sure. Am I doing this right? What do we do on invoices from states with no sales tax?"

He tapped the screen, and I went to help him. I'd never teach him as much as he'd taught me, but I spent the rest of the morning trying.

‟

**—*What are you doing right now?*—**

Adam texted the question at four in the afternoon. Dad was gone. Since McNeill-Barnes had been legally mandated to do nothing but tread water for thirty days, my to-do list was short and boring. All task, no work.

*—Very busy doing your job—*

The phone rang. It was him.

"Is the office door closed?" he asked without greeting.

"Yes."

"Blinds to the hall? Shut them."

I got up and twisted the rod that closed the blinds.

"Are you done closing the blinds?"

"Yes."

"Good. Put the phone on the coffee table and put me on speaker."

"Done." I hoped he heard the anticipation in my voice.

"Pull up your skirt."

"I'm wearing pants." I unbuttoned them.

"Down all the way then. Bend at the waist and put your hands flat on the table. Do all the things we talked about. Put your ass up and your knees apart."

"Yes, sir," I whispered, letting my jeans fall around my ankles. I bent over the table and spread my feet apart. The exposure was enough to arouse me, and when he spoke, I rubbed myself against the sound of his voice.

"How does that feel?"

"I wish you were here."

"I have to go to Philadelphia tonight."

*No.* I didn't give voice to the cry of my heart. We didn't have time for a night apart. *I* didn't have time. Not a minute to spare.

"I know we only have a few nights," he said, reading my mind again, "but I have to go."

"I understand."

"I'll make it up to you."

"You better."

"You're getting five strokes for that."

I wished he could have seen my face, because it reacted to a strong flow of tingling pleasure that ran from my waist to my knees.

"And you left the package home," he said. "You're supposed to carry it with you."

"I'm sorry."

"I want you to open it, but you have to earn it. Do you understand?"

"Yes, sir." I bent my waist more and leaned close to the phone, whispering, "Packing tape is sexy."

"Not as sexy as your ass. So listen to me carefully. Tonight, don't take a shower. Take a bath. A hot bath. Use your fingers between your legs until you're wet and you want it."

"I'll be wet already if I'm in the bath."

Did he chuckle? I heard nothing more than a pause, but he might have.

"I'll clarify, but you're still getting punished for the wise mouth. When you're wet with your own juice, make your fingers wet, and I want you to put one in your ass."

I stopped breathing. "I—"

"Yes, you can. When you're loose, put in a second finger. When it's all the way in, you can come."

Suddenly aware of my exposure and position, I curdled. I wanted to pull my pants up and stand. I must have waited too long. He knew I was balking.

"Huntress?"

"Will it hurt?"

"The first time? Yes. But it's nothing you can't take."

I rested my cheek on the table. "You like it when I hurt. Why?"

"Because you do it for me. You hurt for me. Because I say so. It means you trust me, and there's nothing like that. It makes me want to push your pain harder and keep you safe at the same time."

"I don't want to hurt there."

"That's why I'll make it as pleasurable as possible." He cleared his throat. "This is training, Diana. And you're doing great, but you need to get more comfortable with that part of your body. Get dressed. Dominic will be outside to take you home."

"Adam," I said, sitting halfway straight. "I think it's fine. With Insolent. I really think he got the message."

"I'll see you tomorrow night."

The screen went black.

As I pulled up my pants, I wondered if I could get away with skipping the bathtub exercise.

# CHAPTER TWENTY-EIGHT

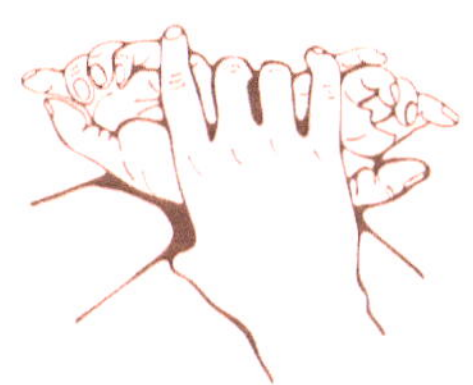

WHAT FREAKED me out most wasn't the pain, but the violation. He'd used my mouth for pleasure more than once, and I enjoyed the feeling of being no more than a convenient object for him. The submission involved in removing my personality and desire from the equation was almost spiritual.

That was probably an exaggeration, but at the same time, it wasn't. I was focused on nothing but him and my objectification.

Anal was a different thing entirely. The size of his cock wasn't a joke, and he was bound to rip me open. Anal wasn't just about submitting to him and his desire. I was submitting to the risk of damage and pain.

He was going to tear me apart for his pleasure.

As much as pain and blood and shredded tissue scared me, what scared me more was the sight of him enjoying it. There was more than a touch of sadism in his appetites. This could be where we found the limits of my masochism.

I knew I could refuse him. I could take as many redlines as I wanted. But I wanted to be trained. I wanted to do it right, and yes, I wanted to finish.

A thousand years before, when I was engaged to a man named

Brian, I'd agreed to anal. It was the night of our engagement party, and I was a little more than a little drunk.

The night was winding down, and as we were kissing and stumbling down the hall, he pushed me into the men's room. There were five stalls with heavy wooden doors. We went into one. I sucked him a little. He got under my Lacroix gown and fingered me until I came. Then I put my hands on the door and bent for him. He pulled my underwear down, and when he said he was going to fuck me in the ass, we both laughed.

A big gob of spit landed in my crack. That was all the lubrication I got, and I didn't know any better. Neither did he. He shoved his dick in my ass, and the pain was brutal. It came from inside me. I screamed and told him to stop.

He did. He pulled out and apologized, but the pain in my gut stayed for another five minutes. We agreed to not do that again.

And that was that.

Now here I was being trained to take anal for someone else's pleasure.

Yeah. I was scared.

"Diana?"

I jumped. Kayti stood in the doorway.

"What's up?" I asked.

"We're going to dinner. Wanna come?"

"God, yes."

"Awesome! We were going to catch the N up to 49th and go to Gerdie's?"

"Yes, yes, yes." I was already closing windows on my computer. "I'm starving."

"Great."

"Wait." I closed my laptop. I couldn't take the train with her. Adam had gotten me a bodyguard and a car. Because he was afraid I'd picked up a rogue Dominant. Who I'd called. Because Adam hadn't wanted to train me. Even though I was submissive. And we were still getting divorced but were acting as if we weren't.

I couldn't seriously explain half of that.

"Meet me out front," I said. "I have a driver."

Kayti; Frank, her fiancé who worked around the corner; and Zack piled into the back of the car. I got in the front next to Dominic.

"Do you know where Gerdie's is?" I asked when the back door slammed shut.

"Sure do." He glanced at me sidelong.

I was supposed to go to Murray Hill, but I was hungry and with friends. So I shot him a look back, and he pulled away, turning uptown.

"What's with the private car, Di?" Zack asked.

"She's the boss, Zack," Kayti protested. "It's the boss life."

"No hack license," Zack continued. "That's not a driver." He changed his tone so it reached Dominic. "You a bodyguard?"

We loved having Zack at McNeill-Barnes because he was sharp and perceptive. That was the exact reason I didn't care for him in the car at that moment.

"Zack, you're being an ass," I said, turning halfway. "If I say he's the driver, he's the driver."

What was that tone? I heard myself as if I were someone else, and I sounded like Adam Steinbeck telling me to get on my knees.

And Zack heard me loud and clear. He actually nodded and shut the fuck up.

I could get used to this.

Gerdie's was packed, but Kayti had magical mystery reservations. Zack to my left. Kayti to my right. Frank across from me, and Dominic somewhere in midtown. He'd said he'd "stay close," but he had to put the car somewhere, and this was not a neighborhood known for legal parking spaces.

Everything was normal on the surface. We talked about work. Kayti showed off her ring. Frank blushed like a schoolboy. Zack leaned two inches too close to me and I jabbed him with my elbow while I brought the fork to my mouth. As the courses came and went, I started to think about taking a bath when I got back. I wondered what my fingers would feel like, what position I'd put myself in. How silly I'd look. I wondered if I could get away with not doing it and saying I did.

I'd missed the last three jokes and I was now laughing because everyone else was. I was ready to get home and just do this thing.

I got up and handed the waiter my card.

"I'll get this ready," he said.
"Where's the bathroom?"
"Downstairs, to the left. Ladies' is the last door."

***—Dominic says you're out—***

Adam's text came as I pushed open the door to the single toilet.

*—Dinner. Why? Do you miss me?—*

***—I need you to be careful—***

I wanted to be careful, but I also wanted to eat. I texted him as I sat.

*—I'll be careful. I'm getting the bill
and going home—*

***—And taking your bath?—***

*—Yes—*

I stood, straightened my clothes, and washed my hands. The light was terrible. Blue green and dim. I looked like a ghoul. Had I stopped thinking about Adam since I'd gotten there? Had I laughed with my friends freely or been fully present for one second?

No. I hadn't. I wasn't finished. I was incomplete. In process. Waiting. And I hated it. Maybe that was why I never finished things. The in-between place where the marriage got hard, or school was a drag, or the project was in production were empty and easy to leave.

I couldn't this time.

*—I'll be thinking of your fingers—*

***—I'll be thinking of your ass—***

*—I need you to love me, I'm going to*

~~die if I do all this and you still leave.~~<br>~~There's no one else, Adam. No one~~<br>~~I'd let do what you want to do. I've~~<br>~~never loved another man and~~<br>~~I promise I've never trusted another.~~<br>~~I can't live without you. If we split up~~<br>~~after you train me I'll set myself~~<br>~~on fire I swear—~~

Highlight>select all>delete.

—My ass is yours—

~

I crawled into bed victorious. Slowly, I'd gotten two fingers in. My ass stretched with the second finger, then closed around them like a vise. I brought myself to orgasm with the other hand, and the involuntary pulsing around my inserted digits shocked me.

Ten o'clock. Was he back at the hotel? Or was he exploring Philly's scene?

I scooted under the covers with my phone.

—I did it—

The reply came immediately.

**—Good girl—**

**—I'll take it easy on you
tomorrow night—**

—I have to go to the Literacy thing<br>at the Intercontinental—

**—That's tomorrow?—**

Nobody's perfect. Not even Adam, who never seemed to forget anything. He'd probably scraped the event from his mind when he moved his stuff out of McNeill-Barnes. In his bones, he was a real-estate mogul, not a publisher.

> *—I'm going with Dad, then we'll
> probably go back to Park
> and I'll crash there—*

Not that I was looking forward to sleeping in my old room, but that was how it usually worked when Dad and I went out. Even when I was married.

**—I'm taking you—**

> *—No—*

—*(...)*—

Whatever he was typing, I didn't want to hear it.

> *—If we're seen together they're going
> to say the divorce is off. And so if we
> split up after the 30th day it's going
> to hurt to have to tell everyone again—*

—*(...)*—

> *—Just let dad take me—*

*Fight for me, Adam. Fight for me.*
I thought he'd never answer. The dots crawled on the bottom of my screen, but whatever he was typing, it didn't make it to my screen.
*Fight. For. Me. You fuckwad!*
He was taking too long to answer. Way too long. What was the problem already? All he had to do was fight the tiniest little bit.

Maybe this wasn't worth it. Maybe I was climbing a tree without a foothold.

*—Just talked to Lloyd. He
doesn't want to go. Be at the
apartment at six. I'll help
you get dressed—*

I practically danced under the covers and, I admit, I squealed with happiness. He was fighting for me. Maybe it was one night and not a lifetime, but he was fighting.

*—Put the box on the night table.
And carry it with you tomorrow.
Got it?—*

*—Yes, sir—*

Yessiree-fucking-bob.

# CHAPTER TWENTY-NINE

## DAY TWENTY-EIGHT

Long white ones for high cholesterol. *Click click.* Yellow once a day as a last resort to keep it from getting worse. *Click click.* Aspirin for blood. Albuterol inhaler—full.

"Then Jesse Helms tells her he'll be a dead man before he puts a woman like that on the NEA committee." Dad snapped the paper.

He had the ability to read something and talk about something completely different at the same time. I could barely count pills and have a conversation at the same time.

"He was a bastard," I grumbled, recounting the little pink pills.

"So I'm glad I don't have to go."

"Just want to make sure, Dad. Adam can be pretty persuasive." I shook the bottle of cholesterol meds. There weren't enough.

"I like seeing you two together."

"You're running out of yellow ones," I said. "You should have another week."

"No," he said with a cough and a short wheeze. "I took what I was supposed to."

"Are you sure?" I was alarmed suddenly. I'd asked him to take over the company and done nothing to help him manage his meds. "When I was gone, are you sure?"

"Loretta's a professional."

His nurse came once a day and she wasn't his daughter. She was a hired hand. Yes, a professional, but what the hell did she know?

I stood and flipped through the calendar by the back door. He'd gotten a new bottle just when I remembered, and a new prescription had been called into the pharmacy in the meantime. Besides, the idea that he'd taken double the dose of his medication was ridiculous. He would have noticed.

I kept counting the weeks, not because I distrusted Loretta or my father, but because something about the way the time had passed stuck in my throat. Why did it matter? I knew when the thirty days ended, so why did I keep knotting my brows about the calendar?

I dumped his yellow pills and counted. Those were a week short as well. I'd carefully counted the days in Montauk, but the weeks before had blended into one.

"Dad?"

He looked over his half-moon glasses. "Yes?"

"I have to go." I slid the pills back into the bottles. *Click click clickclickclick.*

"Everything all right?"

"Yeah."

Dad didn't have to say a word. I stopped at the door and looked back at him. His belt held up his pants, and his shirt folded under the arms. He was soft around the middle and thinner than he used to be.

"Did you..." I took a sharp breath before getting on with it. "Were you happy with Mom?"

He took off his glasses and leaned back. "Why are you asking me that?"

"Because. I don't know."

"I loved your mother. She was better than me, and I blamed her for that, but I loved her. She forgave me. Which proved she was even better. But I still loved her. I wasn't self-destructive enough to let her go for loving me."

I kissed him on the cheek. He grabbed my wrist as hard as he could, which wouldn't have held me if I didn't want to be held. He didn't have that kind of strength.

"And I love you," he said. "I won't lie and say that didn't factor in."

"Got it."

I ran out, grabbed my coat, and didn't slow down until I got back to the loft. I ran so fast I felt scared and excited at the same time, balancing them on opposite sides of my brain without worrying about dropping them.

# CHAPTER THIRTY

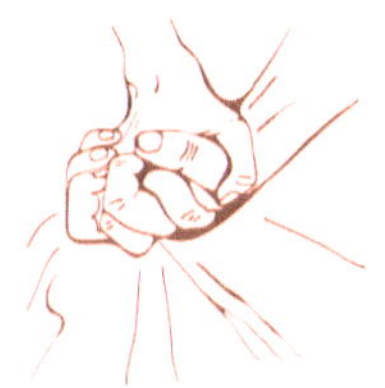

I was supposed to go to Murray Hill right after my dad's, but I didn't. The loft was a short cab ride, and I could make it in time.

I ran in, slammed the door, and stripped my coat and scarf, leaving them in piles on the floor. Kicked off one boot. Took a step. Kicked off the other boot. Unbuttoned my pants. Got into the bathroom. Ripped the package open. Skimmed the directions, which were printed in four-point type. Yanked my pants down all the way, sat on the bowl, and peed right onto the stick.

*What do you want?*

I knew what I wanted. I wanted to have a baby before I got cancer. I wanted to just do that one thing, then they could remove every body part that made me a woman. They could turn me into a flat-chested Barbie doll. I was all right with that. Take it. If it made me live, just take it.

And what about Adam? What about the knot of conflicting feelings we both had? What about the compounded opposites? The love that flicked off like a light switch for one of us just as the other's flicked on? It was a disaster. A complete disaster. I couldn't bring a child into the mess we'd created.

I sat on the toilet with my hand trapped between my closed thighs. I couldn't look.

What did I want?

Was it important to know before I looked at the stick? The result wouldn't change.

But I had to know what to hope for. I had to believe something before I knew something. How else would I know how to feel?

I didn't want to be pregnant. I didn't want a baby now. Of the dozen reasons a woman could miss a period, I didn't want it to be the most likely. Anything but. I wasn't ready. *We* weren't ready.

"One line. Just please, give me one line."

I opened my legs and lifted the stick to eye level. The wet, grey wave had passed the first line in the little window and made its way to the other side in a serrated procession, passing where the second line should have been, to where it never would be, to the edge.

No happy second line appeared.

One pink line.

Not.

Pregnant.

A sob shot out of my lungs like cannon fire. I threw the stick in the trash as if I could break it. It just made a cracking noise against the plastic bag. So ineffective. Everything was ineffective. Everything I tried to do was a goddamn joke. Even the things I didn't try failed. Even when I was handed everything in life I barely made it work and here I fuckingwasinthisfuckingbathroom—

I stood and kicked the bottom of the pail. It upended and spilled toward me, dropping a couple of cotton swabs by my socked feet and a failed pregnancy test on my foot. I kicked it off, lost my balance with my pants around my knees, and fell ass-first on the bathroom floor.

Tears came. Breaths hitched. I had a decent amount of snot happening. I let it go for a long time, but no matter how hard I cried, I couldn't touch the bottom of the pool.

I stayed there, curled up, and cried. I pulled out all the stops. I dipped deep into the well of pain to find I was emptying the ocean with a slotted spoon.

~

My phone dinged. It was getting dark, and I was still on the bathroom floor. My back pocket was folded under my waistband, tucked somewhere behind my knee. I wrestled the phone out.

*—Where are you?—*

I was mad at him. I was mad that he'd given me a broken baby last time and hadn't gotten me pregnant this time. I was mad that he didn't love me enough to be a father to the non-baby. Or that he would be a fine father, but not on terms I understood. I was mad that I loved the wrong parts of him, and that I felt closer to a sadist than a kind man. I was mad that he'd opened me up and I couldn't close the wound without him. I was mad that I could only really cry when he hurt me.

*—At the loft—*

I wasn't ready to tell him why I'd run to the loft, but I felt the compulsion to explain.

*—I had to get shoes—*

Lies. The marriage had collapsed on an underpinning of lies, and there I was, trying to set that same foundation again.

My reasons were irrelevant. Lies were lies.

*—Come here before we go
to the Intercontinental—*

Dominant voice through the text. I sat up on the tiles. My eyes throbbed from crying, and the muscles around my mouth hurt from an hour in the weeping grimace.

Was it wrong that I wanted to please him? That in my misery, the idea of satisfying him was comforting? In obeying him, giving him that pleasure, I could soothe my own pain. I could stop worrying about the future for a few hours and do nothing but make him happy.

*—Yes, sir—*

I scrambled up and got my pants back on. I put the test and the bathroom junk back in the garbage can. I had this. I pulled my hair out of its clips and brushed it down, taking a good look at my face.

My eyes and lips were swollen and puffy. The whites of my eyes were webbed with hot red. He'd know. He'd ask. I couldn't lie to his face. I'd tell him about the failed pregnancy test, and he'd be relieved. I wouldn't be able to bear it.

***—Bring the box—***

Apparently my curiosity was about to be sated. Well, that would be a nice distraction.

If I just focused on pleasing him for one night, I might not be sad tomorrow. I could let it all go, and tomorrow I could be the adultingest adult in New York City. I could tell my husband, lover, Dom, ex, everything, and he could soothe me or not. I'd have it under control by then. I'd be able to see a way forward.

We had cold packs in the freezer. I took the softest and pressed it to one eye, then the other as I went about the house, gathering a long slate-blue dress and matching shoes. Navy lace garter. His pearl collar, just in case. I pressed the pack to my eyes the whole ride to Murray Hill.

# CHAPTER THIRTY-ONE

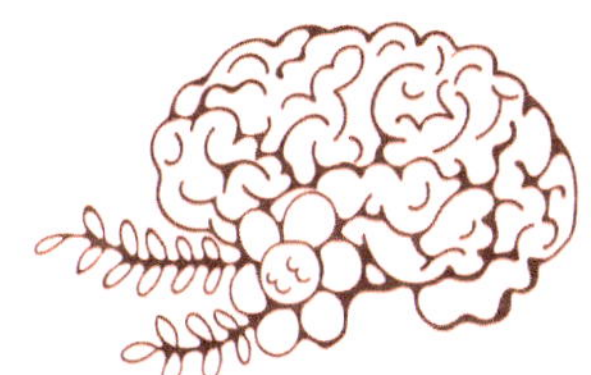

I'D GOTTEN COMPLACENT. I let myself think I'd won him back. That our separation was over and we were about to open a new chapter in our marriage. I'd let the idea of a future with him get real when I took the pregnancy test, and he was so perfect, so comforting in his dominance, I let the hope solidify.

Because who could be so intimate and still walk away?

What kind of person played a woman's body like a well-loved instrument without caring about the woman inside it?

I had him. He wasn't going to say good-bye. I couldn't imagine being without him, and in my little cocoon of self-reflection, he felt the same way.

Complacency is the prologue to calamity.

I was going to be diligent. Stay on task. This wasn't the time to get distracted by a pregnancy test that changed nothing.

The strategy was to make sure he understood that he loved me. The tactic was to submit. To show him that even in submission, I was still the woman he loved.

*Buck up, buttercup. There's work to do.*

Him: Trousers open. Shirt buttoned. Tie draped, not knotted. Socks. Watch big as a dinner plate.

Me: Wet hair. Stockings. Garter. Bra. He'd taken away my panties. I wasn't clothed in much more than his stare.

"Where's the box?" he asked, doing up his cuff. I'd seen him do it a hundred times, and it was never as sexy as it was that night.

"In my bag, sir."

"Get it and present it to me."

I padded out to my bag in my bare feet. As soon I was out of his sphere, I remembered the single pink line. What it meant. The years I'd have to wait to start a family. As soon as I was back in the bedroom with the box, those years fell off me. He didn't make me forget, but his presence protected me from myself. Even saying nothing, he gave me permission to not worry. I needed that or I was going to cry again.

I got on my knees, looked down, and held it up to him. The corners were blunted and the tape had curled at the edges, but I hadn't opened it. I was proud of myself.

He plucked it out of my hands. "You did good with this."

"Thank you, sir."

"You all right, huntress?"

"Yes, sir."

Seeing outside myself, I was saying sir more than usual. I was more compliant in attitude as well as action. If I kept this up, he would realize something was wrong before I had the empty, clear feeling I got from making his will my own. That would be a lot of wasted sirs.

He took a small knife from his pocket and slashed the paper and tape off an edge, then down at a right angle.

"You conquered your curiosity." He handed me the slashed box. "Go on."

I opened it to find a small velvet box with the top on a hinge. I creaked that open. The shiny chrome object inside was a four-inch-long bulb with a ring on the end. I took it out, hooking my finger in the circle.

"Is this what I think it is?" I asked.

"What do you think it is?"

"A Christmas ornament."

He looped his finger inside the ring and took the toy from me. "Exactly right." He put the end against my lips, running the curve of the object along them. "Lick it." His voice was so soft and so stern at the same time.

I put out my tongue and tasted the hard metal.

"Open your mouth." When I did, he slid it in and out along the flat of my tongue until it went all the way in without gagging me. "Close it."

I sealed my lips around the base, leaving the ring outside my lips.

"The way it's in your mouth is exactly the way it's going to fit in your ass. You'll want to lubricate it with your spit. Be generous."

I tried to swallow my fear, but the plug kept my throat from closing. Adam took my hand and led me to the bed, guiding me onto my back. He opened my legs and pushed my knees back, squeezing the flesh of my thighs to expose me to his eyes.

My throat hummed, but I kept my lips locked and my tongue curled around the bulb. I eased into submission, and sexual pleasure merged with a rightness that washed away pain.

Adam bent down and licked the length of my seam. He sucked and kissed me without reservation or pause. He used his fingers to move the lubrication to my ass and back again. I groaned, eighty percent of the way to orgasm.

He stood and slid his finger in the metal ring. "Open."

I opened my mouth, and a thick line of spit tethered the plug to my tongue.

"Hands and knees." He slapped my bottom as I complied. "I'm putting this inside your ass."

"Then what?"

He couldn't fuck me if there was a plug in me. Right? I didn't know how it was supposed to fit in the first place.

"Then we're going out."

"With it in me?"

"Yes. Trust me."

He slid it across my ass, back and forth. There was plenty of lubrication on it, and the twenty percent of an orgasm I had left pounded at the gate.

"I'm going to take this slow," he said. "If there's more than a little pain, you need to speak up. It shouldn't hurt. Just breathe."

"Okay."

He slid it in my ass so slowly it felt as if it wasn't moving at all. I pushed against it. It went in a little, stretching me.

"Breathe," he whispered, putting his hand on my lower back and guiding me toward him. I stretched farther. "Does it hurt?"

"No. It's definitely something. But no pain."

"That's the widest part," he said, and with one last push, he got it all the way inside. My body closed around the base. "It's in."

I twisted around, looking at him over my shoulder. He had his cock in his hand.

"Make it hurt," I whispered.

He drew his hand down my back, considering it.

"Later," he said, sliding into me.

He fucked me hard from behind. I'd never felt anything like it. The weight. The stretch. The way his cock rubbed it through a membrane wall. I was completely full and fully complete, reaching orgasm with my whole body. He bent around me, his hand on my throat, gentle and firm as he came inside me.

His hoarse whisper seemed involuntary, straight from the gut, bypassing heart and brain. One word.

"You."

I closed my eyes and let him kiss my neck and whisper in my ear. I was perfect. I was beautiful. I was so very good.

One pink line perfect.

One lonely line beautiful.

One single line good.

I didn't feel inadequate for not being pregnant.

I felt inadequate for not creating a marriage worth being born into.

# CHAPTER THIRTY-TWO

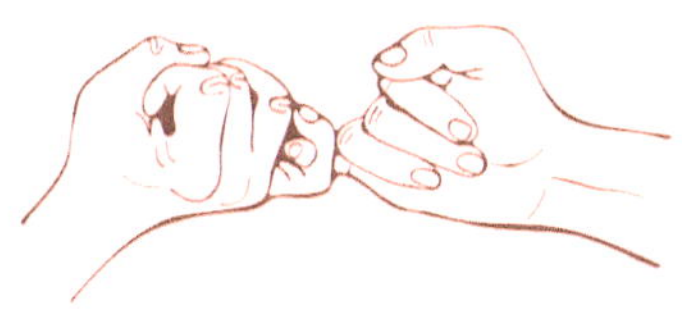

THE EVENT at the Intercontinental was the same as always. Bright lights. Little bronzed nametags. Red carpets that looked good on video but, in real life, were worn and gum-spotted. None of it mattered. He was on my arm and in the core of my body was a solid weight of shiny silver metal, stretching me for him.

"How's that thing feel?" Adam asked once we were out of range of the flashing lights.

"Not bad." I pulled him closer.

He gazed down at me, and what should have been a long, warm look into my soul ending in a kiss was actually short and interrupted by his need to talk to someone across the room.

We'd been married business partners long enough for me to regret the loss of that warm moment at the same time as I understood it. The nametag on the end of my ribbon lanyard said McNeill-Barnes Publishing, and it meant business. I could still play company owner. I could still be a businesswoman. I was always the heiress to an iconic publishing house. Even with a butt plug inserted in my ass.

I had to bite my lips to keep from laughing. We were talking to Giulio Fenestro, who was a shoo-in for a Pulitzer. Not the time to giggle about walking around pretty-as-you-please with a hunk of precious metal in my rectum.

*Do. Not. Laugh.*

Adam yanked me to the silent auction tables.

"What's so funny?" he whispered.

"Nothing." I snapped up a clipboard.

"Am I going to punish you for lies of omission?"

I wrote my name and a number on the sheet. I didn't even know what I was bidding on.

"Put my address. You'll be there for the duration."

"So sure, are you?"

I put down the clipboard. He took me by the chin and looked deeply in my eyes. I tried to hide the pain of the pregnancy test. First, with defiance, then submission as I looked away. I couldn't bear to look away for long. When our eyes met again, he wasn't seeing at something that pleased him.

"Talk to me."

"I'm nervous about later, I guess."

He let my chin go and broke eye contact.

"Well, well," he said. "Look who's here."

I followed his gaze to Stefan, who was talking to Thalia Jonson from Breakneck Books.

"Krovite published his catalogs, right?" I asked. "That must be why he's here."

Adam didn't wait to answer but approached the pair with his usual confidence and grace. He didn't take my hand or give me his arm. His fingers didn't brush my neck as they often did when we were at a party together. He just went, and I dragged my butt plug behind.

Five minutes before, I would have had to stifle a laugh, but now I felt small and infantile with the sophisticated humor of a twelve-year-old boy.

I shook Thalia's hand and did a double-air kiss with Stefan. We talked about the future of plated art books versus art textbooks for a few minutes before Thalia excused herself.

"Just like old times," Stefan said then turned to me.

"Are you moving to Breakneck?" I asked quietly. "They just bought Havershim's old plant in Norfolk."

We engaged in a light, gossipy business discussion about Breakneck's color plating abilities, during which Adam didn't touch me or look at me. I could hold the conversation, but the weight of his inattention kept me from breathing right. Kept me from thinking clearly.

"Can you excuse us?" Adam said, offering me his arm.

"Of course."

He pulled me away from the crowd in the ballroom and up a set of beige marble stairs. My stockings felt saggy and my shoes bit the soft parts of my ankles, but I continued. I needed to focus on pleasing him.

We slipped past a velvet rope, into a narrow hallway lined with paintings of beautiful Victorian women and a deep blue carpet. He wasn't looking at me. Just walking fast and looking ahead. The avoidance hurt more than my shoes.

"Stop," I said. "What's the problem? Wait—" I interrupted myself, looking at the floor and putting my hands up to fend off his voice and his face. I'd melt for either. "You're going to ask me what I'm talking about, so let's just skip that part." I stood straight and took a deep breath, balling my fists and girding myself against his brutal charms. "If I thought you were taking me to fuck me, I'd follow. No problem. But I'm getting the sense there's no sex at the end of this walk."

My voice sounded shrill and desperate, and everything about him was simply rock solid and right with the world. Even in his confusion, as all the things he could say flashed across his face, he was perfect and I was a little girl who wanted to rip a piece of metal out of her ass.

"Just say it, Adam. Whatever it is."

"Your eyes."

"What about them?"

"They're swollen. Just a little. You probably put ice on them before you came, and now they're swollen again. You were crying. Don't deny it. I want to know why, and you haven't told me. So that means one of three things. Either it's something you don't want me to know, it's someone you don't want me to kill, or it's me."

My eyes swelled up again. My palms became as wet as my mouth. I was going to explode in a cyclone of spit and tears, so I clamped my lips shut.

"And I know it's me," he said. "It's what I said. It's what I didn't say. I don't know which. I can't get this right. I mean, at the Sheepshead house, when I made love to you, I felt it again. I thought..." He closed his eyes slowly and opened them again, looking more composed. "It doesn't matter."

"It does. It matters."

"It makes me crazy when you cry."

"Why?"

"I want to hurt whoever hurt you. Then I realize I might have to hurt myself. And I would. I will. Why were you crying?"

My feet hurt and my shoulders were suddenly stiff. Remembering the bathroom floor, I felt like a brittle statue in a fancy dress. I was made of shell and soft tissue. No lie I told would change that.

"I thought I was pregnant."

His eyebrows went up, and his face took on an urgency I'd never seen before. Part confusion and part smothered joy. "You—"

"I'm not."

"Ah."

"But it made me think. This baby. It doesn't exist, but it had parents. And I don't know if his parents have a future, so those babies won't ever exist. I feel like I killed children."

"What does that mean?" He brushed a hair from my cheek. The gesture was tender and sweet, somehow protective, existing in a land between Manhattan and Montauk.

"I didn't want it," I said fiercely. That was the only way. "I told myself to hope I wasn't. I know hoping one way or the other didn't affect the results, but the hope told me something. I don't want to be pregnant. But when I wasn't, I was disappointed. And that told me something too."

"You wanted to be pregnant," he said. "But not with me."

"I want children with you, but not in this situation. I don't know whether I'm coming or going."

"Maybe you're doing both." His fingers caught the ribbon lanyard, stroking down to the name tag. Diana Steinbeck. Our names were merged on the little white rectangle.

"I don't know how to fix all this."

"It's amazing that you left me in the first place without thinking about how terribly inconvenient it would be."

"I'm impulsive. If it didn't take three sponsors to get into the Cellar, I'd be—" I cut myself off, but it was too late.

He increased the downward pressure on the lanyard just a little. "Excuse me?"

Fuck it. I had to stand by my actions or dance around them like an adolescent trying to get away with adult behavior. He wasn't my father.

"I started the process before you redlined it." I didn't say how many minutes before, or how easy it would have been to halt. Maybe I was an adolescent. I yanked my lanyard away. I wouldn't be physically threatened by him.

"Did Charlie write a letter?"

"I asked Stefan and—" Fuck it again. We said no lies of omission. He couldn't hurt me anymore. "Serena."

Adam let the tag drop, took me by the hand, and pulled me behind him.

"Adam, wait!"

"Don't let go."

He held my hand so tightly I couldn't have let go if I wanted to, then he slapped open the door to the main hall and cut into the crowd. He didn't slow down long enough for me to say help to someone I knew or cut a turn on my high heels.

"Adam! The floor is marble!" I barked after I slipped, avoiding a fall but not shame.

He stopped and, with the force of inertia that kept me moving forward, wrapped his arm around my waist. Then he kept crossing the room as if he were saving a life.

"What are you doing?" I hissed.

"Stefan. That's what."

"It's not his fault."

"The fuck it's not."

I followed more readily in an odd, unbelievable need to protect Stefan. "You introduced us. You made it possible."

"Exactly," he said. "I'm the only one who can undo what I did."

"It won't go through until after the thirty days."

"Irrelevant."

"You're being unreasonable."

He couldn't lodge an objection because Stefan came into view. I didn't know the man he was talking to. Looked like an old-school publishing guy with a comb-over, a five-thousand-dollar suit, and red tie.

I smiled at him as we approached, and since we were about to bulldoze his conversation, I mouthed the word, "Sorry."

"Isn't it funny how I don't see you for years and now you show up here?" Adam said the second he was in earshot.

"Nice to see you too," Stefan said. "Adam Steinbeck, this is—" he indicated the man with the comb-over but didn't have a chance to make the introduction.

My husband was made of fuel and fire. "And the Greens too. Everywhere she is, you show up."

Comb-over excused himself. Not that anyone noticed.

"It's nice to see her." He directed his words to me. "Do you want to see me?"

Adam didn't let me answer. "No, she doesn't."

"I think he's kind of interesting," I said.

Adam leveled a finger at Stefan. "Rescind your sponsorship."

"Is that what this is about?" Stefan faced me. "Are you all right?" He seemed genuinely concerned. He deserved an answer, but Adam didn't give me a second.

"She's fine."

"That's enough!" I said, pushing Adam's arm off me.

"She's mine, you understand? I'll decide if she's in or out." Adam growled it as if it were deadly true, but we'd just had a conversation about how I wasn't his. About how he could never love me and be happy at the same time.

"I am not." I was flat serious. Not yelling, almost too quiet for Adam to hear through the rage in his ears.

"I'm watching you," Adam continued. "And I'm watching her. So—"

"I'm not yours."

"—if I ever see you near her again—"

"I'm not yours." I raised my voice just a little.

"—I'm going to make it my business to —"

"I'm not yours!"

The ballroom gallery fell silent. The string quartet hit a speed bump and played again. Interrupted conversations continued. The world spun on its axis for everyone else, while I stayed suspended in time. Gravity stopped, and I floated in the space between us, where the tension between his shock and his rage vibrated.

"I'm not yours," I said. "We talked about this."

"For two days, you are."

I shook my head slowly. I couldn't utter the words releasing him from his last half week with me, but it was done. Something inside me had snapped under the weight of his words, the pregnancy test, and the burden of keeping love alive for the both of us. The charade was ending.

I held out my hand. "I need my coat check ticket, please."

He gave it to me. "I'll get you home."

I snapped the ticket away and pushed through the crowd. He would follow. I knew him at least that well. If I turned around, I'd encourage him. I just wanted my coat and a cab—alone. Then I wanted to go to my father's place and cry for a few hours. Maybe I'd cry hard enough to excavate my grief. I wouldn't tell Dad why I was crying. I wouldn't tell him how I knew we were finished. I wouldn't talk about the submission or my own needs. I'd only tell him how bad I felt for fucking this up.

"Diana." Adam sidled up to me when I handed the girl my ticket. "Let me take you home."

"No. Just no."

"Why not?"

My coat came. I pulled it over the counter. "Because I'm sad. And I feel hopeless. And trapped."

"By me?"

"You want me to answer that?"

He guided me away from the coat check window. His jacket still smelled like Montauk snow and his body smelled like fennel as it pressed against me.

"Don't answer," he said. "Just listen. We have a few days. Only a few more before things get even more complicated. Will we be together? Apart? Some middle thing? Something so painful we can't even imagine it? These few days we have, they're precious. It's all unknowns after that. So let's just lock ourselves away. You and me. We trust each other. We'll close the door on love and celebrate trust."

Running my fingers along his lapel, I avoided meeting his eyes. He pressed his lips to my cheek, then my neck.

"I want to tie you down one more time."

"What's the point?" I was arguing about nothing. I was going with him. I just wanted him to work a little harder.

"The way you try so hard to stay quiet when I hurt you. That moment of hesitation before you get on your knees." I felt the line of his erection against my thigh. "I want it as long as I can get it. I can keep you on the edge for fifteen minutes. I want to see if you can stay quiet before I let you scream." His lips traced a line across my forehead.

"I hate you."

"But you trust me."

I pushed him away, looking into his eyes. "I do. And if you break that trust, it's broken forever."

"I won't."

I walked past him, pushing my arms into the coat sleeves, tying my scarf, my heels clopping and echoing in the cavern of stone. A doorman opened the brass doors, and I went out into the cold.

# CHAPTER THIRTY-THREE

I GOT into the cab with the word *trust* written on my heart. But it wouldn't stick. Trust didn't want to be on the heart. It was in the mind. Maybe it was in the hands or voice, but though I knew we trusted each other, it wasn't the same as love written on the heart.

We got to Murray Hill before I decided what to do about it. So I abdicated to complicity. Trust would have to write itself wherever it wanted.

When we got into the apartment, he took my coat like a gentleman.

"Go into the bathroom. Take the dress off and put your hands on the vanity."

All the command and dominance were there. All the confident intonations that ensured my obedience were present. I should have hopped off to the bathroom to do his bidding.

If it were Montauk, I would have.

The day before, I would have.

But it wasn't Montauk or day twenty-three. It was the night of day twenty-eight, and something had changed. I went to the bathroom with my chin high and my shoulders back. Not to please him, but because I wanted this dead weight out of my ass and I didn't know how to get it out myself.

Naked, leaning over the vanity with nothing but the French stone countertop in my sight, I laced my fingers together and bowed my head. The diamonds on my wedding ring pressed hard against my fingers. After the first meeting with my lawyer, I'd put it back on. He'd had his ring on, and it seemed disrespectful to take it off before papers were signed, or he took off his, or we both agreed that the marriage didn't exist anymore.

It was as if my world had always revolved around his pleasure.

He came in behind me. We made eye contact in the mirror. When he put his hand on my lower back and pressed down to get my ass up, I turned back to the top of the vanity, pressing my forehead against the cool stone.

"You're perfect. Don't let anyone tell you otherwise."

"Not even you, sir." *Sir* was marbled in sarcasm. Damn. I didn't want to show my hand. I didn't want my words painted in four coats of my feelings. I wanted to hide, and didn't.

He wasn't stupid. He heard it, but he chose to ignore it.

"When I take this out, you're going to be open for a few minutes. I'm going to lubricate you." He leaned down and whispered in my ear, "It won't hurt when I fuck you. Not more than a few seconds, maybe. You're going to come like you've never come before. Are you ready?"

"Yes, sir," I whispered back with my eyes closed.

He stroked my skin, warming me, then tugged gently on the plug. "Push out a little."

I did, and the thing slid out. He wrapped it in a towel and snapped up a bottle from the cabinet.

"How does that feel?"

It felt odd. It felt as if my body was doing its own thing. I felt stretched, empty, as if I'd made room for something that wasn't there anymore.

He squirted lube on me.

I wasn't scared. I thought I'd be tense at the prospect of getting fucked in the ass, but it wasn't the fear of pain or humiliation that caused my anxiety.

His buckle clacked and his zipper hissed.

"Do I say pinochle, or can I just say stop?" I asked.

"Don't think about that yet."

"No. I mean *now*."

"Why are you safeing out?"

"I just am. I'm not in the mood."

He continued to massage my bottom. "The sub doesn't get moods, Diana."

I stood up straight. Naked in the mirror with him behind me, we looked like normal people. But we weren't. Everything was wrong.

"Pinochle." I said it without question. I said it like he said *get on your knees*. And just in case he missed it, I repeated it. "Pinochle, pinochle, pinochle."

"Why?"

I faced him. "Because this is too intimate for how I feel right now."

"Diana, I—"

"I'm moving back to the loft. This..." I put my hands on his lapels. "This is a complete waste of time. I mean... it's not. It's fine. It's what I signed up for. But I'm just saying pinochle to the whole thing."

I gave him a little push and brushed past him to get to the bedroom. The afternoon's jeans hung over the back of the chair. I couldn't wait to get into them. I couldn't jam my legs in fast enough. My foot got tangled in the fabric and I nearly fell before he jumped to steady me. His hand on my arm, perfect pressure, just enough to hold me up but not hurt. His posture and expression were pure concern for my bodily well-being.

Oh, to be taken care of by a man who loved me. Something I'd never desired because I never wanted to be taken care of was now a lofty and far away fantasy.

"Let go," I said. "Let me fall, okay? Just let me fall." I stood straight, buttoning my jeans. I was still naked from the waist up, but his only interest was my face.

"Stay," he said. "Stay tonight and go tomorrow."

"No. I'm getting a cab." I snapped a shirt out of a drawer and pulled it on. No bra. Didn't care. The coat would cover me. "I'll come back for my stuff in the morning."

"Wait."

I didn't wait. I went to the front door. A pair of boots and the heels

I'd worn to the event were under my coat. I stuck my bare feet into the boots.

"Diana!"

"What?"

In his nice blue suit, tie halfway undone, sock feet, and unbuttoned trousers, he looked like a man falling apart at the seams. He looked the way I felt.

"I want you to stay with me." The desperation in his voice was new, and I was upset enough to be immune to it.

"Whatever." I got my coat on.

"You're acting like a brat."

"I'll be one by tomorrow."

I turned the knob, but he leapt for the door, pressing his hand on the seam between the door and the jamb.

"Adam. Let. Me. Go."

"Stay tonight. Please."

"Look, if you can't love me, I get it. It's fine. I can save you the trouble. Just save me the trouble too. Save me the heartache."

"Just stay."

"Why? What's the difference?"

"I want you to finish what you started."

He said it with all the Dom bells and whistles, but it landed like a squib, not a bomb.

"I'll decide what's worth finishing. Me. I'll decide. Now let me out."

I yanked the door with all my might. His hand came off it, and I swung it wide with everything I had. It slapped the wall so hard the bell rung. I didn't waste a second, getting out into the indirect, warm lighting of the hall just as he put his arms around me. They grabbed nothing, sliding away like a scarf that wasn't wrapped tightly enough.

# CHAPTER THIRTY-FOUR

## DAY TWENTY NINE

THE RAIN SOUNDED like a percussion section. I wrapped myself in my covers, alone at four in the morning. Wide awake after three solid hours of sleep.

I'd walked out on him to save my dignity. He'd made sure I had a car home, but I could barely look at the driver.

I'd reveled in feeling like a piece of meat with Adam. Rejecting my identity for a few hours. Existing for his pleasure. I didn't know what had changed. Something enormous and abstract. I couldn't put my finger on it. I got on my stomach and put my arms between my chest and the mattress, trying to squeeze out the panic that Adam and self-respect were incompatible.

I took my journal off the night table and scribbled in the half light.

*At some point, it was going to come to this.*

*There was never hope for it. I'm running west to chase the sun. It's going to set, no matter how fast I go.*

I'd stopped writing questions in my journal. I was making statements. I didn't even notice the change for the first two pages. I didn't realize something had broken until the third page, when I was unable to get the stream of consciousness back to questions.

*Take a page from Adam's book. He didn't need love all those years. I don't have to love a man to get satisfaction from him either. Maybe. What would it be like?*

Finally. A question. And yet, it was unanswerable because I couldn't imagine it. Couldn't sink deeply into a fantasy about some Dom I'd never met, seen, spoken to.

*What was it like for Adam? How did he give himself to that intimacy without being intimate?*

Practice.

Maybe.

Maybe peeling Serena and subs like her down to the core built him up until intimacy wasn't intimacy anymore.

The valid, even productive train of thought veered off the rails as I imagined him fucking Serena. Eating her pussy. Pulling her hair. Pretending to rape her by a creek.

My heart was a spool of emotions spinning as the thread was pulled faster and faster. She wanted him. She could have him again. I'd known it before, back when I was confident that I'd win him back, but all my imaginings of them weren't an imagined past, but a possible future.

I grabbed my phone.

His green dot was planted solidly in Murray Hill, in his kitchen, if the satellites were dead on.

That should have helped, but it didn't, because Montauk Adam wasn't limited to a single room. If he could take me anywhere in the house, he could take Serena too. She'd said she was going to Tel Aviv, but wasn't she back already? Or he could be with someone else. Or texting her. Or thinking about how he was going to get her in bed.

"For the love of God, Diana. Get control of your life," I said, tossing the phone back on the table. I hugged my pillow. It was a sad substitute.

*Get control.*

All right. Well, the first thing I had to get control of was the next few hours. Because sleep wasn't in the cards, and I wasn't going to lie in bed and mope like a freaking loser. If I was awake, I was going to do something. I put on sweat pants and a hoodie, laced up my sneakers, and went for a fucking run in the fucking rain.

The utter, blanket stupidity of this move wasn't apparent until I got around the corner and stepped in a puddle that left one sock soaking wet. The other didn't meet the wetness challenge until the next block.

Yet I felt better. Cold. Wet. Slipping every dozen steps, I still felt as if I'd gotten control of a few minutes of my life. All I needed to do was tack together more minutes, hours, and days.

I heard splashing footsteps behind me about four blocks from home, on a cobblestone stretch of Crosby. New York never sleeps, but it does go into a fugue state in the wee hours. A few cars splashed past. The bakery lights were on. But I didn't see another soul on the street. I turned. A man jogged half a block behind me, but not jogging. Not really. He was in jeans and a T-shirt. His hood shadowed his face.

What a pain in the ass.

I wasn't afraid. Not at first. At first I took the normal precautions. I turned onto a wider street with more traffic. He was still there. Then I had the good sense to be scared.

My heart raced. My vision closed up in the rain. I picked up my pace, but not that much. Not enough to force him to run. I wanted him to be complacent, because I had to think.

Assume it's not a coincidence. Assume it's not a random guy minding his own business. Run into a public place. Except there are no public places at four in the morning.

Run home. Then he'd know where I lived.

The thunder cracked and the rain picked up as I chose home. Crosby Street was narrow and dark, but I could get behind a locked door.

Headlights from a slow-moving car lit up the sidewalk, and I avoided another puddle. As I turned, the same headlights shone ahead. I turned. The man in jeans was still behind me, and astride him, a car kept pace. He glanced at it. Stopped as I kept going. When I turned back again, the man in jeans was running away from me, and the car sped ahead.

What the hell?

Had the driver chased the man away? I hadn't heard anything. Was it just the presence of the car? What had just happened?

*You know exactly what happened.*

I got under a scaffold and took out my phone, quickly opening the phone tracking app.

Adam's green dot was two blocks ahead of me, turning off the street I was on, left onto Crosby. Must have been Dominic's car. Or a hire. Something he'd grabbed fast when he saw me move. Something he could park by the loft and wait in, because according to the dot, that was exactly what he was doing.

If I started jogging, I'd get home from the other direction. He'd already be watching.

I could have gone and gotten a hotel room just to fuck with him. But I wasn't feeling spiteful. Having taken the run, I was truly tired.

I jogged home, looked at the car long enough to note it was Dominic's, and went into the lobby without even waving at my husband. I didn't want him to know I knew he was there, and I wanted to give him the gift of thinking I was safe because of him. Whether it was true or not, whether he deserved it or not, the gift was still mine to give.

# CHAPTER THIRTY-FIVE

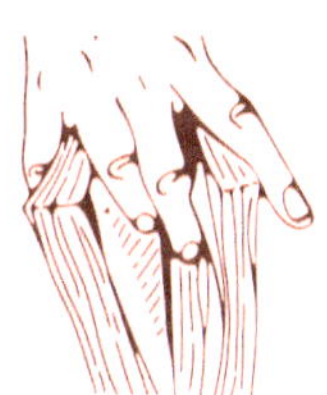

I TRIED TO WORK. I had an essay to read, a box full of emails, and checks to sign.

Though I'd slept soundly for a few more hours, my adrenaline was pumping by the time I got to work. Pictures of Adam and Serena danced in my head like sweaty, grunting sugarplums. I didn't want that shit in my brain. I felt violated by my own thoughts.

So of course I had to check his green dot.

It was like an addiction. I craved the rush of anxiety. I was both miserable and comfortable in the heady, unpleasant pain of panic.

It was day thirty. If I was going to get him back, my last best chance was during the next sixteen hours. After that, we'd live on the same planet, but we would be unbound.

And yet, it was over.

He loved me and couldn't admit it. He could chase away stalkers in the middle of the night, throw a fit about another Dom's advances, but he couldn't admit he loved me. Did I even have time for this? With or without Serena breathing down my neck, how was he serving me as a lover? Was I chasing him out of fear that she'd scoop him up? If he was wrong for me, what was the damn difference?

My hands shook too hard to sign the checks. I answered emails. The essay was good enough. I sent it to Zack for further review.

Nadine's son wasn't in, but his little space was carved out, waiting for him. I wished he was there. He cheered me up.

Dad sat at the desk across the room. I could hear his wet breaths behind the mask. Humidity was tough on him, even if it was cold. The air became a solid thing.

"Dad?" I said.

He said *yes* from behind the mask and kept his eyes on his keyboard.

"Do you want to go home?"

He tapped a few more keys then pushed the mask to the top of his head. His grey hair got caught in the strap and stuck out at odd angles. The shape of the mask left a red oval around his nose, cheeks, and chin. "Why would I want to go home?"

"You don't sound good."

"You always tell me that, and I'm always fine."

"I'm sorry, I just don't want you to feel obligated."

He shut off the oxygen tank in three angry turns. "I am not obligated. Stop it. You make me crazy. Like you got nothing better to do than henpeck me your father."

"You're fine. I know."

"You don't. I taught you everything you know about this business before you were sixteen, but I haven't taught you everything I know."

I put my elbows on the desk and folded my hands. "Fine. Tell me something you know that I don't."

"Tell you something?"

"Yes. Tell me something. Surprise me."

"Management rule number one." He stuck his pointer finger at the ceiling. "If the person sitting next to you isn't complaining, don't ask them to. They're probably very happy to be working." He slipped his mask back down and turned on his oxygen.

Zack knocked and poked his head in.

"Hey," I said. "I just sent you the camorra essay."

My email beeped, and I looked as a matter of habit.

"I don't think it's expandable," he said, closing the door behind him. "Not unless you want to do historical forensics, which is fun but doesn't sell."

"Forget it." I opened the email and read it. "Oh!"

"Good news?"

"I won the silent auction. I forgot I even bid."

He leaned into me. I could smell his cologne. "Dinner for two at *Le Bernardin*. Very nice." He smirked and looked me up and down in a way that was wholly inappropriate.

"Yeah." I didn't want Zack to ask me who I was taking, because I wasn't taking Adam and I wasn't taking him. "Dad?"

He pushed his mask back. "I'm fine! Stop asking!"

"I know. Do you want to go to dinner with me?"

Zack stood, getting his breath off my neck. He really needed a good poke in the ribs with a very sharp stick.

"When?"

"I don't know. I haven't gotten the voucher yet."

"Sure." He looked from me to Zack and took the snap out of his tone. "Fine. Yes." He put his mask back and got to work.

"He really is a fun date," I said, and Zack and I laughed.

With a knock on my desk, he said, "I'll take you some other time." He winked and turned to leave before I could gracefully decline.

But then, why should I? Why not go with Zack? He was handsome and smart. He'd taken care of his mother when she was sick. He didn't seem particularly broken or so whole he was boring.

Wasn't I happy enough before I started crawling?

Why not just live? Why make it all so complicated? Why make every single thing about sex? Why not just fuck like a normal person? Was it so antithetical?

I couldn't stretch my limited experience over the drum of the question.

Two birds lined up, right then. And I had a stone.

All I had to do was throw it perfectly the first time.

# CHAPTER THIRTY-SIX

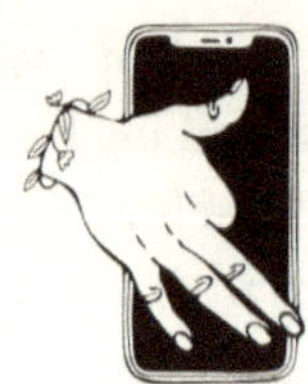

## DAY THIRTY

I'D NEVER BEEN to the Cellar outside a tryout night. Without the amateur population, it was much emptier and had the feel of an exclusive gathering place, rather than a nightclub.

Stefan met me in the lobby, wearing a sweater with his collared shirt and a pair of slim slacks. He'd told me to wear whatever I thought would help me achieve my goal for the evening. I didn't tell him my goal. He was trying to get it out of me.

I'd chosen a long silk skirt and heels. The skirt covered me to the ankles but was so tight my goose bumps showed.

Adam had started texting me at four thirty.

*—When am I seeing you tonight?—*

I didn't answer the first time.

*—Diana? I can still punish you—*

*—No, you can't—*

I hoped he felt his power waning. I hoped he felt the weight of day thirty. I hoped he wanted to make it the most memorable day of the past month and I was thwarting him by not giving a shit.

Which was untrue. I gave a shit. Just not the same shit.

**—*Stay there. I'm coming
to the office—***

*—I'm leaving now, so have at it—*

I called Stefan. I lobbed the ball high assuming he wouldn't catch it, but he did. That was the problem with asking people to help you do crazy things.

Sometimes they said yes.

~

Stefan signed me into the Cellar as a guest.

"I want to tell you something," I said in the elevator ride up to the Cellar's sixth floor.

"Yes?" Stefan answered, hands in his pockets as if it were the only way he could keep himself from brutalizing someone with them.

"Serena's after Adam. She thinks she can make him happy where I failed."

"And vice versa."

The elevator doors opened, and we went to the bar.

"You knew?"

"I know her. Inside and out."

Could I say the same of Adam? Did I know him inside and out? I did, but it hadn't helped me one bit.

"You can stay close to me," he said.

"Okay."

Stefan pulled a chair for me at a little table by the window and ordered two ginger ales. At the bar, I recognized the young Dom from my first visit, when I'd gotten pulled into a dark room to watch a woman get paddled. He was in a crisp white shirt open at the neck and a grey sports jacket, talking to a woman in a business suit.

"If you have any plans," Stefan said when he saw me watching the young Dom, "consider me first. For your own safety."

Stefan was still Stefan. He still didn't care for Adam, yet he tied himself to a man he didn't like in an obsessive knot I didn't understand. If I could hazard a guess, Stefan didn't understand it either.

"Really? Safety?"

"I'm less of a wild card than you think."

I'd have to consider it. If I was going to continue experimenting in this world, I would have to weigh my options. Stefan was attractive. He respected me. He was probably more hardcore than I was ready for but—

"Well," I said, sitting up straighter. "You might want to turn around."

He raised an eyebrow, finally turning when I nodded.

Serena stood in the doorway, looking so confident a normal person wouldn't believe she was submissive. I wanted to look that confident. I wanted to fully submit and fully dominate at the same time, just like Serena.

Stefan only had eyes for her.

I didn't want what they had. Their relationship walked too many wires, was too high maintenance, too brutal and servile.

Locking eyes with her, Stefan grabbed my hand across the table. "Now. Please."

The *please* was more of a command than appeal. She turned her head away and went to the bar.

Stefan took his eyes from her and met mine. "I can give you what you want, however you want."

"Are you trying to make her jealous?"

"Come." He stood and held out his hand.

His Dominant voice had no effect on me. He was good, but he wasn't Adam.

I stood without his help. "Listen to me, you need to try something different. She's not coming back to you over sharing. Give her a reason to want you."

"I know her," he hissed.

"Apparently not. You're invested in keeping Adam and me together so she comes back to you. Get her back because she loves you."

Stefan and I were locked in a dead heat when an Australian-accented voice came from behind me.

"I just got the most interesting text." Charlie leaned on his cane.

"Let me guess," I said, letting Stefan watch Serena get a drink. "*Is my wife there?* You said yes. He said he was on his way. How long do I have?"

"This is getting old," Charlie said, leaning on Stefan's chair.

"At some point, he's going to have to just deal with the fact that I have a body and I'm going to do what I want with it."

"This is his club, missy." Charlie's voice was unusually sharp. "This is his safe space."

"Missy?" I sat so I could be eye-to-eye with him. "Who the fuck do you think you're talking to?"

"I'm talking to one half of a hot mess. The closer you get to what makes you happy, the more miserable he's going to be. And the only way for him to be happy is for you to forget all this and be miserable. What you two need is a few miles between you. Indefinitely."

Fuck him. He was butting in where he had no business butting. I sipped my ginger ale to hide the tension in my mouth. Scanning for Serena, I caught the eye of the young Dom in the white shirt. He raised his eyebrows just a little. Enough to let me know he wasn't looking at me by accident.

"He's like an alcoholic." I looked back at Charlie. I could have made a speech about my explorations and self-actualization, but I didn't. Couldn't. They were too abstract. "He's addicted to ideas about who he can love. You know the best thing for an alcoholic? Hit bottom."

Hit bottom. Make it worse by far. Take it as far as it would go. Was that the answer? Or would it make reconciliation impossible? And if it did mean Adam and I were finished forever, did that also mean that was best for both of us?

"People break up all the time. We're not inventing anything new."

"On the contrary." He leaned both hands on his cane. "You two are definitely inventing something new."

"Then let's not pretend to follow the old rules." I picked up my bag and coat and walked past him.

He laid his hand on my arm. Not a hard or threatening gesture, but it made me stop. "Where are you going?"

"Winning the race to the bottom."

I walked to the bar before he could ask me to explain. I made sure the young Dom saw me, but he was talking to a woman. I couldn't approach directly.

I needn't have worried. He met me halfway across the room.

"Hello," I said, folding my coat in front of me.

"I was hoping I'd have a chance to talk to you."

"About?"

He didn't pause a beat. "About where our needs intersect."

"I have a need."

"Tell me."

"My husband."

"Your husband?"

"You might know him. Adam Steinbeck."

"Adam Steinbeck?"

"Is there an echo in here?"

He laughed a little. Nice smile. Nice face. I convinced myself I could do this.

"You intrigue me past original thought," he said. "Tell me more."

"I was with him when you paddled a sub in one of the rooms back there."

"And?"

"And it looked like fun."

He raised an eyebrow, tilting his head slightly. "I like fun as much as the next guy. Adam hasn't been around in years, now his wife shows up wanting a paddling? Is he allowing it?"

"No. But he doesn't want me. He dropped me. So I can get my paddlings anywhere I want."

He crossed his arms. "What's your end game, Mrs. Steinbeck?"

"Honestly?"

"Honestly."

"Get him pissed enough to do it himself. He won't because I'm his wife. I need him to address our intersecting needs, as you say. If you do it, he might wake up out of his stupor."

"You know how foolish that is, right?"

"He's on his way."

His grey eyes lit up, and he put on a mischievous grin. "We'd better get to it then. My name is Chris."

"Diana. Nice to meet you."

He led me to the back. When I looked back, Charlie was no longer at the table. Serena was at the bar. I turned the corner with the vision of Stefan five feet from her, standing stock still as if afraid to approach. Three weeks earlier, I wouldn't have believed Stefan was afraid of anything, Serena least of all. Maybe it would be a night of shattered assumptions.

# CHAPTER THIRTY-SEVEN

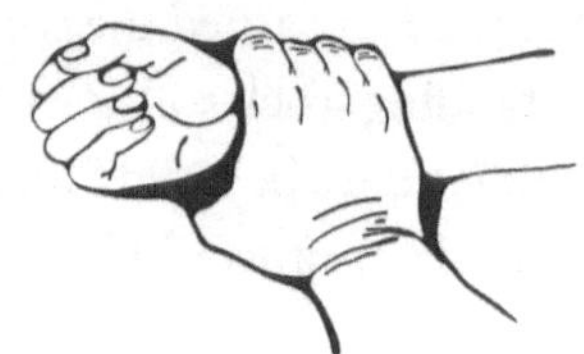

*IF I EVER LOVE A SUB, it's going to be you.*

Desperation was a terrible mentor. Desperation covered the pitfalls in soothing colors, made everything outside of itself look more sensible. Desperation pretended to be calculation, but it was terrible at math. Desperation denied it was desperation until it hit bottom.

*I can't love you.*

"Your cheeks are red," Chris said when he closed the door behind us.

He'd led me through the long hallway with the rug of naked bodies to the same viewing room I'd seen him in last time. It was smaller from the inside, dimmer, both cleaner and more run-down than it looked from the other side of the mirror. Cables ran from the back of a box to a beige power strip with a red light at the end. The door on one of the cabinets didn't sit quite flush with the frame. The upholstery in the luxurious wingback chair had a tear that was shaped like an eye.

*I felt close to you. Very close. And at the same time, I can't, Diana. I've tried.*

"I'm nervous."

"Let's take away as much of that as possible. Let's set limits. One. You're a married woman."

"For now."

"I'm not going to touch you."

"Okay."

"And you can keep your clothes on."

"I want it hard," I said, surprising myself. "Don't waste my time with love taps."

"I wouldn't worry about that." He slid a paddle out of a leather case. The same one he had when I'd seen him before. Light-color wood. Three holes. Worn leather handle. He placed it on the table. "Ten strokes."

I nodded. "Yes."

"Yes?"

"Yes, sir."

When I called him sir, I was hit with the gravity of what I was doing. *Every time you submit to me, it's like I'm waking up from a dream and the reality is that it's just not there anymore.*

"Lean against the edge." He tapped the table. I did it. The height came right to my waist. "Now, bend."

I did, getting my elbows under me. The paddle was right below my face. He crouched by my feet and fastened my ankles to the legs of the table. I had to stay on my toes to stay forward, creating a forward thrust to my posture.

When both were fastened, I got scared. I wasn't supposed to be scared. I was supposed to be aroused in anticipation.

Chris came up and looked at me. "You all right?"

"Yeah."

"We're playing a game, Diana. It's not more serious than that. And no matter how hard you say you want it, I don't know you well enough to really get in there where it hurts."

"Just don't bore me, okay?"

He laughed again. I was torn in ten places. He wasn't Adam, but he seemed all right. He was safer than my husband in a hundred ways, yet he was as dangerous as they came.

"Kiss that paddle," he said. "And spread your arms out."

I put my lips to the paddle and opened my arms. He pulled leather cuffs from under the table and tied down my hands.

"Now, if you want to stop, just say stop."

"I can remember that."

"Pick your head up."

I did, and he slid the paddle out from under me.

"Back down."

I put my forehead against the warm wood of the table. He tapped my ass with the paddle, and for the first time, I felt vulnerable and exposed. My heart pounded, and I took a deep breath.

"Count with me," he said.

He tapped my bottom again.

"Count," he said.

"You're joking. I'm not even counting that."

"Mister Adam Steinbeck has his hands full," Chris said before thwacking me good and hard.

I grunted. "One."

Again, harder. *Whoosh-thwack*

"Two."

"You really meant it."

"I got this."

He hit the breath out of me, *whoosh-thwack* sending waves of pain from skin to core.

"Three," I counted through my teeth.

"That's your sweet spot, right there."

Again, *whoosh-thwack*, a little lower. I let out a deep *unh*.

"Four."

I wasn't turned on sexually, but I was on fire with challenge. I could take this. I could take whatever he dished out.

I could finish. But that was all it was. He couldn't break me. He couldn't find me. He wasn't my master, and I wasn't his property. Not even for a minute. All he could do was test me.

On the wall above, a red light I hadn't paid any attention to turned green.

"You're doing great," he said before he hit me again.

Multiple strokes made each one hurt a little more as fresh pain laid itself on top of old pain.

"Five."

The next *thwack* came without a *whoosh* and the pain arrived out of cadence.

"Six."

The sound of the last *thwack* hadn't been a *thwack* at all, because it repeated itself. Deeper, more resonant, farther away.

Someone was pounding on the mirror.

"Well, well," Chris said. "I suspect—"

"Don't stop."

*Whoosh-thwack.*

Harder. I curled my toes and strained against the cuffs. "Seven!"

"You sure?"

The pounding was accompanied by shouting, but it was all muffled a million miles away.

"Yes!"

*Whoosh-thwack.* Searing pain.

"Eight!"

Again. Tears shot from my eyes, but someone else was crying. Someone who didn't care if she ever got to ten. A woman in the moment. I wasn't that woman for the next stroke. I was the huntress, and completion was my prey.

The pounding on the mirror stopped. The green light on the wall went back to red. Had he gone away? Had it been someone else? Did he decide to stop trying to love me?

"Nine!"

So busy in my thoughts, the last stroke came as a surprise and I cried out.

"Ten." It came out as a groan.

"Good girl."

Chris laid the paddle down and came to the side of the table. Past my tears and the limitations of a head resting on a table, I couldn't see much besides the full-sized boner under his trousers.

He undid a cuff then crouched to meet my eyes. "You're really beautiful."

"Thanks."

He walked around the table again and undid my other cuff. "If it doesn't work out with your husband, I'd really like to hurt you sometime."

On the wall, the light went from red to green.

"I know where to find you."

My wrist came free just as a crash deafened me. I twisted, wobbling to feet that had been paddled for ten strokes, to hear another crash as a garbage pail came through the two-way mirror, opening a three-foot-high hole.

Adam was on the other side of it.

My husband looked like a savage. Borderline feral with his jaw clenched and teeth showing. His jacket was open, exposing a chest that heaved with breath, stretching his shirt. His hair was askew, and his fists were clenched. The fire in his eyes was directed over my shoulder, at Chris, who I'd stupidly gotten involved in something that didn't concern him.

"I asked him to," I said.

"I'm going to kill him anyway." Adam stepped through the hole in the mirror, swiping the cracked edge of the opening. A spray of broken glass clicked to the floor.

"She was lovely," Chris taunted. "Too good to throw away."

"Chris," I said, turning slightly, "thank you, but can you go? Please?"

Chris backed away. Adam lunged at him in one fluid move. I put my hands on my husband's chest and pushed as hard as I could. The moment when his body parted with my fingers was the moment I realized how sore my bottom was.

Chris grabbed his case and his paddle. He didn't seem bothered at all. "Take care. And I mean that."

He left. I pushed Adam as he tried to charge out the door after him.

"Back off," I said.

Finally, he looked at me.

"Blame me," I said.

"What were you thinking about?"

"My future. My life. What I want."

"I won't watch you become a whore."

When rage surged from my glands, it bypassed my heart and mind, going directly down my right arm, which shot out and slapped his face with every bit of strength I had. His face moved with the velocity of the blow, but not enough. I swung again with the same force, but he grabbed my wrist mid-stroke.

"Diana."

The rage wasn't done flowing. It rerouted through my left hand, which caught him by surprise. I slapped him again. And again, when my left hand went to slap him a second time, he grabbed it midair until he was holding both of my arms up by the wrist.

I wasn't done.

I'd been raised in privilege, but I was still a New Yorker. When I spit in his face, the aim was as perfect as the thrust, and a formidable mass of throat gunk landed right between his eyes.

"Stop it," he growled though his teeth.

There were voices in the hall on the other side of the broken mirror.

"Fuck you, Steinbeck. Fuck you. You made me like this. You woke me up. You dragged me out of the darkness and now you don't want me in the light. Well, fuck you." I jerked away, and he let me go. "I don't fit in that box anymore, and you don't love me outside it. Fuck you. Either love me or set me free. And if you let me go, don't think for a minute you can dictate how I live without you."

He pulled a handkerchief from his pocket and wiped his face, and I took the opportunity to spin on my heel and walk to the back door, grabbing my coat and bag. I walked fast as I pushed my arms through the sleeves, into the back hall with the rug decorated with nudity. People looked at me, or I thought they did. I was a stranger, but for how long? Forever? Or was I already kin?

I was nothing. Nowhere, in the middle of a jump from one world to the next, midair, legs pumping at nothing above the chasm of in-between-ness. Neither-nor-ness. A yawning gape of indecision. A life without an identity.

The hall was a tunnel, soft and out of focus at the edges like a vintage portrait.

Only forward.

I had to make it to the other side. The other side of who I was. The other side of my life. The other side of the hall.

I clung to the million paths to success and came up with a chest full of anxiety. Go back to vanilla. Go full bore into kink. Get another Dom immediately. Remain faithful until death. Be present at the Cellar. Move to Tahiti.

Every path was a fantasy. A road not taken because it didn't exist. I couldn't decide what to do with my life based on how he'd react, but I couldn't imagine doing anything without loving him.

He'd asked me for much more than I thought I could give. He'd asked me to love him when what awakened my love was the very thing that killed his love. There was no path to reconciliation. They weren't just less traveled, knotty, bracken-blocked road. They'd been demolished by our crossed purposes, and we had so much work to do to find our way back. The thought of it made me tired.

Adam's fingers hooked in my pocket, and when I turned, he looked so anxious I could feel the coil twisting around his lungs, squeezing out all the air. He was trying to get to the other end of something, but our paths were perpendicular. We'd cross once and never meet again.

"Please." He took his hand from my pocket and held both out as if showing me he had nothing left to offer. "I love you."

His words blocked my forward momentum, and the bucket of my heart filled with rage.

"Don't you dare pull that trick. I'm over it, Adam. I'm over not knowing which end is up. I'm over letting you control me. I'm over being a puppy dog to your moods. I can't play anymore. I'm done. Finished."

He put his arms around my waist, his lips on my shoulder, then my chest, his arms around my thighs as he kneeled before me and held me still.

"I love you, Diana."

"No, you don't."

In the hall of the Cellar, with his peers playing their parts as props on our stage, Adam knelt in front of me, hugging my thighs, wrapping me in his need.

"I'm sorry, Adam. It's midnight. Day thirty. Time's up."

# ADAM

# CHAPTER THIRTY-EIGHT

THE FIRST TIME the garbage pail crashed into the glass, the window shattered like a windshield. A hole in the center webbed out in a series of tempered glass cracks that looked like her eye, ocean blue, trapped in a white net. I smashed it again, breaking the web.

I was supposed to know how far to push a sub before she broke, but I didn't. I'd misjudged. I loved her. I knew I loved her. I didn't know how to express it, but she knew. She knew.

She knew everything. She'd intuited it in my old bedroom, even before I digested it. The path closed behind me, and if I stopped, the inertia of the past would run me down.

I'd realized my error too late, because it was the first of so many.

Up to a point, I'd been honest with myself and Diana. That point had been in my grandparents' reinvented porch in Sheepshead Bay. I'd gone to hell after that. Right to hell. I didn't know what to tell her, because I was barely on speaking terms with myself. I kept my silence to buy time. If I'd bought enough, there wouldn't have been lies, only delayed truths, but the mistake went from emotional to tactical. I'd made the mistake of not recognizing that my love had never left and a second mistake of not telling her.

I'd wanted to be sure. I didn't want to lead her down a path she couldn't finish walking without me.

When I saw her in that room with Chris, I broke.

I was jealous. When her toes curled and I could see the bottoms of her feet, I pounded the glass. Fuck the glass. It wasn't stronger than I was. It wasn't thick enough, tough enough. It was a thin layer of bullshit.

If I could just talk to her. Tell her I got it. I was jealous. I'd admit that. I'd cop to a ton of shit. Paddling Serena because I thought Diana didn't even care. Stupid. I'd opened that door with my own actions. Me. My fault. All of it. I'd drop all my shit and apologize. I knew how it felt. And I'd tell her, for a goddamn second if I could, that the jealousy was bad but not the worst of it. I could handle jealousy. It was seeing her hurting herself that broke my heart. She was a new sub. An open wound. I'd let her down, and she did what any sub would do. She tried to find an answer, and for the love of fuck, there was no good end to this for her.

She was in that room because of my failures. She was trying to preserve her dignity with indignity.

As I stormed out of the dark room, I understood it all. I saw inside her because she was my sub, and she saw that I still loved her because of a bond I'd forged and ignored.

We were in sync. I got it. Now to destroy the thin layer of glass between us.

Heaving the pail, I hit the glass so hard my arms vibrated. It cracked into an eye-shape. I couldn't let that cracked eye bore down on me for another second. I smashed the window again, and it came apart in a layered symphony of glass cracking, breaking, falling. A jagged hole opened from knee to chest height. I walked through it ready to connect with her. Ready to tell her I loved her. I'd always loved her. I'd fight for her.

"She was lovely," Chris taunted. "Too good to throw away."

The little fucker just had to poke me. I went in with the best intentions, and he'd picked at the scab like a toddler, flicking away the healing so the wound bled. I would have done something stupid if she hadn't stopped me long enough to let him leave.

"What were you thinking about?" I asked as if I didn't know. She was working on her own wounds.

"My future. My life. What I want."

"I won't watch you become a whore."

I had more to say. Nicer things. How she didn't have to hurt herself. That I'd take care of her. Take care of everything.

But I lost control. She was the sub. I was the Dom. For fuck's sake, why did I lose control with her constantly?

She hit hard. I'd give her that.

"Diana," I said as I held her wrist.

She wasn't a lefty, but she hit like one. I held both her wrists. I could explain this. I could tell her what the fuck was happening if she'd just stop slapping me for a second. Then she spit in my face. I should have been enraged at the humiliation. Any Dom would have punished her hard or broken it off right there. But she was more than a sub at that moment, and I was less than her Dom.

She was the huntress, and I admired how she'd found a way to slap me without her hands.

"Stop it." I maintained a deep control of my voice, but she wasn't receptive. Couldn't say I blamed her.

"Fuck you, Steinbeck. Fuck you. You made me like this. You woke me up. You dragged me out of the darkness, and now you don't want me in the light. Well, fuck you." She jerked her arms. I let her go and went for my handkerchief. "I don't fit in that box anymore, and you don't love me outside it. Fuck you. Either love me or set me free. And if you let me go, don't think for a minute you can dictate how I live without you."

I heard her. Every word. She'd said similar things before, but I hadn't heard her the way I heard her then.

I opened my mouth to tell her, but in the moment I closed my eyes to wipe off the spit, she was gone.

I had to tell her the most important part first, but she was walking so fast and there were people everywhere. I hooked my finger in her pocket as if her clothes might accept me where her body wouldn't.

"I love you." I'd said those words before, but I was sure that was the first time I'd understood them.

"Don't you dare pull that trick. I'm over it, Adam. I'm over not knowing which end is up. I'm over letting you control me. I'm over being a puppy dog to your moods. I'm done. Finished."

The moment when I crashed and all my resistance broke into sorrow, I had nothing to do. I didn't have a plan to execute. The frustration of that note on the counter went from sharp as newly-broken quartz to smooth as a rock pounded by the sea for millennia.

*Tell her. Tell her everything. Stay up all night picking it apart.*

I just got on my knees and held her as if she was a buoy in a rising tide.

I had the same urgency to make it right, to do *something*, but I was powerless to do anything, and despair filled the space where determination had been. My attempts to love her kneeling form had worn away the need to get her back, and the intensity of my need to protect her pounded away at my ability to leave her.

Both. Neither. All.

She put her fingers in my hair as I knelt in front of her. I was going to have to get up, stand. Walk down the hall. Deal with the broken mirror and leaving my wife. I was going to have to get her back. Keep her. Turn my back on her. Let her go. Insist on possessing her. All of it at the same time.

I was exhausted. I needed her, and denying it had tapped me. I was empty. I had no will outside her anymore.

When she stepped away, I stood and walked briskly behind her without slowing down until we faced the closing elevator doors. It was full of people, and we had five floors to go. I couldn't wait.

"Please," I hissed through my teeth.

She didn't answer. The doors slid open and more people got in. The floor got light as we began our descent.

"Stop playing around," I said.

A Domme looked at me, then Diana. I didn't know her and I didn't give a shit.

"Not here," Diana said, watching the numbers flicker on and off.

When the doors opened on the first floor she burst out and I rushed behind her. She and I burst into the cold, wet air of Gansevoort. Cabs waited in a line of coward yellow. She opened the door of one without looking at me. Panic gripped me when she sat and reached for the handle to close the door. I held it fast.

"What do you want?" I asked.

She started to answer, stopped herself, shut her mouth, moved her jaw a little as if she needed to chew and swallow what she had been about to say.

I shouldn't have asked. Shouldn't have put it all in her lap. And the question was meaningless. What is it to want? Wanting is compulsive. Want sneaks up in the middle of the night and infests the soul with dissatisfaction. Want becomes an obsession. Want isn't real.

I needed her. My need was physical. It came in chemical bursts of sexual desire and protective rage. Did I love her? Did it matter?

"It's midnight," she said again. "Day thirty. Time's up."

What could I say to that? I couldn't argue that she needed to finish her training or that we needed to stop this disaster before we both did something even more stupid.

"I don't care," I said.

"I can't live like this."

"Me neither. But I can't live without you. I can't live with how I acted. I was trying to break what we had, but I didn't. I made us better, and I couldn't see that. Please forgive me. You have to forgive me."

"Okay." Her voice was husky in those two syllables, as if the word was made up of half-digested pieces of other answers.

The cabbie's voice came from the front seat. "I'm turning on the meter. Where to, lady?"

"Come back to Murray Hill," I insisted.

"Out or in?" the cabbie said urgently.

Her eyes, the color of tempered glass that shattered when I cared about her more than myself, had never looked more opaque.

"In." She tried to close the door, but I held it.

"You shouldn't do this alone."

"Let go." Her voice came in the loudest whisper I'd ever heard. "I mean it."

"Please!" the cab driver begged. "Out or in? Pick one!"

"Let go," she said.

"Come to my place. I'll make you believe I love you."

"No, you won't. It's not about how much you say you love me. I'm ashamed of what I just did. I won the game, but at what cost? I degraded myself. Not sexually. I degraded myself morally. I used to be better than that. Now I'm an awful person. I hate what I've become. I hate being a winner, and I hate playing games. I can't do this anymore."

"We're going!" The cabbie shouted.

The car jerked forward as he put it in drive. The door came out of my hand and she slapped it closed. The cab took off.

Maybe I should have chased it, but I thought a few hours away from me would be good for her. I'd let her stew, then look for her little green dot on my phone. I'd go wherever she was.

As Rob and Carol came toward me, I took out my phone.

"Mr. Steinbeck," Rob said, "there's a big mess in observation seven. Serious damages. Your name came up."

"Yeah." I smiled at him while my tracker app opened. "That would be me. Let's settle up."

I went inside without a fight. I'd pay through the nose for the glass then go to Diana. The green dot of her phone appeared on my screen, making a turn east onto 14th street.

I was about to put the phone away as I entered the darkness of the club, but before I could, the green dot disappeared. She'd cut me off.

# CHAPTER THIRTY-NINE

THE SUN ROSE with me alone in my bed and Diana half a city away, I just didn't know in which direction. The green dot hadn't reappeared. I stood outside the loft, but the lights didn't come on. I went up to Riverside Drive, but I didn't see her in Zack's window. I went past her father's building on Park. The doorman said he hadn't seen her.

The thirty days I'd demanded had been more crowded than I'd intended. I'd planned to fall out of love with her but hadn't planned on her falling back in love with me. I'd planned to leave her but hadn't planned on wanting to stay.

*—What do you want to do?—*

My finger hovered over the send button. If I asked her like this, I'd find out when she woke up in a few hours. Yes, no, maybe, or a torrent of a hundred texts slicing what had happened between us and what it meant for our future.

But it could be no. A flat no.

Until I got a flat no, I had hope, and I needed it. I wouldn't forgive myself otherwise.

So she wasn't going to decide through the phone. She was going to tell me to my face, and I was going to remind her why I was the only man who could dominate her.

It was five in the morning. I had a couple of hours to answer some emails, go for a run, make myself presentable, and ask her what she wanted face to face.

# CHAPTER FORTY

I WAITED IN HER OFFICE.

Our office.

I got there early and sat on the couch, answering email from my phone. I felt strong and sure. Ready to grab her, hold her, convince her that I was back one hundred percent.

But she didn't come. I built a tower out of Legos and still she didn't come.

Kayti didn't come.

The office was empty as a church on Monday. A temp sat at reception. She was as surprised to see me as I was to see her.

"Where is everyone?" I asked, tapping my watch.

"Don't know. Just got a call from the agency. Should I get someone on the phone for you?"

McNeill-Barnes was my company and I didn't need a temp receptionist to find out why the fuck no one was in the office on a weekday.

I called Diana while I waited for the elevator. No answer. Got in, hit the button, and sent a terse text asking after her whereabouts. Undelivered, naturally, because I was in a fucking elevator.

By the time I got down the block to the loft, I'd texted three more times and none had been delivered. All my calls went to voicemail. She'd been in my sights eight hours before, but she'd disappeared. New York was playing a shell game with me, picking up all the cups one at a time only to reveal she wasn't under any of them.

I was about to open the door of her building when the city turned the first shell again, and there she was. Through the glass, wrapped like a Christmas present in light refractions from the moving doorway, she stood near the elevators.

She was with a man. He was so close to her, I thought he was moving past her to get to the elevator. But he wasn't. He held her in his arms. I couldn't see well. Was it a hug or a kiss? Or, in other words, did I want to kill someone?

Which I'd wanted to do the night before.

I craned my neck to see who it was. If it was Chris, I would break another window. I would break windows all over Manhattan. I would pave the sidewalks in broken glass.

It wasn't Chris.

If it had been Chris or any other Dominant in the known universe, I would have done harm to myself and others. If she was going to have a Dom in her life, it would be me. But as the light refraction moved, I was relived of that burden. It wasn't a Dominant I knew of.

It was Zack.

# CHAPTER FORTY-ONE

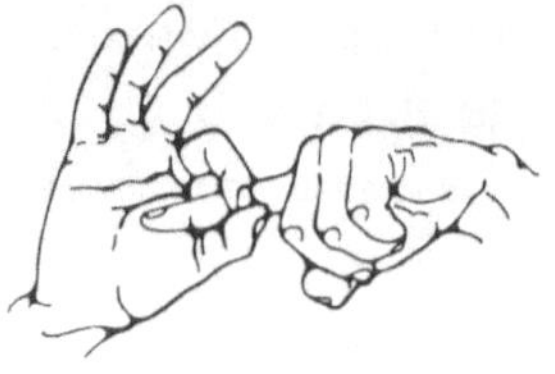

## TWO DAYS LATER

I WALKED to work every morning. Two mornings since I'd seen her, but it felt like a year. I kept intending to hop the subway or grab a cab, but my legs kept moving, rotating the wheels in my mind with a push-pull-push-pull.

Push—She was mine. She'd always be mine. Even as confused as I was about what love meant between us, she'd never stopped being mine. Not for a second.

Pull—I couldn't compete with vanilla. I could never go back. If she wanted the old me—but not *me*—I was powerless to change her mind. And though the feeling was much the same as the day I'd found her note on the counter, there was less I could do about it.

I texted her and heard nothing. Her green dot didn't reappear. She'd blinked out.

I'd lost the love of my life. I had to accept that.

Acceptance was freedom. I went with it for two days. I pushed down a pain in my chest that said *wrong wrong wrong* until I couldn't bear it. Couldn't sleep. Ate nothing. I was sucked dry. I texted again. No answer.

Freedom sucked. Freedom wasn't more than losing the fight. Signing a treaty of complete surrender. Giving up the homeland to the opponent and watching it burn day and night from a foreign land.

I said my good mornings at R+D. Push-pulling down the hall through a tunnel that led to my desk.

I didn't like losing. I wasn't used to it. Not in business and not in the personal. Losing this fight was like walking the length of a swamp and coming out on the other side covered in leeches. Each one had to be pulled off painfully. My pride. My sense of self. My imagined future. My culpability. My love might never come off. That one would bleed me the rest of my days. I'd hemorrhage love.

I closed the door to my office and opened the top drawer, where I'd put her divorce papers. They clearly outlined her ownership of everything. She'd earned it. She'd tried to make it work. She'd come back from her own swamp, gone through it again, and come out the other side. I'd thrown her efforts back in her face.

Well, fuck me.

I clicked my pen and hovered over the dotted line. I had to release her if I was ever going to be free.

I didn't want to be free, but she did.

A knock came at the door, and Eva poked her head in. "Adam?"

"Yes?"

"I set up a meeting in half an hour. We're doing the Theesen property projections. Have you looked at them?"

"No."

She stepped all the way in and closed the door. "Are you all right?"

"Not really."

"Is it Diana?"

"That's a personal question. We don't do personal questions."

She wasn't put off. She came deeper into the office, pink from head to toe in a wide lapel jacket and flowing silk pants. She was a beautiful woman I couldn't be attracted to. How many more would there be?

"If you didn't want me to ask a personal question, you would have said you were fine."

"I'm not lying anymore. But that doesn't mean I'm explaining."

She sat on the chair in front of the desk and crossed her legs. Her pumps were pink. "Noted."

I signed the divorce papers. Dated next to my name. Initialed by the tabs. Folded the pages in threes. Regretted it then let it go, then regretted it again.

"Do you know why I decided to work with you, even though you were younger and had shit for brains?" she asked.

"My acumen?"

"You had no fear. You pitched me projects so risky, no one had even thought of them."

"I was young and stupid."

"And lucky. But I didn't know that yet. What I did know was that you had real upside. You were a winner."

"Well, you were right. Up to a point."

"You're still a winner. Even when you lose."

There were a few occasions over the years when Eva had tried to be a big sister to me. I hadn't been able to let her go there because I needed to be her equal in the office. Had the distance been necessary? Had I distrusted her with my confidence, or myself?

"Thanks," I said. "Can you have Britt send these?"

She took the papers and tapped them on the heel of her hand. "It's hard to see now that this can be a new start."

"Noted."

"You can make your life whatever you want from this moment."

"What if I don't know what I want?"

"You can figure it out. You're handsome. Successful—"

"Are you making a pass at me?"

"You're too good a catch. I prefer pathetic losers." She stood. "It's a weird fetish."

"You can make your life whatever you want from this moment."

"Touché."

"I'll review Theesen and see you in the meeting."

"Good."

She went out and left me alone with a life of infinite choices, minus one.

# CHAPTER FORTY-TWO

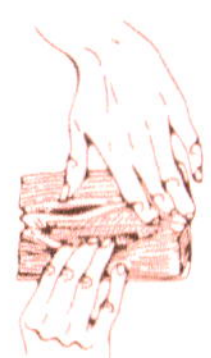

I COULDN'T SLEEP. A full glass of whiskey didn't cure the insomnia. I went to Crosby Street and watched the loft window for signs of life, but even at eight in the morning, four hours into my vigil from the coffee shop, I saw no sign she was even there. I asked the doorman if he'd seen her and he hadn't.

I was supposed to be letting go. Signing the divorce papers had done nothing to quell the anxiety that screamed *wrong wrong wrong.*

I went back to the coffee shop and ordered another. I just wanted to see if she was all right. That was what I told myself. But by nine thirty, I knew she wasn't coming home. I went back to Murray Hill to get ready for work.

So much for being free. So much for the breadth of choices. So much for giving up on her. Maybe I was tired, and in the exhaustion, I fell back into old patterns. I was married. She was mine. My wife. My lover. My sub.

Even though I felt the truth, I knew another truth. Equally accurate yet diametrically opposed.

She was less mine than she'd ever been.

When I got out of the shower, I took off my ring and put it in the medicine cabinet. My hand didn't feel any lighter. The skin at the base of my finger was pressed smooth and shiny. Even after I rubbed it, an indent remained. Even in winter, the bottom of my finger was a lighter color than the rest, as if the metal was gone but the ghost of the marriage remained.

I got dressed. I didn't have the energy for formality, so I put on jeans and a sweater. Then I decided that maybe today was the first day of a new life, so I put on a charcoal-grey suit that was narrower in the shoulders. Back when I dressed for Diana, I'd avoided it. It was time to stop caring what she liked. It was time to be alone with my preferences.

Single Windsor knot.

Shit.

Wrong shirt for that. It looked dinky with the wide collar, and the wide collar wasn't right with the jacket.

Double Windsor or change the shirt?

*Jesus Christ, asshole. Get it together.*

The doorman buzzed the intercom.

"Yeah," I said into it, pulling off the tie.

"Good morning, Mr. Steinbeck. I sent a guy up with a package."

"Thanks."

I made coffee. Fuck the suit. Fuck the whole thing. Let it all unravel. Maybe I'd just go to Tahiti for a year and wear nothing but cut-off jeans and puka shells. I could learn to surf. Sit in the sun and tan this white ring off my finger. Let it burn this pain out of my chest. Maybe I could throw away this damaged soul and grow another. One that worked right.

When the bell rang, I went to the door. I signed for a small package, not looking at it until I'd tipped the delivery guy and closed the door.


*Mrs. Steinbeck - Congratulations! Your silent auction prize is enclosed. Thank you again for supporting the Literacy Project.*


I'd forgotten she'd bid on something at the event. What had it been? Who even knew? I dropped it on the front table. I could send it to her. Or I'd deliver it personally. I could ask her how she was doing. See if she was with Zack. Ask if that meant she was going vanilla. Pretend I was all right with whatever she said. Look right into her eyes and see if she was lying when she said she was fine. Maybe I'd see Zack at McNeill-Barnes and commit murder. Get myself arrested before noon.

Talk about a new life.

As I finished getting ready, going back to sweater and jeans, I decided using the package as an excuse to see her wasn't in line with starting fresh without her.

Having used my entire store of willpower in the decision to send the package rather than deliver it, I was powerless against my desire to see what was inside the box. Maybe she was sending me a message. Hope could be in the bottom of that box. I opened it. A certificate lay on top.

Dinner for two at *Le Bernardin*. I knew the place. Sauces swiped across white plates like impressionist pigment and cooked scallops placed back in the shell. Lighting so dim the menus came with little gold-plated flashlights. Nice. Great. She'd probably take Zack. Maybe her father, but if she was sleeping with that weasely little motherfucker, she'd have every reason to take him.

I didn't have to deliver it at all. Then she couldn't take Zack out to a six-hundred-dollar, pre-fuck dinner.

Maybe she hadn't won this thing. She had no way of knowing, and I wasn't made of stone. The money would go to the charity whether she went out for dinner or not.

I was being an asshole. I was being petty and immature. I was jealous. Ravenously jealous.

I folded the voucher to remove it from the box. I was throwing it out. I only had so much patience for this shit, and it had just run out.

If she wanted to go back to vanilla and it had just been me she didn't want vanilla sex with, I would let her have that.

I hated it.

The thought ate at me.

I had no choice.

Like a bell from a heavenly host, my phone dinged. It had buzzed and dinged all day long. I didn't stare at it or answer it when I was doing something else, but this time, I looked at it.

· · ·

*Hello,*


*Sorry for the mass email. This is going out to all contacts.*

*As some of you know, two days ago, Lloyd Barnes passed away from complications associated with emphysema. He was a fearless leader and a shining light. We will miss him.*

*The wake will be at Costa Bros. Funeral Home. Address and viewing schedule are enclosed.*

*Thank you so much for your constant support.*


*~Kayti McTeague*


*PS: Business at Mc-Neill Barnes Publishing will continue on Monday. Please forward all inquiries to this email.*

# CHAPTER FORTY-THREE

LLOYD BARNES HAD HAD a long life. He'd made hundreds of friends, and every single one of them seemed to have shown up at his wake.

The funeral home was huge. Located in a double-width brownstone off Lexington Ave., it was a study in small rooms and dark woods, still life paintings and noise-absorbing carpets. She'd be in the front, by the casket. I had to push through a press of people and perform a thousand niceties before getting there.

Lloyd was laid to rest with a rosary in his folded hands. I'd forgotten they were Catholic. They had too. Even when Diana and I were married at City Hall, no one had brought up a church even though I was Catholic too.

"She's not here," a voice said from behind me.

It was Zack. His hand was out to shake. I looked at it. Considered ripping it off. But it was a funeral for fuck's sake. I shook his hand. I could break his face another day.

"Where is she?"

"I don't know. No one does. Apparently she didn't go to her mother's funeral either."

"What did she say?" My throat burned with bile to ask, but I had to swallow it back. Let it burn again. None of this was my choice, and it wasn't about me. It was about Diana. "Anything? Last night? This morning?"

"Nope."

"Why aren't you trying to find her?"

"I don't know what you think—"

"This is her father. He was everything to her. And you don't know why she's not here?"

"I'm not her keeper."

"Yes, you *are*." My promise to keep my shit together was falling to pieces. I gripped his elbow as hard as I'd ever gripped anything. If I didn't, I was going to rip off his balls.

"What are you doing?" He tried to wrench away but was as cognizant of the crowd as I was.

"You're supposed to take care of each other," I hissed. "If you don't hold up your end—"

"I'm not fucking her. Jesus."

I loosened my grip enough for him to get away.

He rubbed his elbow. "You're a damn psychopath."

"I saw you in our lobby." I was as good as calling him a liar. I was also starting to doubt he was lying at all.

"A few days ago? Lloyd was sick, really sick, and I took her home. Look, I tried. I admit it. Her ring was off, so I tried. But she's all yours, okay?"

"It's not..." I stopped myself and straightened my cuffs. I didn't want to be misunderstood. "It's not that she's mine. She needs to be treated right. That's all. No more than that."

"What do you want me to say?"

I looked around. We were being watched. They'd seen my vise grip on Zack's arm. I felt like a criminal.

"Ask around, all right? See if anyone knows where she is. Please," I said.

"All right. For her. Not you, because you need help." He tapped his temple, saying I was crazy. Which I was. Completely out of my mind.

"I'm sorry about your arm."

He waved it off and went to talk to a group of three young women

Diana had known in college. I forgot their names, but I knew they wouldn't know where she was.

I looked at Lloyd, painted in repose. The middle-aged woman kneeling in front of him made the sign of the cross and got up. Before I could think twice about it, I took her place, putting my knees on the pink velvet bench and my elbows on the brass bar.

"Lloyd, buddy," I said so softly I didn't know if the dead could hear me. "I'm sorry I couldn't get her back. It's complicated."

*She missed her mother's funeral too.*

I felt stupid, but I couldn't keep myself from talking to a dead guy. I was out of control, but not in a frightening way. "She's going to be really broken up about you, and it's not going to kill her. I know. But I don't want her to be alone."

*She missed her mother's funeral too.*

"I'm not a praying guy. I don't believe in miracles. But I want to make sure she's okay. So—"

*She missed her mother's funeral too.*

I didn't have to finish the sentence. Of course. I knew exactly where she was. Finding her there was a shot in the dark, but darkness was all I had.

"Lloyd. You're all right for an in-law. See you on the other side."

# CHAPTER FORTY-FOUR

I was aware she was an adult woman who was perfectly capable of taking care of herself. That unimpeachable truth sat in my consciousness right next to the fact that she needed someone to take care of her. The best someone for the job was me, but if not me, someone. Even adults who could take care of themselves needed to be taken care of.

I didn't try to make sense of it. The two ideas would never sing in harmony. Fuck it. I could own them both.

Manet's *Luncheon In The Grass* was in Paris. She could have caught a flight. The airport was my next stop, but first I had to check the Impressionist gallery at the Met. It was a short hop to Central Park.

I didn't get past Madison Avenue because I ran right into the beating heart of a protest.

The street was blocked by blue sawhorses so police could keep traffic away from the throngs of people holding signs (Christians Against Blasphemy! Some Art Is SIN!) and chanting slogans I couldn't understand.

"Go around 84th," a female cop told a family of tourists. "Back that way. Left. Left. Straight. Can't miss it."

"What's going on here?" the father asked.

"New exhibit. People don't like it. There're pamphlets all over the street if you want to grab one." Not wanting to get embroiled in a discussion, she held her arm out to someone lollygagging. "Move along. Move along, everyone."

I picked a pamphlet off the ground.

## IS THIS ART OR BLASPHEMY?

Under the headline was a color picture of Serrano's Piss Christ.

I smirked. The Piss Christ was a big joke on everyone. Maybe. A photo of a white plastic crucifix that was (possibly) in a glass of (what could have been) urine meant to drive everyone batshit while the artist sat back and watched. Pure genius.

I wasn't an art guy. Not the way my wife's family was. Pieces like Piss Christ made me laugh, because they didn't put food on the table. Didn't solve any problems. Didn't make money for more than a couple of people. It was art. A conversation starter. You want to poke everyone? Say you're defiling the crucifix.

Holding the pamphlet over a trash can, I stopped. The photo glowed red and orange. If you forgot it was supposed to be urine, it was beautiful. If you didn't think about the corruption of purity, the oranges and reds had a hallowed life of their own.

As if the cross made the urine holy.

And I thought, why did I think it was my filth that ruined Diana?

Why did I not think Diana purified me?

Why wasn't *she* cleansing *me*?

Like a checkerboard that you always assumed was black on white, but once you saw the possibility that it could be white on black, you couldn't unsee it. The mind goes back and forth with the opposites, melding them into an agreement of inverses. The way a grown woman could take care of herself and need to be taken care of, she and I could ritually defile and purify each other, black on white, white on black, spinning like a pinwheel faster and faster into constancy.

I let the pamphlet drop into the garbage. She and I were linked like black and white as long as the world spun, and I knew that on the day of her father's funeral, she wasn't in the museum.

# CHAPTER FORTY-FIVE

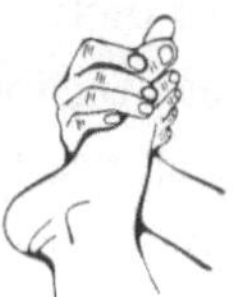

"I don't have the key," I repeated to the doorman. "Look at me. You know me. I've never needed a key. I've been coming in and out of Lloyd's co-op for five years and I haven't raped or killed anyone."

The doorman knew me. He also knew Lloyd had died and had admitted Diana was in her father's apartment.

"Tell me what you're checking for and I'll look for it," he said.

"My wife. Please. She's not answering the phone, and I know she's upset."

He didn't know I'd signed and sent the divorce papers. He didn't know I hadn't seen Diana in days or that I'd given up on us. But he knew I wasn't going away, so he unlocked the little cabinet behind the lobby desk and took a key off the hook.

I followed him to the elevator and up to the front entrance with the plant in the hall.

He knocked, waited forever, knocked again, waited an eternity, then shrugged. "Sorry, Mr. Steinbeck, but I can't open it if—"

"The back way. She could be in the kitchen."

He looked at me with narrowed eyes. "I have to get back to the lobby."

"If she's hurt herself and you didn't open the door, I'll do worse than sue you."

"Fine."

We walked down the hall, around the corner, and through the door to the back stairwell. We heard a muffled, high-pitched squeal.

"The teapot," I said, knocking before he had a chance to raise a goddamn objection.

No answer.

"Open this door," I said. "At the very least, the stove's on."

He opened the door, revealing a kitchen washed in twilight, the blue flame of a gas burner, and a violently whistling teapot that rattled. It must be almost empty. I reached for the knob. That was when I saw her.

She was no more than a shape under the window, barely visible in the darkening room. Knees to chest, back to the wall, arms around legs.

"Adam?" Her voice was soft in disbelief.

"Ma'am?" the doorman said. "I'm sorry to bother you."

"Get the fuck out." She said it softly, but with conviction.

He left, snapping the door closed. I crouched to see her. She was cast in twilight shadows. Blocks away, a car alarm went off. A crosstown bus ground the brakes with a deep grumble a New Yorker would barely hear unless they were trying to listen to their wife's soul cry out.

"Can I turn a light on?" I said.

"No."

"Were you going to leave the teapot on there all night?"

"I meant to get it. Did you go to the wake?"

I sat on the floor with my back to the stove and one leg bent. "Packed. Wall-to-wall people."

"I should have gone."

"Why didn't you?"

She played with her fingers in the dark, worrying at corners that weren't there. "They'd all wait for me to cry, and I can't. I don't want anyone to see."

"See what? That you're not crying?"

"They'll think I'm a monster."

"Everyone knows how much you loved him. They'd think you had superior self-control."

"That's me. Self-control girl."

"Are you hungry?"

"No."

"Do you want me to finish making the tea?"

"I don't know what I want."

"I'm making you tea." I got up on a hand and a knee. "I don't even care if you drink it."

After standing and straightening my jacket, I put the teapot under the faucet. When it was full and the sound of the water left us in the semi-silence of New York, I heard her whisper.

"Get out." Her voice had a flat conviction, almost dominant in its command.

"I'm going to stay here and take care of you," I said, flipping on the burner. "You don't have to like it. I'm staying. You've gone through too much alone already." I shifted the teapot as if it would make a difference. "You had no support in Montauk. None when you got home. Maybe Lloyd was here when you got the signed divorce papers. I don't know. What I do know is I'm depleted. If I had to face something like this right now, I'd have nothing left."

She sat on the floor, unmoving, staring into the middle distance.

"You need me," I said, "and you're taking everything I can give you."

She blinked. No more. Watching the teapot had the expected effect, so I kicked off my shoes by the back door and sat in front of her. I took her bare foot in my hands and rubbed it, digging my thumbs into the soft part. She groaned and woke up a little. I dug harder, pushing out the tension, letting her know I was there. She flinched from the pain but came around, making eye contact in the dark room.

"I love you, Diana."

"I don't want you to."

"Tough."

The teapot hissed. Her head moved so slightly I could barely perceive her saying *no*, as if I'd misunderstood.

"I want you to hurt me," she said.

I dug my thumbs in harder. She didn't resist or react.

"Take it from me." She pulled back her foot.

"What do you mean?"

"What you did to Serena. Give it to me. Take it. Make everything hurt. Make me do things."

The teapot whistled, and my dick swelled.

"Do you know what you're asking?"

"Yes. I'll say pinochle if I have to. But no means yes."

I stood and turned off the burner. I hadn't gotten a cup or a teabag. I hadn't made a plan or a list of limits. We hadn't had a cold, honest discussion to protect us from each other.

"It'll work out better this time," she said from below me.

"No." I had to put my foot down. She was in no condition to give up her will so completely.

"Do you know why you scratch an itch?" she said, getting on her feet.

"It's still no."

"Because an itch is pain." She peeled off her T-shirt. She wasn't wearing a bra, and the streetlights on her nipples cast long shadows across her breasts. "A scratch is greater pain. It drowns the itch out."

"Diana. What you're asking for takes hours of negotiating and talking."

I didn't want to talk. Didn't want to turn on the lights. I wanted to give her what she asked for, and though a part of me cried against it, I couldn't help but play the scene in my mind. Her body was so beautiful in the soft light, her skin satin, waiting to be marked. I could destroy her utterly and put her back together.

"I trust you." Her voice was a velvet blanket I wanted to rip into a scream.

"Do you?" I reached for a hard nipple and pulled it.

Her eyes fluttered closed when she gasped. She couldn't have known how bad it could get. She couldn't have foreseen it. "Yes."

But I could play it out. I could give her what she needed. But I couldn't.

"Please," she implored. "Make me."

I could.

I twisted her nipple until she grimaced. I ached for more, and I was going to get it. I took a deep breath of acceptance. I was a sadist, and a masochist was asking to be hurt. I loved her with every bone in my body, and if giving her what she needed broke that love, I could at least give her what she needed.

As if she knew I'd come to a decision, she pulled away and pushed me aside, dodging to get to the door.

The first move was the hardest because it set the tone, and without preparation or discussion, I was playing it by ear.

I took her by the throat before she got past me and pushed her against the refrigerator. She clutched my arm.

"This what you want?"

"Fuck you," she spit.

"No, huntress. Fuck you." I stuck my free hand down her sweat pants. She was soaked.

She fought me. She fought hard, twisting and punching. So hard I wondered if this was what she wanted. Wrestling her to the floor, I got her on her stomach and put my knee between her shoulder blades, gasping for breath. I pulled my erection out but left my pants on.

"What's your name?"

"Diana. Get off me."

I grabbed a handful of hair and jerked her head back so I could see her. "How old are you?"

"Twenty-eight-fuck-you."

I held her hair, moved my knee, and got her pants off. She hit me so hard I saw stars. She made it two steps before I got hold of her wrist and threw her over the kitchen table.

"Self-defense advice," I snarled. "Don't end up on your stomach."

She growled and twisted. I had control of her for a moment, but I knew I'd let her get away again. It was how I exerted control and how she surrendered it.

I could do this.

I could keep it safe. I could be the master. I could play the game. I had no rules, no contracts, no list of hard limits, but I knew her. I knew her better than I knew any other human being. All I had to do was trust that.

I jammed my hand between her legs, sinking three fingers in her. "You're so fucking wet. I could just fuck you right now like a nice guy.

Just fuck your cunt sore and make you come. But that wasn't what you wanted, was it?"

A rack of cooking supplies sat by the fridge. A bottle of oil was stuck sideways between soy sauce and salt. I grabbed it and opened it with my teeth, spitting out the cap. I dumped it onto her lower back, letting plenty fall into the crack of her ass. She'd need it.

"We could have done this nice. But have it your way."

Two of my wet fingers drove into her ass. She held back a scream. I pushed her face into the table, stretching her ass. I didn't have plugs or tools. I didn't have time or cooperation. This wouldn't be painless, but it wouldn't be without pleasure either.

"No!" she said.

But no meant yes, and though I thought I'd stop when she said it, I didn't. I trusted her and myself.

"You're taking it. All of it. I'm going to tear you apart."

She rocked back and forth violently, kicking and flailing.

I let her go before driving her to the floor. She crawled out of the kitchen. I snapped up a towel, throwing it around my neck.

I found her in the dining room with her back to the table. The front door was steps to the right, but she backed away in the other direction.

"Get on your knees and I'll take it easy on you." One step forward.

"No."

One step back.

A horn honked outside. She got distracted, and I lunged. Her foot slipped on a bead of oil on the floor. I caught her and drove her to her knees at the same time, pushing her face on my erection. When she opened her mouth to scream, I shoved my cock in it. Her face went beet red as I pushed down her throat. Her hair was a mess. Her fingernails dug into my thighs. When she looked up at me, her eyes were webbed with red and she was so close to utter submission, I almost came in her mouth.

She gulped air when I pulled out. Before she could get away, I was on her, twisting her onto her side. I put my forearm on her head to keep her still. Her leg flailed over my shoulder. With my other hand, I put my dick at her ass. Held her still. She bucked. This was going to rip her up if she didn't stay still.

I could feel her heaving for breath under me.

"Get off me," she gasped. "Fuck."

I'd stopped to think too long. She was getting restless. I needed more control, and I wasn't continuing without it. I snapped off my belt and buckled it around her neck as she cursed at me.

Grabbing her ankle, I stood and dragged her across the dining room floor. Her free foot kicked.

"How old are you?"

"Twenty-eight. Let me go."

She grappled with the belt, but the buckle was in the back and she didn't have enough time to undo it before I got her into her childhood room. It had been stripped of posters and photos. The full-size bed with the white wood head and footboard was dressed in a white, pink, and blue duvet I hoped she wasn't too attached to.

Closing the door behind us, I got my hand around the front of the circle of the belt and put our faces close together. "Be good."

"No."

I let her go and pulled an extension cord out of the wall. The next five minutes were spent tying her hands together. She was slippery and strong, but I was stronger. I got her on the bed and bound her hands to the headboard, above her head. I could turn her front or back while keeping her more or less still.

I got off the bed and undressed while she watched, lying on her back.

"You've got to calm down," I said, pulling her ankles apart. "You might even like it."

"I won't relax. I won't let you."

The fire in her eyes said otherwise, and I had to trust that. I put my knees on her thighs, keeping her motionless with my weight.

This wasn't about getting my dick in her ass. It never had been. This was about taking her so low she could let go of her pain, and it would take more than a fight against penetration. When I leaned over her, she turned her head. With one hand, I took her by the cheeks and made her face me.

She wasn't close enough. She was physically drained, but her guard was still up emotionally. I had to break her. We had no map for this. No list to check off.

I had to trust myself to know what she needed.

I had to trust she'd tell me if it was going wrong.

"So we're clear," I said. "I want this to hurt. Every time you cry, my dick gets hard."

I put my fingers in her mouth, down deep with my clean hand until she made gurgling sounds. I removed them, and I slapped her cheek. Not hard. Just enough to hurt her feelings.

Her eyes got wide with shock.

"You like that? It's what you wanted."

Before she could answer, I slapped the other cheek a little harder.

Her eyes welled up with tears. Her chin shuddered. I did it again, and tears flowed.

That was it. The train pulled out of the station and we were on it, speeding toward her breaking point. I got off her thighs and turned her onto her stomach. She didn't have a hell of a lot of fight in her. I slapped her bottom so hard my hand hurt.

I didn't need to torment her with cruel words. I didn't need to make her tell me to go fuck myself again, but I needed to finish this with her.

I put my fingers in her ass and stretched it. She was still lubricated enough. It would hurt for a minute, but if I took it slow, she'd be fine.

The head of my dick stretched her. She screamed into the pillow and resisted. I held her still and slowly, inch by inch, took her ass.

The extension cord slid down the vertical bed railing. I pulled her hair back but fucked her gently.

"Up on your knees," I said, slapping her ass.

She did as she was told because she was breaking and she knew it. I could feel her falling apart. Falling into me. Opening like a flower. After the second stroke, she was released from pain and she pushed her hips back into me.

Turning her on her side, I bent her leg on my shoulder. Her face was so puffy and tear-streaked, I didn't recognize it. I reached between her legs and rubbed her clit. She made a vowel sound that was half surrender and half battle-cry.

"I can't! I can't come like this."

"You can." I leaned into her face. "You can, and you will."

It wasn't long before she bucked and stiffened under me. When she came, her ass clenched around my cock over and over until I exploded inside her.

When I pulled out, she cried harder than I thought possible.

I needed to get us into a bath. I needed to clean up. I needed to feed her. I needed to check every inch of her body to make sure she was unharmed. But once I untied her and she put her arms and legs around me, she wouldn't let go. She wept long and loud from the floor of her heart to the ceiling of her soul. Not one ounce of sadness was left unpacked.

When I tried to let go of her, she clung harder.

I gave up and held her as tightly as I could, rocking back and forth. The scene finished and I had nothing to add to what I'd done. I was all right. I'd kept it under control and given her what she needed. I knew her. I loved her. Through the entire thing, I'd loved her, and it was the love that kept me from breaking along with her.

I was safe and sane, giving her a gentle, guided ride back to the reality of her power.

# CHAPTER FORTY-SIX

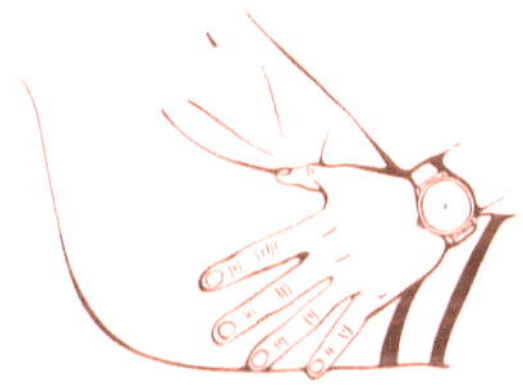

WHEN SHE WAS TOO tired to cry another tear, I took her to her little bathroom and managed to hold her off the floor while I drew her a bath. It was a hilarious comedy of errors she only had the energy to smile about.

"I just want to go to sleep," she said as I put her in the hot water.

"I know."

"This feels really nice."

I washed her legs from toe to thigh, then I got in the tub, sitting behind her so her shoulder blades were to my chest. I had more cleaning to do, but it could wait a minute while I wrapped my arms around her.

"I'm going to miss my father." Her voice was husky. "Knowing he doesn't exist anymore. Not even anywhere. Gone. I can't visit. Can't say hello. Can't play cards anymore. I don't know what to do with all the things we did together." She leaned her head on the bend in my arm. "I'm not his daughter anymore. I'm... I don't know who I am."

I kissed her behind her ear. "You're mine."

"I'm still sad."

"I'll break you again when you can't stand it."

"Before," she said sleepily. "Did you mean what you said before?"

"That I was going to rip you apart?"

"No. I know you meant that. The other thing. In the kitchen."

"What thing?"

She didn't answer. The sound of dripping water echoed off the tiles, and I felt her breaths on my arm.

"That I love you?" I asked.

"Yes."

"I meant it."

"Really?"

"It's probably the only thing I've said all day that I really meant. It might be the truest thing I've ever said. Even more true now today than all the other times I've said it."

She turned as much as she could to face me. She was cried out, empty of her grief for now, but somehow fresh and new. "I love you too."

"Good."

"All of you. And you don't have to love the submissive me."

"Diana—"

"It's okay." She turned, getting on her knees to face me, clouds of suds dripping off her breasts. "But if you just love the regular me—"

"I love the regular Diana, and I love the submissive Diana. I love all the Dianas yet to be discovered. If you just stay with me long enough to show me all the parts of you I don't know yet, I'll prove it to you. I can love you more than you even thought possible. I'll love you until it annoys the hell out of you."

"I dare you to try."

"Challenge accepted."

We kissed. She tasted like rosewater. She tasted like freedom and captivity. She tasted like the rest of my life.

# CHAPTER FORTY-SEVEN

Thirty-five days.

They'd sped by so slowly, I barely had time to digest them, and yet, they'd filled me completely. I didn't know so much change could be packed into such a short time, yet when I held her the morning after I took her body completely, I was a different man than I'd been on day one. Every fiber of my being had been torn down and rebuilt. I'd gone bankrupt because of her, and I'd reorganized into a functioning human for her.

A bird chirped outside the window as the sun came up. The window of her childhood room looked across a narrow alley, into the building next door. We'd crawled into her old bed the night before, leaning into each other to keep from falling off the smaller space. Her neck was bruised from my belt, and her eyes were puffy with tears. I still had to check her anus for damage. I had to care for it if I was going to use it again.

Her lashes fluttered on my arm, letting me know she was awake. Even after that, she didn't move and I didn't rouse her. The world could wait.

A phone rang from the other room.

"That's you," I said.

"Let it go to voice." She took a deep breath, her body expanding and contracting against mine. "The freeze is over and we have to get the business going again. Fill the slate. Find new writers. There's so much. So much."

Her face took on a distant look, as if she was reading the to-do list inside her head.

"We should go so you can get started."

"One more hour."

So we stayed there. I stroked her hair. She stroked my arm. I touched where she was sore, and she groaned. She touched where I was hard, and I pinned her wrists together behind her back.

"Straddle me," I said. "Face the other way."

She rode me. Her ass was sore, but it clenched when she was close. I pulled her hair and made her wait to come. I made her beg. I made it impossible for her to wait, then I let her release, touching her so gently her orgasm went on and on in waves.

"You're so good," I said when she was back in my arms. "So perfect."

"I wish I could unsay all the things I said about not loving you."

"No. I don't. I'm glad you did it."

"I was a bitch."

"I was an asshole."

"You still are."

I rolled on top of her. "Really?"

"Master Asshole, sir."

I laughed, but the words, even in jest, made me hard. So I fucked her again, good and slow. Plain old missionary vanilla style. Because I could.

Her phone rang again.

She groaned. "Can you get it and tell them I'm indisposed?"

"You have to get up to go to the bathroom anyway."

"How do you know?"

"You're human. Come on, I have to look you over. This is dereliction of duty."

I slapped her ass. The sound of it made me want to fuck her again, but we'd never leave the apartment if I started fucking her as much as I wanted to.

The ringing stopped and started as we got into the bathroom. I heard it while I checked her throat, the bruising on her arm, and her anus, which didn't look half bad. I'd been more gentle than I thought.

By the time we were dressed in the previous day's clothes, my phone joined the chorus.

"I'm afraid to answer this now," Diana said, holding up her ringing phone. The name *Kayti* was on the screen.

"How bad could it be?" I said.

"Don't tempt fate." She slid her finger across the glass. "Hello," she said into the phone.

I pretended to read my email while I watched her reaction. A sigh. Resigned. She rubbed her temples. Sat down. Got her little pad out of her bag and scribbled, mostly saying, *yes, all right,* and *I don't know.*

"Is the building burning down?" I asked when she hung up.

"Not quite. What are you doing today?"

"Besides saving the world?"

"I can't... I can't deal with this myself. Can you come to SoHo with me?"

I took her by the shoulders and made eye contact. She looked lost, panicked, and determined at the same time.

"I'd fall off the edge of Manhattan with you."

We got in the Jag and headed downtown.

# CHAPTER FORTY-EIGHT

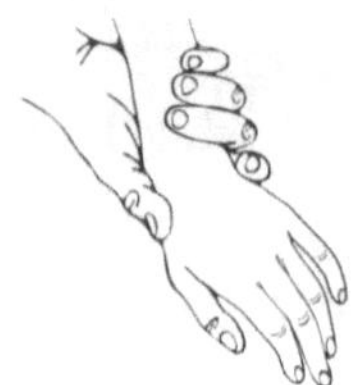

THE ENTIRE STAFF of McNeill-Barnes had gathered on the sidewalk, clutching coffee cups in the fresh spring air. The entrance to the building itself was behind police tape, and traffic was diverted to the other side of the street.

The sidewalk was littered with broken glass from the front window, opening Ticky-Taqui—the high-end shoe store on the first floor—to thieves, who had taken their pick. Kayti ran up to us, folder tucked under her arm.

"Hey," she said with laser focus on Diana, ignoring me and rattling a string of words without punctuation. "Okay, so they confiscated the security video and I'm sorry if you didn't want us to but the lawyers said—"

"It's fine," she said.

"—we should and Ticky's saying they're going to sue us those shoes are—"

"Have you spoken to the police?"

"—two grand a pair yeah I talked to Officer Gareth right over there he's super hot so I have no idea what I said." She let out a little giggle and turned fire-engine red when Officer Super Hot approached.

"Hi," Diana said. "I'm Diana McNeill-Barnes. This is my building."

He shook her hand. I kept mine in my pockets.

"Let's go inside," he said. "I have something to show you."

She followed him under the tape, but turned as she got to the entrance. "Adam? Are you coming?"

"You have this."

She swallowed then stomped toward me, heels crunching broken glass, knuckles a tight white on her shoulder bag. "Okay, look," she said when she was close enough to speak softly, "I know you're not part of the company anymore. I get it. But I need you, okay?"

How could I deny her? I'd tried and failed so many times.

I got under the police tape and went with Diana to meet Officer Gareth by the front door.

"Are you an owner, sir?" he asked.

Diana and I exchanged glances. The deed was in the company name, and the company was in the process of moving back to her family trust. So technically, yes. But actually, no. Lying or fudging with law enforcement was probably the stupidest thing a person could do, even if they hadn't done anything wrong.

"No."

"Yes," Diana interjected. "He is."

"Can I wait for her in the office? I have the key."

"Go ahead." Officer Gareth held his arm out so I could get in.

"It's fine," I whispered to her as I passed.

She nodded. I kissed my ex-wife on the cheek and went upstairs.

# CHAPTER FORTY-NINE

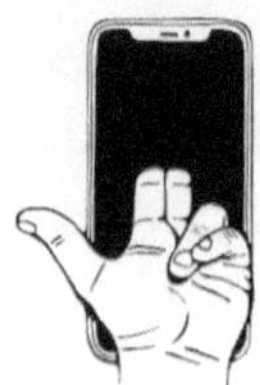

HER DESK WAS TOO CLEAN. That was the first indication that something was wrong. My Lego tower was exactly where I'd left it. I pushed an errant brick onto the blanket.

Lloyd's desk was organized but busy with piles of paper, as befitted a man whose career had started before fax machines. It would have to be sorted and cleaned out and it would hurt Diana to do it. I didn't want her to hurt. I texted Kayti.

*—Who's cleaning out Lloyd's desk?—*

**—The office has been closed
since he got sick. So. No one?—**

*—See if they'll let you up here—*

**—They won't—**

How did Diana deal with this level of daily obstruction? I thought Kayti resented me because she didn't report to me and I still asked her to do things when "things" equaled her fucking job. She'd move mountains for Diana, but everyone else? They could fuck a duck.

*—Ask again—*

I went to the freight elevator and grabbed some discarded boxes, stopped at the supply closet for packing tape, reset the thermostat, and went back to Diana's office.

Diana was already there, leaning against the back of the couch with her arms crossed.

"Where were you?" she asked, spinning like a lawyer intimidating a hostile witness.

I dropped the boxes by Lloyd's desk and put the tape on the chair. "Back hall. How did it go?"

"They asked me if Dad owed anyone money. If he had gambling debts. If he had a girlfriend. I mean, really? As if they shouldn't be interrogating Jason Taqui."

"I'm sure they are."

"My father was a fucking pillar of the community."

"Yes. He was."

"He didn't have any enemies. Not one. No one would come here and break a window because they were pissed he what? Died without paying a debt? What. The. Fuck?" She was pinched and raw, buzzing with emotions she couldn't hold in check.

I closed the office door. "Huntress."

"How dare they. How dare they try to soil his reputation over a stupid broken window."

I held her face. When she tried to jerk away, I held her tighter.

"You're all right," I said in my dominant voice. Then more softly but with just as much conviction, "You're all right."

"How? You don't see it. I haven't told you. This whole thing is falling apart. I can't think of new projects. There are bills on top of ledgers and I don't know what to pay unless accounting points at a dotted line. I can't handle it. I can't. And now? I was keeping it together for him. Why am I here *now*?"

"You've been training to run this company since you were sixteen. You've run it the past five years. You have this."

"With you," she said, then her face lit up. "Are you coming back? Will you? Please."

I didn't know how to answer her. I hadn't even considered it. The publishing business wasn't interesting to me. I'd saved the company for her and only her. Without her in the picture, the entire building would have been turned into third-party-managed condos and the backlist would have been sold in bulk to an aggregator who couldn't give a shit. I'd walked away from what was profitable and walked into what was satisfying. I'd done everything I could to rebuild a failing publishing house; and I never failed in business. Never. Not for myself and especially not for her.

No matter what she said, McNeil-Barnes Publishing was in good shape.

Its owner and president? Less so.

"You don't need me." I didn't think she'd believe me, but it was the truth.

"How can you say that?"

"Listen to me. Breathe and listen. You have this."

"I don't finish things."

"Yes." My hands slid to her shoulders. "Yes, you do. I won't let you fall. But I won't let you undermine yourself either." I pointed at her seat. "You're going to move that desk so the window is at your back. You're going to sit framed in the city like the queen you are. You're going to take Lloyd's stuff and go through it. You're going to respectfully pack what you have to keep and throw away what you don't. Then you're going to run the shit out of this place. By yourself. You were born for this. And me. You were born for me."

She bit her lip. Consternation or arousal? Both? It didn't matter, because I'd broken through the fear for the moment. We slid our arms around each other.

"I don't need a pep talk, Steinbeck."

"What do you need?" I grabbed her ass so hard she let out a sharp *ah* of pain.

"That."

She was so hungry for it. In the past month, she'd been willing, but I'd been too wrapped up in my own doubts. I hadn't seen how right she was for what I had to offer. Sex tangled with violence and I fisted her hair, settling her into my cock as it hardened.

"I was too easy on you yesterday," I said in her ear.

"Yes, sir."

"Take off my belt."

I held her head so she couldn't see it, leaving her fumbling for the buckle. Having her so uncomfortable, trying to please me despite what I was doing to her, excited and calmed me at the same time.

She got the leather belt through the loops.

"Very good." I took it and let her hair go. It stayed knotted in the back, a reminder that I'd controlled her. "Are you wet?"

"Yes."

"Prove it. Touch yourself and show me."

She made short work of her fly, unbuttoning and unzipping in seconds, getting her hand down in there as if it was her job.

She held up her slick hand, trying to staunch a smile. I brought her fingers to my lips and tasted her juice. Then, because I suddenly had no self-control at all, I kissed her so I could christen her mouth with it. I tasted every corner, touching her deepest crevices with my tongue. I wanted to make sure every soft surface she had knew I owned her.

Taking the belt, I pushed her against the window, pressing my body against hers.

"I liked working with you," she said when we separated to catch a breath.

"You made me crazy." I pushed my erection against her until her lids fluttered.

"You loved it."

"Regardless. I'm punishing you for it." I stepped back and pointed at the window. "Face New York."

She turned to face the window. The people walking up, down, across, around the street looked like boats on a currentless grey sea. Across the way, the windows of the office building sat in silent witness.

"Let me see your ass."

She hooked her thumbs in her waistband. I made a plan for the perfect ovals of her bottom if last night's marks were gone. Another plan for a series of light pink welts, and yet another if it turned out she was still bruised and red. All involved pain and pleasure. All were meant to satisfy her need to forget herself.

I slapped the belt against my palm when her pants were halfway down, and in response, a sharp knock came from the door.

Her head whipped around to look at me even as her bottom remained in my direction.

"Who is it?" I called.

"Hi. Hey. It's me? Kayti. Have you seen Diana?"

"Yes. Why?"

"Officer... um... the hot one wants to see her? They got the security tapes."

I looked at her, still bent but without the look of anticipation. I knew the moment had been stolen from us.

"I better take this," she said. When I nodded, she stood straight and called to the door, "One minute, Kayti."

"We'll reconvene tonight." I put my belt back in the loops.

"My place or yours?" She pulled her pants up and fastened them.

"Ours."

She smiled for a second then looked at her father's desk. The sadness wasn't there, but something more businesslike. I didn't know exactly what she was thinking, but I had a clear sense of what she was feeling, and it wasn't fear or hopelessness. They'd be back while she grieved for Lloyd, but she had a handle on it.

"You're not getting the condo for free." She went for the door. "I earned it fair and square. Now you have to earn it back."

"Oh, really?"

"Yes. I demand one hour. Tonight. If you can make me pinochle out in one hour, you get your half of the loft back."

I'd missed her. I didn't realize how much. "If I do, I'm moving back in."

"Yes, sir."

"And the car," I added.

"Forget it. Go get the Mustang off blocks."

She opened the door wide enough for me to see Kayti, who smiled like a schoolgirl. She practically jumpy-clapped when she saw me, then she fell into line behind her boss, who walked to meet Officer Gareth like the world's only badass.

How was I going to get a woman like that to safe out?

# CHAPTER FIFTY

It took me fifteen minutes to get back to the R+D office. I spent fourteen of them devising ways to push Diana's limits while staying within my own. I had a few ideas, but they'd take more than an hour. My wife was stubborn. If she knew she only had to last an hour, she'd last an hour. Then she'd demand more and more opportunities to sign over the loft. Each time, her limits would expand and the game would get harder to win.

I didn't care about the deed to the loft. I had plenty of property.

I cared about winning the game for our mutual benefit. I wanted to live with her.

"You look chipper today," Eva said, all in red as I came through the back entrance.

"First day of the rest of my life, et cetera."

"Does that have anything to do with the long-stemmed rose in reception?"

Odd. Why would Diana send me a flower? I could use it later on her body, certainly, but it wasn't her place to make suggestions.

"Have Britt leave it on my desk."

"Not a real flower." Eva's words stopped me as I tried to walk off. "Don't be so literal."

I knew who she was talking about before she'd even finished the second sentence. "Thanks, Eva. And no."

We walked toward my office together.

"No?"

"I'm not chipper because of her."

"That's almost an answer to a personal question."

I texted the receptionist on our messenger service.

*—Send her in—*

"I'll give you one more question," I said without thinking. And fuck it, because I loved making her smile that wide.

"Can I save it?"

"Save it and you get interest." I held up two fingers as I got behind my desk.

"Two questions? Please. No more. I'll die of happiness before I can make a list."

"Don't die. I need you."

"Now you're getting mushy. I'm leaving before you embarrass yourself."

"Thank you."

She passed the long-stemmed rose on her way out. I'd been right. It was Serena in black slacks and sage-green polo shirt. Even Eva turned to look at her when they passed. My ex-sub usually walked around as if she was well aware of that fact that she was the most beautiful woman in the room. She moved with precision when she walked down a runway and when she kneeled and opened her mouth for a cock. She spent her life striving for aesthetic perfection and came close to achieving it.

It was boring as hell, but that wasn't my problem. I didn't have to live with her.

"You can close the door," I said.

When she did, I held my hand out to the chair on the other side of my desk. I had a perfectly serviceable couch, but I didn't want her to get the wrong idea. By checking on her so often, I'd already given her enough reasons to think I wanted her.

She sat in the chair and crossed her legs so that one of her feet hit the floor, resting sideways in her stiletto, and the other stretched to the side of the chair. Her crossed legs were not decorous and demure. She was tense and engaged. Purposeful, yet somehow fragile.

"What brings you?" I asked.

"I know something." She played coy, adding a sheen of seduction to her expression, running her finger along the crease of her pants. "I thought you'd like to know too."

"Maybe. Depends on what it is."

She broke into a self-conscious smile. "This seems silly. I didn't ask how you were. Didn't tell you what a nice office this is."

"It's just an office. It's for business."

She cleared her throat and turned back into a sophisticated supermodel in the blink of an eye. "Of course."

My hands were folded on the desk. I tapped my thumbs together. "You said you had something to tell me?"

She uncrossed her knees, letting the cross fall to her ankles. "I had an experience the other night. When you were kneeling in front of your ex-wife?" More than the knowledge that she'd seen me kneel, I bristled at *ex-wife*. "Stefan saw it. It inspired him."

"To what?"

"Kneel."

"I'm sorry?"

"Yeah. The exact same thing. After you left."

I didn't believe what I was hearing. I'd gotten on my knees for Diana in a moment of unbearable pain. I knew Stefan loved Serena, but apparently I hadn't known how much. "What did you do?"

She cleared her throat and lifted her chin, making eye contact. "I was shocked. I was anxious. It turned everything upside down, but he wouldn't get up. He's a very stubborn man."

"Apparently."

"Then something changed. I felt kind of... gratified... from the inside out, instead of the outside in. And that... well, there's no other way to put it. I got turned on. Very turned on. I couldn't keep my eyes open."

"Ah." The pieces clicked together in my mind.

"It's not like he was there for twenty minutes. The whole thing took seconds."

People evolve. Sexual urges and needs can be unlocked at different life stages. Stefan and I hadn't seen Serena's inner Domme because she wasn't ready, or the Dominant side didn't exist. Had this side of her been conceived in Montauk? Or before? Or had she been gestating for years? And did it matter?

"I don't know, but subbing hasn't been working for a long time. It doesn't feel right anymore. When I heard you were back and you'd been vanilla all those years, I thought I could try it. You wanted to try it with me and I rejected you. But when Stefan kneeled, I knew vanilla wasn't what I needed."

She was all balls. I was proud of her on the one hand. On the other, I couldn't leave the door open half an inch for her, or she'd burst through and insist I train her as a Domme.

"I can't help you explore this, Serena."

"I know, I know. But I've had three masters, three real ones I care about, in my life. You're one of them. I want your blessing."

"That's very submissive of you."

"Do you want me to kneel for it?" She raised an eyebrow, as if the prospect had appeal despite everything she'd said. But the expression also had a tinge of a dare, as if she was the one in control.

"No." I stood. "You have my blessing and my encouragement."

Her grin was worth ten thousand dollars. Literally. "Thank you!"

"Now you can top from the top."

We shook hands as equals. I didn't realize we hadn't been equal in my mind, but until I showed her out, she'd been a pest or a toy. That guilt was on my shoulders, not hers. Not the community's. I knew in my head that the sub was an equal partner, even though they gave up power.

I'd been operating under some kind of delusional fog.

Had Diana cured me of it? Only the fear of her being beneath me had driven me away. I could never see her as anything less than an equal. Had Serena just been the proof of the truth as I came to know it? How many more years of loneliness and upside-down thinking did Diana save me from?

Thank God for her. Thank God for her a million times.

# CHAPTER FIFTY-ONE

How do you break a masochist? If receiving pain is part of their identity, how do you cause so much pain they forget who they are? Reveal their secrets? Bare themselves to you?

One hour.

I didn't want the loft anymore. I did. I wanted a life with her inside that loft or outside of it, but the loft was ours. It was *us*. And there was no *us* without the truth.

Once I decided to trust her with submission and then trust myself with her self-determination, the resistance washed away like years of caked-on dirt because I loved her. I'd give her anything she wanted, but not without letting her enjoy the fight.

She kept a mug of pens on the bar, next to stacks of paper and business cards she'd never get to. I picked out a pen, made sure it worked, and put it in my pocket. She was mine, and her body was going to announce it.

I was snapping the last of the blackout drapes closed when I heard her keys jingling outside the door. I shut off the last lamp. The loft went black.

The darkness was cut by an arrow of light from the hall. I grabbed her wrist before she could flip on the hall lamp.

"Close the door," I said.

She did, and I clicked the deadbolt.

"Hello to you too," she said to the sound of her bag falling on the floor.

My watch glowed when I touched it and beeped when I set it. "One hour."

"Yes, sir."

I was in the same darkness she was, but I'd been in the loft for a couple of hours. The darkness was mine. I knew where everything was. So when I stepped away from her, I knew where to go.

"Strip down. Quickly. Then put your hands behind your back and stand with your feet apart. Close your eyes."

Her clothes rustled and her boots *clonked* on the hardwood. When the rustling stopped, I flicked on a very small, very powerful flashlight and pointed it in her eyes. She put her hand up to block it, a porcelain statue in a dark room.

"Ow, hey."

"Close your eyes or you're going to be punished in a way you don't like."

She scrunched them tight. I shut off the flashlight, took her by the wrist, and put her hand behind her back. She gasped with arousal.

"Your safe word?"

"Pinochle. But forget it. I'm not saying it."

A silver cuff set that looked like two intertwined rings sat by the coats. I crisscrossed her wrists behind her back and snapped it closed around them. "The Jag says you're wet already."

"I'm not taking that bet."

I put a black velvet hood over her head and tied it around her neck to keep her eyes from adjusting. "Do you know where the credenza is?"

"Yes."

I smacked her ass hard. The darkness seemed to echo the sound more than the light ever did. "Yes, what?"

"Yes, sir."

"That was for forgetting." I smacked her ass again. "That's for not closing your eyes." Again and again, I felt her ass give under my hand and the sharp clap of pain. "For not keeping your hand behind your back. For trying to make deals, and three more just because you love it."

*Smack, smack, smack.* She was already panting. I held her up so her knees wouldn't buckle under her.

"The credenza," I said. "There's a window to the left of it. Can you walk to it?"

"Yes, sir." She took a step.

I stopped her, pushed one shoulder toward me and one away until her feet twisted and turned. I spun her again and again, leaving her facing the kitchen.

"Go then."

She stepped toward the kitchen, which was nowhere near the credenza, and yelped in pain. "What...?"

"You said you wanted children. I'm giving you a taste of it. Keep walking."

"I don't... ow!"

I put the flashlight at her feet. The black Lego brick was stuck to the bottom of her foot. She rubbed it against her knee, and it clacked and bounced on the floor.

Letting the flashlight run up and down her body, I soaked in her submission. Hands behind her back, off balance, fighting every painful step as she tried to avoid the bricks I'd covered the floor with. She was the picture of ungainly, awkward, unsexy obedience. It was the most arousing thing I'd ever seen.

She bumped into the back of the couch and growled in frustration. "Which direction am I facing?"

I smacked her ass.

"Sir. What direction?"

I put the flashlight on her face. I couldn't see her expression past the hood, just the bottom of the fabric going concave, convex, concave with her heavy breaths. Her chest heaved, nipples like pebbles. I put my hand between her legs, and she opened them for me, squeaking when she stepped on a Lego. Soaked. Her arousal was dripping inside her thigh.

"I'll tell you on one condition."

She groaned. I pinched her clit. A long N sound came from beneath the mask. That was new.

"Okay," she gasped, rotating with my finger, "what's the condition?"

"You get there on your knees." I slid two fingers inside her, hooking the fingers until I found the bundle of nerves just inside. She cried out. Back to vowels.

"There're these things on the floor all the way there?"

"Yes."

"You're a sadist."

I touched her nose through the hood. "Correct."

"Or you won't tell me which way I'm walking?"

"Nope."

She turned her head right, where she'd bumped into the couch, then left, where she'd started. She was calculating where she was, and if she managed to do that, she'd find her way too easily and we'd have no fun.

"Also, I moved the furniture," I said, still rubbing between her legs.

"Jesus."

I didn't know if she was praying for relief from my cruelty or for release from my fingers. I took them away from her sex, and she jerked toward them as if on a string.

"If we spend the whole hour with me knocking around here, you're not going to get your pinochle."

"You underestimate how much these things hurt the twenty-fifth time."

She didn't answer. Without seeing her face, I was only guessing at what she was thinking, and my guess was she was thinking she could kill an hour.

I was right. She stepped forward, right onto a nasty two-by-two brick.

"Ow! Shit!" She lost her balance trying to shake it off, but without her hands, her foot landed hard on another brick. She screamed.

"I'll tell you what," I said as she rubbed it off, letting it bounce. She put that foot on top of the other. I allowed it. I wanted her safe word, but I didn't want to be a brute. "They're hard on the knees. But if you crawl, I'll clear the way under your knees." I let my pause hang. "On one condition."

"I thought this would be easier."

"You want to stop?"

"Hell, no."

"Do you want to hear the condition?"

"Yes." She caught herself just in time. "Sir."

"You tell me the truth when I ask you a question."

She barely let me finish my sentence. "Yes."

I turned her ninety degrees. She was a straight line to the blackout drapes on the center window, which started a foot above the floor and ended higher than either of us could reach. I removed the cuffs, and I used my foot to clear a space in front of her.

"On your knees."

She fell to her knees. She didn't land one at a time, nor did she drop cautiously. She trusted me, and I was filled with satisfaction. There in the dark with her naked and unsure, I felt a contentment that everything inside the space was under control. My control. She was my partner, giving me everything she had so we could trade pleasures.

She put her hands down. Squeaked at the sharp edges I'd never promised to move.

"Straight."

Standing behind her, I put the flashlight on her back, watching her go two paces and stop when she got a brick in her knee.

"You're supposed to wait for me to ask a question." I took the brick out of her skin.

"Right. Okay."

"When you went to the Greens to meet with Insolent, did you intend to let him touch you?"

"I knew you were the only one. I kept trying to think of myself taking an order from another man. I let Insolent boss me on text, but I pretended it was you. And the thought of someone else breaking me... being vulnerable in front of them. It's not supposed to be creepy. Right?"

"Creepy isn't your kink."

"I told myself I'd let you go after thirty days but I knew I wouldn't. I'd fight for you to the end. I'd put off the fight until later, but never, ever give up."

I reached under her and cleaned the space in front of her knees. She took two paces, using her fingertips to avoid the sharp bricks, and stopped before she got her knee on one.

"Go."

She took one step on her hands and knees then stopped.

"Will you do whatever I ask?"

"Yes."

Another painless crawl forward. I had about four left before she reached the window, and she wasn't getting to the window without safeing out.

"Serena came to my office today," I said. "Do you want to know what she said?"

She tensed.

"You all right?" I asked.

"That's not even a question."

"Do you?"

"I trust you."

"I know." I crouched beside her and ran my fingers along her spine. "That's not what I asked you."

"You're asking me if I'm curious?"

"Yes." I caressed her bottom then thwacked it. "Now answer."

"Fine. Tell me."

"Is that how we ask?"

"That's another question."

She was particularly on the ball so she'd make it the hour. I was going to have to go outside her comfort zone very quickly.

I swooped some bricks away, and she moved forward a pace.

"No," she said. "That's not how we ask."

Good thing she couldn't see my face, because I had to bite back a laugh. She was a formidable and worthy opponent. She was going to make me earn my Dominance over her for the rest of my life.

I put my hands between her shoulder blades and leaned close to her ear. "Do you want to know what she proposed?"

"You're scaring me."

I took my hands off her, kneeling back on the balls of my feet, waiting. I had fifty-five minutes, and I'd take all of them if I had to.

"Okay. Tell me."

"She's changing sides and wants a try at you. What do you think?"

She tilted her head, making the tie of the hood drop between her shoulder blades. "What?"

"She can tie you down and fuck you. I'll watch."

She got up on her knees and grappled with the hood's tie. "Fuck you. Get this off me." She made the knot worse, and I didn't move. "Stop it now, all of it. Let me out."

"You're breaking the scene."

"Fuck the scene."

"Fuck the scene?"

I put the flashlight on the floor, facing the ceiling, then undid the string on the hood and lifted it off her. She was sweaty and beautiful, panting. Her eyes were crystal-clear blue, the lenses refracting the hard, limited light from the flashlight.

"You're considering—?"

"Nah."

"What?"

"She's flipping, but she didn't bring you up. Or me either," I said.

"You made it up?"

"Yes."

"Why?"

"I only had an hour, Diana."

Her eyes went wide and her mouth opened enough to reveal the little crease in her bottom lip. I tried not to smile and succeeded.

"You..." She drifted into silence where all the worst insults lived.

"Yeah, well. I want to live with you. I want to share a bed and a couch. I want to use that blue pot to make us a dinner just because you put a hole in the wall with it. I want to share your air again. Your space. Everything. So yeah, I played a trick on you, but Serena gave me the idea—"

"Serena what?" She'd gone utterly white. Her face practically glowed in the dark.

"Don't freak out."

"You really spoke to her?"

"She came to the office. I'm not pursuing her."

"Were you ever?"

"No. And she's not pursuing me. She needed my approval to feel right about becoming a Domme."

"You think you're so indispensable."

I laid my hands on her arms until they unfolded. I caught her fingers and laced them in mine. "I am indispensable."

"To me."

"Goddess of the hunt." I kissed her fingers one by one, leaving the left ring finger for last.

I hadn't intended to make any big gestures during our hour together. I only intended to win the game. But being with her in the darkness and talking of mundane things reminded me of what I'd longed for from the minute I met her. Before the lies. Before the games. When I met her and the sky opened above me, I wanted to possess her in a way that ached so badly, I had to deny it for five years. All I'd wanted to do was share her life, please her, care for her, mark her as mine.

"I am going to spend the rest of my life with you," I said. "That's non-negotiable."

Her smile was magical, unintentional, a reflection of her body and heart. Not all of her smiles had that glow of truth. She was undeniable when her expression so matched her true desires. "Thank you."

Her gratitude took my breath away. Never had she been so beautiful. Never had I needed to own her so badly. Not even in the deepest colors of my blind infatuation. Not even when I thought I'd saved her company and her family and done everything I'd set out to do with her. Not even the first time she opened her heart in submission and I tried to deny that I loved her.

I placed her left hand on mine and spread the fingers, isolating the fourth. I kissed the pad of it, ran my tongue along it, took the whole thing in my mouth and sucked it. She groaned until I bit down on the base. Then she gasped and tried to pull away, but my teeth held. I sucked hard, and I saw from the twist of her hips that she was moving inside the space between arousal and pain, pushing her finger in my mouth and yanking to the side at the same time, as if she wanted both and neither sensation. Or as if she understood that from now on, she'd associate one with the other.

I let go and held her hand to the flashlight. A layer of spit and the indents of my teeth were on her ring finger. "The bruises will last until you put your ring back on."

"That really hurt." She observed it closely in the beam of light, like a curious nude painted by Caravaggio in layers of glaze.

"I have forty minutes to get your mind off it." I got on my feet and stood over her.

Looking up at me, her eyes clear and open and ready for anything, she placed her hands behind her back and looked down.

"I'm going to push a limit," I said. "Can I trust you to safe out if it's too much?"

"I'm not going to safe out twice in one scene. Even if you cheated the first time."

"We have a lifetime of pushing boundaries together."

She sighed. "You're right, sir. We do."

"The flashlight. There's a hinge on the bottom panel. There's a strap inside for your wrist."

She picked up the flashlight and poked at the bottom, more curious than obedient. She opened the bottom, took out the four-inch plastic loop, and closed the compartment. Opening the loop, she started putting her hand through it.

"No," I said. "It goes in your teeth. The strap."

She bit it, letting the light swing below her chin, illuminating her breasts in a kinetic glow.

"Now you can see." I stepped out of the way. "Crawl to the window and open the drapes."

Between her and the window stretched a path of black bricks. It was worth the extra cost to get the single color. They looked painful, and anticipation of pain was where the sex was.

Behind her, watching her crawl with her ass up as the light swung, stopping when sharp edges went into soft skin. The way she kept going because I wanted her to, without complaint, not out of fear. She endured the pain because she wanted it, and she wanted it from me.

The power was laced with adrenaline and gratitude. I wanted more. I wanted to take her places only I could guide her to, because I'd own them. Open her in ways she'd never imagined, because she'd let me. Care for her because she'd given me a gift no one else had. She'd given me the gift of my true self.

I was bursting out of my skin for her violation, her degradation, and her honor.

She raised herself on her knees, shook off sharp little bricks, and opened the blackout drapes. The loft was flooded with the nighttime light of New York. We were above the streetlights. Their illumination was soft and shadowless. The lights from the department store across the street had a warm bite that slit Crosby sixteen hours a day, casting long shadows in the evening, and dimmed down to romantic-dinner levels after closing. Before the neighborhood changed, the building across the street had had the same use as our loft—a factory with big casement windows for free lighting and ventilation.

"Stand," I said, pushing her gently onto the six-inch-high ledge under the window.

She stepped up, and I stepped back. Her body was silhouetted by right angles. The black grid of the window panes. The yellow glow of the department store windows. The uneven colors of the bricks across the street. She was a goddess on the hill, staring down at the field of battle. She took my breath away.

I put my hands on her hips, ran them along her ribs and down again, trying to locate the source of her supremacy. She shuddered under my touch, transferring her power through my arms to my heart.

Why couldn't I love a sub before? Because they made me no better than a Dominant. Diana, the goddess of the hunt, loaned me her power and made me her equal.

"Turn around." My voice was pitted as a broken stone. Her existence pushed my limits, challenging my ability to dominate her, and in that moment of awe, I was surprised and honored that she obeyed.

On the ledge, she was almost my height, but she kept her gaze down and let the flashlight display the glorious velvet of her skin.

I needed to lift myself to her level. I needed to mark the moment. Put myself on her, in her, with her. Degradation had its moments, but as I pulled the pen from my pocket, I felt only the reverence of a supplicant writing their name on a piece of paper and putting it at the feet of a sponsoring saint.

Brushing my hand across her left bicep to her right and back again, I took stock of the room I had to say what needed saying.

"I'm not a poet," I said, taking the flashlight out of her mouth. "But I want you to indulge me. Repeat after me, but only if what I'm telling you to say is true. Do you understand?"

"Yes, sir."

I clicked the flashlight off and put it away. "This isn't a game. I'm taking you at your word."

She glanced up as if checking my sincerity. She nodded and put her eyes back on her feet.

"I belong to Adam." Third person sounded comedic coming out of my mouth, but I needed to hear the words exactly that way from her.

"I belong to Adam."

I bit the cap off the pen and spit it to the side. I started at one of her shoulders and wrote across it.

I BELONG TO ADAM

"He belongs to me," I said.

She looked at me, eyes dark in the night, and bit her lip. "He belongs to me."

I wrote under the last line.

HE BELONGS TO ME.

I thought I had a unifying line for the bottom, which would fall just above her breasts and over her heart. But as I drew out the last E, the sense of the words left me, and I tented my fingers on her sternum as if I could draw the intersections of our feelings through them. "I want to say, 'When I write it here, it's real.'"

We stood still with it for a minute, then she said gently, "On this body and in the book of life, it is written."

"It's perfect, but it may take two lines."

She shrugged, and a smile curved her mouth. "Take all the time and space you need."

ON THIS BODY AND IN THE BOOK OF LIFE, IT IS WRITTEN.

I stepped back to look at my work, placing the pen on a side table and crossing my arms. "Too dark in here. Turn around. Let the city see."

When she faced outside, I got up on the ledge and put my back to the window. I could see how she was marked, her hard nipples, the glow of the street on her skin.

"Do you know what I'm feeling?" I asked.

"Sexy and dominant?"

I brushed my fingers along the letters and across her breasts. "Proud and honored."

Her eyelashes fluttered when she looked down, and she pressed her lips together to keep from smiling. I enjoyed humiliating and hurting her. I was who I was, but those acts made her moments of fulfillment all the sweeter.

"Thank you," she said, pausing before the last word. "Sir."

"Put your hands on the glass and show me my options."

Her breasts hung as she bent to get her hands on the cold window. I got the flashlight from my pocket and tucked the strap away, facing the window with her.

Sometimes, after closing, people milled around the floor across from us. Designers, store buyers, renegades from a cocktail party on the third floor.

That night, with Diana no more than a body in a window, a young couple had split from what looked like a meeting on five and were chatting in the empty store with a row of white and silver mannequins behind them.

"They'll see you if they look," I said, clicking the flashlight on.

She sucked air through her teeth. "Can I say something?"

"Speak."

"You're so fucking filthy." She said it as if she had bacon fat and brown sugar rolling around her tongue. "If I'd known that when we met, I never would have married you."

"I know. Now open your mouth." I put the back end of the flashlight as far down her throat as I thought she could take. "They won't see your face with the light here. But your body's lit by the street. Be their inspiration. Their north star."

I took my cock out, fisting it for her. I needed her to see it, accept it, before I tore her apart with it. She acknowledged it with a low *nnn* in her throat, and I got off the ledge.

Grabbing the place where her ass met her thighs, I opened her to me.

The couple across the street faced us, but they weren't paying attention to anything besides each other.

"Watch them," I said, putting my dick where she was wet, sliding along her slick line. She bucked. "Watch for when they see your light."

I rammed inside her, and a split scream and growl came from her as I buried my cock as deep as I could. As if he heard the pressures of the mass and volume of the universe shift, the man across the way looked at his reflection in the window and straightened his tie. I dug my fingers into Diana's hips and thrust twice. The second time was so hard, the flashlight tapped against the window, and though he likely couldn't hear it, the young man across the street had definitely noticed the light.

Diana went *hmp* around the shaft of the flashlight, her head turned slightly toward the couple. She saw him looking.

"North star," I said. "Are you ready?"

She made a bouillabaisse of sounds around the flashlight. A sentence.

"Are you safeing out?"

She shook her head.

I took a handful of hair and bent over her to whisper in her ear. "Then just take it."

I rammed her, driving so hard and so fast I had to hold her hip to keep her steady. With every move, I aimed for her heart, to go deep enough to touch it, own it, crawl into it and expand it. My life was written there. I wanted to enter her and explode, covering the world in all-consuming fire. Inside. Deep. So deep we became linked at the soul.

"*Ook!*" she grunted, spit dribbling off her chin.

So sexy, the depths of her debasement. How far down she had to crawl to love me. I followed her stare to the couple across the street. They were watching. Her fingers were at her throat. His were in her hair as he said something in her ear.

"They're going to worship you." I reached around her, getting four fingers on her hard clit.

He was behind her now, rubbing his dick on her ass. Saying dirty things. One hand on her breast and the other reaching for the hem of her skirt. An R-rated version of the goings on in heaven.

"Look what you're doing to them. God, Diana, you're that sexy. That powerful."

The woman pulled her skirt up as he dug his fingers down her underwear. She buckled at the same time as Diana. My wife's voice came in a stream of long sounds. Her fingers curled against the glass.

"You want to come?"

She nodded.

"Wait for her."

It didn't take long for the woman's back to arch. Her mouth opened, and he had to hold her up. Diana let loose, pulsing around me, knees stiffening, her legs going out from under her. She trusted me to hold her up, and I did, lightening the pressure of my fingers so her orgasm sat on the edge of pain without crossing into it.

She fell against me, limp and boneless, folding to her knees like a map.

I did that. I gave her so much pleasure she couldn't stand, and she gave me the control to do it. I felt wrapped and right with the world.

"Beautifully done." I took the flashlight out of her mouth.

"Oh, God. Thank you." Her words were molded around her breaths. "For that. Sir."

I looked in her face. She was high on endorphins, pliable and pleasured.

I was bigger on the inside than the outside. My dick was going to explode.

Taking her cheeks in one hand, I forced her mouth open and guided myself into it. She took it. All of it. Marked with ownership of her heart. Sweat-streaked. Mascara running black. Spit dripping, messy-haired, she opened her throat for me. I got two strokes in then pulled out.

"Look up." I jerked myself with her body's juice.

When she exposed her chest, I came on it, marking those words true.

I BELONG TO ADAM

HE BELONGS TO ME

ON THIS BODY AND IN THE BOOK OF LIFE, IT IS WRITTEN.

# CHAPTER FIFTY-TWO

"Last night, you tried to tell me something. While I was fucking you."

The morning sun cracked the skyline at a little after seven. The days were getting longer, pushing out the nights of the longest, most miserable winter of my life.

"Which time?" Diana replied with sleep in her voice.

"In front of the window. With the flashlight in your mouth."

"Mmm." She didn't say anything after that. I thought she'd forgotten the question. "Oh yeah. The north star."

"What about it?"

"It's steady in the sky. So if you were going to make me move around, you missed the point."

"Thank God for the flashlight." I kissed her shoulder and got out of bed. "I'm making breakfast. What you do you want?"

"You're cooking?"

"I'm ordering in." I got into last night's pants

"Coffee. And scrambled eggs."

"Okay, fifteen minutes."

"And bacon."

I kissed her. "Anything else?"

"Two pancakes. No. Three." She held up three fingers. The bite mark on her ring finger was gone, and the bruising wasn't more than a pale yellow. I was going to have to do something about that.

"Are you sure you're not pregnant?"

"I'm not. Just hungry. I've been too sad about Dad to eat."

Laying my lips on her shoulder, I closed my eyes and told myself how much I loved her. More than the day I met her. More than the day she left me a note that hurt more than any other betrayal. More than I deserved.

"I'm going to knock you up or die trying."

"Challenge accepted."

When I was almost to the bedroom door, she stopped me. "I never filed the deed transfer, by the way. So half the loft is still yours."

"A win for me."

"The gospel according to Adam."

"Amen."

I left it there and called for breakfast. Serena was going to have to be dealt with. And Stefan. Their gossip could only be destroyed face-to-face. Probably with Diana present. I didn't want her involved in that crowd. It had been a hard limit. I'd told myself it was because I didn't trust the culture, but that wasn't true. I hadn't trusted *her*. I hadn't trusted her stamina as a sub. My instincts had told me her submission wasn't real.

The doorman buzzed as I set out the plates. Diana appeared out of the bedroom, hair still wet, wrestling her sweater on over jeans as she walked. She hit the button on the intercom with a flat slap.

"Is it food?"

"Yes," the doorman squawked.

"Send him up." She let the button go. "Hide the furniture. I'm going to eat anything that doesn't move."

"Sit." I held the chair out for her.

She sat. I put the cloth napkin on her lap, but just as I was pushing her in, the doorbell rang. She was up like a shot, slapping the door open to a delivery guy holding a huge thermal bag with a receipt on top.

"Ah. Yes! Mine!"

"Sign, please," the man said from behind the bag.

Diana slapped her pockets, looked around. "Pen."

"I can't get it," said the delivery guy. "If you reach into my pocket—"

"I have it." I got the pen I'd used to mark her the night before and signed on the dotted line. When he took the paper back, I noticed a tattoo on his hand and was inspired.

I wasn't going to put a ring on her finger. I was going to do better.

She dug into her eggs and toast first. Watching her eat food I'd provided gave me a flood of satisfaction. She moved to the pancakes before I'd even finished my toast.

"Oh," she said around a mouthful. "I found out about the window. So sad."

"Really."

"Yes. Are you going to drink your coffee?"

I popped the top off my cup and poured my coffee into hers.

"Remember Nadine?" She jammed a bite into the corner of her mouth while she spoke and sopped up maple syrup with a triangle of her next bite of pancake. "The kid with the blanket and Lego... hey. Wait a minute. You didn't steal that child's Legos?"

"I did not. Those were all new."

"That would be truly sick."

"The window, huntress. Stay with me."

"Nadine's soon-to-be ex-husband. So sad. It's just getting uglier and uglier." Her pace slowed. She poked at her next bite instead of shoving it in her mouth like a hostage.

"Do you think we could have become that?" I asked.

Her head cocked at a slight angle. One eyelid dropped a few degrees. She was trying to read me. "I don't know. Except that you broke a window."

I laughed. "I forgot about that."

"Are you serious?"

I nodded and she laughed, dropping her fork as if she'd just heard the craziest thing she'd ever hear in her life.

I tapped my finger on the edge of my coffee cup, bent the plastic edge, then let it find its shape again. "Insolent," I said.

"Can you drop it? How long are you going to—"

"I lied." I interrupted her because she was upset at me for the wrong thing. She'd be plenty upset at the right thing in a minute. "Not technically. He did live in his mother's co-op, but he inherited it and it was really very nice."

"Okay? So?"

"I let you think he was a threat so you'd be scared of other Dominants, but he wasn't. At least not to your safety."

"What kind of threat was he then?"

She wasn't going to cut me any slack. She was going to drill down until I scraped the bottom of my worst behavior.

"I gave you the impression that he was a slob who never left the house."

"And he's not?" She squeezed more syrup onto her pancakes.

"He was... no. He's not."

"He was what, Adam? Come on. Don't hold out on me. Was he tall? Handsome?"

Insolent had been sharply dressed, handsome if you're into that kind of thing, calm, and well-spoken. He was Dominant without being a dick, and he'd had a good sense of humor about the entire thing. But I'd walked away from him with a nagging fear.

"I was pretty sure you could fall in love with him," I said. "So I made him sound unattractive. It was petty, and I'm sorry."

"If we see him at the Cellar, I want you to point him out. I'll be the judge of who I can fall in love with, thank you." She took a stack of pancake slices in her mouth and let the fork scrape her teeth on the way out.

"I'm letting my membership to the Cellar lapse," I said, changing the subject.

"Why?"

"I have you. I don't need the scene."

She flipped open a Styrofoam container with the edge of her fork, revealing a stack of bacon in a napkin. The move wasn't motivated by curiosity or hunger. It was too contemplative for that. It replaced words she wasn't ready for.

"What?" I asked. "Nothing you say is going to turn me off."

She smirked and speared a strip of bacon. "When we met, I didn't think people needed to talk about sex. Then, five years in, I felt like I *couldn't* talk about sex and I wanted to. And now, well, I guess I'm surprised by what I'm about to say."

I let her bite the bacon and put the rest on her plate. I didn't need to encourage her to finish her thought.

"Whether it's the Cellar or not, it doesn't matter. But..." She took a deep breath and looked down at her lap. "When people watch, it really turns me on. They can see you dominate me, and it's like... that makes it valid and real. Three-dimensional. But because it's you, it's safe and I can get lost in it. Being your toy in front of people is like a drug. I see myself through their eyes and through yours. And I go out of myself..." She shuddered. Her eyes met mine, their blue as clear and intentional as the tide. "If you don't want that, I can live without it, but I really like it. The Cellar seems like the best place to get it."

I didn't want to smile. I didn't want to tell her what letting people watch did for me. The way it multiplied the effects of my domination exponentially.

"Can I think about it?" I asked.

"I'm not going anywhere."

She wasn't. I'd claimed her. Earned her back. She'd been mine to accept or reject for weeks, but I hadn't believed she'd stay until she did what she'd been too afraid to do when we were married. She told me what she wanted from our games.

# CHAPTER FIFTY-THREE

ONE WEEK LATER

I'D LEFT Diana at the loft with instructions to finger herself for five minutes every hour, but not come. No matter where she was—the store, the street, the office—she had to find a private place and think of me while she touched herself.

The Greens was packed for a weekday. I nodded at the maître d and walked right up to Charlie's table. He was sitting with a sub I didn't recognize. She was in her twenties with wavy brown hair spilling over her shoulders. Her posture was off, and she looked nervous with her skirt around her waist and her hands flat on the table.

I sat across from her.

"Hello to you too, mate," Charlie said.

"I have to talk to you."

"Of course you do." He didn't take his eyes off the sub. "Scarlett, open your legs and say hello to Adam. You'll address him as 'sir.'"

She shifted. I couldn't see under the table, but I assumed she was spreading her knees.

"Good afternoon, sir."

"You staying for lunch?" Charlie asked.

"Nah. I came to thank you."

"For?"

"Giving her that card. Insolent."

"I thought you'd try to kill me."

"I almost did, but I've heard about that cane."

He smiled and yanked the handle off the cane halfway, until the silver blade was visible. "That cane?"

"Yeah. I'd have to disarm you then kill you. It's way too much trouble."

"You drove all the way from Montauk to tell me she loved you. You looked like a man who'd found a seam of gold. Then you turned into a massive twat. I should have put the knife in you."

He had been happy. He'd practically handed me a cigar. When I told him I thought we could do it without being part of the community, that I could keep her safe from others seeing her submission, he'd agreed it was possible. Doable. Others had done it, so could we. I'd sped back to Montauk like a man on fire, only to find the kinky community had already infiltrated our relationship.

"Scarlett, sweetheart," Charlie addressed the sub, "pick up your shirt. Show me those lovely tits. Let everyone see how hard your nipples are."

Scarlett's sharp breath rolled with arousal and shame.

"Then put both your hands back on the table for sixty seconds. Then use your right hand to touch yourself and be very quiet about it. Understood?"

"Yes, sir." She grabbed the edge of her shirt.

I didn't watch her finish. I didn't want to see her tits. My exposure to other women was going to have to be dealt with.

"Good girl." His last word drifted into the glass ceiling and a smile crossed his face.

I followed his gaze to the door. Serena was walking through the tables where people could only fit single file. This was where subs trailed Doms by three paces. She was only one step ahead of Stefan, who held her hand behind her.

Stefan saw us and tugged on Serena's hand, then he whispered in her ear when she stopped. They both looked our way.

There was something different about her. She was dressed the same, in a spring-yellow polo and black slacks. Her heels were sensible and didn't trip her up. Her hair was up in a twist and the bangs were pushed back. When she smiled and waved at us, the nature of the change became obvious.

"She did it," I said.

"Apparently topping from the top is better than topping from the bottom."

"What about Stefan?"

"He's not going to change." Charlie waved them over. "They're going to try sharing subs. Scarlett's about to try it. Aren't you, Scarlett?"

Scarlett nodded, though her face was scrunched in pre-orgasm tension.

"Hold that thought," Charlie said to her. "Until you're told to let go."

Serena walked as if marking territory. Surveyed the room as if it were her property. Took stock of Scarlett as if she could own her any time. Stefan looked like a proud parent. We greeted each other with kisses and handshakes. Serena kissed me quickly on each cheek.

"Hello," she said, trying Dominant confidence on for size. She was about to sit at a table with her three Masters, as a Mistress. The difficulty only showed for a second.

"Nice to see you, Mistress."

Stefan held the chair out for Serena. "So," he said, "you've come to meet Scarlett?"

"No," I replied, pushing in my chair. "I'm leaving. It's been fun. Nice to meet you, Scarlett. Don't boss these two around too much."

Scarlett's face twisted in strain. "Okay. Yes. Sir."

"Will I see you in the club?" Serena asked, posture straight and commanding. Had that always been there? No, I was sure it hadn't been. People could change. They did it all the time.

"I don't know."

We said another quick good-bye, and I walked to the door. Turning for a second, I saw Serena whispering in Scarlett's ear while Stefan and Charlie conducted business as usual.

I was about to get in the car when Serena caught me outside.

"Adam, are you... back there, you looked unsure."

"I'm not."

"Really? This doesn't bother you?"

My approval was important to her. It was no more than that, and no less.

I hadn't realized the extent of her hurt. She'd been nineteen, new to the scene, sheltered, a virgin, and as defenseless a sub as I'd ever handled. I'd been reckless. I knew enough about her to know what would make her vulnerable, and I'd exploited her need for acceptance and her desire to please the way I'd exploited those desires in any sub. For pleasure, pain, dominance. But she was new. She'd needed more care. She'd chosen me. She'd chased me. She'd topped from under Charlie and under me, and we'd let her hurt herself through us.

"Yes. Diana's waiting. I have to go."

She seemed relieved for a second, then she straightened up to a Dominant posture that would eventually become a habit. "Say hi for me."

"I will."

She went back inside, and I hurried to Diana. She was my chance to right old wrongs and turn mistakes into successes. She was my chance to win in a way that was real and permanent. Every minute without her was empty. Every minute wondering if I could spend eternity by her side was meaningless. A life without her was a life wasted.

# CHAPTER FIFTY-FOUR

SIX WEEKS LATER

THAT MORNING, I'd tied Diana up before she was fully awake and fucked her while she sang "Happy Birthday to Me." She couldn't come until she finished the song, but I made her start over and over until she was in tears and I was ready to explode inside her.

We went our separate ways. She went to McNeill-Barnes to publish books. I went to R+D to buy and sell property. A month after we wrote our names in the book of life by christening her body in sex and felt tip pen, we went about our daily business as partners, and our nightly business as master and servant.

I never looked back unless I wanted to remember how stupid I'd been. She was everything I'd ever wanted in a woman. She was smart, bold, intrepid, principled. Everything I could admire in another human being, I admired in her, and she was all I desired. Warm, yielding, open-minded, honest, submissive, and perfectly masochistic.

Sometimes, when she fell asleep in my arms or when we went to the Cellar and some well-meaning cocksucker of a Dom asked if I'd share her, I thought I was kidding myself. She couldn't possibly want to deal with my shit. Couldn't be letting me fuck her face while who-even-knew watched from behind the glass. But she did. Time and again, she let me break her and rebuild her. She gave and gave. I struggled to keep up, taking better care of her, giving her more of what she needed inside and outside the game. The score was never even. I was always down, owing her more than I could ever repay.

But, goddammit, I wasn't going to stop playing.

"Rings?" she said when I told her what she was getting for her birthday. "Are we having a ceremony?"

It was six thirty on the Thursday before a long weekend, and half her office was gone already. The air felt thin with electricity as the days got longer and the temperature invited bare throats and open toes.

"This is even better." I pulled out her chair, and she let it roll back. "Come. It's something new."

"Really?" She seemed intrigued.

"Stand here. Arms on your head. Legs apart. Come on."

She did as she was told, eyes cast down as she'd been taught. I could do whatever I wanted to her and she'd let me. She'd beg me. That knowledge alone was enough to send a rush of rousing chemicals through my blood.

I opened her fly. "Look at me, birthday girl."

Her tempered-glass eyes flicked up. I felt around my pocket for the little silicone toy. It was the size and shape of a flattened walnut.

"We're going to see someone I trust. That's all you need to know."

"Yes, sir."

I ran my finger along her folds until she was wet, then I laid the toy between her underwear and her pussy. I snapped her underwear in place and closed her pants.

"What was that?"

"Surprise." I kissed her. "Let's go."

Once we were in the elevator, I fingered the remote control in my pocket with one hand and held her hand with the other.

"Stay calm," I said as the doors whooshed open to let in half the accounting staff.

"Why?"

She barely got the word out before I pressed a button. She gasped, even at the lowest setting. Everyone turned around to look at her. She was bright red, smiling, the owner and visionary of the company with a vibrating egg kissing her clit.

I shut it off when everyone was out of the elevator.

"Oh my god," she said as I led her across the lobby. "What are you doing?"

"Giving you a birthday present. Remember what I said about trusting me?"

I let her go through the revolving doors in front of me, and she held her question until we were spit into the street where a black car waited. Thierry opened the back door.

"Why?"

"It's not fun if you don't trust me. That's why."

"Hi, Thierry," she said.

I helped her into the car. She looked both intrigued and worried, just the way I liked her.

"What is this thing?" she asked after I slid in across from her and Thierry closed the door. "Some kind of vibrator?"

"How does it feel?"

"Good, but—"

I flicked the button to buzz her, and she jolted.

"Open your mouth."

I took an envelope from my inside pocket and put it between her teeth. She bit down.

"Happy birthday."

Her expression was precious. Curiosity plus incredulity plus struggle. I had to laugh.

"Open it. Go ahead."

She plucked it from her mouth and ripped it open, making a mess out of the envelope.

"I'm so intrigued," she said, sliding out the card. She opened it, and a smile crept across her face. "This is my present?"

"Part of it."

"You're filthy."

"I'm sick of signing you in."

She held on to the invitation to membership at the Cellar when she hugged me. "Thank you. It's what I always wanted."

"If always equals a month?"

"What else? Is there more? I love birthdays. Dad always made them feel like national holidays." Her face crinkled. She blinked hard. She was working through her father's death one tear at a time.

"That's my job now. Slide to the edge of the seat and open your knees. Keep your feet on the floor, but I want a hundred-twenty degrees between your legs." The car lurched to a start, and we headed downtown. "Hands behind you on the seat. No talking."

She complied beautifully, and a calm settled over me.

"I'm not giving you something you can unwrap. We're past that. This will be the first birthday where I get to give you what you truly need. I'm going to give you what I should have given you in the first place."

She ground her hips into thin air.

"Did you hear me?"

"Yes, sir."

"What did I say?"

"Birthday. Something. Can't wrap it. Something. *Mmmm*."

"Do you want me to tell you?"

"Sure."

She was fully pliant, in the drunken space just past manageable arousal where my patience and violence found their outlet. But she was also complacent.

I fisted her hair and pulled her to the floor at my feet.

"Take it out," I said as she got her knees under her. "Take it out and suck on it."

She fumbled with my belt, hook, zipper, cock. She'd been at this long enough to know I didn't want her to suck like a hooker. She opened her mouth and her throat.

"Don't come," I said. "Or the punishment's going to fit the crime."

I pushed her head onto my lap, rubbing my head on the back of her throat. I hadn't felt guilt about my cruelty in weeks, even as I remembered the sound of remorse in the back of my head. She wanted my cruelty as much as my kindness. Needed both as much as I did.

I pulled her head off me, and she gulped air.

"I should have had you alone in Montauk. This weekend, I will."

Before she had a chance to react, I pushed her face on my dick and she took every inch like a fucking champion.

"You and me alone." I pushed her down, let her breathe, pushed her down again. I pulled her off me so I could look in her eyes. "That's the first half. Are you ready?"

"Yes," she whispered with spit dripping from the bottom half of her face. "If you think so."

"I do."

She was in heaven. With her clit vibrating and my fist in her hair, she snapped deep into a sexualized high. I was responsible for keeping her safe while she was like this, and I always would. Her protection was my pleasure.

"Swallow." I put my cock back in her mouth. "All of it. Good girl."

I came in her mouth just in time for Thierry to turn onto Ludlow Street.

We'd cleaned up before letting Thierry open the door. He knew damn well what was going on in the backseat, but I paid him to not care.

"Wait," Diana said. "We're going in here?"

She pointed at the religious artifact storefront. I'd turned off the egg. She seemed more awake and aware.

"In the back."

We were ignored as we walked through the cluttered room, past the seven-day candles, incense, and Holy Books. Figurines carved in wood with bone skulls on top, wreathes of money, dancing skeletons with red bulbs in the eyes. A stone fountain tinkled as a stream of water came from the mouth of the monstrous death mask carved into the top. The water fell into a bowl shaped like a rib cage. A stone heart sat in the center. Diana stopped in front of it and dug into her pockets.

"I want to make a wish." She came out with a quarter.

I held her hand back and drew out my own coin. "Switch."

I gave her my quarter, and she gave me hers. We both made a wish. I didn't know what she wished for, but I hoped it was the same thing I did.

I wished for her to be happy.

"You're the Steinbecks?"

A guy with a long beard and plaid collared shirt stood in the doorway to the back room. He wore a leather collar with a silver ring in the front.

"Steve?" We shook hands.

"Missus," he said to Diana. "I'm your artist."

Before she could ask, he snapped open the black velvet curtain to reveal a barber's chair and a table with instruments of torture. The walls were covered with snakes, crests, lions, knives, dragons, and skulls.

"A tattoo?" she asked. "I'm getting a tattoo for my birthday?"

Steve went into the room to work on preparations, which was good. I was suddenly nervous. I didn't think she'd refuse me. I wasn't nervous about her. I was nervous about me. That I'd make the moment less than perfect. That I'd misread her and that gentleness would be a liability.

Facing her, I ran my hands down her arms and back up again. "We did everything right the first time, you and I." I cleared my throat. "We had a wedding. We had a reception. We wore rings. We didn't work. It was our fault. I'd love to blame it on the tired traditions, but it was us. We broke what we built and then we blew it to dust. We have something now. We're unbreakable. We're non-negotiable. Do you feel it? I know it's not just me."

"It's not just you. I thought I trusted you before, but this is different. You're different. And the same."

"Both."

"Neither."

"I want everything to be different."

"I love this already."

"Are you ready for it? I have plans. I don't think you're ready."

She looked into the tattoo room, where Steve waited, then back at me. "Challenge accepted."

I took her by the chin and made her look at me. "If you pinochle out, you'll safe out of the scene, but you'll never safe me out of your life."

She pressed her lips between her teeth, then smiled as if she couldn't hold it back another second. "Will it be fun?"

"I think so."

"So what's the tattoo thing?"

I surprised her and myself by picking her up under her arms and knees, carrying her to the chair, and setting her on it.

Steve put his phone down and sat straight. "So!" He slapped his hands on his jeans. "Here's what I have so far."

He opened a folder in front of Diana. I sat next to her. I felt her excitement and the tug of her curiosity. I wanted her to know she was safe.

"We're tattooing big red targets on your butt," I said. "One on each cheek."

I slapped the back of one hand into the palm of the other. Steve laughed, and she let herself smile a little.

"I'm going to assume you're joking," she said.

"Maybe I'm not."

"You are. You'd never cover the pink it turns." She smirked coyly at Steve. She was safe with him. His collar told her everything she needed to know.

I relaxed when she did.

Steve opened the folder. "All right. I worked on these based on your names."

He handed her a page with the outline of two left hands, one smaller than the other. On the ring finger of each were our names. The smaller hand said ADAM'S and the bigger hand said DIANA'S.

"Oh. These are... Adam. They're perfect."

"I'll get you another diamond ring, but under it—"

"No, this is it. This is what I want. We can't ever take it off."

"I worked up other designs." Steve pulled other papers from under the folder.

"I want to see all of them."

Had I wished for her happiness five minutes before? Had I put a time limit on it? Because I wanted her to stay exactly like this, reacting to my silly gift. It wasn't expensive or flashy, but she understood it because she understood me. She knew I wasn't after a big gesture but a solid signal of permanence. We would die with each other's names on our bodies, wrinkled, grizzled, papery, and old, our marriage couldn't be taken off. It couldn't be hidden. We couldn't walk away ever again.

I'd meant to use the egg while she was getting inked, to pair pleasure and pain with shame and safety, but she was so childlike when she talked to Steve about the design, showing him her hand, that I couldn't disrupt her. I didn't even know what they were talking about. I didn't even care. She was happy with me. Because of me.

"Which one?" She held up her favorite two designs.

"Whatever you like." I couldn't work through an opinion. They were both good enough. What mattered was the way her eyes sparkled.

"Boss me," she said with her mouth behind the paper. "Sir."

Every time she looked at the tattoo, she'd remember this day. She'd remember what I demanded and what I acquiesced. Keeping her happy meant not always letting her get her way. It meant making sure she knew she was safe in the world because I was in charge of a corner of it.

I pulled a third option from the pile. I didn't even look at it. For all I knew, it was the ugliest one in the bunch. It didn't matter *what* I chose, it mattered *that* I chose. "This one."

"That was my favorite," Steve said.

Diana's eyes stayed with mine as she let Steve take her choices away. "Yes, sir. Who goes first?"

"Me."

I held my hand out for Steve. He swabbed it, and Diana and I began our journey for the hundredth time.

Every day we'd start all over. A journey to oneness and independence. Stability and uncertainty. Happiness and melancholy. Pleasure and pain. Shame and confidence. Opposites locked in permanent tension. We would hold our worlds together with the ribbon of love.

# EPILOGUE

## SIXTEEN MONTHS LATER

"It has to be hot all the way through," she said, not for the first time. I held the phone between my shoulder and ear while struggling to free a five from a roll of twenties. "If it's not hot, I'm going to go down there and shove it up someone's ass."

"I'll do the shoving." I redirected my words to the round guy with the doughy skin and sweat-stained hat who plucked the five from my hand. "They hot?"

"Hot. Yes." He slapped open the metal door. Steam escaped the silver compartment, gathering under the umbrella. The humidity by the little pushcart was as thick as taffy. "Since this morning. I put them in." He wrapped two knishes in wax paper.

"Mustard," I said.

"Brown mustard!" Diana said from the phone. "If it's that yellow shit, I'm gonna—"

"I know, I know. Give someone a mustard enema."

The doughy guy raised an eyebrow.

"Mustard. Not French's," I said to him. "You got Gulden's?"

"This New York or what?" He pulled a rod out of a silver container.

It was coated in brown mustard. He rubbed it on the knishes, wrapping them in a practiced motion.

"Are they hot?" Diana asked.

"Yes."

"Did you check?"

Doughy Man handed me a brown paper bag already soaked with grease. I took it and headed back into the building as fast as I could without making a scene.

"No. I did not check."

"How could you not check?"

"He said it was hot." The elevator was already open, and I squeezed in just as the doors were closing.

"He lies. You have to check yourself."

"I'm not sticking my finger in a strange knish."

The businesswoman next to me smirked.

"If it's cold—"

"I know, huntress. I know."

The signal cut out.

As infuriating as she was when she demanded I manhandle food, when I burst into the pink-and-blue waiting room, dodging out of the path of a woman in a lab coat, I was reminded why I'd run all over Manhattan to soothe her.

Diana sat alone, hands woven together in her lap, hair half in-half out of the ponytail, skin blotchy from the hormone stew in her blood.

She was beautiful. Everything about her. From her ever-rounding belly to the way she dropped into bed after dinner. Perfect. The only thing marring a perfect pregnancy was her anxiety about the baby.

Today, we were getting rid of that. She was going to start enjoying this.

I sat next to her, put a napkin on her lap, and opened the bag.

"I'm not hungry," she said, wringing her hands and staring into the middle distance.

"Yes, you are."

"It's not hot. I know it isn't. Cold potatoes are gross."

"They're delicious. Can a million Irish mothers be wrong?"

"Our appointment was fifteen minutes ago. They don't want to see me because of last time."

I put the bag to the side and took her hands, prying the fingers open. She was strung tight enough to break. "Would you like me to set the building on fire?"

"Stop."

"I can shove a clock up someone's ass." I rubbed the tattoo on her left ring finger. ADAM'S. Always mine. Her hand relaxed into my palm.

"I need this to be over with."

"Tell you what. I can do that thing Superman did in the movie. The old one."

"Pick up a car?"

"That. But also, he flew around the earth to make time go backward. But I can go the other way. Make it go forward. Any time between the sonogram and when he graduates from college."

"That sounds great. Skip right through."

"If you say so." I leaned back. "We'd miss a lot of sex."

"Oh. Yeah."

"And the actual parenting part."

She pointed at a dark-skinned technician in pink scrubs sharing a clipboard with a guy in scrubs. "Can we skip to Dolores coming here and saying we're next?"

"Yes."

The technician nodded, took the clipboard, and approached us. "Are you ready?"

This wasn't our first rodeo, though every time felt like it. Diana didn't want to hear the heartbeat. She didn't want to see anything, so she clamped her eyes shut so she wouldn't see the screen. She didn't want to fall in love. She'd wept with joy when she heard the first *whoosh whoosh* of the baby we lost, and she didn't want to cry again over something she couldn't have.

So though this was her third sonogram for this pregnancy, only the tech had heard the heartbeat. I'd seen the grey blobs on the screen, but Diana acted as if she was just gaining weight. Dolores knew our history and knew how shut down Diana was. She handled us personally, making sure the gel was warm and her earphones were plugged in before the sound of the heartbeat came through the speakers.

"You understand today is it," she said, rubbing the gel around with the sonogram wand. "The issue you're worried about, if it doesn't show today, it's not going show up at all."

"I understand," Diana said.

I sat next to my huntress, holding her hand. Actually, she was holding mine in a death grip. I didn't complain. That's what I was there for. Death grips were my specialty.

"There could always be something," Dolores continued as she adjusted knobs, sliding across the linoleum on a round stool.

"I understand." Diana had done a lot of robotic understanding in the past months.

"Even during the birth, things can go wrong."

"I understand."

"Child could also be a brat. Not our fault."

"She understands. Brattiness is her fault," I said.

Diana's eyes were still squeezed shut, but she faced me. "You love my brattiness."

"I do."

"Right," Dolores continued. "Do you want to know the sex?"

"No," I answered half a millisecond before Diana said, "Yes."

"I see you guys decided." She flicked a switch, and the screen lit up. There was our baby in glorious lo-fi black and white, swimming in static. "All right. Let's see." She leaned into her screen, moving the wand. "Well, knock me over with a feather. Happy to report Baby Steinbeck is as right as rain."

"Diana," I whispered, "did you hear that?"

She nodded but her eyes were shut so tight her upper lashes dovetailed with her lower.

Dolores marked numbers down, shifted the wand, clicked buttons and switches while Baby Steinbeck hovered behind me.

"You can look," I said.

"I'm scared."

"You don't have to be." I put my body between her and the screen. "Here. I'm between you and the screen. Open your eyes."

She took a deep breath and did it, hanging her gaze on mine as if my attention was a six-inch-ledge over a hundred-story drop.

"Good girl. Are you ready to meet your... Dolores? Boy or girl?"

"Congratulations. You're carrying a boy."

All of my wife's anxiety rushed out of her in the form of tears. "A boy?" she choked out.

"Are you ready to see your son?"

She nodded.

I moved out of the way, letting the light of the screen shine on her. She looked full and round, swollen with a joy she'd been holding so tightly she couldn't let it go until it got too big for her fist. Her face twisted into sobs and spit, becoming more beautiful in relief and release.

"Do you want to hear the heartbeat?"

"Yes," Diana answered before Dolores finished the question.

The whooshing came through the speakers, loud, strong, and steady.

"Heartbeat's just about perfect." Dolores continued, showing us where the spine was (exactly where it should be), where his penis was (same), and his placement in the placenta (just fine).

But we weren't listening. I was watching my wife let go of months of taut apprehension, and she was staring at the screen through sheets of tears.

Dolores said something about leaving us alone. She froze the image and left, clicking the door behind her.

"It's over," Diana sobbed.

"It's over." I wiped her face with a handkerchief.

She turned away from the screen to make eye contact with me. "I finished."

"Not quite, huntress."

Every tear the handkerchief wiped away was replaced with two new ones. I kissed her cheeks, tasting brine and perfume. I couldn't help it.

They were the stuff life was made of. Salt of clarity. Water of growth. The elixir of change.

She put her arms around me, and I held her. I didn't comfort her with pats or hushes. I didn't tell her it was going to be all right, because it wasn't. Life was messy, and God was an irresponsible parent. None of it mattered. I held her to keep her company. I was her companion, her complement, and her protector. The celebration of her light and the consummation of her darkness.

We were no more than bound, no less than gods, creating life from the love between us.

THE END

—————

# ACKNOWLEDGMENTS

I've been thinking about this story for a long time. Over a year ago I sat in the front seat of my car in a Starbucks parking lot, breaking the story with Lauren Blakely. Many moons later, it's completely different, but without that first breakout with her I never would have been able to start it.

So first, thank you Lauren for taking that time with me.

I pitched the story and release concept for *Marriage Games* to Mary Cummings at a poolside bar in Hawai'i (it wasn't that glamorous, truth. My feet hurt and I was unprepared for a presentation the next day....but doesn't it sound so delicious? *pitched at a poolside bar in Hawai'i*— Glitter just pours off that sentence).

Turns out, she was about to pitch me a release concept, and it was the exact same one. It was like we were puzzle pieces. Mary and Ever After have been what a publisher should be. Supportive, unintrusive, constructive and collaborative. Kudos to her, Taylor, Sarah, Fiona, and the entire Diversion team.

My husband has done me the service of just being himself, and supporting me in his quiet way while I work. My kids think all I do is work. In fact, they get hours of my time a day. They're greedy, and I love them for it.

My early betas, Joanne and Diana helped me mold the first half because I didn't know what the heck I was doing. Because of the care they took with me and my work I figured it out. There's never any "good enough" way to thank betas, especially the early ones because they're like Tim Robbins in *The Shawshank Redemption*, trudging through miles of shit.

Laurelin Paige stayed up until 4am reading the first draft. She had a million other things going on, but she beta'd it and then, unbelievably, she did it again after I chopped off the ending and replaced it with the one that wound up here. If you want to know what the original ending was, you'll have to wait until I'm dead. Laurelin's not telling.

Cassie Cox, my tireless editor, rushed the hell out of this so I could get it to print. I bow low, because she caught more than a few clunkers. As always, I sound like me, but with better grammar.

My Camorra, ladies and one gentleman, thank you for your support. You guys went into the breach when I had to check out of social media for awhile. Thank you.

Late betas Jenn McCoy and Amy Vox - thank you. You read a late draft and gave me the confidence to release this nerve-wracking book.

Jean Siska checks this and all my books to make sure I at least sound as if I know the law.

Janice, Erik, and Candace – (blows kiss) thank you for the fast turnaround on the proofs.

Jenn. Speechless. Wind beneath my wings and all that corny shit that makes me gag. I'm sure by the time this is released I'll want to kill you because of all the parties, but you'll be feeding me coffee so I'll forgive you.

And you.

Yes, you.

Blogger. Fan. Supporter. Service provider. Advice-giver.

I'm forgetting you.

I'm sorry.

# ALSO BY ME

## THE EDGE SERIES

*Rough. Dark. Sexy enough to melt your device.*
*He's her husband but he's rougher and more dominant than the man she married.*

*Rough Edge | On The Edge | Broken Edge |*
*Over the Edge*

## THE SUBMISSION SERIES

The *USA Today* bestselling Series

*Monica insists she's not submissive. Jonathan Drazen is going to prove otherwise,*
*but he might fall in love doing it.*

*Submission | Domination | Connection*

## THE CROWNE BROTHERS

*Five alpha brothers—each dominating their own standalone.*
*Iron Crowne | Crowne of Lies | Crowne Rules*

9 781942 833727